The Thirteenth Sigil

J.L. O'Faolain

SECTION
13 Case
Files

Dreamspinner Press

Published by
Dreamspinner Press
382 NE 191st Street #88329
Miami, FL 33179-3899, USA
http://www.dreamspinnerpress.com/

The Thirteenth Sigil

Cover Art by Paul Richmond   http://www.paulrichmondstudio.com

ISBN: 978-1-61372-603-7

Printed in the United States of America
First Edition
July 2012

eBook edition available
eBook ISBN: 978-1-61372-604-4

To Caty. Thanks to you, "Captain Sharky and the Magical Treasure Cave" lives!

Whether you like it or not!

THE phone was ringing.

It took Cole several tries before his hand closed around the infernal device buzzing mindlessly on the nightstand next to his bed. Several more seconds passed as he struggled to find the right button that would answer it. In any other situation, he would not have bothered. The phone would have likely wound up bouncing off the wall at the far end of his private chamber, far from him, while he nestled back deep under the covers.

One thing prevented him from doing that, however. The clock on the nightstand next to his phone was showing the time. It was after three in the morning. No one ever called at 3:00 a.m. unless it was important, and Cole had been hoping for a certain call these past three weeks.

"Hmm?" he grunted, his voice thick with sleep. "Hello?"

"Get dressed."

The voice on the other end of the phone belonged to Inspector Joss Vallimun, the commander in charge of Section Thirteen and Cole's maybe/maybe-not boss... and lover. Cole had been a special detective with Section Thirteen, a clandestine group of officers within the NYPD working to solve the unsolvable. The Section had been brought back together just a little more than two months ago, revived after a decades-long sabbatical. Their job was to keep supernatural crime at an all-time low while providing the ignorant with plausible explanations for why strange things happened.

Internal Affairs, it turned out, had been watching them from the get-go under orders from the higher-ups. It had led to more than one sticky situation, one involving a rampaging ogre in the holding cells of the precinct where they were stationed and another all the way out on Staten Island. Cole had been placed on indefinite suspension without pay as a result, right after he'd just managed to secure a decent team to work with, and Joss Vallimun, his lover, had been seriously hurt.

Joss was doing fine now, though. A quick kidnapping from the hospital where Joss was under constant surveillance had ended with him regrowing a whole arm in the depths of the sithen that was Cole's home. They hadn't seen much of one another since then. Now Joss was calling him in the wee hours of the morning. Somehow, Cole seriously doubted he was getting news of where they could meet for what humans these days called a late-night hookup.

"Get dressed?" Cole was usually far sharper on the uptake. At the moment, however, his brain was finding it difficult to string his thoughts together into something that resembled sense. Blinking a couple of times, he cleared his head and tried again. "Why?"

"There's been a robbery," Vallimun told him in a clear tone. "Someone broke into a high-tech storage facility a few hours ago and made off with a canister. The company who owned it has been reluctant to identify what was inside."

"Right." Cole nodded even though Joss couldn't see him. "And how does that concern me, or even you for that matter? It sounds like your basic case of theft."

"The sealed doors were torn right out of the walls," Joss elaborated gravely. "Whole chunks of concrete are missing. The inside of the storage area looks like it was swept clean by FBI agents riding on tornadoes, but the crime happened in the space of less than two minutes. No room could have been gone through like this in such a short period of time, at least by anything human."

Sleep was leaving Cole's brain in a hurry now. "Very true," he said.

"Oh, and forensics found claw marks all over the place. Preliminary analysis suggests they might have been caused by a tiger, or a whole bunch of tigers."

Cole sat up fully now and began processing what Joss had just told him. "So a bunch of tigers riding on tornadoes broke into a heavily fortified storage building and stole something? I'm beginning to see why you called. The chief must be having kittens by now."

"He is," Joss replied. "For the moment, though, we aren't his biggest concern. He's too distracted by the mayor pitching one hell of a hissy fit. It seems your suspension has been lifted."

Now Cole was completely awake. "What?"

"Someone called the governor last week," Joss went on. "I know only a little more about it than you do right now. Word is, the governor received a phone call from somebody important. They insisted you were being wrongfully punished for what happened on Staten Island and insisted he investigate."

"No one would go to bat for me," Cole said, even as he crawled out of bed. "Nobody that important, except…."

Joss was silent as Cole stared blankly at the wall ahead of him in the dark room. "Except?" he prompted when Cole didn't finish.

"Nothing," Cole said. "Absolutely nothing. I can be dressed and out of here in fifteen minutes."

"Make it ten," Joss advised. "Nobody down here is happy to see us, as usual. Internal Affairs sent some of their boys over as soon as word got out that we'd been called in. I'm sure they'll be thrilled to see you."

"I'll dress to impress, then," Cole told him, smiling now. "Now that I'm officially a member of the NYPD again, does this mean we can be seen in public together?"

"We can probably arrange something," Joss said coyly. Then his voice grew serious again. "We need to be careful. You might be back on the team, but IA won't hesitate to look for an excuse to run you off again. I haven't quite figured out why but they seem to think you are a serious threat."

"I'll be careful," Cole swore.

"Behave," Joss warned. "That's what I need to hear."

"Fifteen minutes," Cole told him, avoiding the unspoken question. "Once I collect my next paycheck, we'll have to do something special together to celebrate. Just the two of us."

"We'll talk about it later," Joss said, sounding rushed now. "I have to go. Speaking of your paycheck, though, you're being given retroactive pay from the time you were suspended."

Joss gave Cole the address and hung up before he could say anything more. After laying the phone down, Cole marched over to the closet for a change of clothes. Because of the amount of junk Cole had accumulated over the years, the sithen had made a walk-in space for him. As Cole searched for something to wear, there was an abrupt gust of air out of the floor next to him, despite no vent being present.

Mal materialized beside him dressed in army fatigues and wearing face paint. "Up and at 'em, soldier!" he shouted before blowing on a bugle. "That there war ain't gonna be fought on its own!"

"You were listening in on my calls again," Cole stated, giving Mal a dark look. "What did I say about that before?"

Mal's wardrobe shifted to an evening gown worn by a 1950s starlet. "I'll never tell," he insisted melodramatically. "Never!"

Cole fought to maintain an even temper. There were moments when the ex-sorcerer could really try his patience. It had gotten especially bad these past few weeks, with him having so little to do.

"I realize you are connected to the sithen," Cole said, breathing in deeply. "And being that my cell phone was a gift to me from the sithen, that means you can naturally hear whatever is being said on it. Still, I can't believe that such a powerful sorcerer, even the spirit of one, would have such a hard time blocking out incoming signals."

"I'm bored," Mal stated, shifting back into the butler uniform he wore as a default setting. "There hasn't been anything to do these past few weeks. I was hoping the phone call might be good news."

"You already know it was." Cole paused as he located something promising. "I've been reinstated."

"And with retroactive pay." Mal appeared thoughtful for a moment. "Does that mean what I think it does?"

"It means I'll be receiving pay for the time I was suspended," Cole said. "They'll pay me even though I didn't do any work."

"Woo!" Mal cheered. "I love this country."

That wormed a smile out of him. "Yes," Cole admitted. "It does have the occasional perk from time to time. Would you mind getting out so I can change now?"

Mal gave Cole a once-over. "You're already naked. We've been talking for the past five minutes while you were in the raw. Why should it matter if I stand here and watch while you put on clothes? Besides that, I thought the sidhe didn't have a problem with casual nudity?"

"We don't," Cole replied. "And ordinarily it wouldn't bother me, but I have to get ready and go to a crime scene now. The more you talk, the more it distracts me. Therefore, please leave."

Mal bowed and then disappeared without further comment. Seeing as how his soul had once been trapped inside a book, then later a computer hard drive, Cole supposed it only made sense that Mal would act more exuberant now. Still, having nothing to do for these past three weeks had meant that Cole was forced to endure his spastic personality. He could always have gone for a drive, left the sithen for a couple of hours, but the Internal Affairs goon squad was forever on the lookout for him.

So Cole had stayed inside and watched TV. He had seen more of it in the past three weeks than he had in the previous three years. The experience had left him feeling soiled and reminded of why he'd given up on it more than once already. Pushing the thought aside, Cole began to dress himself. He had gone with the traditional black leather pants that were usually a staple of his attire and a long-sleeve shirt that laced up the front and on the sleeves. Lastly, there was the hat over the long silvery hair that trailed down to the small of his back. Long hair was a symbol of pride among the sidhe, whereas the hat was an accessory he'd picked up and worn in the fifties for a brief period of time. Cole had found it in his closet the other day while searching for an old Super Nintendo that had somehow gotten lost. The sithen refused to help him find it. The hat still fit well over his head.

Satisfied with his clothes, Cole marched back out to his chamber and snatched up his cell phone, wallet, and the keys to his car up off the table. More importantly, though, he gathered up his weapons. His two bastard guns, Bandersnatch and Jabberwock, fit in the holsters hanging just below his hips while Aed Deigh, the ancient faerie weapon whose twin blades fit into one hilt, fit neatly in the horizontal sheath he'd had made for it years ago. The sithen was kind enough to rearrange itself so he could reach the garage faster. Apparently, it sensed how important reaching the crime scene was to him. Mal had already beaten him to the garage. Being able to traverse the labyrinth that was their home at the speed of light was a perk, of course. Mal had done Cole the favor of warming the modified black Camaro up for him. The driver's side door was already open and waiting.

"Have a safe journey, sir," Mal said in a snooty, faux-British accent. "Shall I have some tea waiting for you when you get back?"

"Please," Cole replied, climbing into the front seat. "Maybe a fresh bagel while you're at it."

"Very good, sir."

The Camaro was actually a carriage left over from one of the old Wild Hunts. It was a minor power, nowhere near as strong as the handful that Cole had seen growing up, before his exile. In the mortal realm, however, it could still punch straight through a stone wall without getting so much as a scratch. The engine roared as he stuck the keys into the ignition. On his signal, the garage doors opened, showing themselves to be somewhere in the lower half of Northern Manhattan. The garage had the ability to appear anywhere it felt would be convenient to Cole.

Usually, anyway. The powers of the sithen were often unpredictable or flighty at best. Cole had learned the hard way not to depend too much on them. He suspected the sithen just didn't like being taken advantage of, which was something he could relate to. Joss had asked once right after Cole was suspended how the sithen could be located beneath Bowling Green and still have the garage appear halfway across the island.

The short answer Cole had given was "it just could." Cole never tried explaining faerie physics to a mortal. It gave everybody a headache.

At this hour, traffic was manageable. The bigger problem was the snow falling steadily on the asphalt. New York City had been having strong snowstorms for the past month. It was another reason he hadn't left the sithen a whole lot. Driving alongside humans who didn't share the same reflexes as him made Cole nervous. He had resisted buying a car over the years for that very reason. Having one that could mystically glide over the surface of ice made things a whole hell of a lot easier.

Cole managed to reach the address in good time. He did a quick drive-by to assess the situation before getting out. Cop cars were everywhere. Many members of the NYPD were standing outside on the sidewalk looking at what may have been a door at one point. Now it was just a huge, gaping hole that looked to have been torn right out of the building. Cole slowed down enough to where he could scan the faces of the uniforms there. Joss wasn't among them, or anyone else from the Section, for that matter. Either they were waiting inside for him or somebody else had already run them off.

Cole parked his car behind one of the patrol cars at the curb and got out. One of the officers was coming his way as Cole came up the sidewalk. The man stopped short as he got a closer look at Cole and appeared dumbstruck for a moment. Cole already had his badge out and held it up to the man's face while walking past. The uniformed officer shook his head as though trying to clear fog out of it and followed in Cole's footsteps.

It was a common side effect for humans. People in this realm still spun tales of his ancestors, who had fled here to escape Oberon's tyranny centuries before. One of the things most talked about was how beautiful his kind appeared. Humans who looked upon a sidhe for too long could sometimes become besotted by them. It especially happened in those who were deeply linked to the spirit plane or weak of mind and heart. Their befuddlement faded after a while, normally, but Cole had noticed it happening a lot more often lately. Something told him the officer dogging his steps would be enduring quite a few tasteless jokes after he'd left.

No one tried to stop Cole when he held his badge up and stepped over the police line. A few of the dirty looks they'd been throwing his way even softened a little. Now that he was at the entrance, he could make out several familiar voices from deeper inside the building. It looked like the others had gone in without him. Cole stood at the opening for a moment and listened as the sound of Rainette's sharp tone drifted toward him, letting him know where they were. The inside of the storage building had indeed been demolished. Everything was scattered all over the place, to the point that Cole couldn't begin to guess what had once belonged where. Packages and crates had been smashed open, and expensive-looking electronics were scattered in pieces. Moreover, several areas were coated in a colloidal gel. That was something Joss had neglected to mention. One sniff told Cole what it was, which brought his hackles up instantly. Sweeping the area now on full alert, he spotted Rainette DuBois having an argument with Marcel halfway down an aisle.

Marcel was the ogre who had broken into their precinct last month. He'd been under the influence of a device Cole had dubbed "black rings." The fey on Staten Island had been enslaved, thanks to them, as part of a larger plot. Cole had been able to wrestle Marcel free from jail and convince both him and Rainette to join the Section. Rainette was a witch whom Cole had become acquainted with a couple of years back, thanks to a mutual friend. At the moment, Rainette didn't look happy with Marcel. She was also on the verge of being crushed to death.

Cole charged forward without thinking and snatched Rainette up in his arms. The witch barely had time to shriek in outrage at being manhandled before the crate that had been falling toward her smashed to pieces on the floor. Cole stopped, set Rainette back onto her feet without another word, then turned around to check Marcel.

"You okay?" he asked.

Marcel dusted the shrapnel off his chest. "Just a few scratches," the ogre replied calmly. "I notice you didn't try to save me."

"You're a lot tougher than she is," Cole told him. "Rainette would have been flattened by that thing. And she might have complained all the way into the afterlife."

Marcel nodded as Rainette scowled. "Very true."

"You're back," she stated flatly.

"I'm back," he affirmed. "Joss called me less than an hour ago and filled me in. How have things been going so far?"

"Horrible," she snapped, stomping back over to the crate that had almost crushed her. "It's been like that ever since the normal forensics team told us we were free to check the place out. Things have been falling off the shelves left and right. What wasn't smashed by whoever did this, anyway."

"A number of the falling items have gravitated toward Officer Rainette," Marcel added, adjusting the big-and-tall jeans he was wearing. "Inspector Vallimun asked me to go with her to ensure nothing else happened."

"I was almost buried under a bunch of cheap junk earlier," Rainette groaned. Rainette looked like she was dressed for a party. Her clothes were inexpensive but stylish.

"I think they were parts for somebody's computer once," she went on. "Anyway, there isn't much left, and I've been wandering around the place trying to get a reading on whatever did this."

"How has that been working?" Cole asked.

"Terrible," she said. "There are some very faint signals, residuals from when whatever did this was still inside the building, but I can't get a fix on them. It's like… whatever did this just gave up and left or was never here to begin with."

"Nothing at all?" Cole surveyed the damage in their area again. "That isn't possible. There should still be something even if the human forensic team couldn't locate it."

"There is," Marcel told him. "We've been finding it all over the place. It just hasn't done anyone much good."

Cole looked at the ogre. "Ectoplasm?"

"Right," Rainette said, looking surprised. "This whole place is covered in ectoplasm. The forensics team was finding it in nooks and crannies everywhere, enough to where it's actually visible to people with no Sight whatsoever. They can see, feel, and smell the stuff."

"That's how I knew about it," Cole informed her. "It's thick enough to where the smell is difficult to miss."

"I'm still not convinced a bunch of ghosts did this," Rainette insisted skeptically. "A ghost's body, for lack of a better term, is made up primarily of ectoplasm, and the substance always carries a fragment of the ghost's persona with it. None of the ectoplasm carries any kind of signature whatsoever. It's completely blank."

Cole was confused. "That doesn't make any sense," he said. "You found ectoplasm, a lot of it, for that matter, all over the crime scene, and yet you don't think ghosts were responsible?"

"The ectoplasm doesn't have a signature," Rainette repeated, like she was speaking to a kindergartener. "All ghosts leave behind a kind of footnote of themselves, similar to how humans have auras. A ghost's ectoplasm will share an imprint of who it was. If you can read that imprint, you can learn more about the ghost and what it wants. Ectoplasm is just the substance ghosts are made of, after all. The principle is more or less the same when using thaumaturgy in location spells."

"We keep coming back to the same conclusion," Marcel added, sounding bored. "Rainette has explained this to us several times, but the only conclusion we've been able to draw so far is that ghosts were responsible. Not that there is much evidence to work with, for us or the regular forensics team."

Cole surveyed the area again. "I just don't see how there could be ectoplasm in a crime scene and no 'signature', as you call it," he said after a moment. "If ghosts did do this, and that's highly uncharacteristic of ghost behavior as I know it, you should be able to track them easily."

"And yet we have nothing," Rainette declared, throwing her hands up. "There's nothing here for me to sense. It's like the ghosts don't exist to begin with."

"I find it all very confusing," Marcel confessed. "Is there an expert in the field of ghost study we could ask? The police data bank has consultants on just about everything."

Cole gave Marcel a look, followed by a wry smirk. "You're really getting into this detective work, aren't you?"

Rainette surprised Cole by defending Marcel. "He's been a big help," she insisted. "I hate having to fill out police reports. Marcel makes it look easy."

"So why were you two arguing?" he wondered, looking back and forth between them.

"Oh, that." Rainette didn't look as though she wanted to answer at first. "I was having trouble getting any kind of reading from the ectoplasm, like I said before. He thought it might help if I stuck my hands in the stuff. I refused on the grounds that it can overload a witch's senses."

Cole nodded. "I've heard that," he said. "Something about it overpowers untrained witches and makes them susceptible to a spirit's influence."

Rainette looked less than pleased at the mention of "untrained witches." "And it's gross," she added.

"That too."

Curious, Cole stuck his head in closer to one of the shelves. He didn't have to look far at all for the ectoplasm Marcel and Rainette were talking about. Whole clumps of it were stuck between the metal girding of the shelves and between whatever fragmented remains had been placed there. It was indeed so condensed that a regular human would find no difficulty spotting it. Most humans ignored this kind of thing. With the room in chaos, however, it would have been almost impossible to ignore.

Movement behind him tore Cole away from his observations. Looking up, he felt his heart skip slightly as Inspector Vallimun stormed down what was left of the aisle toward them. It had been a while since Cole had seen the mortal, though that term was still debatable. His eyes drifted down to the right arm hanging casually at the inspector's side. The same color flesh as the rest of his body coated it. By outward eyes, there was nothing different about it whatsoever. Cole knew better, though, since he had been the one who aided the Goddess in regrowing it.

Joss was avoiding looking at him. It shouldn't have bothered Cole at all, yet it was. The fact that his heart fluttered as Joss had approached irked him fiercely. The man shouldn't matter that much to him so soon, yet he did. Cole should have known from the start not to let his feelings for Joss get the better of his judgment, yet he had. He was growing soft, and that frightened him. Fey who were exiled to the mortal realm had to be very cautious, particularly when it came to humans. Surprisingly, however, none of that bothered Cole as much as the fact that his boyfriend, whom he hadn't seen in days, hadn't said hello to him yet.

"Anything?" Joss asked. His voice was tense, and he didn't sound happy. Cole had to remind himself that it was probably after four in the morning now and not a good time for overworked inspectors to be awake.

"Nothing," Rainette told him, sounding unhappy herself. "It's the same here as it was everywhere else."

"Hm." Joss sounded angry, though not specifically with Rainette. "Well, maybe when the forensics team analyzes the stuff, they can tell us something."

"Not likely," Rainette countered. "I tried to warn one of them before. The ectoplasm will dissolve quickly, even faster once it is taken from the place it condensed at. The minute I used that word on them, though, I got 'the look' and they pretended like I wasn't there."

"We have to be careful about what we say in front of them," Joss reminded her. "They won't take us seriously if we talk about ghosts tearing up storage buildings."

"Despite the fact that it seems as though this is what actually happened," Cole chipped in, looking at Joss directly now. "How have you all been, incidentally?"

Joss glanced at Cole. "Lousy," he replied, turning away again. "Internal Affairs has tied us up in so much red tape that we can't even piss without them breathing down our necks. The chief informed me personally that we aren't to speak a word of things like monsters, ghosts, zombies, or fairy-tale creatures committing crimes in this city ever again. Our job is to find out what really happened and report it in a believable and scientific way."

"He actually used the word 'scientific'," Rainette added for Cole's benefit. "I wanted to laugh."

"It was a good thing you didn't," Joss said, looking strained now. "I haven't seen him or the mayor so wound up in ages. If I didn't know better, I'd say someone higher up is putting serious pressure on them."

"The Order," Cole said flatly.

"We can't know that for certain," Marcel replied quickly.

"We can," Cole insisted, leaning against the shelf. "They were involved with the incident on Staten Island last month. It was their technology that Daniel Whittaker used to establish himself as the Lord of All Fey. They had me suspended indefinitely to cover up the incident inside the police and get me out of the way."

Everyone looked at Cole now. "I was left to rot in the sithen for weeks," he pointed out irritably. "Anytime I left, someone from Internal Affairs or probably the Order itself found me and had me followed. There was nothing to do but sit on my ass and think."

"It does make a weird sort of sense," Rainette admitted. "And it would explain why we've been spied on so much since that whole Staten Island fiasco. Why is the Order so intent on keeping you out, though?"

"The Order despises the fey," Marcel answered automatically. "It is how they have always worked. The fey are a threat to them and their power as master magicians of the human Craft. So long as something exists in this world that is stronger magically than they are, the Order will never rest."

Cole nodded emphatically in agreement. "The fey, especially a sidhe, working in the NYPD must have set them all off. They can't have us inside the law enforcement. It would be regarded as a taint, and I was the one who insisted Marcel be allowed to serve the Section as a way of paying off his debt to society."

"Which makes me wonder, why didn't they just get rid of Marcel?"

The question seemed to be for Cole, though Joss still wasn't looking at him. "I don't know," Cole said finally. "I could harbor a guess, though I'm sure Marcel would prefer I didn't."

Marcel looked at Cole. "Go ahead," he insisted. "I am listening."

Cole chose his words carefully. "The sidhe were the highest ranking race in fey society. That didn't change once for hundreds of thousands of human years. Even the people of this realm know it to be true. Perhaps the Order saw Marcel as the lesser threat and easier to control."

Marcel frowned as best he could and nodded thoughtfully. "It does sound like them," he admitted. "And by the by, I take no offense from that statement."

"What was offensive about it?" Rainette asked, looking up at Marcel. "I don't understand."

"You wouldn't," Marcel said. "You were never raised in Faerie. Neither was I, for that matter, but some of my older family still recall a time when the sidhe treated us as slaves and little more. They are still sore about it. I doubt very much they would be thrilled to hear I was working alongside one now."

"I never agreed with the Order," Cole stated flatly as he felt his temper rise. "Even less than the other fey did. Their methods reminded me too much of how Faerie worked before I was exiled."

"I see." Rainette was giving Cole a look the whole time. "Well, if we're done with the PSA on Faerie racial relations, there's something all of you might want to know."

"What's that?" Cole wondered as he felt something behind him shift.

"The ectoplasm behind you is moving," she said, pointing. "In fact, now it looks kind of… angry!"

Cole backed away from the shelf very quickly and drew out Aed Deigh. The red-hot blade extended from the hilt as Joss took point with his .357 Magnum. Joss aimed his gun at the goop as it moved around as though surveying each of them. When its head, or the lump that passed for it, settled its gaze on Cole's smoking blade, it abruptly went berserk. The goop flattened itself into a puddle, then went wild, bouncing around and stretching itself out in all directions at once. With a squeal, it shot off away from them like a jackrabbit.

Joss lowered his gun. "Go after it," he said. "It might be a clue as to what happened here."

"Even if it isn't," Rainette said, giving chase with Marcel hot on her heels, "it's still fascinating."

Joss watched them go, keeping a safe distance between himself and Cole as he put his gun away. "I wonder what set it off?" he said quietly. "Was it you?"

Cole didn't answer. "Can I see you for a minute in private?" he asked instead. "There's something we need to discuss."

Joss finally glanced his way again, but only after a moment's hesitation. "There's nobody else here but us," he said. "Staffelbach is back at the station checking on some leads for us. I thought it wasn't a good idea to leave the station alone without one of us there. It might keep Internal Affairs out of our files and personal effects for a little while, at least. Oh, and Corhagen has the night off. Something about him going to see one of his kid's preschool shows."

"I was wondering where he'd gotten off to," Cole muttered. "How did he take having you put back in charge of Section Thirteen?"

"He was quiet," said Joss. "I think it bothers him more than he's letting on. He's the one guy Internal Affairs seems least interested in. So far, though, he hasn't given me any trouble."

"That is strange."

"Hold on, Marcel! I've got it cornered!" Rainette's voice echoed from somewhere on the far end of the room. "Idiot, you missed!"

What followed was a "splorch" kind of sound, echoed by many things crashing to the floor at once. Joss had gone back to looking around the room. Cole observed this for a moment before deciding he didn't have to take it anymore. Grabbing Joss by the collar of his shirt, he yanked him in until they were eye to eye.

"We have to talk," he said flatly. "Outside, I think."

Cole released him and stomped off toward the big hole in the building that had once been a door. He could hear Joss's footsteps behind him, though at a distance, and tried to act as if none of it mattered. Cole was a carefully trained sidhe warrior, even though he'd barely been acknowledged as one among his own people. His movements should have been silent and unreadable, yet a nagging whisper told him Joss was monitoring his mood very carefully from farther back.

Cole didn't stop when he reached the outside. A few of the officers guarding the place were still too close for his comfort, so he made a right and headed down to where there was a nearby alley. Once out of sight, he waited in the shadows for Joss to catch up. Joss had barely stepped into the alley before Cole was on him and pushed the inspector's body up against a wall.

For once, perhaps the first time all night, the inspector gave Cole his full attention. "I almost shot you," he stated in a tone that hinted at his anger.

"You would have to have aimed for me first," Cole replied, staring daggers at him. Joss immediately looked away, which set Cole off completely.

"*Look at me*," he growled. Though his voice hadn't been much louder than a normal speaking tone, the words somehow reverberated off the walls.

Joss met Cole's eyes then, and Cole was stunned to see the man appeared close to tears. Joss wound his arms around Cole's back and clung to him like he was the only vessel at sea. Cole leaned in slightly and breathed in his lover's scent as he felt several light kisses on his shoulder through the fabric of his shirt.

"I couldn't," Joss whispered softly. "They are watching us all the time. Yesterday, I was held inside an interrogation room for seven hours. They were asking questions about you. They wanted to know everything I knew."

"About our...." Cole paused as the word stuck in his throat. "Relationship?"

Joss shook his head, moving back now to look Cole in the face clearly for the first time. "That was the one thing they didn't ask. They didn't want to know about us. They wanted to know where you went every day. Apparently, Internal Affairs is getting frustrated with the way you keep disappearing."

"Did you tell them the truth?"

Joss smirked. It was the first time he'd looked the least bit happy all night. "Finally, I did. They weren't too pleased with the part about how your house is under Bowling Green park, or that your garage door can appear anywhere in town. I think they thought I was making it up."

"The Order will believe otherwise," Cole said. "Don't worry, though. They might have found out some other way, and knowing won't give them any power to control me. You told them everything and nothing."

"I've been scared," Joss admitted. "It makes me sick to admit it, but this whole mess is scaring me. The monsters we deal with are nothing compared to the people we answer to."

"I believe you," Cole said, still holding onto Joss tightly. "And I feel like a fool for not realizing it sooner. It's…."

"…just that we haven't been able to see one another," Joss finished for him. "I feel the same way. Before I found out you'd been reinstated, I was ready to punch someone. Rainette told me that if I didn't loosen up a little soon, she would smack me upside the head, superior officer or not."

The surprise was apparently evident on Cole's face because Joss laughed. "She's all right," he told him. "I haven't had any problems with her outside of her not having much experience. Really, she's easier to deal with than most other new recruits fresh out of training."

"That *is* a surprise," Cole mused. "Perhaps it really is just me, then."

"Probably."

The smug smirk Cole had come to recognize was adorning Joss's face again. Cole brought him in for a slow, sweet kiss, then pulled away.

"Come over once we're done here," he said, pressing their foreheads together. "You can give me a detailed report on what's been going on during my absence. Preferably while we're naked and I'm fucking you into oblivion."

"Can't," Joss said sadly. "I want to, but after all this, my ass is going straight to bed. I'll probably be asleep for the rest of the day, and after that there are reports to fill out and so forth."

"You could always move in," Cole offered, gripping Joss tightly now. "There's still plenty of room. The pixies barely take up any space at all, and Mal is… well, everywhere."

Joss sighed as Cole pulled him in for another kiss. "Let me think about it."

Cole kissed him again, harder this time. Joss responded, but all too soon he pushed Cole away again. Standing at one another's sides, they marched back to the crime scene, walking for all intents and purposes like soldiers readying for battle. The only thing missing in Cole's mind was some suitable background music.

"You and your boyfriend patch things up?" one of the officers called out sarcastically as they stepped over the tape.

"I had to ask him something," Cole answered calmly. "We didn't sneak away from the job to go make out, assuming that is what you're implying."

Cole distinctly heard one of the officers snort. "Yeah, right. He was over there taking it up the ass again."

Cole turned around even as Joss tried to snag him by the arm. Sniffing the air, a smile began to spread across Cole's face as he sauntered over to where the group was watching. The one who had spoken immediately went rigid and set his cup of coffee down. His hand was drifting toward his gun even as he tried to appear relaxed. Cole spotted the name on his badge as he drew in closer.

"I would ask your friend standing next to you about taking it up the ass, Officer Conclehnn," Cole told him in a low voice.

Officer Conclehnn frowned and looked at Cole, confused. "What?"

The grin on Cole's face spread wider. "Two days ago," he said as the color drained from Conclehnn's face. "Tops. You don't look like a submissive to me, so I'm guessing he must have been the one taking it in the ass. Besides, I can still smell the lube you used on him. You might want to consider switching brands. I could make a recommendation if you'd like."

Everyone was watching as Conclehnn stepped back, away from Cole. The officer's face was as white as a sheet. He looked as though he might be sick.

"Just a thought," Cole added loudly before he turned around.

"What did you say to him?" Joss asked once they were inside the building again. "I thought he was going to start screaming."

"You may recall that my nose does more than center my face," Cole said as they continued farther in. "Conclehnn and his friend there have been seeing each other for a while now, from what I smelled."

"Right," Joss said, looking back over his shoulder. "Well, I'd heard rumors. Speaking of your nose, have you smelled anything strange in this place?"

"You mean like what did this?" Joss nodded, to which Cole responded with a shake of his head, causing his hair to sweep around him. "That is another thing that has been bothering me. Rainette could sense nothing from the ectoplasm left behind, and I cannot catch even a trace of scent left by anything other than the forensic team that searched this place before. This thing, or things, whatever did this, they can't be detected by our usual means."

"That isn't good," Joss said gravely. "No one is going to be happy to hear we're dealing with something that can't be tracked down. Internal Affairs wants us shut down, but no one can deny that we've gotten fairly good results."

"Except for that one time with the slime cube in the sewers," Cole reminded him.

"We agreed never to speak of that again," Joss replied sharply. "The guys in vice squad still won't talk to me. Anyway, we need to keep solving the cases handed to us quickly and quietly or they'll use that as an excuse to separate us."

"I have a more immediate concern," Cole said as they rounded yet another corner.

"What is it?"

Cole stopped and gestured around them. "This isn't an especially big place, at least as far as storage facilities go."

"I've seen bigger," Joss agreed. "What are you getting at?"

"We've nearly walked all the way through it," Cole went on, his voice darkening. "So where are Marcel and Rainette? They were only supposed to catch that escaping glop of ectoplasm that came to life behind me."

Joss's face went stone cold. "I think I might have an idea," he replied, pointing to something behind Cole. "Look over there. That wasn't here before."

Cole turned around and immediately spotted what Joss was talking about. Near the twisted remains of what had once been a metal shelf was a solid chunk of concrete. Cole walked down the aisle and picked the piece up off the floor, testing its weight.

"It looks like one of the pieces of the wall from the front," Cole said to Joss as the inspector approached. "But how did it get here?"

Before Cole had finished his sentence, he was already looking up at the answer just a few feet away. Another large hole, not as big as the one they'd come inside through but big enough, had been torn into the side of the building. There were traces of goo around the edges.

It looked as though the ectoplasm had vacated the building and was now running loose on the streets of New York City.

Cole stuck his head out beside Joss's as they surveyed the damage leading out through the hole onto the loading dock, where the unseen thing had escaped to, and beyond.

Cole turned back to Joss. "This is going to… 'suck', isn't it?"

"Yes, it is."

Off in the distance, a car alarm rang out along with what sounded to Cole's ears like screeching metal over a ton of swearing. "At least we know where the others will be. Assuming they're alive, finding them shouldn't be a problem. We just have to follow the carnage."

"We will," said Joss, stepping through the hole into the loading area outside. "And when we get back, I want to have a brief word with the boys who were supposed to be watching this place while we were gone."

THE trail wasn't long, nor was it hard to follow. Cole didn't even have to use his nose. He had been tempted to shift forms as he took point beside Joss, but in his wolf form he wouldn't have been able to use any of his weapons. Cole wanted to be ready in case whatever had broken out of the storage facility was watching from the shadows. "What are we dealing with?" Joss asked as they raced through the back alleys in search of their prey.

"It was likely the ectoplasm from before," Cole explained, keeping his pace even so as not to outdistance Joss. "Given the size of the exit it made for itself, the thing must have gathered the rest of the ectoplasm lying around into itself and formed a body."

"Great," his lover muttered. "So now what?"

"That means we're were dealing with a largely unknown creature," Cole went on as they crossed an empty side street where several parked cars had been turned over. "Whatever this thing is, it can potentially assume any form it wants, provided it has the sentience to do so."

"And Marcel left with DuBois without calling for backup?" Joss cursed loudly as they swerved around a mound of broken glass. "Rookies!"

"Rainette will have wanted the thing contained," he explained. "Most likely, anyway. When you think about it, this thing is the only real clue we have to work with."

"Of course," Joss moaned. "So destroying it is out of the question unless we absolutely have to. I wonder what else will go wrong?"

Cole frowned as they turned a corner. "You should know better than to ask such things."

The ground was slick with ice and snow. They reached the end of the trail a few minutes later. Joss nearly fell as Cole came to a stop. Up ahead was a large warehouse with another gaping hole in the side. Sounds could be heard coming from inside it. Cole pointed Joss in the direction of it and ran on ahead, sliding to a stop as he reached the hole.

There wasn't much light to work with, but Cole didn't require it. Parade floats and equipment, old tents, cotton candy machines, and carnival rides were shoved tightly next to one another inside. Cole recognized some of them as he slipped in under the shadows. This was where the city stored some of its parade floats when not in use. Apparently, Coney Island park had been renting the area as well, to tuck away some of their worn-out equipment.

Not far away, there came the sound of cheery circus music blasting over Rainette screaming at the top of her lungs. Cole made tracks for the sound of her voice as Marcel let out a furious roar. As he rounded a corner in front of Donald Duck's head, he heard a crash that sounded like metal colliding with flesh and bone. Marcel roared again, this time in pain, and came sailing toward Cole just as he came up on the small open space where they were fighting. Marcel almost crashed right into Cole as he dodged to the side. "How is it going?" he asked as Marcel began pulling himself free from Snoopy's nose. "I've been better," Marcel grumbled, accepting the hand that Cole offered. "We chased it here after it escaped out of the storage facility. Rainette had it cornered, but then it leaped inside the merry-go-round."

"Merry-go-round?" Cole turned to find Rainette holding on for dear life to one of the plastic horses as the hovering merry-go-round spun faster and faster toward them.

"Help!" Rainette had to scream very loudly in order to be heard over the grinding of the machine's gears. Her lungs, it seemed, were up to the challenge, however. *"Get me off this thing!"*

"Merry-go-round," Cole affirmed, drawing out both guns now. "Got it."

Rainette caught a glimpse of Cole taking aim as she clung to the merry-go-round spinning high over his head. "Don't shoot at it!" she shouted, her voice growing hoarse now. "You might hit me!"

Cole fired anyway. None of his bullets came close to her, instead striking the interior of the ride's mechanics. There was a high-pitched whining sound that made both Cole and Marcel shudder as one of the bullets got stuck between the gears. The merry-go-round ceased spinning so fast and began wobbling while still up in the air.

"Jump," Cole said loudly to Rainette. "Before it starts back up again."

Rainette didn't hesitate. Releasing her death grip on the plastic horse, she flung herself over the side and plunged toward the dirt-covered concrete floor below.

"If one of you doesn't catch me," she shouted on her way down, "I swear I'll never forgive—"

Rainette's threat was cut off abruptly as she landed in Marcel's arms. He was quick to set her back on her feet. Rainette wobbled for a moment as she struggled to regain her balance. Above them, meanwhile, the merry-go-round of doom was fighting for all it was worth to expel the intruder lodged within its gears.

Cole watched the mechanical beast, his hands slowly going toward Aed Deigh as the monstrosity began to force itself back to life again. Down below, Rainette was giving Marcel a strange look.

"Thanks," she said, staring at him cross-eyed. "For catching me, I mean."

Marcel frowned in confusion. "What else was I supposed to do?"

"I'm sorry to interrupt," Cole called out, holding Aed Deigh in both hands now. "But the two of you might want to move away from there."

Marcel grabbed Rainette up in his arms again before she could move a muscle and hurled them both out of the way. The merry-go-round came crashing down, missing them by inches and sending Rainette falling forward on a broken high heel with Marcel tumbling after her in a desperate attempt to catch her again. Seeing they were safe, for the most part, anyway, Cole charged forward with a battle cry in his native tongue and Aed Deigh raised high over his head as both blades sprung out in opposite directions from the hilt in the center.

The plastic horse Rainette had been holding onto was promptly decapitated. Cole hacked and slashed his way around the false creature as the merry-go-round of doom began rising up off the floor again, spinning in a fast circle. Seizing one of the metal poles, Cole spun himself around and attacked what might have been a replica of Santa's sleigh as he continued in a roundabout path for the center.

"Come out of there!" he shouted angrily, taking another plastic horse's head off. "Come out and face me, you coward!"

Calling the machine a coward proved to make it angrier, exactly what Cole had been hoping for. He could smell the thing controlling it from deep inside. The ectoplasmic monster had too strong a defense while it lurked inside the carnival ride. Cole needed to damage it enough to make it think he was too serious a threat and make a run for it. This plan proved to contain a fatal flaw a moment later. Sidhe or no, immortal or no, there were some things Cole had no power against in this realm. When the merry-go-round increased its speed and then suddenly tilted sideways unexpectedly, he was caught by the anomalous movement. Something caught his eye as he was flung at an awkward angle down past the artificial constructs he'd destroyed before.

Cole snapped his arm out and grabbed one of the headless horses before he could fall out of the merry-go-round completely, and he clung to it for dear life.

"Where's Don Corleone when you need him?" Cole grumbled as he felt his hand slip due to the moisture in the warehouse. "Or Tom Hagen, for that matter?"

Rounds from a Magnum reverberated off the walls like thunder. Cole heard the shots strike the underside of the merry-go-round and let go. As his body glided through the air, he spotted a deflated parade balloon and aimed toward it as best he could. It looked reasonably soft, but upon landing, Cole discovered to his painful displeasure that it was merely a colorful piece of tarp concealing a float. The structure collapsed upon impact, leaving Cole to pick himself up out of what was now sure to be an expensive pile of junk.

Joss, meanwhile, was standing atop another parade float across from him and firing more bullets into the possessed merry-go-round. Cole got to his feet as quickly as he could and charged the merry-go-round with Bandersnatch and Jabberwock at the ready. Together, the two pumped the thing's inner works full of lead. Joss had to reload several times, owing to the fact that his gun did not have infinite ammo. Each time Joss stopped to reload, the merry-go-round would swoop down and try to squash him flat. Cole managed to keep it away from Joss with the help of Aed Deigh until the contraption turned around and swatted him back like an annoying fly.

Cole rolled to a stop where Marcel was looking after a barely conscious Rainette. "Is she all right?" Cole asked wearily as he stood up.

Marcel watched as Joss fired at the merry-go-round again. "She is coming around," he said. "But I think you need my help more."

"We'll manage," Cole insisted. "She can't fight in that state."

"Shows what you know," Rainette muttered, raising herself up slightly. "See for yourself."

Cole drew his guns again and lay down cover fire so Joss could dodge another attack by the merry-go-round, then glanced back. On the concrete a foot or so from her hand, a magic circle had been inscribed into the dusty floor with Rainette's blood. "Don't you dare tell anyone from my coven that I used blood to do this," she warned in a weak voice. "They'd never let it go."

"You're too weak," Cole said, crouching down beside her. "Marcel, go help Vallimun. Whatever happens, do not let that thing get near him."

Marcel stood up to go, but Rainette caught him by the foot and held him in place. "Don't get hurt," she said meaningfully. "I'll never forgive you if you die fighting a merry-go-round."

Marcel simply nodded and charged forward with a battle cry that shook the room. Cole took Rainette by the hand as the ogre tackled the merry-go-round with both arms spread before it could connect with Joss. Joss dove to the side as the machine collided with the floor where he'd been standing. Rolling back to his feet, the inspector fired off a couple of warning shots as Marcel pounded the mechanical beast with his fists.

"That's my man," Cole responded wryly.

"Indeed," Rainette agreed. "Now, I think I can expel the thing inside. The problem will be mustering enough power. Usually, this wouldn't be a problem, but I'm hurt, and the damn thing is moving around too much for me to get a lock on it. I need you to back the spell up. Can you do that?"

Cole gave her hand a squeeze in answer and let his power flow through her. Being a sidhe, he had energy to burn, and handing a small bit over to Rainette so she could turbocharge her spell was child's play. The circle on the ground glowed a ruby red color. The light covered Cole's albino skin and reflected off his snow-colored hair. Rainette squeezed his hand in gratitude before moving their hands into the space above the circle. Quickly, she began chanting in Latin. Cole did not recognize the dialect, but the intent was clear.

Marcel had reached the merry-go-round's center and was hammering into it savagely while Joss kept the machine busy by dodging its attacks. Each time the merry-go-round came near him, Joss would duck to the left or right out of the way. The merry-go-round appeared to regard Marcel as the primary threat, though each time it focused its attacks on the ogre, Joss would open fire on it again to draw its attention away.

On the ground, a red mist had formed around Rainette and Cole. Human blood mixed with sidhe power was a potent mix, one not to be taken lightly. The mist swirled for a moment before lashing out toward the battle not far away. When it reached the merry-go-round, the mist wrapped itself around the contraption and solidified, taking the shape of red chains.

"Marcel!" Cole called out as the ogre continued to rip out the machine's innards. "Get out of there now!"

"Hurry!" Rainette added, getting the ogre's attention.

Marcel shook off his rage and leaped free just as the spell took effect. Everyone watched as the chains rose up off the merry-go-round into the air above it. As they left the machine, so did something else. Rainette gasped as the creature within was torn free from its host. The merry-go-round let out a feeble tune as though taking one last breath before dying, then crashed noisily to the floor in a heap. Marcel and Joss both scattered as pieces went flying. Cole gave the ogre a silent word of thanks as he used his body to shield Cole's lover from harm.

Then he got a look at the thing Rainette's spell had extracted. Inside the circle of red chains, there were faces, thousands of contorted faces screaming silently in pain as they flowed in and out of a mass of writhing, quivering tendrils. Between the ropes of tentacles were mouths, each bearing razor-sharp-looking mandibles that snapped angrily.

Cole withdrew his gaze and focused on helping Rainette contain the thing. Though the ectoplasmic spirit had been drawn out of the machine, the battle was far from over. If the clicking mandibles and staring eyes were any indication, the creature was far from happy. Marcel's assault on it had done little to take the fight out of the creature. Even bound by mystical chains, it continued to struggle as Cole added a bit more power to the spell, hoping that would be enough to subdue the entity.

The circle shone like a beacon now. Cole felt the energy pushing against his hand. Rainette was chanting faster, but it didn't appear to be enough. The creature, its form changing every few seconds, fought against her spell as the chains surrounding it tightened. The more it struggled, the more visible Rainette's pain was.

"It isn't working," Cole told her, drawing his hand away slightly. "You're going to hurt yourself if you keep this up."

"I can do it," she insisted; then she went right back to the Latin chant.

"It's out of the machine now," Cole insisted. "I can destroy it."

"We need to contain it," Rainette hissed between words. "It's our only clue."

Something rippled in the space between where their flesh connected. The sensation was cold, like death, sparking Cole's left hand awake. Feeling like a fool for not thinking of it before, he switched hands with Rainette and poured magic from the Hand of Cold Death into the spell. Ectoplasm was the stuff of ghosts. Though he couldn't be sure that the thing had actually "lived" before, it was still made from the essence of spirits. Cole had dominion over all forms of the long dead. Therefore, it was possible for his power to exert some manner of control over it.

He hoped!

As energy from his hand of power entered the spell, the ectoplasmic monster let out a roar of pain. Light poured from the circle beneath them, forming a beam of red light that touched the ceiling. Both Rainette and the creature howled at the same time. Something rushed out of the ground and into Cole, making him go stiff. In that moment, he saw through the creature's eyes. The warehouse was a dark, empty place, not unlike himself. He wanted out, wanted to be free.

Then he saw himself kneeling on the floor beside Rainette and knew the source of what was trying to contain him. The creature dove at Cole while he was still witnessing everything from the creature's eyes. Someone cursed before the entity collided with him. Cole could hear Joss screaming his name, ordering him to move. There was a flicker of white light, and then something struck him in the gut. Cole saw the blow through the creature's perspective at the same time he felt it slam into him.

The blow made Cole whip back, severing the connection between himself and the creature. In the process, Cole released Rainette's hand from his. Looking around for Joss, he spotted the inspector behind the creature, pounding away at it. Joss's right arm was glowing a mixture of silver and ebony. The flesh was like liquid silver poured over obsidian, forming a tribal design. Surrounding the arm was a bright glow that flickered each time Joss moved.

The entity roared as Joss attacked it again. Cole sat back in wonder as a phantasmal armor formed around Joss's right arm and slammed into the creature over and over again, pushing it back. Joss's face was screwed up in rage.

"This way," Cole called out to him.

Joss didn't appear to hear at first, but a moment later he landed another blow against the creature that sent it sprawling backward. Grabbing Rainette up in his arms, Cole moved them both out of the way as the creature landed over the blood circle. Aed Deigh was in his hand a second later, the frost-covered blade extended.

"Power of winter," he called out in an authoritative voice. "Seal this being within your icy womb."

As the blade tip touched the floor, its power flared to life at the same time the mist from the circle poured free. The anamorphic being roared one last time as it struggled to free itself. Each time it changed shape, the mists would adjust themselves accordingly. Cole watched as Joss and Marcel came over to stand beside him. Cole passed Rainette to the ogre without a word. When the mists had completely enveloped the entity, it began to shrink. All of them looked on as the creature was forced into itself. The shrinking didn't stop until the creature had been reduced to the size of Cole's fist. Without making a sound, the mists crystallized and fell to the ground as a chunk of red ice. Cole retrieved it and held the lump up to his ear curiously. Inside it, he could still hear the creature moaning softly. "I think it's crying," he explained to the others matter-of-factly. "When Rainette gets better, she'll want to take a look at it."

Joss looked over to Rainette, still being held in Marcel's thick arms. "Any idea where we can keep that thing in the meantime?"

"A freezer would be my first guess," Cole replied. "To change the subject, when did you learn to do… whatever it was you just did?"

Joss shrugged, though Cole spotted the pleased smile on his face. "I've been practicing," he said in a nonchalant manner. "It worked much better this time than when I was trying to fetch beers from my refrigerator."

Marcel was looking down at Rainette, meanwhile. Deep concern covered his face as his finger brushed lightly over the wound on her forehead. "She needs medical attention," the ogre said. "We should go now."

"I agree," replied Joss, taking the lead. "I don't look forward to writing up this report."

"Nor do I," said the ogre as they all headed toward the hole. The foursome was nearing the exit when Cole smelled something. More light was spilling out of the hole than there should have been. He could hear footsteps outside beyond it, as well as what sounded like a police band radio crackling. Before he could grab Joss by the shoulder and stop him, however, several armed men in SWAT gear spilled into the warehouse.

"Freeze!" one shouted, taking aim with the assault rifle in his hands.

They all stopped dead in their tracks. "Of course," Cole said, keeping his hands close to his hips. "What else would happen?"

ONCE the SWAT team had packed up and driven off, things settled down a bit. An alarm had apparently been tripped when the entity tore a hole in the wall of the warehouse. The first cops on the scene had heard the battle going on inside, thought World War III was being fought, and called dispatch in a panic to send over the SWAT team. Cole was grateful for Joss's diplomatic skills in this situation. He seriously doubted he could have smoothed the events over as easily. Of course, his first instinct had been to reach for his guns and blast his way through. Being suspended had forced Cole to fall back into bad habits. He hadn't been a special detective for the NYPD very long, and even now it felt strange to think of himself as a cop.

Joss had someone radio for an ambulance just as one of the agents from Internal Affairs drove up. Joss spotted the car and motioned for Cole to step back slightly. It annoyed him, but after hearing what the last several weeks had been like for Joss and the rest of the Section, Cole wasn't about to make trouble this time. The IA agent spotted him nonetheless and came to an abrupt stop. Something occurred to Cole as the agent hesitated a moment before motioning the inspector over. It looked as though the stories about the grotto appearing inside the precinct had spread. Chances were, no one from Internal Affairs wanted to come near him after that fiasco, despite him not knowing how it happened. Wild magic was like that, though Cole still couldn't fathom why it was so interested in him all of a sudden.

Rainette, meanwhile, was being helped into the ambulance. Marcel wanted to ride with her but was forced to stay behind upon realizing the ambulance was not big enough to fit his large frame. Cole patted the ogre on the arm and promised to give him a lift as soon as they were done. Fortunately, it looked as though whatever conversation Joss was having with the IA agent was coming to a close. Joss left the agent standing on the street and passed Cole without saying a word, though they did exchange meaningful looks for a brief instant. Cole let his lover go without drawing attention to either of them. Whatever they had to say to each other could wait until they were alone.

The IA agent waited until Joss was farther along before coming up the sidewalk. His eyes remained fixed on Cole, determinedly avoiding Marcel, however difficult that was. When there was a good five feet or so of space left between them, the IA agent stopped short.

"I understand a member of the Section was sent to the hospital," he said in an unexpectedly sincere tone. "You all have my condolences. Which officer was it?"

Cole gave the man a once-over before answering. "Officer Rainette DuBois," he replied. "She sustained moderate injuries while helping to subdue a possessed merry-go-round."

The IA agent blinked. "I see," he said blandly. "I shudder to think the amount of paperwork that will be needed to close this case."

"It's barely even started," Cole said. "You'll undoubtedly find out about this sooner or later, but this wasn't an isolated incident. The thing we chased here was connected to the break-in at the high-security storage facility a few blocks away."

"I see," the IA agent repeated. "Is that something you should be telling me without permission from your superior?"

Cole shrugged. "You're with Internal Affairs," he said. "You can go into any police file or dig through any private reports you please. Keeping something like this a secret from you is pointless."

The IA agent smiled then. "I am Agent Willhiem," he said, offering Cole his hand. "I've been wanting to meet with you for a while, Special Detective MacColewyn."

Cole accepted his hand and felt something flicker along the edge of his skin. "You're a practitioner of the Craft," he stated as the man withdrew.

"And you truly are one of the Fair Folk," Agent Willhiem replied. "I had heard the stories but wasn't sure of them myself. You know how rumors go in this town. When word reached me that you were working inside the NYPD, I assumed somebody was having a laugh at our expense."

"'Our'?" Cole narrowed his eyes at the slip and sniffed the air closely. "You are a part of the Order."

Agent Willhiem grinned. "Guilty."

Marcel was frowning hard now. He had been quiet during the whole exchange and didn't appear put out at being ignored. Now, though, he watched Agent Willhiem with a shrewd sort of glint to his eye. "So the Hermetic Order of the Golden Dawn has spies within Internal Affairs," the ogre summarized. "I understand a great deal now. You've been working to make sure we don't expose you because of what happened on Staten Island."

"And to you in the precinct holding cells," Cole reminded for his benefit. "Someone put that black ring on you, and I still don't believe it was Daniel Whittaker."

Agent Willhiem sighed and removed his thick coke-bottle glasses. "The technology for the 'black rings', as you call them, was labeled top secret and a high security risk," he explained while wiping his glasses clean. "Their creator couldn't get the mechanisms to work right, so the project was shelved. It never occurred to the Secret Chiefs that the answer lay in the mind of a preadolescent."

"Shortsightedness on their part," Cole quipped. "Incidentally, you seem awfully forthcoming about all this."

"I have nothing to hide," Agent Willhiem said as he slipped his glasses back into place. "A secret organization lurking within the upper echelons of Manhattan society who dabble in mystical arts? You'd have better luck convincing the public that creatures from fairy tales were serving as police officers."

Marcel tilted his mouth in what almost passed for a human smirk. "That's what happens when children become jaded by television," he said.

"Indeed," said the agent, giving Marcel a proper look at last. "There is far more to you than what your report says. I think the Order should be made aware of that."

"Don't threaten him," Cole warned, motioning for Marcel to follow as he turned away from the IA agent. "I really don't like it."

Agent Willhiem chuckled as Cole and Marcel walked away. "Believe me, Detective MacColewyn, the Order doesn't waste time making threats."

Cole ignored the man and led Marcel back to his car. The drive to the hospital was uneventful save, of course, for Marcel having to lie on the backseat in a fetal position. There was simply no other way for Marcel to ride in the vehicle, which didn't sound happy as it trudged along through the snow-covered streets. When they at last came to a stop outside St. Mary's Medical, Marcel crawled from the car on his hands and knees and made a beeline for the front doors.

The security officer keeping watch took one look at the approaching ogre and immediately began having a major freak-out. Cole saw the man reach for something in his pouch and rushed forward.

"Special Detective MacColewyn and Officer Marrowdrinker," he said, flashing his badge so the security man could see. "A fellow officer from our division was brought in not long ago. We've come to see how she's doing."

The security guard hadn't taken his eyes off Marcel the whole time, nor had he taken his hand away from his belt, which Cole now saw contained a canister of pepper spray. "It's a disguise," Cole added, gesturing toward Marcel, who was watching the security guard closely. "Officer Marrowdrinker is actually much older."

At first, it didn't look as though the security guard was going to look away from Marcel. When Cole held his badge closer, the guard finally dragged his eyes away from the ogre. Upon getting a closer look, his body seemed to relax ever so slightly.

"That was careless of me," Marcel said quietly as they passed through the automatic doors, leaving the stunned security guard behind. "Becoming an officer of the law has made me a little too comfortable around humans."

"It beats trying to pass you off as a former circus freak," Cole pointed out as they stopped at the front desk to find out which floor Rainette was on. "Like we do at the precinct."

The two made their way over to the elevator amid several startled patients in the waiting area.

"Please don't remind me," Marcel said quietly.

Cole pressed the button and was rewarded when the elevator doors parted almost immediately. "Hey!" a woman shouted as he moved to step through. "I was waiting there and...."

The woman was dressed in a hospital robe and froze when she finally took notice of Marcel. "I'm so sorry," she whispered, backing away. "I didn't realize this was an emergency. Please, go right ahead."

Cole allowed Marcel to go first, then stepped into the elevator after him and ignored the woman as she tried to get one last glimpse of the ogre. "Twice in the space of five minutes," Marcel muttered while Cole pressed the button for Rainette's floor.

"Honestly," replied Cole as the elevator moved, "I'm starting to feel a little left out."

There was no one outside the elevator when it stopped and the doors opened. Stepping out, Cole looked around and, seeing the nurse's station was deserted, reached over the counter to pick up the list of patients for the floor. As he did, someone cleared his throat loudly. Cole glanced up and spotted Joss standing a couple of feet away, looking very tired. Marcel was already facing him.

"She's fine," Joss said by way of greeting. "There are some pretty bad bruises here and there, and the doctor wants to keep her overnight in case she has a concussion, but it's not as serious as we thought."

"Go on ahead," Cole told Marcel. "We'll wait out here."

"Room 402," Joss said as Marcel eased past. "There's no one else in there right now."

Marcel nodded his thanks and continued on. Cole waited until the ogre was gone before drawing his lover in close. "The IA agent wanted to have a word with me," he whispered, holding onto Joss tightly. "He's a member of the Order."

Joss stiffened and pulled back. "What?" he asked, looking Cole straight in the eye. "Are you sure?"

"He told me," Cole replied in a flat tone. "I suspect he wanted me to pass the information along to you."

Cole waited while Joss processed this new info. "I wasn't especially shocked," he confessed, when Joss remained quiet. "We know the Order has us under surveillance, along with Internal Affairs. The fact that the Order has spies inside the NYPD actually makes things much simpler."

Joss rose up at that. "How?"

"It's much harder to watch two different enemies in two different places at the same time," Cole pointed out, pulling his lover back into his arms. "We know Internal Affairs is working with the Order. More than likely, the Order controls them from within. Our enemies are in one place and we know where the attack will come from, whenever they decide to strike."

Joss groaned and buried his head into Cole's chest. "You're starting to make sense," he muttered, breathing Cole's scent in deeply. "That worries me, for some reason."

"It'll pass," Cole promised, wearing a smile as he patted Joss on the head. "In the meantime, why don't we head home?"

"I want to wait here a few more minutes," Joss told him, rising back to his full height. Cole noticed that whatever weight had been bearing down on the man seemed to have lifted somewhat. "The doctor insisted Rainette will be okay, but I don't want to leave her here alone. She asked me to call some members of her coven. They should be on their way."

"Good," Cole said, nodding. "Marcel can stand in a corner awkwardly while her coven members overreact to his presence."

Joss chuckled as Cole gently ran his fingers through the golden locks flowing from the top of the mortal's head. "One thing really bugs me," Joss mumbled after a moment. "Why does the Order want to get rid of us?"

"We're there?" Cole suggested. "They've gotten rid of things that were no threat to them before."

"It still doesn't add up," Joss said. "I know we're the police, but I've been a cop long enough to know how the system really works. The few of us alone wouldn't be enough to hurt a group like that, not without some powerful evidence, which they must realize we don't have by now."

"True," Cole said, pulling his hand away. "I honestly don't think the Order wants us out of the way. I think this is about them controlling us."

That made Joss pause again. "Explain," he said. "I'm on your train of thought, but I can't quite see where it's headed yet."

"The Order is all about power," Cole elaborated. "Most things are, but the Hermetic Order of the Golden Dawn is about amassing power and influence mystically, politically, and financially. They want to control Section Thirteen, not do away with us."

"That makes sense," said Joss as the pieces came together in his head. "Politicians have always kept cops in their pocket in case of an emergency. If the Order is as powerful as you said, I can see where they might think of us as an asset, especially considering what circles they run with."

"In both the human society and the supernatural, as you call it, the Order has considerable influence." Cole hesitated and then stepped back against the wall as a nurse came down the corridor toward them. The woman took notice of both him and Joss and smiled slightly, but gave no further indication. Once she was gone through the elevator doors, Cole relaxed and continued.

"Incidentally," he went on, "there's something I've been wanting to ask you for a while now. Did you ever find out who originally started Section Thirteen?"

Joss turned away from the elevator and looked back at Cole. "You've seen the files that were stored in the evidence warehouse," he reminded him. "All the names of the members were kept in there."

"Right," Cole said. "But who came up with the idea? Who did it all originally start with?"

Something passed over Joss's face then. "What are you getting at?"

Cole glanced around again and quickly threw up a veil of glamour to prevent them from being overhead. His glamour skills were not the best, especially around so much man-made machinery, but it would suffice for the time being. "I wonder if the first Section Thirteen wasn't founded by someone in the Order in the first place," he said, lowering his voice for good measure. "If the Order controlled the first Section from the beginning, it might explain why they lasted for so long."

"Because they had a powerful group with money backing them from behind the scenes?" Joss looked as though he wanted to protest but then hesitated. "Actually, that would explain a lot."

"It might explain why the first Section Thirteen was written off as expendable in the end," Cole added. "If the Section started out under the Order's thumb but then tried to distance themselves from the organization's influence as time wore on, the Order could have had them disbanded for their insubordination."

"Or because the first Section knew too much," Joss pointed out gravely. "You've made it pretty clear that the Fair Folk in this city like staying in the shadows."

"It's more that we've learned to survive longer by doing that," Cole corrected him. "Still, you aren't wrong. Plus, the Order loves keeping secrets."

Behind them, the elevator dinged again. "It's just a suspicion of mine," Cole finished as a familiar-looking group spilled out into the hallway. "But one worth thinking on."

Cole dropped the glamour around him and Joss before the group of practitioners could walk into it. The lady in front smiled when her eyes landed on Cole. Marianne, the high priestess of Rainette's coven, had always been friendly toward him.

"Tuulois," she said, greeting him with his true name. "It's been a long time. We missed you at Katalina's funeral."

Inwardly, Cole flinched at the mention of his deceased roommate. Katalina had been his friend and confidant, as well as a member of Marianne and Rainette's coven. Her death was still a raw wound. Only Joss seemed to notice the change in him. The other coven members stood behind Marianne, looking grim at the mention of her name. He would have liked to share in their grief, but Katalina had died because of him.

Nevertheless, Cole took both of Marianne's hands in his when she extended them toward him. Marianne had always enjoyed touching him. "I was in the background," he explained as she squeezed his fingers warmly. "You were sitting on the third row, if I remember right."

"Katalina's family almost didn't let us in," a woman standing further back added irritably. "I wish you had been there with us. You could have bewitched them into thinking we were the pallbearers."

"It's good to know you were there," Marianne went on, letting go of Cole reluctantly when he pulled away. "I wish we were meeting under better circumstances."

Cole nodded and reached over to pull Joss into the forefront beside him. Joss had been standing off to the side the whole time, though nowhere near as inconspicuously as he wanted. Several members of Rainette's coven were eying him, in particular the waves of sun-kissed hair concealing his face.

"It's good you are all here," Cole said, giving Joss's shoulder a squeeze. "Rainette is in with Officer Marrowdrinker at the moment, but they should be finished soon. Incidentally, this is Inspector Joss Vallimun, the police officer who helped rescue her."

Joss gave Cole a look as the coven members stared. "So Rainette really is working for the NYPD now?" someone in the back asked. "I thought she was joking this whole time!"

"Do you know what happened?" Marianne asked worriedly.

"She wasn't hurt badly," Joss assured her. "A few bruises here and there, but nothing too serious. The doctor wants her to stay here overnight for observation, just to make sure."

"She got attacked by a merry-go-round," Cole added.

Someone snorted. "Leave it to Rainette to piss off the only merry-go-round in Manhattan with a nasty disposition," she muttered.

"As long as she's all right," Marianne stated. "Does this mean you're working for the NYPD again as a consultant, Cole?"

Cole's mouth turned upward slightly in a wry smile. "Actually," he said hesitantly, "I'm a member of the NYPD now. I joined as a special detective. Inspector Vallimun and I work together in the same unit."

No one in the coven blinked.

"I'm very…." Marianne managed to hold it together for a second longer before she burst out laughing. "What now?" she demanded, laughing hysterically.

Cole glared as the coven members laughed in unison. Something behind him caught Marianne's eyes abruptly, and when Cole and Joss both turned to see what it was, they found Marcel standing halfway out the door to Rainette's room, looking at them curiously.

"I was wondering what everyone was laughing at," he said before ducking back in quickly.

"That's Officer Marrowdrinker," Cole explained to the wide-eyed coven members.

"Amazing," said Marianne. "I didn't know ogres were allowed on the police force. Rainette never mentioned she worked up close with one."

"Please don't stare," Cole asked as they began marching past him. "It makes him very uncomfortable."

"We won't," Marianne told him as she led the group along, though somehow Cole didn't believe her.

Once they were alone again, Cole pulled Joss forward and placed a small kiss on his lips. "You're coming home with me," he declared. "I want to see you tonight."

Joss started to protest, but Cole cut him off. "We haven't seen each other in almost a month," Cole reminded him, somewhat flatly. "This isn't an angle for sex. I just want to be around you for a little while."

In the end, Joss consented to ride home with Cole. Cole stepped inside Rainette's room to check with her and confirm she was indeed all right. Rainette reassured him by way of insults while the other coven members assured him that they would keep an eye on her. Marcel would be staying overnight, along with one or two others to insure the hospital staff didn't bother him. Marianne had already offered to give him a ride home once Rainette was released. Cole made sure she swore not to ask him too many personal questions. The fey were not a modest bunch, but Cole knew Marcel's experiences among humans had been less than appealing. He would most likely not find Marianne's questions flattering. Reassured, Cole left the room and marched purposely toward the elevator, snagging Joss by the back of his long coat as he passed by. His lover came along without protest.

Despite Cole's reassurance that he didn't want sex from Joss tonight, the sidhe had a difficult time keeping his hands to himself. The elevator was deserted except for them, and it was one of the few places they'd been alone together the whole night, and without interruption. By the time they reached the bottom, Cole had his hand down the front of Joss's pants while his free hand stroked a nipple through the fabric of the inspector's dress shirt. Joss had been caught halfway between enjoying the attention and trying to move away. When the elevator doors opened, however, he pulled away and marched out with Cole in tow.

A few humans in the waiting area looked up as they passed by, but Cole and Joss both ignored them. It felt good to step out into the cold March air. By now, the sun was rising over the row of skyscrapers in the distance. Before they had reached Cole's vehicle, a sharp wind was blowing across their faces, reminding everyone that the warmth of spring was still far away.

MAL was waiting for them with the hot water primed and Cole's bed already turned back. Keeping to his word, Cole allowed Joss privacy to shower in peace, stretching out nude on top of the covers while he waited. It occurred to him that Joss might get the wrong idea, but nudity was not an issue with the fey, and Cole wasn't about to change himself. When Joss emerged from the bathroom, still wet, he too was naked. Cole smiled, thinking he might have had an influence on the mortal in the short time they'd been together, and also because he was grateful for the show. His own shower felt marvelous, but Cole didn't spend very long under the jets. Joss was waiting for him, and, sex or not, Cole desperately wanted to crawl into bed with him.

After he had dried off thoroughly, Cole reentered his room and climbed in under the sheets. Joss was already there and dozing as Cole snuggled up behind him. Joss mumbled something unintelligible before falling silent. Cole drifted off after him almost immediately. The room and everything in it faded from thought as his body drifted on a cloud. Looking back on it the next morning, he wasn't sure exactly when it started.

At some point, Cole started to dream.

His body didn't feel right. This wasn't the first thing he noticed, yet it occupied his attention for several minutes. The first thing Cole noticed was how close the ground was. His legs were far too short. Furthermore, his skin was a dark blue color, like the sky at twilight, and his hair had turned black. Cole looked around and thought he recognized the place he was standing in. An instant later, he changed his mind, but the thought lingered. He had been transported to some kind of grove, though not one he'd ever visited in Faerie or on the mortal plane. Calling it a grove might have been something of a stretch. At one point, the ground looked like sand found out in the Sahara Desert. Then it was a deep, rich green, like the photographs of Ireland. Each time he wiggled his toes, the grass would ripple like water in a pond and the scenery changed.

There were trees. That much he could be certain about. Though their shadows stretched and shifted with the light, nothing about them appeared overall different, save perhaps for the fact that they were massive. Comparatively speaking, Cole felt like a gnat standing near them. It wasn't a pleasant sensation. Something made Cole turn to look behind him. He had never been this far out before. This was far too close to the kingdom's borders. It took a moment for him to remember why this sounded strange to him. If he'd never seen this place before, then he shouldn't know anything about it. Something in his gut pushed up to the surface, insisting that he turn around and go home. Cole resisted it, more on the grounds that home was nowhere near this place than anything else, but the feeling persisted. In defiance, Cole looked ahead of him. Not far away, he could see row after row of black thorns and burned grass. Everything ahead of him through the thicket looked scorched. This was the place where their lands ended, where he had been forbidden to go. He had wanted to see this place just once after hearing so much about it. One peek wouldn't hurt anything.

Before he knew it, Cole was running toward the place where the grassy earth met with the scorched ground. At the spot where the two met, he stopped short. He teetered on the edge there, daringly. It made him giggle to think he could come so close and not go over. Without thinking, he sniffed the air for signs of danger, just in case. Nothing made him think he was in trouble here. So long as he didn't go past this point, everything would be fine.

Feeling brave, Cole swung his arms back and forth, enjoying the sense of rebelliousness. There was no one here to watch him, to order him back or make him sit up and pay attention. He was enjoying the feeling when something grabbed him by the arm.

It was a vine, and the barbs had dug themselves deep into his flesh as the sharp vine wound itself around him. It had already curled up to his elbow and was moving further while tugging at the same time. The jerk caused him to lose his balance. Blood gushed out of the wounds as Cole fell forward over the line separating his ancestor's lands from their enemies'. The moment his foot touched the blackened soil, everything changed.

Cole's eyes snapped open as he felt a sharp pain in his ass. Gasping, he dug his fingers into Joss's back out of reflex as the mortal buried his cock in him, letting loose a flood of cum. Cole cried out at the same time Joss did, feeling his own unexpected release. Realizing he still had his fingertips dug into his lover's flesh, Cole let go as his own cock finished spewing cum into the mat of curly hair blanketing Joss's abs.

"Whew!" Joss gasped, stretching out alongside Cole. "That hurt! It's a good thing you came when you did. I thought I was never going to get you off."

Cole blinked, rose up to glance around the room, then lay back down. "Where am I?" he asked, knowing full well it was a stupid question.

Joss laughed. "I guess I really did rock your world," he said, sounding pleased with himself. "I suppose it has been a little while for both of us."

Cole took a moment to gather his thoughts while Joss stared at him. "Sorry," he apologized. "I think I must have been dreaming. What time is it?"

Joss frowned but rose up far enough to look past Cole at the clock on the nightstand. "A little after one," he said. "I didn't realize it was so late. Captain Hawkins is going to let us both have it, but I really don't give a shit right now. He can stew for a bit longer. I was on my beat until sunrise. A little downtime won't make me cry."

Cole smiled then and wrapped both arms around his love. "I want to do it again," he stated. "Once wasn't enough after waiting so long."

Joss snorted. "You are insatiable," he said. "But I guess one more round won't kill me. Then again, I don't think there's anything wrong with going out on a bang. Just give me a minute to recover."

"You don't need it," Cole said, rolling over on top of him. "It's my turn now."

He snaked his arms around Joss's neck and pulled the mortal to him for a long, passionate kiss. "Once we're done," he said seriously, while pushing his way between Joss's legs, "you and I have somewhere to go."

"Back to work," Joss answered as he raised his legs obligingly. "Don't remind me."

"Not yet," said Cole, pausing as he aimed his cock at Joss's ass. "We need to pay a visit to the man responsible for getting me reinstated. It's time for you to meet him, I think."

Joss gasped as Cole entered him, then groaned as the sidhe moved back and forth. Cole wasn't giving him time to adjust, but Joss didn't seem to mind. In mere moments, he was panting like a caged dog in heat.

"Wh… who?" Joss managed to get out.

Cole looped one arm underneath Joss's left leg and raised it up to give himself better access. It also gave him a chance to slow down and catch his breath.

"My godson," he answered before picking up speed again. "And my grandson. His name is David Bryne."

Joss said nothing during the rest of their time in bed, save for a few carefully placed swear words here and there. After they'd both cum again, Cole kissed him deeply on the mouth one last time, then reluctantly crawled off Joss so he could reach his cell phone on the nightstand. It was in his hand before Cole remembered he didn't have David's private cell phone number. The cell phone was a recent addition, a gift from the sithen. Cole had never carried one before, so he was still collecting phone numbers from people he'd known over time. The process was infuriating.

Deciding it didn't matter, he placed the phone back on the nightstand, then climbed out of bed. In the past, Cole had often dropped by David's place unannounced. David had never minded before, so calling ahead seemed a little unnecessary. Taking his lead, Joss got out of bed and followed Cole into the shower. The idea was that this would save time, but there was a slight delay as Cole felt a craving for Joss's cock one more time. Joss had to lean up against the shower wall to keep from slipping as Cole sucked down as much of the horse-sized dick as he could. Only after Joss came did Cole allow his man to finish bathing and exit.

Breakfast, or lunch, rather, was waiting in the kitchen when they entered it. A few of the pixies had left their fountain inside the sithen entrance hall, so Mal was attempting to chase them away as he served both men their meals. Being a part of the sithen, Mal could be in as many places inside of it as he wanted. At the moment, the Mal serving them was dressed like a stuffy British butler off an old sitcom, while the Mal chasing the pixies had assumed the guise of an exterminator.

An exterminator who talked like the Crocodile Hunter, to be exact.

"We are now entering the dreaded kitchen stove area of this treacherous terrain," the exterminator Mal whispered. "Pixies are well known for their ability to adapt, so we must be careful. Any sudden movements could set them off!"

As if in answer, one of the rebel pixies jumped out from its hiding place and flipped on the stove eye directly under Mal's hand. The flames came to life, causing Mal to jerk his hand back.

"Hot!" he shouted as snickering filled the air. "Come on, baby, light my fire!"

"I think they already did," Joss commented around his slice of buttered bread.

"Don't encourage him," Cole warned, while the butler Mal was glaring at his counterpart irritably. "When Mal starts getting on his own nerves, something is wrong."

Mal was still chasing pixies when they finished breakfast. Cole and Joss left quickly to avoid getting caught up in the whole affair. The pixies had taken to dropping pots to the floor. The kitchen was crawling with Mal copies trying to pick up the various pots, catch the pixies, and restore order all at once, none of which was working.

A loud crash echoed down the hall as Joss and Cole headed for the garage.

"Come on," Cole said flatly, reaching for the doorknob. "I want to get out of here before the chaos spreads."

The car started for them before either could get inside. Cole drove out into a busy street that he soon recognized as being near downtown. Once he had oriented himself properly, it took only a few minutes to reach the street where his godson lived. The space directly in front of the building was clear, so Cole ducked through a gap between oncoming cars and slid in while Joss held on for dear life.

A security guard was already on his way as both climbed out. "Sir, you cannot park your vehicle there," the man said loudly, in what Cole suspected was meant to be an intimidating tone.

"My name is Tuulois MacColewyn," he said, giving the large man a once-over. "I am here to visit my godson, David Bryne."

The man stared back blankly as if Cole had just spoken to him in Faerie language. "Let me guess," Cole muttered after a long sigh. "You're new, aren't you?"

The man didn't budge, and Cole would have left him bleeding on the sidewalk, unconscious. The only thing stopping him was the fact that Joss happened to be watching. The last thing he wanted to do was leave a bad impression of himself in Joss's mind, any more so than usual, at least. Plus, this was supposed to be a special occasion. One of the very few similarities between human and fey culture was meeting the family.

At last, following several minutes of Cole being given the runaround, a man dressed in a moderately expensive suit came out of the building to see what was going on. Cole immediately asked them to phone Hagen, his godson's personal aide, as Cole did not have the man's number. The building employee took Cole's name and placed the call on his cell. A moment later, the man hung up looking a little paler than before and shooed the security guard away.

"Right this way," said the man, leading them through the front door. "An attendant is holding the elevator for you so you can go right up. I'll make sure a valet sees to your vehicle."

"Will the vehicle try to eat the valet?" Joss asked as they walked across the ground floor lobby. "I remember you saying something about that once before."

"Probably not," Cole replied as they passed through the elevator doors. "So long as he doesn't touch the radio."

The elevator emptied out into a hallway. At the end, a door opened up to a set of stairs leading to the roof. Cole made sure Joss followed closely behind as they exited through yet another door onto the roof. It had been more than two months since Cole had last seen this place, yet it felt like a human lifetime. He had stood here once before, wishing he didn't have to confront his godson about what he knew. Joss gave an appreciative whistle as he took in the scene. "I could retire with the money that was sunk into all of this. How can he have green grass in this weather, and why isn't there any snow up here?"

"David has money to burn, and a flair for the dramatic," Cole said, leading his lover down the path through the green garden to the front door of the castle. "I suspect he gets at least one of those traits from me."

The garden path was a mixture of stone, fountains, and glass as green as emeralds. The sprinklers turned on just before they made it out, which ended with Joss getting soaked. Cole shook his head in pity as he rang the doorbell. To say that things weren't going according to plan was an understatement. His boyfriend was wet, and neither of them was really dressed for the occasion, now that Cole thought on it. They should have waited. He'd always been terrible with these kinds of things. However, it was too late to worry about it. A second later, Hagen opened the door to let them in.

"Master Colewyn," he greeted Cole, lowering his head respectfully. "And I see you've brought a guest with you! This is an event."

"I'm afraid the sprinklers caught Joss as we were coming through the garden," Cole explained to Hagen as Joss attempted to shake himself dry. "Could we have a minute so he can dry himself off before meeting with David?"

"As a matter of fact," Hagen said warmly while helping Joss shrug out of his wet coat, "there is a fire going in the drawing room right now. I just made some tea and biscuits, and we have a dry set of clothes you can both change into if you'd like. I'll have someone send them down along with a few towels so you can dry off."

Joss looked very uncomfortable as he followed Cole, who was being led to the drawing room by Hagen. Cole had been here enough to know where things were by heart, but Hagen had always insisted on doing his duty. Once they reached the drawing room, Hagen bowed slightly to both of them before hurrying off. Joss lingered in the doorway while Cole moved over by the fire. He wasn't cold exactly, but the fire looked inviting all the same. He wondered briefly if Mal would be able to whip up something like this for the sithen.

Looking up, he saw Joss still standing close to the door. "Come over here," he said. "It's warmer. Besides, lurking in doorways is considered rude in more than one culture.

"Also," he added as Joss reluctantly complied, "you should really do something about your expression right now. It looks as though you just bit into something sour."

Joss smiled, and it looked almost painful. "You don't like being here," Cole stated bluntly. "Why?"

Joss opened his mouth as if to answer, then immediately shut it as though thinking better of it. After a moment's silence, he tried again.

"I'm just... not used to all this," he answered at last, albeit clumsily.

Cole glanced around the drawing room. The space was opulently furnished, though the decorator David had hired had possessed the foresight to go with a moderately more subtle approach. Though the room spoke volumes of the wealth in his godson's possession, it was also the most comfortable room in the entire castle, save perhaps David's private quarters. "You don't like being waited on," Cole said, putting it together at last. "You're not comfortable around someone with more than you. Is that why you don't want to live with me?"

Joss quickly looked away, enraptured with a nearby lamp all of a sudden. A maid broke the awkwardness by quietly entering the room and placing a change of clothes near where Joss was standing, along with several towels. Joss stared at the bundle for a moment, like it might strike at him, while the maid quietly bowed out.

Cole sat, not saying a word, as Joss began to change. Once his wet clothes had been set aside, the maid returned to collect them. Joss looked taken aback by her sudden reappearance, in particular because she had caught him au naturel. To the maid's credit, she gave no indication that Joss's state bothered her, though Cole did catch her taking a furtive glance at his crotch before leaving. This made him smile, though it was very brief.

Once he was dry and changed, Joss joined Cole by the fire, though he insisted on standing the whole time. "I never knew having so much would bother you," Cole said quietly. "You should have said something before now."

Joss stiffened at the sharpness in Cole's voice. "It isn't you," he explained softly. "I don't mind being at the sithen, but it doesn't feel as though I belong there. Maybe later on, I'll consider it, but it feels like we're moving a little too fast right now."

Cole stared hard at him. "What do you mean?"

Joss turned toward him. "We just met a couple of months ago. Almost right after I met you, we wound up having sex with a third person, who, incidentally, can't look me in the eye without fighting off the urge to punch me in the face. I don't know what came over me when I… when I was asking you to join the Section. It just seemed like the thing to do at the time."

Joss's voice had gone up an octave or two. Though Cole wasn't bothered by the subject, he had the distinct feeling his lover didn't intend for the entire castle to know about their affairs, or the circumstances behind their initial meeting.

"You followed your instincts," Cole said, letting the calm in his voice drift through the air toward Joss. It wasn't mind control, but a simple trick to bring his lover back down to a more manageable state.

"Yeah," Joss mumbled. Then he took a deep breath. "I did. I've been wondering about that for a while now."

"Have you changed your mind?"

Joss chuckled at that. "If I had, this morning would not have been my way of saying it. No, I didn't change my mind. I just want to take things slower."

Cole was very confused now. "I thought we were."

Someone cleared his throat noisily. Both men turned at the same time to find David Bryne looking stiffly at them from the doorway. A pair of dark shades covered his eyes. The clothes covering his svelte but tightly muscled frame were tailor made and clung to his body like a second skin.

"Inspector," he said by way of greeting before turning to meet Cole's eyes. "Detective. I was told you both wished to speak with me. Would you like to conduct this in my office, or is in here fine?"

"This is fine," Cole said, finding David's behavior peculiar. "You know I've always preferred the drawing room."

David stiffened for an instant. "Yes," he replied curtly. "I remember."

Cole waited while David took a seat in the chair directly in front of the fire. "What can I do for you gentlemen?"

Joss said nothing. Cole kept his eyes on his godson for a moment before answering. "I wanted to thank you," he said in a slightly more formal tone. "You were the one responsible for getting the governor to reinstate me. I thought it would be better to come now rather than later. I hope I wasn't interrupting anything."

Whatever had been on David's mind before instantly left him. A great weight seemed to lift from his shoulders as his body visibly relaxed.

"Did you think we had come to arrest you?" Cole asked, a slight teasing in his voice now. "You would have to be guilty of something for that to happen."

"And you would need proof that I'd done it," David replied, though his voice had lost its edge now. Joss watched the unspoken words pass between them and laughed inwardly at it. It was clear the two had played this game of words with one another many times before.

After a moment of staring each other down, David smiled and turned toward the fire in defeat. "You are welcome," he said. "I felt it was the least I could do."

"To be honest," Cole confessed, "it came as a surprise to me. I had never asked anything of you before."

"You were always so proud," David said. "I wish you had come to me from the get-go. I would have had the mayor's head on a pike for you."

"That's too old-fashioned," Cole replied dismissively. "Don't people serve the severed heads of their enemies on a platter now?"

"Things have gotten a lot more high-tech in the last decade," David joked. "Today, we take photos of the severed heads with our cell phones and e-mail them to the offending party. It's much more efficient."

Joss stared at the two men as they laughed together. "You two are twisted," he said flatly. "I can see where he gets it from, though!"

David observed Joss a moment before turning back to Cole. "You never brought someone with you to visit before," he noted.

There was a definite question lurking somewhere behind the man's words. Cole closed his eyes and nodded as though giving an answer.

"No, I haven't," he replied. "This is Inspector Joss Vallimun, as I'm sure you already knew. Joss, this is my godson and grandson, David Bryne. His grandmother was conceived through my boss's wife, her husband, and myself on the night of Samhain."

"That isn't something you hear every day," said Joss. "So your grandmother had two fathers?"

"It would seem so," David told him, removing his glasses so the inspector could have a glimpse of his three-ringed eyes. Joss's own eyes widened slightly as he caught sight of the topaz, copper, and gold rings lying in circles, one after the other, around the pupil.

"My grandmother had these eyes," he explained, slipping the shades back into place. "So did my mother. They make people uncomfortable, so I keep them covered most of the time."

The room grew quiet for a moment. "So," David went on, looking at Cole yet again. "I have your thanks. Was there some other reason you stopped by?"

"There was," Cole said. "I wanted you to meet the man in my life."

David looked at Joss closely, smiling. "That explains the conversation I overheard before," he said teasingly. "I knew it didn't sound like official police business, unless the NYPD finally decided to drop whatever pretense was left."

Joss looked across the room at David, perplexed. "Every cop on the street is a stripper now," Cole told him, explaining the joke.

Joss rolled his eyes. "Damn Village People!"

All three of them laughed. "So this is your man, huh?" David asked, utterly serious now as he gave Joss a once-over. "I guess I approve, so long as he doesn't treat you badly. Is he good in the sack?"

Joss actually blushed a little. "He's very well-endowed," Cole informed David. "The last time I saw a cock as big as his was on stage in Florida."

"The infamous Doors concert," David said, nodding. "I remember you telling me that story. Is he really *that* large?"

Cole turned to Joss expectantly, who looked back as if he couldn't believe what was happening. "You," Joss said slowly, "can't be serious."

In the end, Joss's penis stayed tucked away in his pants out of sight. David had fun trying to bribe Joss into showing it to him, which only made Cole more determined. The bidding went up to five thousand before Joss put his foot down and refused for the eighth and final time.

"He's stubborn," David noted. "I kind of like that about him."

"I feel like I was brought into a wolf's den," Joss muttered, his face glowing bright red while his eyes darted toward Cole. "Then again, that's probably a fair analogy."

"Have you got time to stay for dinner?" David asked suddenly. "I can have Hagen bring us something. We won't even need to leave the drawing room."

"Sounds good," said Cole, before turning to Joss. "Unless you're ready to face Captain Hawkins."

"He can wait," Joss said. "Food sounds good right about now."

"Great," said David as he pushed a button on his phone. "There was something I wanted to discuss with you anyway."

Hagen entered the drawing room almost supernaturally, and left after hearing his master's request. "A favor returned for one given?" Cole asked suspiciously. "You know, the sidhe have the same aphorism about humans that humans do concerning the fey: never do a favor for one, ever."

"This is a small favor," David promised. "I own a local network station here in Manhattan. Lately, there have been some problems."

"Money?" Joss guessed.

"Money problems, I can handle," David assured the inspector confidently. "These particular problems are geared more toward your line of work."

Cole sat up and gave David his full attention. "We're listening."

"The station has carried a rather interesting history to its name for a number of years," David explained as he leaned forward slightly. "It wasn't always this way, I'm told, but in the last fifteen years, give or take, there have been a number of unusual incidents. Some of the reports made their way to me, but I let them slide. Strange things do occur from time to time, and I thought any publicity it generated would help the station's ratings. People are sometimes drawn to the unexplained."

"Go on," Cole said, nodding.

"Lately, the number of incidents has increased," David said. "Drastically, in fact. Rarely does a day go by that I don't hear about some kind of accident, people claiming they've seen monsters that vanish into thin air, or mechanical problems for equipment that's brand new. The most disturbing reports, however, are the rumors of people vanishing."

"You've reported people missing?" Joss asked, taking interest now.

"Not me personally," David explained. "There was a woman who worked on the station's number one show, but she'd been having problems. The rest of the cast claimed she was difficult to work with and threatened to quit more than once. One day, not too long ago, she didn't show up to work, and everyone assumed she had finally left. Then an intern was sent to the actress's apartment with her paycheck and some forms to sign, legal stuff, mostly, and the place had been ransacked. The door had been left unlocked, and the inside was a mess. According to her, it looked like a fight had broken out, but there was no body and no blood anywhere. The police chalked it up to a burglary and didn't investigate further."

"But you think something else got her?" Joss pressed.

"After I got the whole story and heard about what else had been going on, I hired a private investigator to search for her," David said gravely. "It's as though the woman disappeared off the face of the earth."

"So your TV studio is haunted?" Cole summed up.

"Haunted?" David answered. "Possessed? Cursed? Built on top of a spiritual nexus? Resting over intersecting ley lines?"

"Ley lines?" Joss asked, interrupting.

"They are like veins," Cole explained very quickly, "inside the earth, carrying its energy from place to place."

David shrugged. "I have no idea. I was going to hire a professional, but when you showed up, it occurred to me that this might be more your speed."

"Once you were sure we hadn't come to arrest you, you mean," Cole reminded him. "It isn't that I'm not grateful, or unconcerned for your plight, but Section Thirteen is swamped as it is. Early this morning, something broke into a high-security storage facility and made off with a canister. So far, the company that owned it has been tight-lipped about what was in there."

"Ah," David replied, smiling. "I heard about that. As it turns out, I own the company that manufactured what was inside that canister."

Both Joss and Cole blinked at the same time. "You?"

David nodded. "Word about the theft reached me early this morning," he went on. "If Section Thirteen is working on the case, I should be able to convince my stockholders to give you full access to what was inside the stolen canister. As it happens, I would very much like that business cleared up. The contents of that canister aren't dangerous on their own, but I wouldn't want something like that in the hands of unsavory types."

"So, in exchange for solving the mystery behind the accidents at the TV studio," Joss finished, "you give us the information, putting the Section in your debt at the same time."

David smiled up at Joss's angry face. "I learned never to give away an advantage. You have your new love to thank for that."

Joss scowled at Cole. "You taught him way too well."

Cole shrugged. "The boy was a good listener. It isn't often you run into one of those."

"True," Joss admitted, however reluctantly. "And knowing what was stolen should help us narrow down the search."

"I'll have the information sent to your precinct this afternoon," David said, still grinning like the Cheshire Cat. "It will be waiting on your desk. Oh, and the mayor will be informed of the favor you're both doing for me."

"Wonderful," Joss muttered. "At least we'll have him off our back for a while."

"One thing, though," Cole said, giving David a hard look now. "You tell us what was in that canister here and now."

David opened his mouth. "And don't tell me you haven't got a clue," Cole warned, cutting him off. "I know you better than that."

David sighed. "I wouldn't dream of it," he grumbled. "The canister contains the failed results of an experiment one of my research and development divisions was working on. I had commissioned a private party to do some work for me, completing an unsolved equation. The plan was to download the completed equation into a nanobot colony we'd been testing for the past two years. Unfortunately, the results were less than what I was hoping for, so I had the project shelved temporarily. One of my competitors must have gotten wind of it and wanted to know what I was up to."

"A canister full of microscopic robots?" Joss asked. "Sounds like something out of a bad science-fiction movie! What sort of results were you hoping for?"

"Medical, primarily," David answered at once. "Nanobot surgery is possible, we believe. Refining the process to where it only attacks cancerous cells and programming them with the necessary information on how to repair severely damaged tissue in sensitive areas is the hard part."

"Have the files sent to Officer Rainette DuBois," Cole suggested. "She'll be interested in this sort of thing."

"What do you think stole the canister?" David asked as their lunch finally arrived. "I heard the evidence was... interesting, to say the least."

"Something left ectoplasm all over the inside of the storage facility," Cole told him, digging into the deli sandwiches and tea the maid had left on the table. "We're still looking into it."

"Speaking of which," Joss said, checking his watch, "we should be going once we're done here."

"Before I forget," Cole said, reaching into his pocket suddenly. "There is one other thing I need from you, David."

David froze. "What's that?"

Cole pulled out his cell phone and held it up. "Your number," he said as the screen came to life. "I don't intend to get stopped at the door a second time."

"You have a cell phone now?" David stared at the device in Cole's hands. "It's the end of the world as we know it!"

"YOU thought we were moving slow in this?" Joss asked.

Cole paused in the process of tugging his leather pants down and sandwiched the phone between his ear and shoulder before resuming his efforts. It had been a long afternoon full of an angry police captain making threats that culminated with a phone call from the mayor, which promptly shut the mortal man up. Joss had asked to be taken home, which Cole complied with. Now he was struggling to get out of his clothes while having a conversation with his man, who didn't sound happy for the moment.

"There," he declared as both of his legs were freed, "sorry about that. Now, what were you saying about moving slowly?"

"When we were visiting your godson, or grandson, or whatever, you said that you thought we were moving slowly together."

"Right," Cole said, leaning back on the bed naked. "What about it?"

The line went quiet for a moment. "You think two months is long enough time to spend together before making a decision like moving in?"

"I don't know," Cole replied earnestly. "I've seen humans do it before. I just assumed this kind of thing was normal. How long do humans usually wait before sharing the same place?"

"I…." Joss paused. "I really don't know myself. There may not be a set timespan for this kind of thing."

"I see," said Cole. "Then, how do you know this isn't the right speed?"

"You really are lost when it comes to certain social norms," Joss said flatly. "I keep forgetting that."

Cole shrugged, then remembered that Joss couldn't see him. "Too many of the rules concerning human society change every few years, especially regarding the subject of mating and relationships. Learning them all seems pointless to me. Besides, learning the rules wouldn't help me fit in better. Humans share an instinctive fear of me, in case you'd forgotten that as well."

"I hadn't," Joss reassured him. "The bottom line is, I'm just not ready to move in together."

"That's fine."

Joss waited a moment before speaking again. "That's all you have to say, then?"

"Was I supposed to say something?" Cole asked, raising up slightly. "I thought you would enjoy not having to worry about how I feel."

"So you were lying?"

Cole sighed. "The sidhe do not lie," he reminded Joss in a very tart tone. "None of the fey lie. It's simply not in our nature to do so. We'll paint the truth a whole new kind of blue for you that you've never seen before, but lying outright isn't who or what we are. That's a human trait."

"I see." Joss's voice was vacant of emotion now. "That's good to hear."

After a moment of awkward silence, Cole tried again. "Clearly, I've said something to upset you," he said, thinking back over his conversation with the mortal. "Can we start over again? I'm not upset about you not wanting to move in with me right now."

"Okay," said Joss. "That's a big relief. I guess I was expecting you to react more strongly to it, though."

"There's no reason for me to," Cole pointed out. "Would you want to move in with someone who reacts in such a way over everything?"

"I have," Joss reminded him. "I was married, remember?"

"If you aren't ready to live with me, getting upset won't help change your mind," Cole went on. "I kept bringing it up because I assumed this was some sort of game, or something that humans who have sex together argue about initially. A lot of television shows suggested as much."

"Your knowledge of human relationships in this era comes from TV?" Joss sounded as though he was verbally kicking himself. "No wonder you're so screwed up."

"I'll ignore that," Cole said in response. "Getting back to our earlier discussion, I just wanted to be around you more. We're always busy at work chasing down one thing or another. There's very little time for us to spend alone together, and you're always worrying about paying your rent on time or spending too much money. Living here would be much easier on you, I assumed. I wasn't going to suggest we share the same room. You could have your own private space, and we would be able to hang out more.

"In short," Cole finished, "I would like to see more of you. Living together seemed like the most practical way of doing this."

Joss didn't speak again for several minutes. "Okay."

Cole waited. "Okay," he repeated. "What?"

"I'll… think on it some more," Joss said hesitantly. "If you've got plenty of space, and the pixies don't mind having one more person around. And Mal doesn't mind having a freeloader take up space for a bit, I guess it could work."

"Mal will get to expand the sithen more," Cole said. "He's been looking for an excuse since we moved in here. Apparently, there were a number of rooms he disposed of when we kicked Naryssa out."

"Oh, brother," Joss muttered.

"You should have seen the replica he made of a sixteenth-century street," Cole told him, between fits of snickering. "Complete with buildings. One of the pixies started a fire, and we had to close off that whole section while a thunderstorm extinguished the flames."

"What have I gotten myself into?" Joss asked.

"It's never dull here," Cole assured him. "But we have free Wi-Fi and cable."

"That's something."

"When will you move in?" Cole asked as Mal materialized beside the bed. "Mal can get started on your room right now. Would you prefer a simple bedroom suite, or something along the lines of an east wing?"

"Simple bedroom, if you don't mind," Joss answered at once. "For now, anyway. Will I be able to park my vehicle in your garage? The sithen isn't going to vomit it back out, or drop it out of the sky into a field in the next state, is it?"

Cole hesitated before glancing toward Mal. "It shouldn't."

"I'm relieved." Despite the sarcasm in his voice, it didn't sound as if Joss had changed his mind. "I am going to wait until we wrap this mess up with the missing canister, though."

"Sounds good."

"Speaking of which," Joss added. "I want you, Corhagen, and Staffelbach to work the TV station angle. I've already spoken to the chief and Captain Hawkins. Neither of them will be giving us any trouble, at least for the time being. Rainette, Marcel, and I will handle the canister theft case."

"Do we have to split up?" Cole said, and though he primarily meant it in jest, there was a ring of sincerity to his voice. "You and I make a great team. I was looking forward to us working together."

"The way I see it," Joss said seriously, "the TV station isn't a major problem. Whatever happens there shouldn't be too tough for you to handle. It sounds like a simple haunting, or somebody playing a bunch of cruel pranks, assuming the actress's disappearance was a coincidence."

"I don't believe in coincidence," Cole countered.

"Neither do I," Joss admitted. "But you can take care of yourself. Corhagen and Staffelbach can be your extra set of hands and eyes. The theft of the canister itself might not seem too serious, but whatever stole it tore a piece of that building away before ransacking the place in under a minute. Something powerful and dangerous wanted that canister. Marcel can stop a Mack truck, and Rainette once used her magic to melt through a solid door. Plus, she knows the supernatural real well. I can count on them to watch my back."

"As long as they just watch it," Cole warned teasingly. "Anything beyond that, I want to be a part of."

"Don't worry," Joss replied, chuckling. "I don't think I'm Rainette's type. My tusks aren't nearly so pointed."

"Be careful all the same," Cole warned him. "I came close to losing you once. Rainette and Marcel are both still green with field combat. We're going to have to work on that later."

"I know," Joss said. "And you're right. We'll get this sorted out eventually. Until then, though, I think it's about time I hit the sack. I'm starting to fade."

"Good night, then," Cole whispered softly. "I love you."

Joss only hesitated a moment. "I love you," he said. "I guess I'll see you soon."

It took two more good-nights before Cole and Joss hung up. Mal was still standing anxiously by the bed when Cole set the phone down on the nightstand.

"Can I decorate his room pink?"

"No," Cole replied flatly. "Good-night, Mal."

THE next day, Cole arose bright and early. The address for the television studio was now programmed into his phone, a capability he hadn't been aware of until yesterday. Cole dressed, showered, and ate, dodging Mal's attempts to capture the few stray pixies that were left. When the chandelier that had been hanging in a side hallway came crashing down due to his efforts, Cole ordered Mal to leave them be.

Mal had looked slightly put out until Cole reminded him that he needed to get to work on building a suitable room for Joss.

When Cole left, Mal was still debating with himself on whether Joss would enjoy having a water slide. Staffelbach was supposed to meet them at the TV station. Against Cole's better judgment, he had agreed to pick up Corhagen on the way. It wasn't much of a detour, but Cole couldn't imagine Corhagen looking too thrilled at seeing him back on the force. According to Joss, Corhagen had taken a shine to being put in charge of the Section, however briefly. When the detective had reestablished contact with Cole after a year, he'd hinted at wanting to bring in a group of cops for the express purpose of handling supernatural crimes. It turned out, however, that the city of New York had already tried it once before. Section Thirteen had originally begun back in the fifties. It was Joss Vallimun who had convinced the chief of police that the Section was needed again.

From the start, there had been friction in the group. Cole had initially chalked it up to Corhagen's overall attitude toward sexuality, and the fact that Cole and Joss were lovers. After hearing Joss's side of things in the wee hours of yesterday morning, though, his suspicions had shifted ever so slightly.

Corhagen lived in a surprisingly nice apartment on the second floor in Murray Hill. Cole parked his car outside and then walked across the small expanse of grass buried underneath a blanket of freshly fallen snow. The stairway was slick in spots, but it didn't give Cole any problems. At apartment 202, Cole hesitated a moment before ringing the doorbell. Thinking back on it now, it would have been better to call first and have Corhagen waiting for him outside. Though, to be perfectly truthful, Cole was actually looking forward to this.

A baby could be heard crying loudly behind the door. Cole rang the bell twice, just on the off chance someone didn't hear it, and then stepped back. A moment later, sooner than he'd expected, the door opened slightly and a young girl peeked out at him.

"Hello," Cole greeted her formally, pulling out his badge. "I'm Detective Tuulois MacColewyn, here to see Detective Corhagen. Is he ready yet?"

"Um." The girl hesitated, taking longer than necessary to squint at his badge. "He's in the back with Mrs. Corhagen. Can you wait here a moment?"

The girl was gone before Cole could answer. A moment later, he heard Corhagen's voice. He didn't sound thrilled at the news of Cole being outside his apartment door. When the girl returned, she was by herself and giving Cole a sheepish expression.

"Sorry about that," she said, opening the door wider. "You can come on in. I just wanted to check with them first."

"Smart," Cole told her. "I'm guessing you must be the babysitter."

"How'd you know?" she asked, though there was a hint of coyness to her voice. The girl looked to be about eleven or twelve, with hair past her shoulders that was neither brown nor blonde.

"I'm a detective," he reminded her pointedly. "Plus, Corhagen and I have known each other for a while. You aren't old enough to be one of his kids. Since he's going to be at work today, the only reason you should be here is if you're babysitting for them."

"Mrs. Corhagen has a doctor's appointment," she explained. "My name's Kelly, by the way. I live down the hall from them."

"Nice to meet you, Kelly," Cole said, taking a seat without being told.

Kelly said nothing for all of ten seconds. During that brief span of time, she pretended to be fascinated by a crucifix hanging on the wall above the sofa. Cole watched her and nearly flinched when she turned around fast enough to have inflicted whiplash on herself.

"Can I ask you something?" she blurted out, and then she resumed speaking before he could answer. "Are you really a cop? I know that's a stupid question. I saw the badge. It's just that you looking nothing like a police officer."

"I've never heard that one before," Cole muttered.

"Really?"

"I was being sarcastic," he explained. "It's a nasty habit I picked up when I came to live here. And I'm a plainclothes detective. The badge didn't come with a uniform."

"So the NYPD just lets you dress however you want?"

Cole gave the inquisitive girl called Kelly a droll glare. "Could you imagine me wearing anything but this?"

Kelly frowned before looking Cole over appreciatively. "I guess not," she admitted finally. "But you'd probably blend in better if you'd quit dying your hair."

"My hair isn't dyed," he replied. "It's always looked like this."

Kelly's eyes widened. "How can you have hair like that?"

Cole shrugged, turning away from her penetrating stare. "I take after my father in terms of looks," he said, wishing she wasn't so curious. Except for the constant barrage of questions, she wasn't so bad.

Kelly was still staring when he turned back toward her. "Except for my eyes," he added, though for the life of him, Cole couldn't figure out why. He supposed it had to do with how calm the girl was acting around him.

Hearing this bit of information, Kelly moved in closer to get a better look. "What color are they really?" she asked, staring. "I've heard of contacts that make your eyes ringed like that, but they're really expensive."

"These aren't contacts. My eyes look like this naturally."

Kelly backed away, watching him closely now with even more interest. "Where did you say you were from?"

"I didn't," Cole replied. "I've lived here and there, spent some time down on the Florida coast for a while, believe it or not."

"Where were you from originally?" she asked insistently.

Cole smiled at her. "Long ago and far away."

Kelly was prevented from asking any further questions by the arrival of James's wife, Sarah. Sarah entered the living room wearing a robe and looking very pregnant. The moment her eyes landed on Cole, they bugged out of their sockets, and she emitted a high-pitched squeak of angry surprise before about-facing. Cole watched her scurry off back where she'd come from, laughing under his breath. Kelly, meanwhile, observed this whole exchange with a very bemused expression. "What just happened?" she asked.

A second later, Sarah's angry shouts drifted into the living room, presumably from wherever Corhagen was. James emerged a few minutes later, looking quite harried and more than ready to leave.

"I'm going on ahead," he informed Kelly while deliberately trying not to look toward the chair where Cole sat. "Sarah will be ready to go in a few minutes, I think. The kids have already been fed and changed, so you shouldn't have to do much. Just hold the fort down until she gets back."

"Okay." She nodded before turning to face Cole. "See you around, Mr. Detective."

Kelly was waving good-bye to them from the second floor as they walked toward Cole's car. The Camaro was running quietly all by itself, with the inside nice and warm when they slid into their respective seats. Cole gave the inquisitive girl named Kelly one final wave and smiled as she went back into the apartment.

"How long have you known her?" he asked before pulling out into traffic.

James acted as though he wasn't going to answer at first. "A while," he finally admitted begrudgingly. "She lives three doors down from us with her mother and aunt."

Cole made no further attempts at conversation during the drive. It was clear James was not in the mood to talk. If anything, his disposition suggested he was not thrilled at being assigned to work with Cole. This was hardly surprising, and after enduring such behavior since the year started, he wasn't expecting a change.

As they neared the TV station, however, James managed to surprise him after all. "I heard you were put back in the NYPD," he said. "Congratulations."

"Thanks," Cole replied cautiously, unsure of where this was going.

"They told me you were brought in early yesterday morning to handle some kind of break-in," James went on. "Since when does the Section handle things like that?"

"The perps tore a hole in the side of a building big enough for Marcel to walk through without ducking," he explained. "And then ripped the inside apart. Nothing human could have done that. It's definitely a weird case, but Joss sounds more worried about who might have done it than the actual theft itself. He's working on it today with Marcel and Rainette."

"How is she?" he asked, and to James's credit, there was none of the roughness to his voice that Cole had come to associate with his former friend.

"The doctors made her stay in the hospital overnight merely as a precaution," Cole said, taking a curve sharply. "Joss wouldn't have her working on the case otherwise."

"Yeah."

Cole returned his focus to driving and managed to avoid sideswiping an SUV full of what looked like very small soccer players. The woman behind the wheel flipped him the bird before he zipped through a yellow light ahead of her. Corhagen's hand remained on the door handle until the danger had passed. Only then did he release his grip slightly.

"So, is it just us today?" he asked in a very strained voice.

"Staffelbach is joining us," Cole replied calmly. "We're meeting him at the TV station. Did Joss fill you in?"

"Kind of," James mumbled. "He said something about a TV station being haunted."

"We think it might be haunted," Cole corrected. "At the moment, there isn't any way to tell for sure. The Section is being assigned this case to pay back the guy that got me reinstated. It shouldn't take very long."

Staffelbach was already standing outside his parked squad car with a hot latte in his hands when Cole pulled up beside him.

"Have you been waiting long?" Cole asked, climbing out opposite of James.

"Not very long," the young-looking officer said as James took great pains to avoid coming anywhere near where Paul was standing.

Cole watched, recalling Corhagen's personal demons regarding his own sexuality and the feelings he'd harbored toward Cole for years. It was obvious Corhagen knew about Staffelbach being gay.

Rather than being offended by Corhagen's behavior, though, Staffelbach seemed amused by it. James didn't help matters by stumbling over his own two feet and almost head butting himself against the squad car's rear fender. Both Staffelbach and Cole gave James a moment to pull himself back upright and regain his dignity.

Of course, that wasn't to say either of them refrained from outright laughing the entire time.

"You are a regular twinkletoes this morning," Cole noted as they made their way toward the TV station's main entrance, with James bringing up the rear.

"I didn't even ask if we could stop for coffee," James grumbled, looking thoroughly miserable as an icy wind kicked up.

"That wasn't me," Cole said, reaching for the doors. "Just in case you were wondering."

"I didn't say anything," replied James, though the look on his face said he had been about to accuse Cole of that very thing.

The inside of the TV station was much warmer. The building itself was relatively small, but gave the impression that it did very well for itself. The open expanse beyond the entrance housed a large desk, where a single attractive woman sat speaking into a headset while typing furiously at her keyboard. Beyond that and far off to the side was a very small maze of cubicles. Directly opposite, a row of workstations that looked like they belonged inside a bank and not a television station rested in front of a thick wall. It all felt strangely inviting.

Which made Cole all the more suspicious.

The woman behind the desk froze as she looked up from her computer, and Cole heard her tell the person on the other line that she would call them back.

"Can I help you, gentlemen?"

Cole stepped forward with Staffelbach following close behind. "I'm Detective MacColewyn," he explained, holding up his badge. "This is Officer Staffelbach and Detective Corhagen. We were asked to come by this morning."

The woman didn't appear fazed by the sight of their badges, or so many of them at once. "Do you have an appointment?" she asked crisply.

Cole leaned forward slightly. At the same time, he pushed a wall of glamour around them so as not to be overheard. "It's about the disturbances," he explained. "The actress that went missing and the accidents that were reported. We're here to look into it."

Something flickered in the receptionist's eyes. Cole recognized it as fear and stepped away so the lady wouldn't get the wrong idea. However, the fear in her eyes didn't fade instantly. Fumbling, the woman hit a button on her headset, which dialed a number automatically.

"Yes, sir," she said, her voice warbling slightly now. "The police are here. It's about Ms. Morrison's disappearance and—"

The voice on the other line cut her off. "Yes, sir," she replied meekly.

Cole tried to listen in, but the headset carried a slight distortion through it. It was a common problem for him with most electronic devices that transmitted sound waves. The voice on the other end of the line was definitely male, but beyond that, he didn't have much luck working out what was being said. The person was obviously angry, however, and said anger only increased as the woman tried to explain further. Finally, the shouting stopped altogether, and the receptionist relaxed a little.

"I'll tell them," she said, before the line went dead.

"Could you wait just a moment?" she asked politely. "The station manager is in a meeting, but it should be finishing up soon. Would you mind having a seat until then?"

"That's fine," Cole told her as she looked away.

Rather than sitting down, Cole flipped out his cell phone and hit two buttons. The phone rang twice on the other end before someone answered.

"It's me," he said. "They're not letting us in."

Corhagen and Staffelbach stood near Cole. Their eyes darted back and forth every other word or so from him over to the receptionist watching.

"You wanted me to look into this," Cole pointed out. "We could always work out some other form of payback, if that's what it takes."

Silence, then Cole nodded. "Thank you."

Cole put his phone away with a satisfied smirk. "Two minutes," he said to both men. "Let's have a seat before the show starts."

"What show?"

Cole ignored James and sat down in one of the nearby chairs. Staffelbach took the one next to him, and after hesitating for several seconds, James relented at last, taking the last one on the very end, directly next to where Staffelbach sat.

After a moment, Cole spoke again. "One minute and seventeen seconds left."

"Do you plan on explaining any of this soon?" James grumbled, rising from his chair slightly.

Cole glanced toward James before his eyes drifted back to Staffelbach, who was watching Cole with a very innocent, yet equally amused, smirk. "Look around," Cole instructed. "What do you see?"

Staffelbach raised up far enough to give the area they were in a quick sweep. Corhagen wasn't far behind him. "And?" the younger officer asked.

"Just put together what's right in front of you," Cole went on. "The answers are all around us. Part of our line of work is taking what people overlook every day and seeing it for what it really is. There isn't any question of whether or not something unusual is happening this time. We came into this case knowing that. The question is to figure out the truth behind what is being hidden."

"People look scared," Corhagen noted. "It feels like this whole room is getting ready to jump out of its skin."

Staffelbach frowned as he took note of the receptionist, who was doing a fair job of pretending not to eavesdrop. "She knows something," he said finally. "I'd say she knows everything."

"Or enough to harbor a guess," Corhagen added.

The receptionist jumped at this, though it turned out to be due to a call coming through her headset. Cole nodded as the woman took the call and stood up.

"Time's up," he said. "Let's move."

The receptionist saw them approach and swallowed hard. "You can go on through," she instructed in a very nervous voice. "The station manager said for you to have a look around. If there's anything you need, I can have someone get it for you."

"Do you have any coffee?" Corhagen interjected.

"Um," the woman stammered, looking momentarily caught off guard by the question. "Over by the water cooler. There's cream and sugar inside the drawer of the stand. Help yourself!"

Cole reluctantly waited as James took his time attending to his fix before joining them again. "They have real cream," he said excitedly, pointing back toward the stand. "It's in those little plastic cups like they serve to you in restaurants. And real sugar too, not that cheap saccharine stuff that gives you cancer!"

"I am so happy for you," Cole retorted. "Could we get on with the investigation now?"

"Where should we look first?" Staffelbach asked as they made their way into the sectioned-off area of the station usually reserved for staff.

"Anywhere," Cole answered. "Everywhere. Right now, we're simply looking the place over for anything strange. My source told me this place has enjoyed a rich history of unexplained events for the last decade or so, but that things recently took a turn for the worse."

"Since when do you have sources?" Corhagen wondered as he spilled a drop of coffee on his hand. "Ow! I thought I was the one with contacts and so forth."

Cole turned around to face him. "Very well," he said. "What do your sources have on this place?"

James stopped short. "I don't know," he confessed. "I hadn't checked yet."

Both Staffelbach and Cole stared at him. "Sarah was up all last night," James replied defensively. "She hasn't been feeling well."

Something flashed across Corhagen's eyes, and Cole thought he saw a glimpse of his former friend there for an instant. James looked away before Cole could focus on it, and when the detective finally met his gaze again, it had disappeared.

"You're in charge, I guess." There was no mistaking the tone in Corhagen's voice now. "Do you want me to start looking into this place?"

"After we leave, yes," Cole said before moving along down the hallway again. "We need as many eyes and ears as we can get right now. If things have gotten worse, something is bound to happen if we wait around long enough."

"Yes, sir," James answered, though the "sir" carried a sharp edge to it.

The first floor was mostly office rooms and storage areas. Nothing of interest caught Cole's eye as he wandered through the area to the far back of the building. The three of them had split up to cover more ground, with instructions from Cole to message one another every few minutes whether they found something or not. Cole swept his side of the first floor meticulously but found nothing. Row after row of offices and cubicle space greeted his eyes and nose. Before long, he found himself back in the main corridor next to the elevator where they'd first separated, with nothing to show for it. The others weren't far behind, and both James and Staffelbach shook their heads without being asked.

"Next floor, then," Cole said. "Onward and upward, until we find something."

"Maybe if you...." James shot a look at Staffelbach as they stepped into the elevator. "*Changed*. We could pass you off as a police dog."

"I'm not about to let you put me on a leash," Cole responded, jamming his thumb into the second-floor button. "Also, very subtle there. Staffelbach knows I am not human. I would have thought you knew that already."

James looked at Staffelbach strangely. "When did you tell him?" he asked Cole. "I thought you hadn't had contact with anyone inside Section Thirteen while you were on suspension?"

"I hadn't," Cole replied as the elevator doors parted. "I told him while we were on our way over to Staten Island, before I was suspended."

Cole caught the look on James's face. "He was willing to share with me," the sidhe replied calmly. "And it seemed like the sort of thing I should mention right away. He took it as well as you did."

Staffelbach laughed. "I thought he was kidding at first," the officer admitted.

"So did James," Cole replied, leading them down a different hallway. "But his reaction was nowhere near what I'd expected from him. Believe it or not, there was a time when Corhagen was much less high-strung."

"I wasn't married back then," James grumbled.

Unlike the ground floor, the second had much larger rooms designed to serve as sound studios for programs. Cole spotted one up ahead whose door had been left open. Reaching it first, he backed against the door far enough to allow the others to pass through first.

"It comes as no surprise to anyone," he informed James as the detective slipped by him.

Staffelbach overheard the exchange and laughed out loud. His laughter stopped short, however, when he had gone far enough into the sound studio to see the layout of it clearly. Cole found this strange, but then James followed suit, even going so far as the ogle openly with his jaw hanging open.

"Is something amiss?" Cole asked dryly, coming up behind them.

"I had no idea," Staffelbach whispered.

"Me neither," said James in an equally quiet tone. "I can't believe this is the place. My kids are going to go ballistic when they hear this."

Both men sounded very excited, though to Cole, the room was a bit underwhelming. Off to the side was a setup meant to give off the illusion of a wrecked ship lying sideways against a cluster of rocks inside a cave. The area directly in front of them looked more like an actual cave, or as close to a cave one could get with bad lighting and painted Styrofoam rocks. Something about the area did feel familiar to Cole, though he was having a hard time placing it.

"You don't know where we are, do you?" James asked, grinning from ear to ear as he looked back at Cole.

"How could he not know?" Staffelbach asked, staring at Cole in open shock now.

"Know what?"

James pointed off to the side, toward the setup with the model shipwreck. "This is the soundstage for *Captain Sharky and the Magical Treasure Cave*."

Cole frowned. "Captain Sharky?"

"*Captain Sharky and the Magical Treasure Cave*," Staffelbach repeated, staring around at the soundstage in awe. "I used to watch this show all the time when I was a kid."

"Same here," James added proudly. "I would get up early enough to catch it in the mornings before school."

The excitement in their voices was approaching a sort of critical mass now. Cole's bemusement only grew as the smiles on their faces threatened to split each man's head wide open horizontally. "Remember when the first Captain Sharky died?" Staffelbach asked James, all but bouncing on the balls of his feet now. "It was all over the news."

"My parents didn't let me watch it," James replied. "All the kids at school used to tease me because they knew I still watched the show. That was the first thing someone said to me when I got to class that day. That was on a Friday, and I spent the whole weekend worrying about whether it was true. I woke up a whole hour earlier than usual the next Monday morning so I wouldn't miss it, and he was still there.

"I found out later that they'd filmed several episodes in advance because the actor's health had gotten real bad by that point," James added sheepishly. "I think they said he was a diabetic."

"He was," Staffelbach affirmed. "I actually helped run a fan page for the 'original' Captain Sharky back in junior high. We would have an online charity drive each year to raise awareness for diabetes on the anniversary of his death. Shit, I can't even remember the guy's name now."

Staffelbach promptly turned red. "Wow, even back then, I was a complete dork."

Corhagen scoffed in response. "That's nothing," he derided. "I slept with a Mossy Rock plush toy until I was eleven. Mom finally gave it away while I was off at summer camp. The counselors said we weren't allowed to bring any of our toys, and when I got back, she told me it had been sold by mistake at a garage sale she and Dad threw."

"Harsh," Staffelbach said, wincing. "Say, did you ever get into that *Captain Sharky* collectible trading card game?"

"My parents wouldn't buy it for me," James replied morosely. "When I think back on it, though, those card packets weren't cheap, and someone in college told me the game sucked big-time. It's no wonder, considering how quickly the company that made it went under. I heard that game was why Big Top card games filed for bankruptcy."

Both looked at Cole, who was watching them in bemusement. "*Captain Sharky* is this old kid's show that's still around," James explained, before clearing his throat loudly.

"I know," Cole replied.

Staffelbach frowned. "You do?"

"I was around during the seventies when it first began airing," he explained. "To my knowledge, the show wasn't broadcast outside the local area, but it was very popular at one point."

"Did you know this was the station where they filmed it?" asked James insistently.

"No, I didn't." Cole made no attempt to conceal his ennui. "I wouldn't have said anything either way, though. I didn't realize it was such a big deal for the two of you."

"Sorry, sir," Staffelbach said at once, straightening up.

Cole grinned. "Have you both gotten it all out of your system yet?"

"Yes," James muttered.

"Good. Then why don't we continue with our investigation. You two can come back when this is over and watch the show in the audience with the other children, assuming they still allow that."

James's face practically split open again. "Say! I wonder if they would let me bring my kids down here."

"Later, Corhagen," Cole barked. "I cannot believe I have to be the ringleader of this circus yet again."

"The burden of being the man in charge," Staffelbach joked as Cole approached the stage setup. "You have to be the big boss while we act like kids. Think of yourself as Rodimus Prime right after he inherited the Matrix of Leadership."

"I'm going to pretend that I don't understand what that means," Cole grumbled as he glanced around. "It doesn't look as though anyone else is around right now. Shouldn't there at least be stagehands nearby somewhere?"

"As long as the place is empty, we should have ourselves a quick look around." Corhagen caught the look on Cole's face. "I'm serious," he insisted. "This way, there won't be anyone around getting in our way, and the investigation won't hold anyone up."

"You're right," said Cole, though he didn't sound happy himself. "Just try to keep your minds focused on the task at hand. Don't swipe anything from the soundstage as a souvenir."

"I wasn't going to," Corhagen insisted. Cole didn't believe it for one minute.

"I was," Staffelbach confessed. "But I won't now."

The three split up, Cole taking the area near the shipwreck. A few minutes later, James had wandered over to where he was standing, looking anxious.

"What is it?" Cole asked as he observed one of the smaller models used during the show's opening.

"Huh?" Corhagen asked unconvincingly.

"I asked, 'what is it?'" he repeated. "You looked as though there was something on your mind."

Before James could protest, Cole added, "Also, we're supposed to be splitting up. I can't believe it was a coincidence that you wandered all the way over here for no reason, so what is the matter?"

Corhagen hesitated a moment, then sighed deeply. "Have I ever told you how unnerving it is for me when you do that?"

"You're easy to read," Cole replied, turning away from him. "This is hardly the first time I've guessed correctly that something was on your mind. Spill."

"I...." James began reluctantly. "There wasn't a chance to bring this up before. You were suspended, and everyone in the Section was told not to have any contact with you."

"I know," Cole interjected. "Get to the point."

"I heard that the Whittaker kid disappeared last month." James waited a moment for Cole to say something. When he didn't, the detective cleared his throat loudly, then continued. "There were all kinds of stories coming out of the place he was being held in. Some said he was broken out, and others were going on about him fighting off the guards before vanishing into the night."

"So?"

"No one mentioned you," James finished. "There wasn't a single word in any of the reports about you being there."

"Daniel Whittaker broke himself out," Cole verified. "I had nothing to do with it. My mission was to make sure he left with a decent meal in his hands. That was all."

"You gave him a boxed lunch and sent him on his way?"

"He was leaving," Cole explained, looking over his shoulder as James reluctantly followed him. "That was all there was to it. If Internal Affairs asked you to find out where he is, I'm afraid you'll have to search elsewhere. I haven't heard from the Whittaker kid, and as to where he might be at this moment, I have no clue."

Cole paused. "Also," he added as an afterthought, "you know full well that I don't lie about anything. So if I say I don't know where Daniel Whittaker is, that is the truth."

"I remember," James said, nodding.

"And I am not mad about Internal Affairs asking you to drill me for information," Cole went on. "I suspect they put you into an awkward position."

"They have all of Section Thirteen in an awkward position," James clarified. "If it weren't for the fact that the Section had nothing whatsoever to do with the kid after he was airlifted out of that hospital, we'd have gotten stuck with the blame for it."

"It isn't as though Internal Affairs needs to look for excuses to come after us," Cole said, moving toward a different area of the studio, one with row after row of puppets. "If we don't wrap these cases up soon and locate Naryssa, the Section will likely be shut down."

James opened his mouth to reply, but was cut off by Staffelbach. "Hey, guys!"

James looked around, but Cole instead looked straight up. Staffelbach was crouched down on one of the metal rafters. "How'd he get up there?" James asked, upon seeing him.

"Limber little minx, isn't he?" Cole mused. "Did you find something?"

Staffelbach nodded before pointing to something near where his knee jutted out slightly. "It looks like several of these ropes were cut. There's a ladder in the corner back there."

Staffelbach pointed behind him to the corner of the studio room. "Climb up it," he went on. "I think this might be sabotage."

Cole headed for the ladder with James not far behind. The mortal had a rougher time getting up the rungs than he did, but then, James had always been a little nervous about heights. Cole said nothing, just waited at the top of the ladder for him to climb up before walking across the nearest rafter out to where Staffelbach was waiting. Though he gave no notice of it, Cole was careful not to look down. Before too long, James was standing next to Cole with one hand gripping a nearby wire as sweat poured down his forehead.

"See?" Staffelbach said, pointing at one of the ropes. "Some of them were cut, but not all the way through. The edges are frayed, like the rope just wore out, but the cut itself is still too clean."

Cole nodded at Staffelbach's assessment as he stood up. "My guess is they used a dull knife to cut through the rope so it wouldn't look so suspicious," the younger officer continued. "Whatever the ropes do, it probably means trouble."

"This was definitely sabotage," Corhagen grunted. "Seems kind of cliché, though."

"We should find one of the boom operators and let them know," said Cole, turning around slowly on the rafter. "Then find out exactly what the ropes do, and what our saboteur meant to accomplish by cutting them."

"Great," James said, already facing the ladder. "Can we go back down now?"

Halfway across the rafter, Staffelbach started chuckling to himself. "We're inside of a TV studio, walking across a rafter that has ropes hanging from it, which have been sabotaged," he explained when both men looked over their shoulders at him curiously. "If this were an actual television series, whoever was behind the sabotage would probably show up and attack us."

Something dark and covered in smoke catapulted through the air right at James, missing him by a hairbreadth. Corhagen staggered and was saved from falling by Cole steadying him.

"I wish you hadn't said that," Cole growled, looking back over at Staffelbach.

"What was that?" Staffelbach wondered, searching the space above them as he rotated in a circle with his gun drawn. "I didn't get a good look at it," Cole admitted, pulling Aed Deigh out. "But it will be back. We're far too vulnerable up here. Get to the ladder."

Corhagen did not need telling twice. However, he had barely taken two steps when something happened. Cole wasn't sure what happened exactly. James's footsteps flickered, as though coming through a glitching stereo. There was a loud pop, followed by static crackling. The whole room seemed to fade in and out for a second. When Cole blinked, something made him look in the direction James had gone. Something had caused both him and Staffelbach to look away at exactly the same time. When they looked back, James was gone.

Or rather, was fading away rapidly, and not all at once. The air around what remained of Corhagen's hovering body parts sizzled and smoked. It was like watching a film reel tear slowly in half. The image of James was still there, but not all in the same place. Another popping sound drummed against their ears, and quite suddenly, Corhagen was gone.

The metal rafter shook slightly. Cole looked up at the ceiling as the sound of a faint humming filled the room, followed by what might have been laughter. "What...?" Staffelbach gasped for air and tried again. "What just happened?"

"I don't know," said Cole, holding perfectly still. "Were you able to see what I saw?"

Staffelbach looked at Cole like he had lost his mind, but seeing the serious expression on the sidhe's face made him reconsider. "It was like he was there," the younger officer tried. "Like watching a bad video file. He was there, and then gone, but not all at the same time."

"That was what I saw," Cole replied. "I thought I should be sure first."

"What do we do now?"

Carefully, Cole extended the bright red blade out from his weapon's hilt and prodded the air where Corhagen had vanished. There was no reaction, yet the fabric of the space itself did feel slightly weaker. "Corhagen is alive," Cole stated after a moment. "Of that, I'm reasonably sure. Something opened a kind of hole here for one of us to step through. Corhagen might have just had the bad luck of stepping into it first."

"You don't sound sure," Staffelbach noted. "What if whatever took him did it on purpose?"

"Why would they want him, though?" Cole thought on that for a moment. "I guess this at least solves the mystery of whether the incidents here were supernatural or not. Call the station and let them know we've got an officer missing. Once we get down from here, I'm going to call Rainette and have her send over someone from her coven."

"How are we getting down?" Staffelbach was still watching in case the smoke-covered thing came back. "Whatever took Corhagen is between us and the ladder."

"It's gone," Cole assured him. "Though I hesitate to contaminate the area even slightly, since it's our only clue at getting Corhagen back."

Cole thought on that statement for a second. "Albeit, it has been a while since I ever thought I'd want him around again."

"Comrade in arms, remember?" Staffelbach pointed out. "He can be a jerk, but neither of us is abandoning a fellow officer."

"We won't," Cole promised. "But we are getting down from here, and I'm afraid the only way to do so without endangering the crime scene is to jump."

Staffelbach glanced over the edge. "I hope you can fly," he said. "Because there's no way I'm getting down like that."

The entire rafter they were on shook. Smoke whisked through the air down behind Staffelbach, missing him by an inch or so. The smoke disappeared, then came back up again to swipe the space next to Cole. Cole froze, then saw Staffelbach stagger slightly.

"Don't move!" he ordered. "Whatever you do, don't move!"

Staffelbach regained his balance and stayed perfectly still. "What just happened?"

Cole sniffed the air as he looked around. "We're being toyed with."

The smoke darted down through the air again, this time slicing diagonally through the gap between him and Staffelbach. "It's opening more holes in space," Cole explained. "Trying to get one of us to walk into them."

"Can you see them?"

Cole shook his head. "No, but the air in places smells different. I didn't catch it the first time before Corhagen was spirited away."

The smoke was zipping back and forth all around them now. "It wants to keep us guessing," he explained. "So we don't know which places it's been have open gaps in them. Then it will attack us."

Staffelbach took aim with his gun at one of the places where the smoke trail had just been, and fired. The bullet stopped in midair halfway down and was scrambled into pixels before vanishing altogether.

"That's one," Staffelbach said. "But I don't have enough bullets to pinpoint all of them."

"I have more than enough bullets," Cole replied. "But neither of us has enough time."

As if in answer, the smoke came at them again, this time aiming for Cole's head. Cole spotted it in the nick of time and raised Aed Deigh up to block the attack. A set of claws materialized out of the smoke long enough to strike against the blade. Sparks flew as one of the claws snapped off in a flicker of flame. The claw clanged against the metal rafter before bouncing back up in the air. Cole saw it as he turned around to try and bring his blade across the underside of the smoke creature. Aed Deigh's firebrand passed effortlessly through it, however, as though the smoke creature wasn't there. At the same time, the broken claw piece began dissolving in midair.

Staffelbach took aim again and fired after the creature, only to see his bullets get stuck in the gaps in space around them. The bullets began to pixelate almost at once. One after the other, they disappeared from sight as the smoke monster came back to launch another attack.

In anger, Cole brought his blade around again and swung it through the air. Missiles made of pure flame swept through the air at the intangible creature. Not a one touched it, though Cole's sharp eyes spotted it cringing away as the last flame shot came close.

"It doesn't like heat," he realized. "I can work with that."

As the smoke creature reached them, Cole let loose a burst of fire from his weapon. The flames covered the space surrounding them. Staffelbach shielded his face as the sound of something crying out in pain filled the room.

"Phase two," Cole said, reaching over to grab Staffelbach by the hand. "Jump on my shoulders while it's distracted and hold on tight. I'm getting us both down from here now before it recovers."

Still hiding his eyes from the lingering flames, Staffelbach jumped clumsily onto Cole's back. Cole shifted his weight slightly to help settle the mortal in. The man's crotch was digging into the lower part of his spine, but Cole dismissed it as he retracted the firebrand and brought forth Aed Deigh's frost-covered blade. Aiming it down, he leaped off the edge of the rafter without a word, keeping the blade pointed toward the floor as it raced toward them.

Cole had timed each attack to the point that he was fairly certain the spot from where they'd jumped did not contain any gaps in space for them to fall through. When the ground was about twenty feet from them, Cole forced his power through Aed Deigh's tip, forming a thin column of ice that rooted itself into the tile coming toward them. Grabbing hold, he used the ice column to slow their descent enough to survive the fall. Staffelbach lost his grip and slid off his back onto the floor as Cole's feet made impact on the ground, leaving behind cracked indentions.

Pulling his feet free, Cole turned around to face the smoke monster again.

But it was gone.

Cole sniffed the air to be certain, but there was no sign of it. The room smelled the same as it had when they first entered. No one else was there.

At least for a second or so more. Then a set of doors burst open off to the side. A man with a paper-thin mustache hanging beneath a too large nose looked around and spotted the two of them standing next to the melting column of ice. Behind him were several young people, many of whom looked to be no older than five. All of them gasped at the tower of ice standing proudly.

The stranger with the children, however, was staring straight at Cole in wide-eyed shock. Several of the kids behind him peeked around the man's legs curiously.

"Why do they always barge in at the worst possible second?" Cole muttered.

4

AS BAD as he felt, Cole was relieved when Joss showed up a little bit later. The moment his lover came through the studio doors, their eyes locked on each other. Joss slowed his march halfway across the room to where Cole was and motioned for him to follow, before cutting a detour off to the side where they wouldn't be overheard. The remaining officers had already sealed off the room with police tape and were keeping the irate station personnel back.

"What happened?" Joss asked, once they were far enough away.

"Corhagen has disappeared."

Joss frowned and glanced back behind Cole at the bustling cops. "Did you radio for him?"

"No, I mean that he *vanished*." Cole paused to gather himself. "We found sabotage up on one of the rafters. Staffelbach was showing us where several ropes had been cut, then something attacked us. When Corhagen turned to leave, he disappeared right in front of us. Staffelbach took several men and went looking for him in the off chance he's still somewhere in the building. The security guards offered to help as well, but I don't believe any of them are going to have much luck."

Cole turned to where the column of ice had once stood. By now, it had melted down to several broken chunks and slushy water. Everyone had been curious as to what it was doing there, but Cole had ordered that they ignore it for now. Off in the corner, another officer was guarding the ladder leading up to the rafter where they were attacked earlier. Cole had put him there with orders not to let anyone go up without his express permission. The official story was that Cole had sent for a special forensics team. The truth was that they were waiting on the rest of Rainette's coven to get here. Cole had called her first, before speaking with Joss.

Joss nodded toward the entrance to the studio, snapping Cole free of his thoughts, as Rainette came through with several women from her coven in tow. "Sorry for dragging you away from your case," Cole apologized as they strode back across the room together to meet with Rainette's group.

"We weren't getting anywhere," Joss replied. "I'm glad you called when you did. We need to locate Corhagen as fast as we can."

"I filled them in on the way," Rainette said. "You said it was up in the rafters?"

Cole pointed. "That ladder over there," he explained. "I'll show you."

"This is so exciting," gushed a young coven member that Cole didn't recognize. "Actual spiritual displacement! Maybe he was taken to a separate plane of existence?"

"Eleanor," Rainette warned. "Not now."

The guard watching the ladder saw Cole coming with the group and nodded as Cole signaled him to allow the women to pass. "We'll let you know as soon as we find something," Rainette told him, while the young woman named Eleanor struggled to climb the ladder as fast as she could.

"Make sure she doesn't fall," Cole advised as Eleanor slipped down one rung and had to be steadied by the lady behind her.

"She was anxious to come along," Rainette confided. "Plus, despite her enthusiasm, Eleanor really is knowledgeable in this field. I'll get back to you soon."

"Right." Tipping his head in farewell, Cole turned around and received an unpleasant shock. Sarah Corhagen was standing at the edge of the doorway, attempting to muscle her way through as she simultaneously argued with one of the officers on scene. Her yelling only grew louder as Cole reluctantly marched up to the door to undoubtedly make the situation worse with his presence.

"You!" Sarah shouted once Cole came into view. "What did you do with my husband?"

Joss was coming up behind Cole now. "Mrs. Corhagen?" he asked. "What are you doing here?"

"Someone called me while I was at the doctor's office, claiming my husband had disappeared," she shouted, pointing directly at Cole. "What has that lunatic done this time?"

"Who called you?" Joss asked in a calm, if slightly strained, voice.

"Whoever it was," Cole muttered, "I plan to have a word with them. That word is 'pain', incidentally."

"Let her through," Joss instructed to the officers attempting to hold Sarah back. While they removed the barrier tape to let her through, Joss leaned into Cole slightly.

"Technically, she had a right to be told," he whispered. "The next of kin are always informed if something happens to an officer in the line of duty."

"Does it say 'when'?" Cole asked pointedly.

Sarah was stomping across the studio now, her feet making loud "clomps" that reminded Cole of a Godzilla film he had seen years ago. Behind her, waiting in the doorway behind the police barricade, Cole spotted Kelly, the babysitter, hand in hand with Sarah's children. Sarah, meanwhile, stopped short of tackling Cole head-on and reared back with one hand.

Cole caught it with his own before it connected with the side of his face. "Striking an officer of the law," he reminded her. "Not wise."

"Let go of me," Sarah spat at him. "What did you do to my husband?"

"Mrs. Corhagen," Joss began patiently. "We have men searching all over the building for your husband even as we speak. And I believe the building's security are also helping, right?"

Cole nodded. "I haven't heard back from them, however," he said, releasing Sarah from his grip.

"What happened?" Sarah demanded through gritted teeth.

"Corhagen disappeared," he explained neutrally. "We were asked to investigate a possible case of sabotage along with reports of at least one unexplained disappearance."

Sarah frowned. "Don't you handle ghosts or whatever now?"

"Your husband vanished right in front of one other officer besides myself," Cole explained. "Though we aren't certain actual ghosts are involved yet, that nonetheless falls under our jurisdiction."

"Oh." Sarah paused, then scanned the room quickly. "I want to talk with the officer that was with you."

"He is leading the search team looking for your husband, ma'am," Joss cut in. "I'd rather not call him back right now. Since Officer Staffelbach was with Special Detective MacColewyn at the time of your husband's disappearance, he's one of the few here who would know your husband on sight."

"Oh," Sarah repeated.

Cole couldn't help but think she sounded disappointed at a missed chance to pitch another fit publicly. Sarah was glaring thoughtfully at him, meanwhile, as something else dawned on her.

"Are you sure he had nothing to do with it?" she insisted, pointing at Cole.

"We're fairly certain," Joss replied wryly.

Sarah frowned, then shot a glare at Cole one last time before turning around. "Why they let you become a cop, I'll never understand."

Sarah stormed past the barrier, snatching one of her children away from Kelly as she walked past. Kelly gave Cole a discreet wave good-bye before running after Sarah with the remaining kid. Rainette saw this exchange as she joined him and Joss. "A friend of yours?" she asked.

"She's Corhagen's babysitter," Cole explained. "I have sympathy for anyone who deals with that woman on a regular basis."

Cole thought on that statement for a moment before shrugging. "Usually, that is," he amended. "What did you find?"

"The coven and I would like permission to perform a ritual," she said, looking mainly at Joss now.

"What kind?" Joss asked, giving her his full attention.

"We found several weak spots," she explained. "There could be others throughout the building."

"Weak spots?"

"They're places where the fabric of reality was warped," Cole interjected. "Or torn open altogether. The fabric can heal itself, but it leaves behind a temporary weak point."

"What he said," Rainette affirmed, giving Cole a quick nod. "You said there were others who worked here that disappeared?"

"At least one actress," Joss replied. "Though she was the only one we were informed of. I'm beginning to think we need to question everyone that works here."

"There could have been more," Cole agreed. "Only they weren't reported. If someone didn't show up for work, people could have assumed they'd quit. The only reason the actress's disappearance caused a stir was because she was much more recognized."

"That's going to be a bitch to work out," Joss said, sighing. "See if you can find out what's taking Staffelbach so long in the meantime. I'll get as many men as the department can spare. We can question the employees in groups so it will go faster."

Joss left with Rainette to help clear a space so she and her coven sisters could work as Cole punched in Staffelbach's number. The line immediately went to a recording telling him it was out of service. Cole tried again, but this time, the line didn't even ring. After the third try, Cole put his phone back in his pocket and headed for the door. The phone had been a gift from the sithen, something it could create with the help of Mal's technical knowledge. Cole wasn't sure how powerful it was or what the range on it extended to, but if Staffelbach was still in Manhattan, Cole should have been able to reach him. They'd already had one Section member vanish on his watch. Cole wasn't about to sit through another. He would never be able to face Joss again if that happened.

Something made him head for the stairs. Cole was on the third floor when a strange rippling traveled up through the air around him. Pausing, he realized the ritual spell must have taken effect. Cole's suspicions were confirmed a few minutes later when he came upon a room full of stage costumes. Movement up ahead caught his eye, and Aed Deigh was out and ready before the figure came fully into view. It took a moment of staring before Cole figured out what he was looking at.

A mannequin had been left propped up against a set of boxes. Directly in front of it, however, was a fold in space where the air warped and scrambled. It was like staring into a mosaic on television. The sensation coming from it was so startling that Cole had to blink several times. Part of him wanted to turn away for a moment.

Steeling himself, Cole drew in a quick breath and exhaled, reminding himself that sidhe warriors did not become freaked out over a simple breach in the fabric of reality. He was a proud member of his race, exiled or not, and would act accordingly.

Then the breach pulsated, filling the room with a bright flash. Peering through it, Cole thought he saw something moving inside of the spacial warp. A head materialized, somewhat distorted, but it became clearer as the form inside fought against what looked like several pairs of hands grabbing at him. Again, the breach fluctuated, this time enough for Cole to see who it was.

Charging forward, he grabbed hold of Staffelbach's wrist as the man's entire upper torso exploded out of the breach with a gasp.

"I've got you!" Cole cried out, planting both feet firmly against the floor.

"Pull!" Staffelbach shouted before looking back over his shoulder. "I've got Corhagen with me. They're trying to drag us back in!"

"Who?"

That question was answered as a pair of incredibly long arms rose up behind Staffelbach from out of the breach. The arms were attached to a jester thinner than a sign post, wearing a fool's cap and a mask shaped to resemble a leering grin.

"Oh, what a sweet, scrumptious little boy you are!" he cackled, reaching down with spiderlike hands for Staffelbach's throat. "Did you actually think we'd just let you get away?"

Both blades slid back into the hilt as Cole put Aed Deigh away. Reaching for Jabberwock, he felt something latch onto his forearm as his hand closed around the gun. Another hand, small and wrapped in a plain white glove, was trying to pull his arm away while the jester behind Staffelbach closed in. This hand belonged to a young girl no taller than Cole's hip, who was dressed in a black and white gothic version of Raggedy Ann.

"Don't!" the girl insisted, tugging at his arm. "You'll spoil everything!"

Three things happened at once. The jester behind Staffelbach closed his thin fingers around the officer's throat. Staffelbach jerked his hand back out of Cole's grip in response and struggled to get free. Cole, meanwhile, backhanded the little girl away and drew out Jabberwock, took aim for the jester's head, and fired.

The bullet struck its mark, right between the jester's eyes. Instead of bleeding, however, the head of the jester exploded into wisps of black smoke that wavered in the air for a moment before reforming. The jester released Staffelbach, who turned around to kick the clown somewhere out of sight before falling forward out of the breach. The jester shook his head irately and glared down at the both of them. "That actually almost hurt," he snarled.

Cole drew Bandersnatch from its holster. "Try these, then."

Gunshots echoed around the room as Cole unleashed a hailstorm of bullets at the jester, causing it to blow apart into a swirling vortex of black smoke. Each time a part of it reformed, Cole took aim and blasted it again. Staffelbach stood up, having regained some of his fortitude, and joined in. The jester began to howl somewhere amid all the smoke that was leftover from its intangible form. The smoke spun and whirled, forming a black twister that hovered in midair for a moment, then dove angrily back into the breach.

The girl who had seized Cole's arm before skipped past him as the jester's long arm stretched back out, whole and fully formed again, to grab for her.

"You're a meanie," she jeered, sticking a tongue out at them. "We're going to tell on you."

The jester's hand closed around her, his long fingers surrounding the girl. There was a second bright flash of light. Cole blinked this time, and when he looked up again, both the girl and the breach were gone.

Staffelbach kept his gun raised. "Corhagen," he said quietly. "Corhagen's still back there. I let go of his hand when that… thing grabbed me."

"We're going to get him back," Cole swore, keeping Bandersnatch and Jabberwock out.

A small crack was visible now, where the breach had formed. It looked tiny compared to what had been there before. The tiny split glowed a bright lime green. Cole studied the space for a moment, then pulled out Aed Deigh. The firebrand snapped out at full length. In his other hand, Cole kept Bandersnatch in a tight grip. Hesitating a moment, he lowered his head and began whispering in the language of his birth.

"What are you doing?" Staffelbach asked, stepping away slightly. "Is it some kind of spell to open the portal again?"

"It wasn't a portal," Cole said, pausing in the middle of his Faerie words. "And this isn't a spell. I know of no magics that would open a way to wherever you and Corhagen were. Where was that, incidentally?"

"I'm not sure," Staffelbach replied. "Now that I'm out of it, the memories are a little fuzzy. I know that Corhagen was with me until we got to that portal, or whatever it was."

Staffelbach frowned then. "Why can't I remember?"

"It's not unusual," Cole said, shrugging. "The materials that make up different planes and dimensions are not all the same as this one. I am not sure how to accurately describe it for you. I suppose, in a way, it's like data in a computer. The data for whatever world you were taken to is far too different for your brain to process for longer than it needs to.

Now that you're out, your mind has begun purging the memories from your brain to avoid them causing you harm."

"Where were we, then?"

"Who knows?" said Cole as he studied the crack in space again. "It was a place where both of you could survive, though, so I'm confident I can manage there."

"You're going in?" Staffelbach asked.

Cole nodded as he brought the tip of Aed Deigh's red-hot blade to the split in the air.

"Then I'm going back in with you," Staffelbach said. "I let go of Corhagen's hand."

"Then prepare yourself," Cole warned. "We may have to leave now while Rainette's coven is still making these spaces of torn fabric visible. Hold onto me so we don't get separated from one another."

Staffelbach complied by grabbing onto Cole's arm, the one not using Aed Deigh at the moment. Cole concentrated on the spot where the blade's tip rested, just out of reach of the crack. He poured his power out into that space and hoped. When nothing happened, he tried again, giving it nearly all he had.

"If you don't know how to open it," Staffelbach asked, interrupting him, "what spell were you using before?"

"It wasn't a spell," Cole replied. "I was praying."

The green light from the crack in the air spilled out into the room. Cole held his breath a moment, took aim, and then plunged the tip forward. He had no way of knowing if this would work properly or not, but it was the only idea that had sprung to mind. Staffelbach turned away as the crack split down to the floor and then parted. The room, with its costumes, was filled to the brim with an eerie glow as Cole stared through it into the depths of space and reality.

"Nothing ventured," he mumbled before charging forward.

"Wait!" Staffelbach cried out behind him, but Cole was already gone.

The world ceased to exist for a split second. Everything moved and churned around him. Cole felt like he was trapped inside a washing machine that had been supercharged by a jet engine. The sensation was over before it could really begin. In that time, his eyes glimpsed whole worlds, images of times and places stretching out through the vast ether.

It made him slightly nauseated.

When the feeling stopped, his feet struck against something soft. His boots sank into what Cole assumed was the ground for a moment, before they were met with resistance and pushed roughly back out. The result sent Cole catapulting through the air several feet in a long arc. Behind him came the sound of something else landing on the ground in the spot where he had been. Cole glanced back as his feet touched down again, and he spotted Staffelbach bouncing toward him much less gracefully, at full speed, using his head, shoulders, and ass more than his feet.

As he left the ground a second time, Cole seized the opportunity to have a look around and learn where he was. Staffelbach, however, had caught up with him by that point and crashed headlong into him, causing them both to tumble over each other into a large red block of some kind.

"Not the most graceful entrance I've been a part of," Cole muttered, untangling himself from the smaller mortal. "What made you follow me?"

"You needed backup," Staffelbach reminded him, getting to his feet slowly. "I'm surprised I didn't break my neck there. Why is the ground so bouncy?"

Cole performed one or two small jumps in place, testing the stability of the terrain. It looked to be like this everywhere.

"Have you noticed how the ground is patterned?" he asked.

Staffelbach looked around. As far as the eye could see, it was the same. The ground resembled some sort of gigantic patchwork quilt, stretching out for as far as either of them could see. The problem was that every few feet or so, their sight was obstructed by something. Toys had been left lying around all over the place. Not ordinary-sized toys, either, but ones big enough to belong to a family of giants, though Cole knew from experience that giants didn't bother with such things. There were letter blocks as big as an apartment bedroom, jack-in-the-boxes the size of a small house, spinning tops and model cars the duo could have squeezed into with ease. Overall, it resembled a child's bedroom, if the floors had been made soft enough to function as a trampoline.

"This is… weird," Staffelbach stated flatly. "And familiar. I think this might be where Corhagen and I were before."

"Are you beginning to remember?" Cole asked urgently.

"A little," Staffelbach said. "It's still fuzzy, but I recognize a few things off in the distance. We were running a lot, so he and I might have passed this way at one point."

Cole glanced around again, keeping his eyes sharp for signs of danger. "What's that smell?" he wondered aloud.

"Talcum powder and air freshener," Staffelbach replied as Cole sneezed loudly. "I remember it being here before. This is definitely where Corhagen and I were taken last time."

"This must be their lair," Cole mused through a stuffy nose. "The smell is so overpowering, I can't tell if anyone else is nearby."

"It doesn't look like we have very far to go," said Staffelbach, pointing. "If I'm not mistaken, that's a wall off in the distance. And if you look up, there's a ceiling high overhead. The layout of this area is like a giant room."

Cole looked up to see Staffelbach was right. "Since your memories are coming back, and you've been here before, which way? I'm not going to be of much use so long as that stench is hanging in the air."

"I think it smells nice," Staffelbach replied. "At least, it isn't that bad."

"Maybe for a mortal," Cole muttered, sniffing the air disdainfully as Staffelbach began stepping lightly across the patchwork ground. "It's making my nose itch. Lead on, MacDuff, but stick to the shadows."

"Of course."

Remaining inconspicuous proved more difficult than usual. Cole was not accustomed to traveling from Point A to Point B via Mr.

Springy Boots. Staffelbach was having an easier time of it, yet even he looked unnerved. The man had already made this trip once before, and from the way he reacted, it hadn't been the whimsical journey that the landscape implied. Furthermore, it was entirely too quiet. Not only was his nose useless, there was no sound for them to follow. Cole had to rely on the broken memories of the man leading him, and this left him feeling slightly vulnerable. He hated the feeling.

Farther along, there were more structures that looked right out of a child's toy room, only giant sized. Cole and Staffelbach had just taken refuge inside a row of structures made from massive colored wooden blocks when the shadow of something passed overhead.

"I remember," Staffelbach told him, risking a quick look out from under the archway they were both hiding under. "There were these huge-ass planes that kept circling. They're made out of paper."

"Paper?" Cole looked up as the thing overhead passed over an opening in the roof where he could see it. Sure enough, it was a paper plane big enough to have carried the two of them.

"There are more of them," Staffelbach said as they slipped out through the back. "I'm not sure what they do, but I remember Corhagen saying that they might be scouts."

"Best to stay out of sight regardless," replied Cole as they journeyed further along.

A little later, they came upon a toy airplane fitted to resemble an old World War II fighter. Staffelbach remembered Corhagen getting in to see if it would start, but the engine had stalled on them. Cole was just as content to remain on the ground, since he didn't know how to fly a plane very well and wasn't thrilled at the prospect. The fighter plane might have been a toy, but it was still man-made, and Cole had avoided traveling by human means, especially means that involved metal and combustible fluids, whenever possible. During this whole time, they had kept their eyes peeled for some sign of Corhagen. Cole had been hoping the detective might have left a clue behind for them to follow, but that didn't seem to be the case. Staffelbach was kicking himself verbally under his breath.

"Enough," Cole said gently as they stooped through a tunnel formed from the midsection of a slinky cat. "You didn't let go on purpose. And if you'd held on, that thing that came out of the breach would have probably taken both of you."

"Sorry," the younger officer said, looking morose. "I don't like being back here. There's something about this place that makes me feel—"

"I hear something," Cole cut in abruptly. "Farther up ahead. It sounds like… laughter."

Staffelbach frowned, then took in their surroundings better. "I remember this," he said quietly. "It's coming back to me now. Corhagen and I escaped through here the first time."

"What happened?"

Cole stopped at the same time the mortal did. Staffelbach hung back just a few feet from the exit, the slinky cat's gaping maw, and leaned against one of the huge curving wires. While Staffelbach collected his thoughts, Cole sniffed the air gingerly.

"They had taken us somewhere," the mortal began tentatively as his face screwed up in concentration. "I remember they wanted something. They said something about us, then we were running. I didn't think we were going to find a way out at first. The portal, or breach, whatever you called it, was suddenly there in front of us. I grabbed Corhagen's hand, and…."

Staffelbach straightened suddenly. "You saw what happened next."

"Let's find out where that laughter is coming from," said Cole, giving the man a brief touch on the shoulder for encouragement. "We might learn what we're up against, or even find out where Corhagen was taken."

The slinky cat's mouth emptied out into a racetrack. Thankfully, nothing on the track was running for the time being. Directly next to the track was a dollhouse. Someone had gone all-out with this area, arranging it to where it sported a white picket fence, an above-ground swimming pool, several model sports cars parked out front haphazardly, and a swinging gate opened part of the way out in front. The front yard of the model home was covered in fake green grass. Several people were running around happily, laughing like mad and chasing one another. Off to the side, the same gothic doll girl from earlier sat on the dollhouse's front porch, watching the scene take place with an eerily serene expression, as though patiently waiting on something. Next to her, a large purple leopard sporting an electric-blue mane rested its head in her lap, allowing the doll girl to stroke the mane absentmindedly. A moment later, one of the adults that was playing dropped to their knees suddenly. The woman was pale, even paler and more sickly than several others still moving around her. Cole and Staffelbach both watched as the stricken figure wobbled for a moment, just a few feet away from where Corhagen was skipping double Dutch rope with two others and paying no mind at all to the disturbing scene occurring just a few short feet from him.

When the woman pitched forward suddenly, collapsing face-first onto the fake grass, no one around her took any notice. As Cole watched, he began to see just how wrong the scene was. Corhagen's feet touched ground at the exact moment each time, two seconds apart. The ropes moving over and under him in opposite directions passed by at precisely the same instant. Off to their left, a balding man in a pair of overalls was sitting cross-legged on the ground, bouncing a big blue ball. Each time he bounced, the ropes nearby smacked against the ground. Three other adults, two women and one young man that looked to be about Staffelbach's age, were racing around in circles. They had been playing with the woman who'd collapsed. Cole watched as they ran in the same pattern over and over again, as if ignorant of their playmate's condition. "It's like he doesn't see her," Staffelbach whispered.

"I don't believe they do," Cole agreed. "The girl on the porch is controlling them. They play for her until they drop."

"That's…." Staffelbach paused as the purple leopard on the porch stretched. "Just wrong. Do you have a plan?"

Cole hesitated. "I'm leery of trying anything. We still don't know what we're dealing with."

"I thought they were some of your kind," Paul said, turning back to Cole. "No offense."

"None taken," he replied. "It wasn't outside the realm of possibility, but I do not believe these creatures are of the fey. This place does not smell like Faerie."

Cole noticed the confused look on Staffelbach's face. "My home," he explained. "Where I was banished from. If we were in the Faerie realm, Lord Oberon would have sensed my presence. I could never set a toe anywhere on Faerie soil without him knowing, and if that had happened, he would have sent agents to slay me. And aside from that, this does not smell like my home. The air is stale and dry, like a room that's been sealed for too long. Also, now that I think on it, the creatures we encountered before were akin to humans."

"They smelled human?"

It sounded as though Staffelbach didn't believe him. "Somewhat," he said. "And at the same time, they don't smell like anything at all. It is as though they lack something, and in that absence, carry a unique fragrance unto themselves."

Now Staffelbach was really confused. "I'm sorry," Cole said. "Forgive me for being vague, but I don't quite know how to put it myself. In any case, now isn't really the time."

"Right," the mortal said. "We find a way to get Corhagen and the others out of there, then look for one of those openings to get us back home."

"Agreed," said Cole. "Actually, locating a breach back to the television station might be the better option."

"We can't just leave them," Staffelbach insisted. "What if someone else collapses?"

"They might," Cole admitted. "But for the moment, the others look healthy enough, and the woman can at least rest while we search."

Staffelbach opened his mouth to protest, but Cole cut him off. "If we free them now," he pointed out, "there's still the matter of getting them all out of here. Those people have been forced to move continuously without food, water, and probably sleep. A group of tired, hungry, and thirsty humans won't be easy to escape with. We need to know where to lead them before we draw attention to ourselves."

Reluctantly, Staffelbach nodded. "You're right," he said stiffly. "But I don't like it."

"Believe it or not, neither do I."

"Nor me, personally!"

An eight-foot-long arm with thin fingers swooped down from above, swiping through the space between Cole and Staffelbach like a sling blade. The jester cackled as both men drew their guns and took aim.

"Not here," he jeered gleefully. "Not in this place. Not this time. You can't hurt me like you did before."

Cole fired, aiming straight between the jester's eyes again. The bullet stopped short of hitting its target, however, and burst into a cloud of metal powder.

"See?" The jester sneered down at Cole, revealing row after row of razor-sharp teeth. Each one looked like it belonged inside a baby shark's mouth. "Even magic bullets can't hurt me here."

"Ideas?" Staffelbach asked, not lowering his gun.

"Get Corhagen and as many of the others as you can, then run. I'll hold this one off."

Before Staffelbach could move, the jester jumped down from the overhanging track in front of them. "You know," he jeered, tsking to himself, "not that it's my style, frankly, but if I were going to make a plan, saying it out loud in front of the guy attacking me seems like a really stupid move."

"It is," Cole agreed, putting his guns away. "I've thought so myself."

"Really?"

Cole drew out Aed Deigh, brought the firebrand down in twin strokes, and sent waves of fire out through the air past the jester.

"Really," he said as the flames cut through the giant plastic road, causing the severed piece to plummet down onto the jester's head. "Thank you for noticing, incidentally."

"Ow!" the jester cried out as Cole and Staffelbach planted their feet firmly onto the plastic piece of road. "I think I broke a nail under here."

"He's lucky you didn't give him a concussion," Staffelbach mused as they prepared to long jump across the straight stretch of track toward the dollhouse. "We'll probably face police brutality charges."

"Assuming he can feel pain at all," Cole pointed out. "Ready?"

The first jump was the easiest. After that, they ran into trouble. The last bit of space between them and the dollhouse fence was separated by a descending ramp. Just as they reached it, a cloud of black smoke swept along the ground. As the cloud neared them, something took shape inside of it. Cole's body was dropping back down toward the ground fast, and there was no way for him to stop. Even here, he was susceptible to things like momentum. The purple leopard leaped out from the cloud at them with its jaw wide open and claws bared. With no way of stopping, Cole kicked out and caught the beast under its jaw, causing it to fall back down. The creature managed to land on its feet, however, and was coming for them again as they touched down on the stretch of track.

"Whoa! Can't go that way," Staffelbach said.

"Nor behind us." Cole looked back and spotted the jester advancing with both long arms raised high over its head, reaching for them. "We go up."

The purple leopard was right behind them, as was the jester, using his eight-foot-long arms to crawl up the ramp, keeping pace with the big cat and gaining fast on their heels. Cole heard the cat leap and shoved Staffelbach down onto the track, falling alongside him as the blue-maned leopard sailed over their heads. This gave the jester the chance he needed to catch up, however. As the fanged harlequin loomed above them, Staffelbach clambered for his gun. It would have done him no good, but Cole was now too busy shooting ice missiles at the leopard behind them to bother telling him. As the jester leaned down, saliva dribbling from the bottom row of teeth, Staffelbach raised his pistol and fired.

The leopard froze in its tracks. Confused, Cole turned around to see what it was staring at and felt his own jaw drop in surprise. The jester had a large hole in his chest, much bigger than what a small bullet from Staffelbach's gun would have caused. The hole wasn't bleeding. The area surrounding it was cracked like plaster or glass.

Black smoke curled out from the space. The jester looked down at himself in stunned silence. The gothic doll girl from before came up the ramp behind them, staring at the wound curiously.

Slowly, her eyes turned downward to Staffelbach. "How were you able to do that?" she asked in a calm voice.

"You know something I don't?" Cole whispered softly near Staffelbach's ear. "I'll barter with you to know how you managed that."

"No idea," Staffelbach said as quietly as possible. "But do me a favor and don't tell them that."

The hole in the jester, meanwhile, was slowly closing up, though much slower than the one Cole had put in his forehead before. The process appeared to be giving the clown no small shortage of trouble.

"Boo-Boo, come!" the girl called out.

Behind them, the purple leopard leaped over their heads and slid down the ramp to the girl, stopping short of her and lowering its head so she could pet it. The girl scratched the leopard named Boo-Boo behind its mane for a moment, watching Staffelbach and Cole curiously.

"How did you hurt him?" she asked as if inquiring about the weather. "No one should be able to do that here."

"I think a better question is, what will you do for us to ensure it doesn't happen again?" Cole countered, getting to his feet.

The girl frowned, and for a moment, she actually appeared contrite. It was the first sign of emotion she had shown. Carefully, Cole sniffed the air. It still reeked of man-made fragrances, but at this distance, he could detect the scent of human coming from her. The girl was clearly anything but human, but Cole knew the scent.

In addition, the same scent was coming from the leopard next to her, as well as the jester, who had finally managed to close his wound. Now he was backing away from them, clearly unnerved by what had transpired.

"Set the cat on them," he suggested.

"No," she replied flatly. "They might hurt Boo-Boo."

"Better him than me," the jester cut back, only for Boo-Boo to snarl irritably.

The jester jumped back at this. "Just kidding, of course!"

"Give us the others, and we'll leave," Cole said, stepping forward. "That's the bargain. Otherwise, my friend's trigger finger will get itchy soon."

The gothic doll girl frowned. "I don't like you," she said.

"Honestly, I couldn't care less," he cut back, holding his ground. "Have you got a name?"

The girl glanced up at the jester. "He's Trick," she said, introducing him. "This is Boo-Boo, and they called me Mary Alice, though I don't care for it much."

"Who are they?" Cole asked.

"The ones that made us," she answered as though it should have been obvious. "We were all given names before they threw us away."

"Daddy won't like you telling them our secrets," Trick jumped in, frowning down at her. "You might want to shut that pretty little mouth of yours."

"Daddy didn't say I couldn't," Mary Alice pointed out curtly.

"This is fascinating," Cole interrupted. "But we want the people you kidnapped returned to us. My friend and I are going to walk down this ramp past you, and then I'm going to get them while he keeps his gun on you. If you so much as twitch or make one bad joke, he will shoot you."

"More than once," Staffelbach added.

"What he said."

Mary Alice shook her head. "I don't think that will work."

Something passed overhead. Cole's first thought was that it was another paper plane, but this one moved too fast and was coming in low over their heads. It was also carrying a big green gorilla, which dive-bombed out of the sky toward them as the flying figure swung back and forth erratically. The gorilla, a human-sized beast shaped somewhat like a silverback, but with scaled spikes traveling down its spine, landed in a roll and somersaulted up the ramp toward Cole and Staffelbach. The two dove out of the way to let it pass. As it came to a stop, the gorilla was joined by what Cole could only describe as a blue and gray Frankenstein's monster bat made from different stuffed animal parts.

"Nice landing, Batchwork," Mary Alice quipped. "Are you all right?"

"Fine," the patchwork bat, apparently named Batchwork, squeaked. "Fortunately, I landed on my tail this time."

"I was talking to Daddy," Mary Alice cut in.

"I'm fine, sweetheart," the gorilla answered in a deep voice. "Are *you* all right?"

"They shot Trick," she replied, nodding toward him. "Not me."

"This is one strange family reunion," Staffelbach observed, glancing back and forth between the two groups surrounding them.

"I've been so much stranger than this," Cole said dismissively.

"They've got us cornered. What now?"

"You're the one with the ace up your sleeve," Cole reminded him. "If you think it will work again, by all means, start shooting."

"It's like the *Nightmare on Elm Street* version of *Eureka's Castle*." Staffelbach froze as the gorilla stepped forward, emitting a low growl as it approached them. Flickers of green and yellow fire came from his nostrils.

"Say the word," the mortal told Cole, "and I start firing."

The gorilla behind them let loose a roar. Green and yellow flames exploded from its mouth as Cole grabbed Staffelbach and shoved him toward the edge of the ramp. Both fell over the side as Trick the jester lunged for them, making a wide sweep with his arms that missed while Cole aimed his feet for the ground. Their boots connected with the spongy, quilted ground. The terrain gave way, saving them from broken bones, and flung them back into the air. Both tried to aim themselves for the dollhouse as the gorilla came tumbling after them.

Beneath them, the more solid-looking fake grass was fast approaching. Both men cleared the pointed tips of the picket fence by a mile, coming back down on top of Corhagen and one another in a roll. Corhagen got up first, shaking his head as though coming out of a bad dream, and looked around. "What?" he gasped. "What happened? Where am I?"

"In a world of trouble," Staffelbach said, jumping up. "Help MacColewyn get the others! I'll try to hold them off."

Staffelbach aimed for the incoming gorilla with his gun as Corhagen hesitated briefly, then stood up and grabbed for the first person within reach. Each person he seized came out of their trance after a moment's shaking. Cole was taking a much less gentlemanly approach, giving the men a good hard punch that made each one stagger. "Run for the dollhouse!" he barked, once they were all awake. "It's the closest shelter!"

Staffelbach, meanwhile, had carved several holes into the gorilla, leaving him a smoking pile of Swiss cheese. As Mary Alice drew up to his perforated carcass, something flashed in her eyes.

"You killed my Daddy," she cried out as her body split open down the middle. "I'm going to... kill you!"

"Oh, dear!" said Trick, who had been hiding behind the picket fence until now. "This is bad!"

Something was trying to crawl out of Mary Alice. It looked like two pairs of garden shears attached to a woman's arms. The figure snarled as it tore itself from the young girl's body. What came out of her resembled a young woman, beautiful, with long, dark hair, wearing a white nurse's uniform. Her hands had been replaced with enormous scissors, however, and she was wearing a hospital mask. Her skin was pale, to the point that she could have been a corpse.

"Leave my monkey alone!" the woman roared.

"Staffelbach," Cole called out from the dollhouse's entrance. "This way!"

Cole laid down cover fire, despite knowing it would have zero effect, as Staffelbach ran back toward the dollhouse. Once he was inside, Cole slammed the door shut and sealed it off with a layer of ice. Something collided with the door a second later, splintering the wood and causing the ice to crack. Cole froze another layer over it before giving up and running upstairs, where everyone else was waiting.

"It's me," he called out, just in case Staffelbach started shooting. "I'm coming up."

"We're in the room at the end of the hallway," came Staffelbach's voice. "Get in here. You won't believe what I just found."

Something crashed through a window down below. Cole turned, waving for Staffelbach to move back, and let loose with all the fire he could spare. The flames swept the staircase as the scissor girl that had been Mary Alice ran at them, shrieking at the top of her lungs. The mask covering her face had slipped a little. As she drew closer, batting at the magically enhanced flames from Cole's weapon, he saw that the mask had fallen out of place. Someone had sliced open the flesh at the corners of her mouth. The woman's jaw was hanging down an obscene length for a human's. "Do you think I'm beautiful?" she howled. "Tell me that I'm beautiful!"

"No comment," Cole countered, kicking her in the stomach. "I'm seeing someone!"

Turning, Cole ran the rest of the way up and broke into a sprint once he reached the top of the stairs. "Tell me you have good news," he called out, before reaching the open door at the end of the hall. "Because the bad news is on its way now."

Staffelbach lowered his gun. "I think we found the canister that went missing from that heist the other night," Corhagen said excitedly, holding a metal cylinder up for him to see. "It was just sitting here on the bed, like they'd put it here and then forgot about it."

"Very nice," said Cole. "It doesn't help our current situation, but if we live through what's probably climbing the stairs right now, Joss will be overjoyed."

A green fist punched through the window, cutting Cole off and raining glass down everywhere. The other survivors that had been playing in the yard scattered clear of it, moving as fast as their tired bodies would allow. The fire-breathing gorilla swung upside-down from the edge of the roof in front of the broken glass and looked around until he saw Corhagen with the canister.

"Give me the object," he said, holding one hand out. "And I will save you."

Behind them, the bedroom door splintered as the blade from a garden shear stabbed through the wood. "Let me in!" the scissor woman shouted.

"Get back," Cole ordered, raising the frost-covered blade. "I'm going to freeze her out."

"That won't stop her," the gorilla insisted, even as Cole covered the door in a sheet of ice. "She's too powerful right now. Mary Alice won't come back until she sees that I'm all right. Give me the canister, and I'll see to it you all return home."

"Don't," Cole warned, when Corhagen appeared to consider it. "I'm getting us out of here."

The gorilla outside growled. "You would doom these people to die?"

Mary Alice's scissored hands exploded through the wall beside the door. Rather than trying to break the door down, she was attempting to rip a hole straight through the wall to get at them. Cole whirled around and took aim with Jabberwock, hoping it could at least discourage her. Staffelbach and Corhagen, however, aimed their guns at the gorilla, who was coming in through the window. The beast jerked back, lost his balance on the sill, and fell to the ground, out of sight. Almost immediately, his presence was replaced by that of a flying robot.

"Another one," Staffelbach groaned. "If this wasn't life or death, I would so be geeking out over that right now."

Corhagen kept firing as Mary Alice the Scissor Woman continued bludgeoning chunks of the wall away, making more room for herself to enter. Cole's bullets were having no effect. Corhagen's put several dents in the robot's arms as it smashed the lower half of the wall away, a much easier task for him than Mary Alice at the moment, but the machine simply batted the projectiles away like they were gnats.

One bullet ricocheted off the robot's arm and struck the wall. Light poured in from the crack that formed there, a bright green light that reflected in Cole's peripheral vision.

"What did you do?" Staffelbach wondered.

"It's a breach," Cole said as Mary Alice began to drag herself through the opening she'd made. "Everyone, get ready. We're getting out of here right now!"

"Negative," the robot buzzed. "Remain where you are."

Staffelbach took aim and fired a shot straight through the robot's mechanized eye. The machine recoiled in surprise as black smoke curled up from the wound. Cole seized his chance, took out Aed Deigh, and shoved the blade into the glowing opening. Putting every last ounce of his weight into it, Cole dragged the blade down, tearing a hole not into the wall, but the fabric that made up everything that was. The gap widened as he pulled the blade back into its hilt. Corhagen and Staffelbach were already helping the others up.

"Move!" Cole shouted as the first few people hurled themselves toward the light as though the gates of salvation themselves waited on the other side.

"She's in!" Staffelbach yelled, backing away as he emptied the rest of his clip into Mary Alice. The scissored hands sliced each one in half before they could touch her. The masked creature cackled as her bladed weapons opened and closed menacingly.

"Go," Cole told them. "I'll follow you."

Before either man could move, the gorilla appeared in the opening that had been the window. Cole thought he was springing through the air to attack him, but the beast sailed past without giving him any notice.

"Kongazilla," the robot buzzed.

Kongazilla, apparently, crashed into Mary Alice, sending both of them to the floor. As the gorilla pinned her down with his weight, her eyes rolled up to stare at him.

"Am I beautiful?" she screeched.

"You're so-so," he said. "Just… so-so."

Someone grabbed Cole by the shoulder and pulled him back through the breach. The same flash of light from before clouded his vision, followed by the distortion of falling past so many worlds at once. All of it was over in the blink of an eye. Then he and Staffelbach were lying on top of someone, holding on to one another for dear life.

"Get off me!" Corhagen cried feebly. "Why is it I'm always the one who ends up on the bottom?"

Cole laughed then. It felt good to laugh. "Maybe it's just in your nature?" he suggested as he and Staffelbach stood up.

Cole looked around as Corhagen and Staffelbach saw to the others. Some of them were still having trouble moving around. They had landed in a different part of the station from before, an area Cole didn't recognize. What struck him as odd, however, was how dark it had gotten. The area they had landed in was apparently not in use at the moment. Taking his phone out, Cole punched in Joss's number and waited. The phone rang several times before the inspector finally picked up.

"'Lo?" Joss muttered.

Cole frowned. "Joss?"

It sounded like Joss had been asleep. "Cole?"

"Where are you?" Cole asked. "I found Staffelbach and Corhagen, along with what I think are several missing station employees. We haven't had a chance to question any of them yet, but…."

"Where the fuck are you?"

Cole frowned. "What's wrong?" he wondered. "I'm not sure what floor of the station we're on. It's one I haven't seen before."

"Cole," Joss began slowly, as if holding himself back, "you, Staffelbach, and Corhagen have all been missing for two days. Where have you been?"

"So, what did we miss?"

The entire roster of Section Thirteen had gathered in a spare interrogation room. Joss's office was a little cramped to fit everyone comfortably, so they'd relocated once Staffelbach and Corhagen had alerted their families to let them know they were okay. Corhagen was on his cell phone for a good twenty minutes, listening to his wife yell. No one was surprised. Staffelbach, it seemed, shared an apartment with a friend in Queens, an artist and Internet reviewer of comics known as the Jersey Comic Geek. Once the guy was assured everything was okay, he seemed to take the news relatively well.

Now that everyone had gathered in the interrogation room, Joss was standing front and center. Marcel had taken up space beside a wall, where he was out of the way, with Rainette leaning close to him in a comfortable fashion. Corhagen was resting in a chair by the far left corner of the table, sitting as far from Cole as he could get, who had claimed a spot at the table's edge on the opposite side. Staffelbach bridged the gap between them in the middle. Everyone looked tired, Joss especially. Outside, the sun was just starting to climb the New York skyline. Cole and the others had apparently landed back in the TV station in the wee hours of the morning, before sunrise. It had been a long morning for them all so far.

"Well," Joss began. "Locally, both investigations were postponed so we could look for our missing members."

"Sorry about that," said Cole. "It wasn't intentional."

"I didn't think so. Rainette and her coven were staking out the station every day, thinking that you might have been taken through one of those rifts, or whatever they were called. While that was going on, we managed to learn a few things. It seems the station is scheduled to be shut down next year. Part of its broadcast will be absorbed into other channels, but several shows are being canceled."

"How does that fit in with the investigation?" Corhagen asked.

"We aren't sure yet," Joss said. "But since the three of you are back, we can start finding out. The people you brought back with you were all employees of the TV station that never showed up for work. Some of them were reported missing; others weren't. It seems like most people dismissed their disappearances as evidence that the station was going under. A few had families here on the island, though, so they'll be happy to hear we've located them."

Marcel spoke up. "At least the case behind the missing canister was solved. We were having no luck searching for it."

"We still don't know who stole it," Rainette reminded him. "But having both cases connected is pretty convenient. If I were more suspicious, I'd worry about that."

"It does look like the canister theft and the kidnappings from the TV station are connected," Cole mused.

"So those things we fought are the ones that stole the canister?" Corhagen asked

"Maybe," Cole admitted. "But maybe not."

"The canister theft sounds more like the work of violent spirits," Rainette interrupted. "There was ectoplasm all over that place, and coming into contact with Cole made it run wild."

"Speaking of which...," said Cole. "Have you had a chance to look at the trapped ectoplasm creature yet?"

"Not yet. We've been looking for your sorry asses this whole time!" Rainette smiled then, letting them know she was teasing. "My coven didn't find any unusual traces of ectoplasm at the TV station, though. If the canister was taken by those things, it should have been everywhere."

"The creatures at the TV station are involved," Joss stated. "We just don't know how yet. They might not have stolen the canister themselves, but there's a pretty high chance they were behind the theft."

"They could have gotten some wild spirits to do it for them," Corhagen pointed out.

Staffelbach raised his hand then. "Sorry," he said. "But for the one guy who doesn't have as much experience as the rest of you, what were those things?"

Cole frowned. "None of us knows. They didn't appear to be fey, or any other sort of being I've encountered in my time."

"Our tracking and identification spells weren't working, either," Rainette added. "They kept coming back inconclusive. Marianne thought some of the signs looked human, though."

"I smelled human on them also," Cole told her.

"So they were people?" Staffelbach asked, looking a little revolted by the idea. "Like ghosts?"

"Definitely not ghosts," Rainette corrected. "But something that might have been human once."

"One thing does concern me," Cole said, getting their attention. "The place we were in before, where the canister was hidden? It seemed small."

Corhagen frowned hard. "What are you talking about?"

"It looked plenty big to me," Staffelbach concurred.

"Small by comparison," he amended. "A plane or dimensional space will always feel massive, even if it's a relatively tiny place. This felt cramped, like a cage. The place was big, but it still carried the feel of a small room. Looking back, I cannot help but think that place was something akin to a prison cell."

"How do you know that?" Staffelbach wondered.

"I am sidhe," he replied.

"That's his answer for everything," Corhagen muttered. "Just nod and pretend like you understand."

"It isn't an excuse," Cole replied sharply. "I simply sense things that aren't registered by humans."

"We know," Joss said gently. "So this space felt like a cage to you?"

"Yes." Cole nodded. "A very small one."

"What did it look like, again?" Rainette asked, leaning forward. "Describe it for me."

"Like a giant kid's room," Staffelbach said at once. "There were toys everywhere, but they were massive."

"Building blocks the size of a car," said Corhagen, jumping in. "And model cars as big as regular cars. There were paper airplanes flying through the air, and this big dollhouse the size of a mansion."

"It was surreal," Staffelbach finished.

"You both seem to remember it better this time," Cole noticed.

Both men paused a moment. "Yeah," Corhagen said as he and Staffelbach stared at each other. "That is weird. Maybe you remember more if you've been there more than once?"

"Or have been there a while," Staffelbach pointed out. "You never made it through the breach with me the first time."

"Because you let go of my hand!"

"He had to," Cole said, cutting James off. "The jester named Trick had grabbed him. It would have dragged the both of you back. Be grateful we came looking for you."

"Cole," Joss warned.

"I was just teasing," Corhagen said quickly, waving Joss back. "Sorry about that, though."

"It's cool," said Staffelbach. "I didn't mean to let go."

"Now that *that's* over," Rainette said, giving them all a look, "and we've met our quota of male bonding for the day, let's get back to the place you were being held in. It sounds like it might have been a paracosm."

At once, everyone else in the room turned toward Cole, save for Marcel. "Sorry," Cole said, shrugging. "This isn't something I'm familiar with."

Rainette didn't look the least bit happy. "Honestly," she grumbled. "Why am I even here?"

"We're sorry," Joss said earnestly. "Please continue."

"It isn't really a field I'm familiar with," she confessed. "Marianne knows more about them than I do. She has a degree in psychology and explained the concept to me at one point. A paracosm is an imaginary world, a very minutely detailed one, usually created by children for the purposes of escaping the real one."

"A child's fantasy land," Cole mused. "That could explain a lot."

"It did look like the sort of place a little kid might create," Corhagen said, thinking back. "A place full of toys without any adult supervision around."

"A paracosm isn't real, though," Rainette went on, cutting Corhagen off. "It only exists in a child's imagination."

"What part of that makes it unreal?" Cole asked.

Rainette looked at him. "You're joking, right?"

Cole shook his head and noticed the others, even Marcel, were looking at him. "In Faerie, sidhe children and other types of fey play in what you would call 'imaginary worlds' all the time."

Joss's eyes widened. "Really?"

Staffelbach looked interested. "How does that work?"

"We use glamour," Cole explained. "The first thing sidhe children are taught is how to properly create things with glamour. Many sidhe children weave things from their minds with it. It's not uncommon where I am from."

The silence in the room was stifling. "We're talking about human children here, Cole," Rainette derided. "A human child can't use glamour, not in most cases, anyway."

"But they create worlds for themselves," Cole pointed out. "The principle is the same, correct?"

No one seemed to want to answer. "All right, fine!" Rainette shouted. "Cole, the fantasy exists only in the child's mind. It has no basis in the real world. Maybe it is real to the child, but no one else can interact with it."

"I'm not sure what you mean," Cole said. "Forgive me. I don't mean to be difficult, but I have heard of many human children interacting within the same fantasy together. How is this less real?"

Rainette looked at Joss. "You explain it to him," she said flatly. "He's your boyfriend."

Corhagen looked away uncomfortably at the term, but no one else paid any attention. Joss gave Cole a serious look. "You really are confused by all of this?" he pressed. "This isn't one of your jokes, right? Because now isn't the time."

"I'm aware of that," Cole replied. "I just don't quite understand. Remember, I was not raised in human society like Marcel."

Cole turned to Marcel then. "I assumed that was why you shared in their confusion?"

"It was," he said. "Though I have a better idea of where your thoughts are coming from than they do. If you wouldn't mind?"

"Go ahead," said Cole, motioning for him to continue.

Marcel straightened up as the others looked to him. "What MacColewyn is saying is that he was not raised as a human child," the ogre explained. "He was banished from Faerie as an adult, and does not completely grasp why certain aspects of a human's childhood are the way they are."

"Surely you've been around kids at some point," Corhagen insisted, giving Cole a skeptical look.

"I know some things," Cole answered. "That doesn't mean I comprehend the point behind them."

"Stop for just a second," Joss cut in. "This is getting off track, and I need to know something right now. Are you telling us, Cole, that a fey could have created that pocket dimension, or whatever it was, from a child's fantasy?"

Cole thought for a moment. "It did not feel like a creation of the fey," he began hesitantly. "However, we were only there for a short time, by our time's standards. The two missing days were a result of jumping from one region of space and time to another and then back again. Hours or days can be lost during said jumps, so for Staffelbach and myself, we were only there for an hour or two, at most. Getting back to your question, it isn't impossible that the space was somehow powered by fey magic.

"Though the region did not resemble anything Faerie-made, the power that was maintaining the space could have been coming from a faraway source. If that was the case, then I might not have noticed it right away, especially since we were preoccupied with finding Corhagen at that moment."

"And if it was a child's paracosm brought to life," Rainette brought up, "the region of space would reflect that through all five senses."

"Meaning it would have smelled human," Cole finished, nodding. "Along with anything else in there."

Staffelbach glanced back and forth between Cole and Rainette. "So, what are you two saying?" he asked. "That those things were a child's imaginary friends?"

Everyone fell silent again. "It's possible," Cole said.

Corhagen winced and let out a groan of frustration. "I really don't want to consider the possibility that some poor kid's imaginary friends have been running around stealing top-secret scientific equipment from a high-security storage facility. It makes my brain hurt."

"Especially after what happened a few weeks ago on Staten Island," Rainette said. "They never did find the brat that escaped from the mental house up in Maine. Could he be behind this too?"

Corhagen rose up. "I don't think so," Cole interjected quickly. "Daniel Whittaker was a little too mature by human standards to bother with imaginary worlds anymore. Plus, he was using a combination of human technology and magic to enslave fey, hoping they would retaliate once the police shut his operation down, and die in a more honorable fashion than mere suicide."

"That kid had way too much melodrama," Rainette muttered, shuddering. "So if he's not behind this, that means there's another crackpot kid out there ordering these things around?"

"Or is being used by something far more dangerous," Joss added. "We can't rule out the possibility."

"I find your scenario more plausible," Cole told him. "There is something I never had the chance to explain before. Daniel Whittaker was being manipulated by something other than just the Order. A group of shadows had influenced his mind, darkening it."

"When?" Joss asked. "Why wasn't this in your report?"

"It wasn't something I wanted the Order to become aware of," Cole explained. "I only discovered this after Daniel absorbed the shadow entity into himself. There were a total of twelve shadows in all, and they'd put their mark on the boy in order to manipulate him. For what reason, I don't know."

Joss gave Cole a long, thoughtful look. The others remained silent, giving each other an occasional glance while mulling over this new information.

"We may be in over our heads," said Joss at last.

"I believe we were from the very beginning," Cole said. "It wasn't something I kept hidden intentionally. I was put on indefinite suspension and ordered to keep away from all of you. There wasn't a chance to pass the knowledge on."

"You could have told me before you left," Corhagen pointed out. "Wait. Was that why I got shocked so hard when you were flashing your wang in front of that kid?"

"He was unconscious," Cole pointed out. "And facing the other direction. Besides, charging into a magic circle unheeded is a very foolish idea. You were already aware of that."

"I did try and stop him," Rainette added.

Joss cleared his throat and shifted nervously. It was strange for Cole to see the man looking so harried.

"We've got a lot to do today," the inspector said finally. "Marcel, make sure the canister gets taken down to the evidence locker. I don't want that thing disappearing."

Marcel headed for the door, but was brought up short as it swung open, revealing Agent Willhiem. Cole stiffened and started to go for his gun. It took more willpower than he cared to admit to hold himself back.

"I'm afraid that won't be necessary," he said, wearing the same calm demeanor from before. "Orders have come from above. The canister is being moved to a separate location for safety reasons. The brass feels that something this dangerous shouldn't be locked up in the evidence room. That place has seen enough excitement lately."

Willhiem's eyes drifted to Cole for a second. Joss, meanwhile, was staring at the IA agent as though willing him to catch fire. It occurred to Cole that he wasn't sure whether Joss could actually do such a thing, and he scooted to the edge of the desk and watched the scene closely.

"And will the Section be allowed access to the evidence?" Joss pressed. "It is a crucial bit of information in our case, assuming you were eavesdropping for longer than just the last part of the meeting."

"I wouldn't dream of eavesdropping," Willhiem protested. "I wasn't given orders to. You might want to keep your voice down, though, if something in this room is being discussed that you don't want overheard by anyone. Of course, I'm sure that Section Thirteen has nothing to hide."

"We have plenty to hide," Cole jumped in to say. "Otherwise, we wouldn't have shut the door."

The others found this funny. Willhiem considered as he attempted to match Cole's gaze. At last, the mortal practitioner turned away, back toward the inspector.

"Actually, I came to request that the Section take part in the transfer. Since the canister is, as you put it, a vital piece of evidence in your investigation, you'll all need to know where it's being kept in the event of an emergency."

Joss said nothing. The remainder of the room stayed quiet, following his lead. Finally Joss asked, "When will the transfer take place?"

"Thirty minutes from now," Willhiem replied. "We've already procured an armored van for you and your team. The canister will be kept in a locked strongbox with you. A SWAT team has been brought in to ride in a second van. They will be guarding a second strongbox that will serve as a decoy."

"That's an awful lot of security," Joss noted.

"The canister was first taken from a high-security facility through very violent means," Willhiem reminded him as he turned for the door. "While you might have trouble convincing others in the NYPD of the validity of your work, I am not so blind to the truth. Whatever stole that canister did so for a reason, and will likely try again."

With that said, Willhiem exited, closing the door tightly behind him. Cole leaped away from the table as soon as he was gone and stepped forward to stand next to Joss.

"Is there anything we can do to stop this?" he asked stiffly.

"I'm not so sure we should," Joss replied. "Everything he said is true, and the evidence locker is nowhere near the level of security as the building where the canister was being kept. Whatever stole it tore through that place like it was tissue paper. It'd have no problem getting into this place, and this building is full of people."

"What's wrong?" Rainette asked, looking around the room for help. "No, really. What's the problem? The guy comes off as being kind of a douche, and I know we aren't supposed to like Internal Affairs, but I feel like I'm missing something."

"Willhiem works for the Hermetic Order of the Golden Dawn," Marcel explained to her. "We believe he was put in charge of the Internal Affairs investigation of us by the Order so they could spy on the Section more closely."

"What?" Rainette's eyes grew to the size of saucers. "Why didn't anyone tell me?"

"We didn't find out until a couple of nights back," Joss explained. "It was when we tangled with that merry-go-round. I wasn't there, but apparently Willhiem came right out and told Cole the truth."

Corhagen, of all people, looked the most surprised by this. "Why would he just say it?" he wondered. "Couldn't he have been lying?"

"He is a practitioner," Cole explained. "I felt that much. Plus, it is apparent that the man is hiding something."

"I could sense that much about him," Rainette admitted. "I just thought he might have still been in the broom closet."

Corhagen fell quiet, sitting on his side of the table with a sour frown on his face. He looked deep in thought, and Cole found the level of Corhagen's malcontent to be unsettling. If anything, he and Marcel had more to lose having the Order so close to them.

Joss cleared his throat. "We'd better get ready," he said. "The little turd said a half hour. I want to make sure that canister, and whatever is inside of it, gets where it's going. The last thing we need is for the Order to pull a fast one on us and then make it seem like it was the Section's fault."

THE interior of the armored van was cramped. "I do not like being in this," Marcel grumbled as they attempted to make room for him.

"We should have let you climb in first," Rainette muttered as she was forced uncomfortably against a wall while Marcel attempted to squeeze past her.

"It's moments like this where I'm glad I fall on the short side of things," Staffelbach mused. "Normally, I hate it, but this is one time where it comes in handy."

"Don't remind us," Cole said, holding on as Marcel shook the van slightly in his attempt to get settled in. "How much longer do we have to wait? I thought the little twerp from IA said thirty minutes."

"He did," said Joss, adjusting himself across from Cole. "I just spoke with the head of the SWAT team in the next van. They're ready to go just as soon as Willhiem shows up. Apparently he's coming along with them."

"At least we don't have to deal with him," Cole replied.

"Agreed," added Marcel.

Minutes passed, with no one in the van speaking. All seemed on edge for some reason, though Cole was having a difficult time pinning down why, specifically. Neither he nor Marcel liked the idea of taking commands from the Order. Cole could figure that much out on his own. Joss looked worried, as though he was anticipating trouble, which was sadly a high possibility. Rainette just sat next to Marcel as comfortably as possible, sandwiched between his bulk and the front of the van. Staffelbach and Corhagen were separated by Joss. Staffelbach seemed slightly nervous, but Corhagen was still lost in thought. Whatever was on his mind, it had grabbed his attention and held on with a vise grip. For some reason, that made Cole uncomfortable in an entirely different way.

It was a relief when the van started and they felt themselves ease backward out of the precinct garage. As this happened, Staffelbach lifted his head and looked around at everyone's tired expressions.

"Does anybody else feel like we're being set up?"

Cole looked at him and nodded. "It does appear to be so."

"We weren't told everything," Joss said quietly. "That's for damn sure. This van is supposed to take a separate route through the west side, while the decoy goes through the main part of town. The idea is that, if the perp makes a play for the decoy, the SWAT team will be on standby to make the arrest."

"What about us?" Staffelbach wondered.

"The brass seems to think the Section can handle itself," Joss replied. "Either we've been played and are really guarding the decoy strongbox, or someone is hoping we'll be killed off."

Cole looked down at the strongbox anchored to the floor near all of their feet. Marcel's humongous loafers were blocking most of it.

"There is an easy way to find out," Cole said pointedly. "We open the box and see for ourselves."

"We can't do that," Corhagen cut in, giving Cole a sharp glare.

"No," Joss said, silencing the detective with a glance. "That would be wrong. Still, if we come under attack, and the box is accidentally broken open in the confusion, I won't say a word. I don't want anyone in this van dying for no reason."

"Right," Rainette said, giving Marcel a pat on the arm. "No one is allowed to die unless they have a very good reason."

Staffelbach chuckled. "I should have brought a note from my mom, then."

The mood lightened somewhat, yet Cole felt no inclination to join his comrades in their light ribbing of one another. His eyes remained fastened on Joss while the van rumbled on. Outside, another snowstorm had blown in, snuffing out the promising sunlight that had shown through the windows earlier. While the others made light conversation, Cole observed his lover's face.

None of them were allowed to die, the witch had said. Not without good reason, at least.

When the van came to a stop, everyone went on the alert. The back doors opened to show a team of hazard personnel waiting with their arms raised in surrender. Behind them, the loading dock for a small building Cole didn't recognize stretched out. Each member of the Section disembarked with their weapons out so the hazard team could come aboard and remove the strongbox. "Is this the decoy?" the man in charge, a short, balding fellow with glasses, asked.

"Probably," Joss replied. "Though we were told different."

Cole was watching the area and sniffing every few seconds. "Shouldn't the other van have arrived already?" he asked. "They were coming straight through town. We had the less direct route."

"We haven't heard anything yet," the balding man admitted, marking something on his electronic board. "Someone should have called by now."

Joss watched closely as the box was set down onto a rolling cart. "Everyone, take your positions," he ordered. "Decoy or not, something isn't right here."

Together, they gathered around and walked backward toward the open loading door behind them, where the strongbox was being wheeled through. Something in the air was making the skin on the back of Cole's neck itch. Marcel was having a similar reaction, and kept jerking his head at anything sufficiently loud.

In the distance, the sound of screeching tires echoed through the side streets. The sound grew closer, compounded by something like metal crunching against metal. A second later, a single black car rolled to a halt behind the armored van. Willhiem spilled out of the backseat holding what looked like the canister in his bare hands. Several armed men in suits followed him, taking point on all sides of him as he dashed up the loading ramp on the far right. "Get inside!" Willhiem shouted as he ran. "Get everyone inside and secure the building! We haven't got much time!"

For once, Cole wasn't in a mood to argue. He, along with everyone else, ducked backward under the loading door as Willhiem and his guards bridged the gap between them. Staffelbach and Corhagen were already bringing the door down as the men ducked under it into the building.

"This is an emergency protocol Code Black situation," Willhiem barked once the door was locked down. "No one is allowed in or out from this point on. By the authority vested in me under the Hermetic Order, this structure is to be sealed, and all magical wards activated on full power!"

No one from the Section moved. Everyone else, however, dropped whatever they were doing at once and scattered.

"He brought us to a building under the Order's banner," Cole hissed. "I should have known."

"This is not good," said Marcel. "For some of us, anyway. If the Order has warded the building to keep out the fey, it might see myself and the sidhe as hostiles."

"We're already inside the building," Cole reminded him. "The wards are designed to keep stuff out, not harm things that have already made it inside."

Marcel wasn't convinced. "I still don't like it."

"What's going on, Agent Willhiem?" Joss demanded. "You said that we were the ones carrying the real canister."

"I lied," he replied in a deceptively calm tone. Going by his outward appearance, Willhiem should have sounded close to panicking. His suit had seen better days. Pieces of it had been torn, and it looked as though he was bleeding in several places beneath the fabric. His face had gone pale and looked clammy, even more so with the amount of sweat pouring down it.

"The van transporting the real canister was attacked. I barely managed to escape and call for help. We were followed on the way here. Whatever it was, it is big and very powerful."

"What was it?"

Willhiem paused and gave Cole a look. "I don't know."

Rainette frowned. "Meaning?"

"Meaning," Willhiem elaborated in an impatient tone, "I couldn't see it. No one could see it. Whatever attacked us was…."

"Invisible?" Corhagen tried.

"Yes. No." Willhiem took a moment to gather himself. "It was *there*," he emphasized. "We could all tell it was there, but it was somehow…."

Cole rolled his eyes. "At least he's being straightforward with us."

"Was it transparent?" Rainette offered.

"There isn't time for this right now," Willhiem said dismissively. "I'm not sure if the building's security wards will be enough. When it came for me, I tried throwing spells at it, but the thing shrugged them off like they weren't there. Whatever we're dealing with, magic doesn't appear to affect it."

This made Rainette pale slightly. "Crap."

"Where's the rest of the SWAT team you were with?" Joss asked, stopping Willhiem before he could walk away. "You said that you had to call for help."

Willhiem looked down at where Joss had his bicep in a tight grip. "They're gone," he answered flatly, before pulling away.

"Get your ass back here!" Joss shouted as the man made a beeline for the door at the back of the unloading room.

"What?" Cole called out. "You mean they're dead?"

"No." Willhiem stopped but didn't turn around. "I mean they're simply gone. They vanished while that thing was attacking the van. We could all see it; we could *feel* it, but there was still nothing there. Each time it grabbed one of the men, he disappeared. There were no bodies left at the scene when I left. No bones, no clothing, just the memories of them fading from my mind."

The entire building shook. The walls and ceiling creaked dangerously as everyone jumped back in surprise. Willhiem remained perfectly still.

"It's found us," he said. "Whatever happens, don't let it touch you."

"Could it maybe be taking people to a different region of space or time?" Rainette suggested. "Like what happened with Corhagen and Staffelbach at the TV station?"

"No," Willhiem dismissed. "It doesn't simply take people out of sight. After they were gone, I couldn't remember their faces. The men that I had ridden with started to fade from my mind. I still know they exist, but their voices, how tall they were, the color of their skin? All of it disappeared along with them, but more slowly."

"It takes people out of existence," said Cole, while the building continued to shake.

Willhiem nodded. "Most likely."

The calm in Willhiem's voice struck at Cole sharply. "But even the Sluagh couldn't do that," he insisted.

A low hiss filled the space they were in. It reached through the air, tearing across the flesh of everyone inside, causing them all to hunch forward slightly, as though drawing away from something vile. Nothing in the world had sounded so terrible before. It was like white noise mixed with nails on a chalkboard played in slow motion. Cole felt it worst of all. It made him want to hide. He was a warrior, had been fighting for as long as he could remember. He would not run and hide.

That didn't stop him from wanting to, though. For the first time in a long while, Cole felt genuinely afraid of what was lurking outside the building, wrestling with it while trying to break inside. Slowly, he took a deep breath.

"It isn't the Sluagh," Willhiem replied in a matter-of-fact voice. "I don't know if it can be fought, but it wants inside. I suggest we all prepare ourselves."

Joss looked around at his team. "Any ideas?"

"I don't sense anything," Cole said, trying to expand his senses outward. "I don't smell anything."

"Same here," added Rainette. "It's like there's a great big void outside the building, closing in on us."

"We cannot attack a void," Marcel stated gravely. "A void craves fulfillment."

"That's a place to start." Joss ducked reflexively as the ceiling began to strain against whatever was pressing down against it. "How do we fill a void?"

Marcel shook his head. "It depends on what the void wants."

"It may want us," Rainette pointed out.

"In that case, I vote against giving it us," Staffelbach said. "That wouldn't help things."

"Damn straight," Joss said, nodding. "Come on, people! We don't have much time. If that thing gets inside, we don't have much choice but to fight it, and if what Willhiem said is true, magic won't work on it."

"And if we attack it with brute force, it will erase us from everyone's memories," Marcel added. "Not a good idea. That doesn't leave us with many options."

"Then we don't fight it."

Joss looked at Cole. "What?"

"We don't fight it," Cole repeated. "We go get the canister, wait until that thing breaks through the wards, then run."

The others stared at Cole, slack-jawed. "Cole," Joss said quietly. "We can't do that. There are people inside this building."

"Then make Willhiem give the order to evacuate," he replied. "If they stay here, that thing will get them. It's better for them if they go, anyway. Anyone who stays here and tries being a hero will suffer something far worse than death."

Joss's face went grim as he considered Cole's plan.

"It's… not a bad idea, sir," Staffelbach pointed out. "The fewer people we have to worry about, the easier this will be."

"They can get out through the sewer exit if need be," Cole went on. "Though, knowing the Order, there's probably a secret passage leading out somewhere around here."

The walls were starting to crack. It sounded like the support beams holding the building up were giving way. Whatever was pushing against the building had applied more pressure.

"If we don't hurry," Cole added, "this thing will bring the roof down on our heads, which will most likely kill several of us. The rest will then get picked off at that thing's leisure."

Conveniently enough, Willhiem chose that moment to return. "The wards are starting to give," he told them. "Once they go, the only thing holding that monstrosity back will be the walls, and those are giving way as we speak. We don't have much time."

"Evacuate the building," Joss ordered. "The people here are going to be crushed if we wait around for much longer. They'll be better off out of our way."

Willhiem opened his mouth, then paused thoughtfully before saying, "You have a plan."

Joss ignored him. "Is there a way out of here that it won't notice right away? If so, have everyone escape through it. We're going to take the canister and run."

Something that almost looked like a smile tugged at the corner of Willhiem's mouth for an instant. "You're running away?"

"Would you rather stay and fight that thing personally?" Cole asked curtly.

"An admirable strategy," Willhiem replied. "All things considered. However, I am not authorized to hand over the canister to you."

The monster outside hissed again. It sounded more urgent this time, as though growing impatient with the building's stubborn refusal to fold over.

"You've got two minutes," Joss told him. "Get those people out of here, then take the canister and come with us. Otherwise, you can stay behind and have another crack at it."

The look on Joss's face left no doubt in Cole's mind how serious the man was. Willhiem wasn't oblivious to it either, and immediately ran back the way he'd come to give the order. Once he was gone, Cole moved beside Joss. The roof was beginning to shake again, dropping dust and debris down on their heads.

"Whatever happens," Cole warned him, whispering near his lover's ear, "no matter what, do not leave my side."

Joss looked at him. "I mean it," Cole insisted. "I came close to losing you once and had to beg the Goddess herself for help to heal you. She is not one for granting favors without reason. I do not want to have to ask again for your sake."

"I took an oath," Joss reminded him.

"Fuck the oath," Cole spat. "Your oath almost got you killed by Marcel while he was controlled by someone else. I am sidhe. Out of everyone here now, I stand the greatest chance of surviving whatever that thing is. You are not leaving my side."

Cole hesitated, then dropped his head slightly. "I can't lose you," he whispered. It was barely heard over the noise around them. "Not after so long. I just can't. I don't have it in me to wait years for you to reincarnate so we can meet again."

It looked as though Joss was going to say something, but he was cut off when the ground beneath them bucked upward like an angry bull. The whole world appeared to be shaking all over now. "Hey!" Rainette screamed over the cataclysm. "Jack and Ennis! The wards are coming down!"

Joss stood up, then helped Cole get to his feet. "This is a conversation for another time."

Cole started to protest, but was cut off when a piece of the ceiling came down in front of him, missing the spot where he stood by only a couple of feet.

"Agreed," he muttered. "I can hear Willhiem coming. He must have given the signal."

The building shook yet again. "Over all this?" Joss wondered.

Cole shrugged. "He shuffles with his feet ever so slightly when he walks. It's noticeable."

Sure enough, Willhiem appeared a second later with the canister case tucked under his arm and a gun clutched in his free hand.

"It couldn't hurt," he said, when Cole gave him a look.

Joss cocked his head to one side, as if dismissing the matter. "Marcel," he called out to the ogre. "We could use an exit. Care to make one?"

The ogre did not hesitate. Cole watched with a sense of pride as the seven-foot-tall wall of muscle and force charged at a spot on a nearby wall that had one long crack running down it from the ceiling and several more spreading out from that. Rainette called out to stop him, but the ogre was already slamming into the obstacle with all the subtlety of a freight train. Nothing happened, though several chunks went flying. Marcel didn't let that slow him down, though. His massive fists, each the size of a mortal man's head, began pounding and clawing into the wall, tearing away at more of it. With each blow, he roared loudly enough to almost drown out the terrible hissing sound coming from outside. Cole prayed they didn't encounter their adversary the moment Marcel broke through, and that it wasn't waiting to grab the ogre once the opening was made.

Everyone gathered in closer, despite the danger from flying concrete and plaster. None of them looked optimistic. Marcel gave one final roar as the section of the wall he'd attacked collapsed in around him. At the same time, the creature outside let out one final hiss in what could have been anger, and the world fell silent.

Marcel shrugged off the rubble surrounding him as something thick and fluidized landed on the other side of the wall outside with a "splot" sound. More followed, until it might as well have been raining.

Some of the goop oozed through the gaping hole into the room. Rainette stepped forward after a moment's hesitation.

"It's ectoplasm," she said in wonder. "Like in the storage building before."

"Take caution," Willhiem warned. "It could still be dangerous."

Joss looked at Cole. "Maybe you should keep your distance," he said. "The last time you were near this stuff, we had a problem on our hands."

Cole was already backing away. "Not an issue."

"I don't have any of my supplies or a kit with me," Rainette grumbled, kneeling down near the growing puddle of slime. "I'd like to get a sample of this to compare with the one we took before."

Slowly, she stretched her hand out above the surface of the goo. Marcel stayed close by, ready to pull her back at the first sign of trouble.

"It feels like the same stuff," she noted. "It's as if there is nothing here."

"The creature could have exhausted its supply," Willhiem postulated, moving in closer. "If the thing is able to manifest in our plane of existence by gathering ectoplasm, then its ability to affect our world must be finite."

Rainette was lost in thought now, oblivious to how close Willhiem stood to her. Marcel watched the man but made no movement to swat the nuisance away.

"That would explain why there's so much of it," Rainette mused quietly to herself. "And why it vanished so suddenly. It can only hold its ectoplasmic body together for brief periods of time, and once that body has dissolved, it has to go out and build a whole new body for itself."

"Which takes time," Willhiem finished. "I will alert the Order at once. Perhaps the archives have some information that will shed light on this creature's true nature. Or, at the very least, tell us how we can destroy it."

"What about finding out why it wants the canister?" Cole asked, once Willhiem was far enough out of earshot. "Is that a priority?"

"Yes," Joss replied. "But for right now, we get our asses back to headquarters. Corhagen, find Rainette something she can carry a sample of that ectoplasm in. The rest of us will get the van warmed up."

Cole stopped Joss as he was walking past. "What about the canister?" he asked in a low tone. "Willhiem took it with him."

"Let him have it," Joss growled. "That fucking thing has caused us enough grief for one day. If the Order wants it so badly, they can hold onto it until that thing rebuilds itself and comes looking for it again."

A smile tugged at Cole's mouth. "What about your oath?"

Joss gave Cole's arm a quick squeeze. "The oath was to serve and protect the city of New York and its citizens," he replied. "Not the Order. I don't like getting jerked around by politics, and these bastards nearly got us killed."

"Erased from existence," Cole corrected. "Which is much worse, or so I have been told."

"All the more reason for us to go. We did our job."

Joss gave Cole one final squeeze, then released him and headed for the door. The others were wrapping things up, so Cole followed him.

"I'm with you," he said as a strange sense of warmth spread up from deep inside.

"Why are we here again?"

Cole slowed his pace so that Staffelbach and Corhagen could catch up. They'd all ridden together in his car. It was still early enough in the morning to warrant a stop for coffee. Both men were warming their hands with the largest cup that the shop sold. Cole, meanwhile, had felt a strange craving for a bagel. Swallowing his latest bite, he briefly considered asking for a sip to wet his throat, but changed his mind at the thought of tasting the dark swill in the back of his throat for the remainder of the day.

The three of them were standing outside Cole's car in the parking lot of the TV station. Despite Cole's reservations, Joss had sent them back to finish their investigation. Cole was concerned the thing that attacked them yesterday would be back, but Rainette had assured everyone that this was unlikely. While they knew next to nothing about the creature, the water witch had formed several theories about it after examining the ectoplasm samples.

"It's going to be a while before that... whatever it was, shows up again," she had explained. "The ectoplasm sample was a total blank, just like before, but I think I've worked out how the creature operates. It does need to form a body for itself out of this stuff, and free-roaming ectoplasm can be highly unstable. Each body it forms won't last for very long, and it keeps making bigger bodies to inhabit so it can interact with our world."

"Meaning?" Joss had asked.

"The bigger the body it makes for itself, the more ectoplasm it has to collect," she had said. "This takes time, and the bigger the body, the more unstable it grows. This is just a hunch, but I think this thing is still new at the process. It made a bigger body to attack the warded Order building, but that one couldn't hold together long enough for it to break through. We don't know anything about its physiology, or even if it has such a thing, but this kind of process would be exhausting for some entities. I can't believe it can keep this up for much longer. Plus, as you said yesterday, it was after the canister the whole time. Since it's not with us, we aren't a priority for the moment."

Cole was still reluctant, but Joss had assured him that the entire Section was to remain in contact with one another regularly. This quelled his tension somewhat, and when Joss revealed he was sending Cole back to the TV station along with Staffelbach and Corhagen, he had gone with little protest.

It was Staffelbach who had spoken up next. "We're going to check for more breaches," he explained. "The station refuses to close for some reason, despite the danger."

"It probably has something to do with how you worded it," Corhagen said. "Most humans aren't going to accept that imaginary creatures living in a pocket of space are kidnapping people so they can torture them to death."

"Ordinarily, I would agree with you," Cole muttered, after swallowing another bite. "But we have the testimony from the missing employees."

Corhagen shrugged. "People are stupid sometimes. Plus, I heard that the station is going to shut down soon."

Cole paused in the middle of turning around. "When did you hear that?" he asked, looking back at Corhagen.

Corhagen swallowed a mouthful of hot coffee before answering. "When we were here the first time," he said. "I overheard one of the maintenance crew members saying so."

Corhagen paused to take another sip of his coffee before continuing. "The station's ratings have been in the toilet for a while," he revealed. "The only show anyone tunes in for nowadays is *Captain*

Sharky, and one show won't keep the whole company afloat, so they're in the process of selling it. My guess is the president wants to milk whatever money he can from the place before it goes under."

"Must be why no one was surprised when they thought the kidnapped personnel had up and quit without telling anyone," Staffelbach mused.

"Probably," Cole admitted before attacking his bagel again.

"So what do we do?" Staffelbach asked.

Corhagen reached into his coat pocket in reply and then held up the bottle Rainette had given them. "It's more or less the same thing Rainette's witch friends used the other day," he explained, smiling as he held on tightly to the little glass vial. "We spread this around the perimeter of the building, wait a half hour, and any breaches will become visible."

"The station personnel have already been warned not to approach them," Cole informed them, swallowing his last bite of bagel. "Since they refused to evacuate, we'll just have to work around them and hope nobody winds up falling into a lost pocket of space by accident."

"Funny how that tends to happen," Corhagen joked.

"It's less funny the longer I work with you guys," Staffelbach replied. "I read comic books, and the things we deal with are much weirder."

The three of them proceeded to walk toward the station building. "You still read comics?" Corhagen asked as they neared the building's corner.

"Yeah." There was a note of defensiveness in Staffelbach's voice. "What about it?"

"Cool," said Corhagen. "I haven't had the money to keep track of what's been going on these last couple of years, but I still pick up an issue or two of *Superman* every so often."

By the look on Staffelbach's face, one would think that Christmas had come early. Excitedly, he regaled Corhagen with a full recap of what had occurred in Superman's storyline for the past few years. Corhagen was hanging on Staffelbach's every word as they stopped in front of the station. While the two carried on, Cole took the bottle out of Corhagen's hand and began the tedious process of dabbling a drop or two every couple of feet around the breadth of the square building. Both men were still rambling excitedly to one another when Cole returned from his round trip.

"Done," he declared loudly, to cut them off. "Another thirty minutes, and we can start wrapping this case up."

"How are we going to do that?" Corhagen wondered. It sounded as though this hadn't occurred to him until just now.

"The potion makes any breaches in the building visible," Cole explained, giving Corhagen and Staffelbach each a look with his mouth curved upward slightly. "According to Rainette, it also causes them to close up faster. Once we've marked off where each gap in space is located, I'm going to try and speak with the...."

Cole paused. "Whatever they were," he decided, "one more time. We don't have a prison that could hold them, but if they're willing to stay inside their enclosed space from now on, the department won't report their activities."

"What if they refuse?" Staffelbach asked.

"Rainette already spoke with her coven sisters," Cole went on. "Assuming they refuse, the Shadewater coven is ready to come in and seal off their dimensional space from this world permanently."

"So they either choose voluntary exile, or become prisoners in their own home?" Corhagen wondered.

Cole shrugged. "I didn't say it was a perfect solution."

"It's better than going back there," Staffelbach replied, giving a shudder. "That second trip must have rattled something loose in my head, because I can remember everything now."

"Going back wasn't an option," Cole told him. "We would be fighting them on their home turf. If you still remember what it was like, then I shouldn't have to explain why that is a bad idea."

Staffelbach shook his head. "That place was just too weird!"

The rest of the half hour passed peacefully. No one from security came out to question their presence, meaning they had already been alerted to what the Section was trying to do. Cole still sometimes had trouble relating to the fact that he was a police detective now. In his time on this world, that was the last form of gainful employment he'd ever expected to try out.

Corhagen, meanwhile, had picked up his conversation with Staffelbach on the genre of comics, and both were talking animatedly now.

"Did you ever read any comics, Cole?" Staffelbach asked suddenly.

"Once," he said absentmindedly while keeping both eyes on the building in front of them. "It was some time ago, though. I was always rather partial to *Sandman*."

"Neil Gaiman?"

Cole frowned and looked at Staffelbach. "Who?"

"He's talking about something else," Corhagen quickly interjected, before giving Cole a look. "Wait, you mean to tell me you actually read the original *Sandman*?"

"In the thirties, I believe it was."

Both men's eyes widened. Cole noticed this and shook his head. "Must I remind you both that I've been alive and lived in and out of New York City for almost a century now?"

"What?" Staffelbach hesitated. "No, that wasn't it. I just never met anyone who read the original *Sandman* pulp comics from back then."

"Oh." Cole glanced toward Staffelbach. "My apologies. I didn't read the series through its entire run. To me, the comic was better before the writers tried to make him like the traditional superheroes that were getting popular back then."

"Tuulois MacColewyn," Corhagen announced, chuckling. "The original *Sandman* comic book hipster."

Cole felt a shudder go through him at Corhagen's use of his full name, and went back to ignoring them, maintaining his vigil on the TV station. It was reasonably likely that nothing serious would go wrong, but Cole had always been leery of human spells and incantations.

Katalina, for the most part, had been the exception to the rule. As their waiting period wound down, he noticed the conversation between Corhagen and Staffelbach had died down somewhat.

"If you'd like," he told Staffelbach, not looking at him now, "I will see if I can find the comics for you. They're probably somewhere in my closet."

"What?"

"The *Sandman* comics we were talking about before," Cole explained. "I'm fairly sure I brought them with me when I moved out of my loft. It may take a little while, but when I have a spare moment, I'll go looking for them."

The silence from both men that followed was overwhelming. "Cole," Corhagen began in a voice one generally heard from men standing on a fifty-story ledge. "Those comics were printed decades ago."

"Thank you," he replied curtly.

"What he means," Staffelbach tried, "is that they're incredibly rare. The original *Sandman* comics must be worth several thousand dollars by now!"

Cole frowned as he heard this. "Oh," he said. "I wish I had known that before, when I was struggling to pay my rent every month."

A moment later, the time limit was up. Cole led the two men into the building. The receptionist spotted them right away, but made no move to stop them. All three flashed their badges to be on the safe side, to which she gave a curt nod before ignoring them altogether. It wasn't the same woman as before, but this one had clearly been alerted to the situation.

The trio was barely out of the front area before they located the first breach. It stretched out against part of a hallway wall just past the entrance. Staffelbach pulled out a roll of "caution" tape and began the mundane task of roping the area off. Though the personnel had been warned, Cole wanted to leave nothing to chance. Aed Deigh was out and ready in case something jumped out of the breach at them while Staffelbach worked. Once Staffelbach was done, Cole pulled out a second vial. Uncorking it, he stepped forward to let the blue mist coming from it waver close to the breach. The fissure in time and space glowed a soft blue, ever so slightly darker than the bottle in his hands, before going back to normal. Putting the cork back in place, Cole spotted a security staff member watching, and motioned him over.

"Keep an eye on it," he ordered. "But don't get too close, and make sure no one comes near it. If anything out of the ordinary happens, send for us."

The security guard was watching the breach the whole time, wide-eyed. "What is it?" he asked in a shaky voice.

Cole sighed. "A breach in dimensional space, for lack of a better term," he said. "But if that is unacceptable, just tell yourself it's a rare form of mildew that's harmful to breathe. We really don't have time to explain the issue right now."

Staffelbach was snickering to himself as they walked off, leaving behind the dumbstruck security guard to stare into the breach as if hypnotized.

"It looks like a pixelated mosaic layered over white static," he said. "No one is going to believe that stuff is mildew."

"True," Cole replied as they came up on another breach, "but they aren't going to believe it's a fissure in time and space either, and we have bigger concerns. Corhagen, while he's securing this one, see if you can't track down another member of security. They're supposed to be cooperating with us."

"I was thinking they'd be at the entrance waiting for us," Corhagen replied as he walked off. "Guess we're about as welcome here as anywhere else."

Cole didn't answer. It took very little time for Corhagen to return, by which point Staffelbach had already finished roping the area off. This one had been a little trickier, since it wasn't located along a space of wall, but in the middle of the corridor. Staffelbach wound up taping off the area on either side, effectively blocking the hallway completely.

"Just make sure no one comes this way," Corhagen was telling the man. "You might want to get someone to watch the other side."

"Is this where those people disappeared to?" the man asked, keeping his distance without having to be told to.

"Officially, we can't say," Corhagen replied. "Unofficially, yes."

The man glanced over at Cole for a moment. "Are you boys going to fix this?"

"We are," Cole assured him, retrieving the blue bottle again. "As soon as we finish locating the breaches and secure them."

The security guard watched as Cole waved the uncorked bottle near the breach, which then shimmered and glowed like the one before it.

"What is that stuff?" the man wondered.

"A potion that will keep anything on the other side from getting through," he explained, sealing the bottle again. "It's only temporary, but we have a team on standby waiting to come in and seal the place off permanently."

The security guard didn't look especially reassured. "Is that stuff safe?"

"No idea," Cole replied. "But it can't be any more harmful than falling through one of these."

He nodded toward the breach for emphasis. "Just keep everyone back until we're done."

Though he seemed unnerved, the security guard nodded and stood off to the side. Cole gave the man a nod before walking off to search the rest of the floor. He had several bottles of the potion Rainette's coven had provided for good measure, but having to rely on human magic so much bothered him more than he cared to say. It would be a relief when this case was over. He had been tempted to just bring in the Shadewater coven and seal the place off, but Cole wanted the chance to negotiate. As they stopped in front of yet another breach, not far away, Cole thought back on his conversation with Joss while Staffelbach went to work and Corhagen brought in another security guard.

"Why?" Joss had asked simply.

"Because," Cole answered in a patient tone, "we are, as you have reminded me several times now, supposed to be the police."

"I know that," Joss had replied, frowning. "What do you mean?"

It had been hard, but Cole was determined to get his point across to his lover. "I don't want Section Thirteen to gain the same reputation as its predecessor. The Section of the past was less a division of peacekeepers and more a government-sanctioned team of cleaners. You remember not very long after we first met, I described Section Thirteen as a group of occult Gestapo."

Joss's frown had deepened then. "I guess I wasn't paying close attention," he admitted. "Weren't you joking?"

Cole had shaken his head. "My people," he explained slowly, "the fey of this city, and all the other things that come here, are exiles. They have nowhere to go, so they live amongst humans as best as they can. We have no police to turn to, no one to right our wrongs. Humans have hunted us since ancient times. The creatures you would call monsters live in constant fear. They wouldn't dare contact the police for help. Most cops would shoot them on sight and ask questions later. I don't want to be a part of that."

Joss's face had frozen in place then, as if turned to stone. "Good," he finally answered. "Talk to them, then. See if you can't get them to back off peacefully. If they don't...."

"Then we handle the problem," Cole agreed with a nod. "Rainette's coven can come in and seal them off, keeping them out of this domain. I have no objections, so long as we try a slightly more diplomatic approach first."

Joss had laughed afterward, pointing out the humor in Cole taking a more civil approach to a problem. Cole would have enjoyed objecting, but something told him the evidence to the contrary was overwhelmingly against him.

Their sweep of the ground floor passed without much incident, save for the looks some of the security guards gave them each time they were put in charge of guarding one of the breaches. A few already had someone watching over them. One or two guards had come across them while on patrol and set up a post, assuming whatever they were seeing was dangerous. Cole had to give his props to them for doing so without ending up trapped on the other side.

Several of the studios on the second floor were in session when they arrived. It took a moment to get someone to let them in, which they only accomplished after flashing their badges repeatedly. It was here that the trio received quite a surprise. One of the few studios available at the moment had more breaches in it than any other space in the building. Cole didn't need to ask what the studio was used for. All three of them remembered it from before.

"When is the next episode going to be filmed?" Cole asked a nearby stagehand.

"Later this afternoon," the young woman answered, when Cole showed her his badge. "We're getting ready right now. This is going to be a special live show they're making us shoot to raise awareness for cancer patients."

"This is going to take forever," Staffelbach groaned, looking around at the places where the air was broken apart.

"A lot of them we can't reach without help," Corhagen pointed out. "And we can forget about roping them off. I can spot several hanging in midair."

"How come no one is paying any attention?" Staffelbach asked, looking around as the stagehands walked back and forth obliviously. "I thought the breaches were visible now."

"They should be," Cole mused, glancing up at several hanging above them. "The spell is still working, but it appears the people in this area are immune somehow."

"It's like they can see them, but don't register them," Corhagen noted as a man in a corner wound a strip of cord up around his shoulder, stepping around one breach that would have been directly in his path.

"It's weird."

"You both stay here and get to work," Cole decided, reaching into his pocket for one of the potion bottles. "Staffelbach, give me some of the police tape, and take this with you. You and Corhagen work on securing this place as best you can. Be sure to leave one breach open for us, though."

"Where are you going?" Corhagen asked as Cole and Staffelbach exchanged items.

"To secure the rest of the building," Cole replied. "I have a feeling it won't take me very long. Something tells me this studio is tied into all of this."

Corhagen gave the enormous room a once-over. "You think?"

"Keep an eye on things, and warn me if anything happens," Cole said seriously. "I'll be back as soon as I'm finished, and make a phone call to Joss."

Cole pulled out his phone as soon as he was out of the studio. It rang while he ducked into a nearby storeroom where he wouldn't be overheard.

"What?" Joss's voice rang out.

"Did I catch you at a bad time?"

Joss took a deep breath before answering. "Sort of," he admitted. "I just got finished listening to someone chew my ass out. The worst part was that Willhiem was there to defend me. The little shit's gotta be up to something."

"He's with the Order," Cole reminded him. "That goes without saying."

"Tell me about it," Joss said, sighing. "Go ahead."

Very quickly, Cole explained what they'd found in the *Captain Sharky* studio. "It is no coincidence," Cole insisted. "The three of us were attacked in that place, and it has the most breaches out of any place inside the building that we've seen so far."

"Why there, though?" Joss was silent for a moment. "Could it be the room itself?"

"Possibly," said Cole. "Though I'm not convinced at this point. I want to pull all the information we can find on the *Captain Sharky* show. It's time we got to the bottom of this."

"If the breaches are sealed off, it won't be necessary," Joss reminded him. "The coven is set to move in once you give the word."

"I know," Cole agreed. "But we still don't know what we're dealing with. I have never seen creatures like this before. Their behavior is far too human, yet they resemble nothing of humanity that I've seen before."

"Meaning the coven's ritual isn't foolproof," Joss finished. "Well, I'd be lying if I said I hadn't thought of that already."

"There's something I'm missing," Cole went on. "And I think the answer is connected to that show. It could be the studio room itself, but I want to know for sure. Plus, assuming these things find a way to come back, I want to be ready for them."

"Not a bad idea," Joss said. "So long as you don't mind going through the files by yourself. The system got upgraded while you were gone, and the new operating system is a bitch to navigate."

Both hung up without another word. It struck Cole that he hadn't told Joss good-bye, or exchanged words of affection. This was, from what he'd gleaned through the years, an expected thing among couples. Briefly, he wondered if this was a sign that he should feel concern. Then again, Cole mused as he left the storeroom, now wasn't the time for worrying over such things.

Cole decided to head to the top floor and work his way back down. It had the fewest breaches, he learned shortly: a total of two. On each floor down, that number increased considerably. In fact, the closer he came to the second-floor studio where Staffelbach and Corhagen were, both in floor numbers and proximity, the more breaches he found. When the upper floors had been sealed off, Cole headed back for the studio. Corhagen and Staffelbach had already finished.

"The one behind us is still open," Corhagen explained, jerking a thumb over his shoulder. "Just like you said. Nothing out of the ordinary went down while you were gone."

"Except for that accident on the scaffolding," Staffelbach reminded him. "Though I think the guy that almost fell was just being clumsy."

"The rest of the building is secure," Cole told them. "I asked Vallimun to have someone pull any information on the history of *Captain Sharky*. I'd like both of you to help."

"So you're thinking this has something to do with the show too?" Corhagen asked.

"The show has something to do with this," Cole replied. "Whether because it is filmed in this particular room, or because it somehow connects with the disappearances. This could simply be a weak point in the web of space and time, but I refuse to leave that up to chance. The Shadewater coven will most likely have to perform the ritual, but these things are unlike anything I've encountered before. I want to know why this area is so significant."

Neither man said anything. "Do either of you have any theories?" Cole asked. "You both know more about this show than I do."

"Nothing offhand," Corhagen said.

"Nothing that would tie it to a bunch of extra-dimensional kidnappings," Staffelbach added. "I know, for a while there, the show had a rough patch of history behind the scenes."

"Like what?" Cole asked at once.

"Uh." Staffelbach thought hard. "This was before I started watching, but after the first actor who played Captain Sharky died, there were some problems with the actor they got to replace him. Something about him wanting to leave. I read about that years later, of course."

"There was a scandal where one of the child actors accused a puppeteer of molesting them," said Corhagen. "That was back in the nineties."

"Nothing was ever proven," Staffelbach pointed out. "I don't see that relating to our case, but who knows? Maybe these things were all kids that got abused on set, and are out for revenge. Could they have gotten their powers from somewhere else?"

Staffelbach was asking Cole this specifically. "It isn't out of the question," Cole replied. "Not likely, but we need to keep an open mind. Just because something seems improbable doesn't mean it isn't true."

"Our lives have revolved around that lately," Corhagen said as his eyes lit up. "Wait! What about the banned episode?"

"Banned episode?" Both Staffelbach and Cole frowned at the same time.

"It just dawned on me." Corhagen was talking excitedly now. "Years ago… I think it was in the early eighties, there was an episode that got banned. They had to take it off the air, and sign a waiver promising to never show it again."

Lights overhead came on. The doors off to the side from where the three men stood swung open, and a thread of kids marched in, all wearing eager expressions. Several adults stood by to maintain some semblance of control. "It looks like they're about to start," Corhagen noted.

"We'll continue this later," Cole said. "For now, stay on your guard. I don't feel right about this."

"We should have just gotten a court order to shut the place down," Staffelbach muttered quietly. "These kids could be in danger."

"That would have taken too long," Cole reminded him. "And in that time, these people would have been in even more danger. The breaches we found are sealed off, and they can't make more without exposing themselves. The Shadewater's potion is already closing off their means of travel. For now, we play along and keep the children safe."

The children were being led to a set of bleachers big enough to seat all of them. Some looked around at the studio setup as they were brought along in lines, fascinated by the boom mics and wiring strewn everywhere.

"Couldn't you have just asked your godson or whatever to cancel this?" Corhagen asked. It sounded as though the thought had just occurred to him.

"I did," Cole said. "He can't."

"Why not?" The disbelief in Corhagen's voice was thick enough to choke on. "He's rich."

"He's also under obligation," Cole replied. "Apparently, the studio has several different contracts specifying that it remain on air for so many hours a day. The contracts were in effect before he came into ownership of the place. If he shuts it down, the outside parties will sue, which could only delay things for us even more."

"Of course," Corhagen groaned. "Why would it be that easy?"

Staffelbach snorted. "So much for the theory that money will solve all your problems."

"I was as disappointed to learn this as you are," Cole told him as the show started.

Everyone was quiet, including the children, while the theme song played. Cole suspected they had been promised treats for good behavior, or given outright threats in return for misbehavior. Once the filming formally began, the children in their seats applauded as the actor playing Captain Sharky came out to greet them.

It was, for the most part, an underwhelming performance. Cole got this impression more from Staffelbach and Corhagen's reactions than anywhere else. The children appeared entertained. It was the adults who looked on in disinterest. Cole hadn't been raised with the show, so he had no way of making a comparison. Apparently, though, for the adults, seeing the world of Captain Sharky without the imagination of a child left much to be desired.

However, the real fun began when the interaction between the characters got started. Cole, Staffelbach, and Corhagen were keeping their eyes peeled, but every few minutes, one of them would be drawn back to the stage. Pretty soon, Cole was finding it difficult not to laugh.

"I don't care if nobody wants to be friends with me anymore!" a young boy in front of the camera declared. "I'll go to my room and play. There's all kinds of fun I can have just playing with myself."

Corhagen frowned. "Well, he isn't wrong," Staffelbach mused quietly. "A little young to be knowing about that, but not wrong."

"Don't you want to blow on my pipe, Sally?" a dark-skinned lad was asking another girl with pigtails now. "I promise, it's lots of fun!"

Staffelbach just smiled. "Good luck trying to convince her of that, kid," Corhagen grumbled. A second later, the girl took the pipe from the boy's hand and tentatively began blowing on it.

"You might want to ask him for pointers after the show," Staffelbach suggested.

"Where's Roger and William?" the pig-tailed girl was asking now.

"They're helping Captain Sharky to get up."

Corhagen's jaw nearly hit the floor. "Do the writers on this show not realize their target audience is the three-to-seven set?"

The look of horror on his face was magnified tenfold a moment later. "Don't forget, everyone," Captain Sharky announced to the crowd. "you can play with your balls all by yourself! Or, if you haven't got any balls, try asking a friend if you can play with theirs!"

Cole and Staffelbach were both grinning ear to ear now, as Corhagen's eyes bulged from their sockets. "They…," he stuttered. "They have to know how this sounds. There is just no way…."

A stagehand not far off shushed at them. Corhagen stopped talking but continued looking on in appalled shock as the dialogue grew even more suggestive. The ghost of Captain Sharky was passing out instruments to each child now, which they gripped in one hand and shook. The group of kids started dancing in a circle, holding their rattling instrument before them and shaking them up and down in a more or less straight line.

"My mind," Corhagen muttered, "it is blown. Why did my mother ever let me watch this?"

"This and *He-Man* were the two shows I watched religiously," Staffelbach said lightheartedly as the audience applauded again. "Looking back, I wonder if there wasn't a link between that and my sexual orientation."

Cole, meanwhile, was more disturbed by something else he'd gleaned from watching. "Correct me if I'm wrong," he said, while the stagehands moved in to set up for the second half. "But the moral of this seems to be that doing anything different from the rest of the crowd is inherently wrong."

"That's not exactly…," Staffelbach began, before adding, "well, yeah, I guess it is what they're saying."

"So the children of this generation are told that if they do not fit in with the rest of society in some way," Cole surmised, "the best they will ever have is a life of ridicule and depreciation."

Both Staffelbach and Corhagen gave him a look. "Daniel Whittaker's behavior is starting to make a whole lot more sense to me,"

Cole stated flatly. "I wonder if we shouldn't be more worried about those children in the bleachers instead."

"I'd hold off on that until one of them yanks us into a pocket dimension," Staffelbach replied.

"Speaking of the rug rats," Corhagen cut in. "Have either of you noticed how that one sitting on the edge near the bottom keeps watching us."

"I hadn't," Cole confessed. "Which one?"

Corhagen waited until the girl looked away. "Her, right there," he said, pointing. "The blonde one with the long hair that gets really curly near the end. She's been watching us for almost the whole show."

"Instead of watching the show," Cole summed up. "That is strange. If this were a video game cut scene, I would suspect her of knowing something."

"So remember, kids!" Captain Sharky was saying directly to the camera now. "Always…."

Whatever the children were expected to remember was left open. Before Captain Sharky could finish, the air between himself and the camera began wavering. The actor paused while several of the children standing nearby gathered in close, keeping their eyes on the distortion. Cole realized what was happening a moment too late.

"Move!" he shouted anyway as the pocket of space exploded outward in a brilliant flash of light that blinded the room, sent Captain Sharky and the children flying backward, and broke several thousand dollars' worth of equipment all at the same time. Cole was knocked back as well, sent sprawling on his ass, as the center of the explosion split downward and widened, allowing a familiar face to emerge.

"I'm through!" an overjoyed Batchwork cried out. "Kongazilla, give me a hand!"

A large green hand seized Batchwork by the throat. "Give me a hand first, you bat-brained twit!" the fire-breathing gorilla roared as his head emerged out of the fissure. "And hurry!"

Cole leaped to his feet as both figures emerged from the gap, somehow spreading it wider as they pushed themselves through, then grabbed either side of it to make the opening even wider.

"Pull!" Kongazilla demanded.

"I'm trying!"

The rest of the set and the audience were in a state of pure pandemonium. Children in the bleachers were screaming, and adults struggled to keep the crowd under control as the rest of the stagehands scrambled in all directions. The actors who had been blown back during the explosion, meanwhile, were getting to their feet slowly. The two called Batchwork and Kongazilla kept a close eye on the man dressed as Captain Sharky while another figure emerged from the rift they were fighting to keep open.

"Offworld Outlaw, grab the captain and take him through the breach." Kongazilla ordered as the gray-skinned alien dressed in gunslinger attire looked around. "We can't hold it open for much longer."

"*G'zzter bana k'otcu roa nok*," the alien replied.

"Stop."

Cole forced a note of glamour into his voice as he stepped forward, blocking the alien gunslinger's path. "I am Special Detective Tuulois MacColewyn of the NYPD," he announced.

"We remember," Kongazilla spat. "Outlaw, ignore this idiot and get the captain. Something is forcing the breach closed."

"A spell," Cole said calmly as chaos reigned around them. "To heal any broken places in time and space inside this building. I have come to talk. You have two choices: listen, or be sealed away inside that pocket of space forever."

The duo holding the portal open seemed to hesitate a moment.

"I'd pick the former were I in your shoes," he added.

The alien outlaw drew itself up at these words. Twin guns that looked like they belonged on a science-fiction show flew into its three-fingered hands of their own volition. The Offworld Outlaw, as he was described, stood with both feet spread apart, sizing Cole up. Both blades sprung from Aed Deigh's hilt in answer. A second more passed, then the Offworld Outlaw opened fire.

Cole swung his blades around in alternating arcs, keeping the people behind him in mind, as well as the ones in the bleachers, as he deflected the blasts. Three in succession were sent straight back at the Outlaw, striking him in the chest. The alien gasped in pain as black smoke curled out of the entry points.

"Just like before," Cole mused. "I wonder if this will work."

Bringing Aed Deigh around, Cole charged the red-hot blade until it burned brightly. As the Outlaw looked up, a thin blast of white-hot fire shot through the air into his stomach, burning a hole there big enough for Marcel to put his fist through. The Outlaw cried out in pain as he sank to his knees. Black smoke curled out of him in waves now, filling the air despite the alien's best attempts to hold it in.

"It looks as though you can be hurt here," Cole concluded with a nod. "I wasn't a hundred percent sure."

As the Outlaw cried out again, the front of his hat suddenly glowed a bright red. Cole watched in confusion as the symbol that appeared there spread until it blanketed the whole front of the brown hat. Recognition dawned as the sigil seemed to invigorate the Outlaw. Getting back to his feet, the Outlaw brought his hands away from the gaping wound as it closed shut, sealing the smoky essence back inside.

"Elder?" Cole whispered.

Behind the alien gunslinger, Batchwork lost his grip on the breach he was somehow holding onto and fell to the ground. Kongazilla, in turn, roared as his end of the breach flung him forward on top of the giant patchwork bat. The breach closed with a groan that sounded like metal scraping against metal.

"Sorry," Batchwork mumbled, coughing as he struggled to crawl out from underneath Kongazilla. "I lost my grip."

Cole took a step forward, gaining all three's attention. With the tip of Aed Deigh, he pointed toward the remaining fissure in space Staffelbach and Corhagen had been helping him guard. The two men had been blown back by the initial explosion, but since then had gotten to their feet and were helping to get people to safety.

"That breach is your best hope for getting home now," Cole said threateningly. "If you try to make another one, it will close before you can send for help. I could just have this place sealed off from you forever, but I'm willing to talk. Don't make me regret that decision."

None of them said a word. "Why are you all doing this?" he demanded. "What did this station do to you?"

Kongazilla snorted, blowing a puff of green flame from his nostrils in the process. "They helped make us alive," he growled, kicking Batchwork off to the side.

"Alive?"

Kongazilla considered Cole a moment more, then nodded. "It is because of this," the gorilla said, spreading his arms out to gesture at the studio, "that we're here today."

"You know better than to tell him that, Daddy," came the voice of Mary Alice.

Cole turned at the same time Kongazilla did. Mary Alice was standing near the edge of the stage. Judging by her position, she had just emerged from the last open breach a second or two before.

"The Triskaidekahedron will not be happy with this," she said in a bored voice. "I thought you told me we were supposed to do as they ordered us to."

Mary Alice then looked at Cole. "I supposed it doesn't really matter now," she mused to herself. "As Daddy said, this place helped give birth to us, so we've come to punish them."

Cole sniffed the air quickly, making sure no humans were in the vicinity. The girl called Mary Alice looked every bit as innocent as before, but Cole had seen what lurked beneath the surface. Outside their pocket space, he stood a much better chance of dealing with her, but what he wanted right now more than a fight was information.

"*Rit'zrik dotta hurxi,*" the alien gunslinger jabbered irritably.

"What did he say?" Cole asked.

Mary Alice shrugged. "No idea. He's spoken that way since the beginning. The child who made him must have thought that was how he should sound, because we haven't had any luck teaching him to speak like we do."

Kongazilla turned, picking Batchwork up off the floor as he went, and motioned for the Offworld Outlaw to follow.

"We're leaving," the gorilla told Cole. "But we'll be back."

Cole didn't try to stop them as they marched across the room to the breach. It was nearly gone now. They had to take turns going through. The larger ones took the most time, having to make themselves fit as best they could. Once all of them were gone, Cole pulled the blue bottle of potion out of his pocket and marched over to where the breach stood. Though it was nearly gone, he felt it best not to leave things to chance. Once the blue mist had done its work, he slid the cork back into place, then put the bottle away and brought out his cell phone.

Rainette answered on the second ring.

"Send them," he said. "It's time we closed this place off."

STAFFELBACH and Corhagen were waiting for Cole outside in the hallway. "Security is sealing the place off," Corhagen said as Cole approached. "It looks like we're getting their cooperation after all. Until this is settled, the building is going to be evacuated."

"The Shadewater coven is on their way right now," Cole filled in. "The ritual will take time, but once they've performed it, this area will be cut off from that pocket space."

"So, we're done?"

Cole shook his head at Staffelbach. "I wish it were that easy. So far, they've only opened breaches in this building, but that could be because this place holds a vested interest for them. Plus, there could be other breaches we don't know about, outside this area. We may have made this harder for them, but I doubt they'll stay locked out indefinitely."

"At the very least, we'll be done here," Corhagen pointed out.

Neither Cole nor Staffelbach could argue with that. Now that the havoc had died down, the crowd of spectators was being led out of the building. Cole kept his eyes sharp in case any more openings appeared, but it was quiet now. The potion he had spread around the building was apparently still in effect, healing any potential breaches before they could be fully formed.

It took longer than he would have liked, but the building's occupants eventually poured out into the parking lot. Some were confused by what had happened. Those few that had witnessed the event still looked shell-shocked. Cole was informed that an ambulance was on the way to check everyone for injuries and treat those suffering from post-traumatic shock. While they waited for the coven to arrive, Cole overheard several of the younger children whisper excitedly among themselves. Apparently, the theory amongst them was that it had all been the work of aliens, a secret network of foreign spies, and a magical school for evil wizards.

He was chuckling to himself when Staffelbach noticed. "I'm just laughing at what the kids have to say about all this," Cole explained. "They do have quite the imagination."

One child began insisting his evil wizard school theory was valid due to a book brought to him by his grandmother from Germany. "The evil wizard school was shut down several years ago," Cole called out on a whim, causing the young boy to stare openly in shock. "Sorry to disappoint you."

"I would worry about you saying things like that to a little kid," Corhagen admonished, "but something tells me I don't want to know that there really was an evil school for wizards at one point."

"In Germany," Cole elaborated, earning him a glare from Corhagen. "It was shut down after what you call the second World War."

"So, what?" Staffelbach asked, amused. "Hitler was really an evil wizard?"

"They wouldn't let him in," Cole explained. "His entrance form was rejected, if my understanding is correct."

Cole barely noticed the look on Staffelbach's face. Standing on the outskirts of the group of kids, who'd all begun whispering among themselves excitedly after Cole's loud statement, was the same girl from before, whom Corhagen had pointed out. She was watching Cole now, even more intently than before. Cole stood patiently, waiting to see what she would do. The girl seemed to reconsider but then moved forward as if to approach him. One of the adults nearby noticed, however, and yanked the girl back roughly. The girl rubbed her arm as soon as she was released, begging Cole with her eyes for help.

Cole almost walked over to her, but the Shadewater coven chose that moment to arrive. Whoever was behind the wheel blew their horn loudly. The sound make him flinch, and Cole forgot all about the strange girl as the members of Shadewater hurried across the small strip of grass that separated the parking lot from the street. Each of them was carrying supplies with them for the ritual. The studio employees watched closely, some in amusement and others with dark scowls marring their faces, as the coven set up outside the front entrance.

"We might as well send these people home," Cole mused. "They'll only get in the way otherwise."

Corhagen set off to break the news to everyone. Once he was gone, Cole motioned for Staffelbach to follow him. Marianne was giving her coven members directions as they approached her from behind.

"Good," she said, sensing Cole's presence behind her. "I'm glad you're the one that's here. We were worried about having problems getting set up."

"How long will the ritual take?" Cole asked as three coven members began drawing a complicated circle on the concrete, using blue and purple chalk.

"An hour," Marianne replied, pointing at one girl carrying an armload of handmade broomsticks. "Probably longer. I hate to tell you this, but after this is over, we're going to need some type of compensation from the NYPD. Some of the stuff we had to buy for this ritual didn't come cheap, and the spell by itself will leave all of us pretty drained."

"Understood," Cole assured her. "Joss was prepared for that when he asked you."

"We made a list," she added, pulling it out of her purse. "For tax purposes and so forth. I made a copy of it for you to show, just so he doesn't think we're trying to con him."

"Joss is far more open-minded about such things," Cole said, accepting the paper from her. "It's his superiors who are more likely to accuse you of fraud, but we'll deal with that problem when it happens."

Marianne laughed. "Not like we haven't been accused of worse," she pointed out. "Are you going to stay here?"

Cole nodded. "Until the ritual is finished, in case something goes wrong."

Something occurred to him. "Not that I have less faith in your skills necessarily, but we've been through more than a few surprises on this case."

"I'm glad," she replied seriously. "I don't like this place. It gives me a bad vibe."

The crowd, meanwhile, was starting to disperse. Staffelbach was watching everyone go as Cole wrapped up a couple of details with Marianne.

"So, they're going to wave their collective wands together and, 'poof'?"

"It's a great deal more complicated than that," he explained. "But in a sense, you more or less have the general idea down."

There was a sense of excitement about Staffelbach now as a few humans lingered behind in the parking lot, watching together in groups.

"This never gets old," Staffelbach said after a moment. "A few months ago, I was worried becoming a cop was the biggest mistake of my life. Now, I learn there are real witches and people with superpowers."

Cole looked at him for a moment. "I find your acceptance of this to be a little strange," he remarked. "You still show a sense of wonder toward the world."

"I'm a comic book geek," Staffelbach reminded him. "You have to keep a sense of wonder about you if you're going to accept all the gaping plot holes most writers in the genre leave behind."

After a moment's silence, Cole gave the mortal a nod. "Strangely enough," he said, "that makes perfect sense."

Corhagen was sending the rest of the crowd on their way. One or two people had parked in spaces near where the Shadewater coven was working. As Cole stood there alongside Staffelbach, keeping vigil over the witches, he overheard one woman mutter while climbing into her sports car.

"I can't believe what they're spending our tax money on," she spat out under her breath. "Like the recession isn't bad enough! First they want us to throw money at Tokyo, and now the city is giving handouts to a bunch of hippies."

Cole watched as the car sped out of the parking lot, wheels screeching. "And then there are those who lose their sense of wonder far too quickly," he noted.

"Very true," Staffelbach agreed as Marianne came up behind him.

"We're just about ready to begin," she informed them.

"We'll get out of the way," Cole promised as Corhagen joined them again. "If something happens, I'll be close by."

"Here's hoping nothing goes wrong," Corhagen said quietly while they walked away together.

"Here's hoping if it does," Cole countered, "the witches don't pay the price for it."

THANKFULLY, the ritual was a success. One or two coven members had abstained from participating. This turned out to be so they could function as drivers when it was all over with. Marianne and the others were exhausted by the time the building had been successfully sealed off. Cole stayed behind to ensure they were all right, and promised to have their pay for this consulting job in the mail by tomorrow. Katalina had taught him how important it was to stay in a witch's good graces.

With that done, the others headed home for the day. Cole waited for them to depart before pulling out his cell phone. Joss answered on the second ring. He sounded tired.

"Can I come over?" Cole asked plainly. "I was hoping we could talk."

"Sure," he replied. "I just got in a few minutes ago."

"I'll be over soon."

The drive was complicated by traffic, peppered with just enough snow to make things inconvenient. Cole's vehicle could have handled it, but the roads were congested with human drivers low on patience. He preferred to err on the side of caution. Nevertheless, Cole managed to arrive at Joss's apartment in reasonably good time. Joss had changed out of his work clothes and into a pair of jogging pants when he answered the door. Cole gave the man a once-over as he crossed the threshold, feeling something in his gut tighten at the sight of Joss shirtless.

"How did it go?"

In answer, Cole turned around and grabbed Joss carefully by the side of the head and pulled him in for a long kiss. "I have a few things to tell you," Cole informed him between kisses while his left hand traced idly through the thick patch of hair curling out of Joss's muscled chest. "When we're done."

This was not the first time Cole had stayed over at Joss's apartment. The place was small but kept more or less in tidy condition. The bedroom was to the right after a very short trip down the hall, but they never made it. Joss's swollen cock was digging into Cole's leg enough that Cole dropped down to his knees the moment his mortal lover loosened his grip enough to let him slip through. Cole could have easily broken it, but he sometimes enjoyed letting the man think they were an equal match in terms of strength.

Once Cole had lathered Joss's big dong with spittle, Joss bent him over the easy chair and thrust inside without preamble. The pain was sharp, intense, but Cole was a born sidhe. Pain and pleasure for his kind were interchangeable. Defiantly, he rode back onto Joss's horse-sized cock as the man pushed forward with the strength of his whole body. The thick knob at the tip brushed past Cole's pleasure point, making him gasp.

Too soon, Joss came and slumped forward on top of him. Cole wasn't finished, however, and picked the man up into his arms as though he were a rag doll. Sitting down in the chair first, Cole spread both legs and slumped down so that his cock was pointing directly at the ceiling. Satisfied, he then lowered Joss, whose back pressed tightly against Cole's chest, onto his cock, using one hand to lube his cock up as best he could. Joss, meanwhile, saw the predicament and began licking two fingers. Before Cole lowered him down all the way, he quickly rubbed up against his hole to help make the first few thrusts easier. Cole lay back and watched, finding the sight of his lover preparing himself titillating.

Making a mental note to remember this, Cole gently lowered Joss down onto his fat prick. The head rested outside Joss's entrance for a moment, the sphincter unwilling to give. Then the muscle ring guarding the entry point gave way, and half of Cole's cock slid into Joss in one stroke.

"Fuck!" Joss swore, giving his hair a toss as he threw his head back.

"Like that?" Cole gasped as more of him slid past Joss's tight ring.

"You are not small," Joss hissed in answer, tensing as his body came down to the root of the pole lodged in him. "Give me a second to adjust. I don't think we've ever done it this way before."

"No problem." Cole reached around and gave Joss's thick dick a few careful strokes. "You have a lot to be proud of here."

Joss shook his head at the remark. "You're the first to ever take it all without complaining."

Joss began to slowly raise himself up off Cole's big prick. Cole leaned back slightly, allowing Joss to arch his body back further. The thick curtain of blond hair fell into Cole's eyes, but the sidhe didn't mind. Each follicle smelled of honey and lemons, a mixture of sweet and sour that made Cole light-headed. Still stroking with one hand, Cole rubbed the other up and down along Joss's mat of chest and stomach hair, savoring the feel of it as Joss picked up speed.

"That's it," Joss gasped. "Right there!"

"Here?" Cole braced himself and rammed his hips up into Joss as hard as he could.

"Fuck!"

The sounds of their bodies connecting with each other filled the room. Cole gave no thought to the neighbors. His howls and grunts shook the walls as Joss's own whimpers quickly grew to resemble the sounds of an angry bear.

"I'm cumming," Cole warned, feeling his balls draw up.

"Go ahead," Joss called out between gasps. "I'm there."

Cole felt something splash against his leg. Lifting Joss up, he stood, cock still lodged firmly between his lover's ass cheeks, and fucked Joss standing up. Cum flew from the tip of Joss's dick, splashing against the TV screen. Cole felt himself go a moment later, filling the mortal man's ass with his noble sidhe cum.

Both fell backward into the chair. Cole savored the feel of Joss stretched out on top of him, and once more toyed with the coarse hairs covering the man's front. They were the most fascinating part to Cole, aside from the obvious, of course. Since the sidhe did not have much body hair, Cole loved playing with Joss's.

"Not that I'm complaining," Joss said between breaths after a moment, "but while I recover, what was it you wanted to talk about?"

Cole shifted positions so Joss could turn slightly and face him. "Or was that just an excuse to come over here?" Joss added jokingly. "Because I would have let you in regardless."

"That's reassuring," Cole replied, taking a deep breath. "I was wondering if you were still planning to move in. The last time we mentioned it was before I accidentally disappeared for two days. It occurred to me that this might have changed things."

Joss frowned. "No," he said, giving Cole a look. "Nothing has changed. We've just been too busy these past few days trying to track down things from a piece of pocket space and getting attacked by invisible monsters while a roof threatens to collapse on our heads."

Cole considered his boyfriend's words. "When you put it that way, it sounds like one of our more typical days," he said, shifting his weight in the chair again.

"True." Joss wasn't going to argue over that. "Why were you worried? It really isn't like you."

Cole looked out the window at the flashing lights from a neon sign across the street. Snow was coming down again, more forcefully this time. "It isn't important," he decided. "Just forget I mentioned it. Besides, there are other things we should discuss while I'm here."

In response, Joss climbed out of Cole's lap and led him by the hand over to the couch. Both of them were a mess, but Joss didn't look particularly concerned about this as he stretched comfortably over the soft vinyl for a moment before looking Cole in the eye.

"Now," he said, leaving no room for debate in his tone. "What's this about?"

Cole didn't answer immediately. "I don't want to bring up anything that might cause problems between us," he answered tentatively.

"Don't worry about that," Joss insisted. "There's obviously something on your mind. Tell me. Otherwise, I'll just wonder about it all night and won't get any sleep."

This was not what Cole had envisioned doing all evening. Joss refused to be swayed on the matter, though.

"What am I?" he at last blurted out.

Joss frowned, his eyebrows forming a bridge across the lower part of his forehead. When they'd first met, Joss had been going bald. A night of magically enhanced sex during a dreamscape had restored his hair. These days, he referred to the sun-touched locks as though they were a nuisance, but Cole knew his lover treated the gift for what it was.

"You called me your boyfriend," Cole went on reluctantly. "When James was making insinuations before I was suspended, you told him that I was your boyfriend."

Joss nodded. "I remember."

"I don't understand what that means," Cole stated, looking away from Joss's face at the chair where they'd just fucked like madmen. "I never have. In Faerie, there is no such word."

Cole caught the confused look on Joss's face. "We have words for those who make love," he explained, meeting the man's gaze again. "For married couples, for people who are betrothed, but not for 'boyfriend' or 'girlfriend'."

"You've lived in and out of New York for nearly a hundred years," Joss pointed out.

"I'm aware of the definition," Cole explained. "I know what humans mean when they say 'boyfriend', or say that a woman is 'their girl', but I was not raised with such things. They don't mean anything to me personally. I knew what you meant then, but...."

Cole paused, determined that his words not be misunderstood. "Humans have strange ideas about mating rituals," he said finally, trying to sum up his feelings. "One day, I thought I had it figured out, but then the rules changed again. It seems that for each new generation, you have new ideas about what is acceptable in a relationship, and what is considered taboo."

Joss was hanging onto his every word.

"I don't know what I mean to you," Cole finished as his heart pounded against his ribcage. "I don't know what *you* mean when you say that I am your boyfriend. We never talked about our relationship, or what we mean to each other, and then the IA kept us from speaking for almost a month. To be honest, I was afraid of what I might find when I came here."

Joss's mouth turned up slightly. "You thought I might kick you out?"

"I…. It seemed like a possibility." Cole felt silly now for some reason. "The last man I was with before you was Corhagen, and you are aware of how well that ended. Am I just an experiment to you?"

When Joss didn't answer immediately, Cole elaborated. "Are we just a way for you to get some unresolved feelings out of your system? You don't talk about the people you've been with. The only other man you've shared yourself with was someone named Allen. I don't…."

Cole hesitated, then said, "I don't know what we are to one another, and it frightens me."

Joss said nothing for a moment. When he moved, Cole remained perfectly still, unsure of what Joss had in mind. Joss, however, took him carefully by the shoulders and pulled him across the couch until Cole's head was resting in his lap. Cole could feel Joss's semierect cock pressing against the back of his head, but for the moment, it wasn't significant. Cole was more entranced by the feel of having Joss hold him in such a way. Cole wasn't sure anyone had ever bothered touching him like this.

"I'm not confused about how I feel," Joss said softly. "Allen was the only man I was with besides you. We were young, about fourteen or fifteen, and horny as hell, like all boys are. I just thought at the time that we were helping each other out. It seemed like the smarter choice, given that neither of us was looking to get some girl pregnant. Over time, I forgot about it, and moved on to women. In my marriage, I was most interested in other women than men, though there were a few guys in the precinct locker room that caught my attention, looking back on it."

Joss's cock jumped slightly in response. "But I never thought about acting on it. It just wasn't on my mind. When I met you, when we were together in that place, it felt natural. And afterward, you were always in my head."

"That can happen with some humans," Cole said, looking up from his lover's lap. "They become addicted to sex with the sidhe. You never exhibited the symptoms, though, so I just assumed you were fine."

Joss thought for a moment. "I don't think it was an addiction," he said. "It felt more like I needed you in a different way. I couldn't put my finger on it, but the more it happened, the more I wondered why I didn't just go for it. And then, after the incident in Bowling Green park, I kept thinking about how we might never run into each other. Then I started remembering my old buddy Allen."

Joss swallowed. "He was the one who helped me sort things out."

Cole lifted up slightly. "How so?"

Joss ran a hand through Cole's hair, lowering him back down to his lap in the process. "I hadn't spoken to Allen in a while," Joss continued. "We lost touch with each other following our junior high graduation, but a murder investigation several years ago put me on stakeout in the neighborhood where he'd moved to, and we picked things back up afterward. He was married by that time, and I was going through my first divorce. When I called him, he told me that he'd just finished signing the papers for his own. He and his wife decided to split after she caught him in bed with another woman."

Cole frowned. "She was unaware?"

"Until she walked in on him in bed with his mistress," Joss said with a smirk. "That was a pretty big clue."

Cole nodded and stretched out more comfortably across the couch. "In Faerie," he explained, "we do not have infidelity, as you would call it. Extramarital lovers are common, and even welcomed. Sidhe couples do not find it strange to share with outside sidhe, or bring a third partner to bed with them. It's believed by many that this helps make a married couple more fertile."

Joss found this interesting. "You mentioned this before," he recalled. "In Allen's case, though, she was pissed. He's being denied custody rights for now."

Cole shrugged. "I will never understand human relationships. They are far too complex and contrary for my tastes. It is a wonder I have found someone in this land to share my life with."

Joss squeezed his hand. "Anyway," he went on. "I told Allen about what happened after a few beers. He seemed a little taken aback, but wasn't upset. Before he left, Allen told me I shouldn't let things like gender get in the way of being happy, if that was what I wanted."

"You took advice on love from someone who'd just committed a major human social taboo?" Cole lifted up again. "Somehow, this isn't reassuring for me."

Joss laughed. "Well, Allen could always be a bit dumb when it came to keeping his dick in his pants, but he means well, and he wasn't as bad of a husband as his now ex-wife makes him out to be. Plus, even though he was bad with his own marriage, he wasn't wrong. And I guess even a stopped clock can be right twice a day."

Cole mulled that over while Joss continued to play idly with his mane. "I suppose what I find the most odd is that your friend needed to keep it a secret. Surely some form of compromise could have been attained?"

Joss gave a half shrug in response. "I guess that didn't occur to either of them."

Neither one spoke for the next few minutes. The silence that passed didn't strike Cole as awkward or uncomfortable, but pleasant. Joss ceased playing with his hair, and instead scratched gently over a spot on Cole's scalp. Cole moaned, turning his head so that Joss had better access. Joss's cock had gone back to almost full mast now.

Tired of feeling it poke him in the face, Cole raised up and sat next to Joss. The two wound their arms around one another and squeezed tightly, feeling the strength in one another's body.

"I want to be with you," Joss said at last, giving Cole one final squeeze. "Does that answer your question?"

Cole nodded. "For the moment," he said. "Does this mean you will never want to be with a woman again?"

Joss tensed. "I really don't know," he said stiffly. "For right now, keeping this between us is fine. In the future, I can't say."

"That's fine," Cole replied. "I wasn't bothered by the idea. I just wanted to confirm that being with me wasn't keeping you from something you needed."

"You wouldn't mind?"

"It would depend on the situation," Cole answered at once. "More than that, it would depend on the other party involved. As for whether or not I mind the idea of it happening, not at all. If you are satisfied for the moment with it being only the two of us, though, then so am I. I see no reason to change things right away."

"Me either."

"Good," said Cole, before planting a kiss on Joss's mouth. "Now, as for the other thing I wanted to ask you, I am concerned about the Section."

"How so?" Joss managed to get out before kissing Cole again.

"We are too divided as a team right now." Cole deepened his kiss with Joss before continuing. "We do not fight as a unit, nor do we understand how each other thinks. This could be a problem later on."

"True." Joss took a moment to nuzzle Cole's neck before saying anything else on the subject. "I was thinking about the fight with the merry-go-round earlier today."

"That brings something else to mind." Cole gasped as Joss gave his nipple a tweak. "But if we keep this up, I won't remember it for very long."

Reluctantly, Joss pulled away. "I'm listening," he said.

"Your arm," Cole said, touching Joss's right one. "When did you first realize it could do that?"

"In an alley one night, following a disagreement with some smaller trolls," he said. "It just sort of happened on its own, but afterward, I could control it. I think it still needs work. To be truthful, it kind of scares me."

In response, the layer of flesh concealing Joss's fingers pulled away, revealing the pointed obsidian fingers underneath. The tips almost appeared to glow for a moment in the lamplight of the room.

"Faerie magic can be unpredictable," Cole admitted, watching as the flesh crawled back over the fingers again. "I want to train you on how to use your arm effectively. It would be useful to have someone else in the Section with more magically inclined combat prowess."

"I was going to ask," Joss said. "Thanks for the offer."

The two resumed kissing one another before moving on to outright making out. When Joss's stomach growled unexpectedly, the two broke away and laughed.

"I forgot to eat," he said sheepishly.

"We could make something," Cole suggested. "Or order out? Would you like for me to spend the night here?"

Joss went quiet for a moment. "What would you say to me packing some of my things?" he asked, not meeting Cole's eyes. "I don't have to move everything over in one trip, but having some of my stuff over would keep me content for a few days, until we have time to bring the rest."

Joss met Cole's gaze. "It's not as though I really need to bring the furniture with me," he added. "Or the dishes, even."

Cole smiled. "Order what you want, and we can start packing things up while it takes the delivery boy an hour to get here."

Joss reached for the phone book next to the couch and looked up the number for a decent Thai place they had eaten at before.

"Are you sure?" he asked, after hanging up the phone.

In answer, Cole leaned down and ran his tongue into the piss slit of Joss's horse cock. "Let me convince you," he said, before tasting the salty mix between the folds of skin again. "We can always pack after we eat."

Joss groaned as Cole began to take the length of him down his throat. "I hope the delivery boy is late," he muttered, gripping the back of Cole's head. "Otherwise, he may be in for a surprise!"

JOSS managed to get back into his pants before the delivery boy arrived, despite Cole's efforts. Dinner was a somewhat hurried affair, though Cole did manage to slow things down by insisting on licking the spicy dipping sauce off Joss's balls. Joss, meanwhile, insisted that spilling it had been an accident. When the food was gone and Joss had managed to push Cole off him, they got to work packing up anything Joss might need in the immediate future. It was a rush job, made somewhat difficult by the fact that Joss had no boxes to load his stuff up in. That turned out to be less of an issue than he expected, though, when Cole pointed out that his car could expand the trunk to make more room.

Cole had expected his man to need a moment alone with his living space, but Joss seemed ready to go.

"I'm coming back later," he pointed out when Cole asked about this. "There's more stuff we need to get, and I'll have to tell my landlord that I'm terminating the lease. While I'm thinking about it, is the sithen going to have a problem with me parking my car in the garage?"

Cole stopped short of climbing into his car. That hadn't occurred to him.

"I have no idea," he confessed. "But it shouldn't. If anything, one night won't cause any major disasters. We'll just have to wait and see."

"I can't leave my car parked outside Bowling Green park," Joss said as Cole started his vehicle.

"I know," he replied. "If nothing else, Mal will think of something."

Mal was waiting for them beside the door leading into the sithen when they pulled into the garage. Cole had phoned ahead to let him know about Joss's decision. The moment they killed their respective engines, a troop of Mal copies spilled into the garage space, dressed as moving men.

"They'll handle everything," Mal said as his copies gathered up everything from both cars. "Why don't you two boys come inside and get warm? It's going to be an unusually chilly night."

The moving Mals formed a line and marched out of the garage and into the sithen as Joss watched in amazement.

"I took the liberty of preparing your room," Mal informed him, materializing a few feet away. "If there's something about it you find unsatisfactory, just let me know."

"So long as it's not pink, I'll be fine," Joss told him.

Joss's bedroom was located down a hallway and to the right from Cole's. Cole suspected this could change at a moment's notice, given that the sithen liked to shift things around. Part of this, he knew, was due to Mal's occasional bouts of boredom. Being bonded to the sithen meant he could never leave, so Mal had to find ways to satisfy his curiosity about the outside world. The stories about the hallowed hills in Ireland, however, implied that it was simply the sithen's nature to do so. Whatever the case, though, Joss found his new living quarters appealing.

Mal had fixed a bathroom and shower of Joss's own to use, a four-poster bed with an overhead canopy, several dressers, a full-length mirror hanging from the far wall, and a walk-in closet. Joss gave the space an appreciative nod, earning him a polite bow from Mal before the ex-sorcerer vanished in a puff of smoke.

Just as Cole was reaching for his lover, Mal came back again. "I forgot to tell you," Mal said, ignoring the fact that the two were making out. "Just leave everything where it is for right now. I can put it away after you've finished."

Joss glared at the spot where Mal had been standing. "Is he always going to do that?" he wondered. "Pop in and out without warning?"

"Technically, he's a part of the sithen itself," Cole reminded him. "No matter where we are, he can see and hear what we're doing. Coming and going like that is just habit, I think."

"So he knows what we're about to do?"

Cole shrugged. "He's always known. I had assumed you knew this. Is that going to be a problem?"

Joss looked uncomfortable. "Could he at least give us some privacy?"

Mal appeared back in the room once more. "Certainly!"

Cole pulled Joss back toward the bed as the inspector glared. Standing in front of the bed, Cole wrapped his arms around Joss's front, pulling the mortal into him.

"You are incredible," Cole whispered, giving Joss's ear a nip. "I always want things to be like this with us. More than that, though, I want to take you right now in front of this."

"The mirror?"

Cole nodded. "I want to watch you, to watch us. I want to see all of you."

Joss smiled as Cole began stripping them out of their clothes. "Don't you ever get enough?" he asked, helping Cole with his shirt.

"Of you?" Cole smiled before reaching for the buckle on his belt. "Never."

Joss's smile grew wider as Cole kissed a trail up the length of his neck. "Boyfriend."

THE next morning, Joss's car was missing from the garage.

"What happened to it?" Joss demanded.

Cole remained pressed against the wall, out of his lover's reach. Joss's breathing had grown more labored with each passing second after they entered the garage, whose door had switched to just down from Joss's bedroom.

"Mal," Cole called out softly.

There were no ripples through the air, no puff of smoke, nor any sign of disturbance. "Maybe he didn't hear you?" Joss suggested. "Mal!"

"It doesn't matter how loud you scream," Cole said, giving his head a shake. "We are inside the sithen. Mal can hear us no matter where we are."

"Then he's ignoring us?"

Cole pushed himself away from the wall. "It would seem so," he answered. "For the moment, at least. We, however, are going to be late if we don't get a move on. I will deal with Mal when we get home. If the car isn't back in this garage by then, I will have to get irritable."

That last part was more for Mal's benefit than Joss's. After some coaxing, Joss climbed into the passenger side and buckled in as the garage door opened onto a clear, if bitterly cold, 7th Avenue.

Joss wasn't in a good mood during the drive. Traffic was its usual nightmare of congestion, but the vehicle of the wild hunt appeared to sense this and slipped through several vacant holes before they closed up. Cole gave the dashboard a tap in appreciation as they pulled into the precinct parking garage.

Rainette was waiting for them in Joss's office. "There you are," she said as they came through the door. "I just tried calling your home phone number."

"He was at my place," Cole replied. "We moved in together last night."

Rainette stared in shock. "Oh," was all she could come up with.

"Be careful who you tell," Joss said, getting behind his desk. "You know how things are around here. Plus, we're still being monitored."

"Won't tell a soul," Rainette promised. "It wouldn't do me much good to try. You both have something bigger on me than what you're getting up to after dark."

Joss didn't answer. "She means Marcel," Cole explained. "They're dating now."

Rainette looked around to where Cole was sitting casually. "How long have you known?" she asked.

"Since I came back," he said. "Neither of you did a good job of hiding it."

"I had guessed too," Joss admitted. "It wasn't my business, so I didn't bring it up."

A knock at the door interrupted their meeting. Staffelbach stuck his head through the crack and nodded when Joss motioned for him to come in.

"You didn't have to knock," Rainette told him, before glancing back toward Vallimun. "Right? This is your office, but we're on the same team, right?"

"We are," Joss affirmed. "Unless it's private, this is the Section's official HQ."

"What did I miss?" Staffelbach asked, looking around at them.

"Not much," Cole said. "We were just getting our blackmail material straightened out. Vallimun and I live together now, while Rainette and Marcel have been dating on the side, just to fill you in. Is there anything you'd like to contribute so more of the Section stays deadlocked against each other?"

"Cole!" Rainette interjected sharply.

Staffelbach smiled and gave a casual shrug. "I'm a great big dork," he said. "That's about it, but the NYPD has fired grunt officers for less, so I'm told."

"Moving on," Joss said, chuckling. "Was there some reason you wanted to see me, Rainette?"

"Actually, I wanted Staffelbach here too." Rainette pulled something from her purse and held it up so Joss could see. "It's another sample I took. This one definitely matches the first one from the storage facility, though there wasn't much to work with. I did figure something out, though."

"Staffelbach," Joss commanded, pointing for the officer to shut the door, to which he complied at once. "Tell me."

"It wants to be alive," she went on. "I know that sounds really weird, but I started wondering why the ectoplasm from the break-in went haywire. The thing we locked away in that frozen red crystal Cole made resonates with the sample."

Rainette was talking excitedly now. "When I held the second sample up to the crystal, it started to react. So I did some tests while the reaction took place. The ectoplasm sample was trying to attain sentience!"

"So the creature that attacked us at the Order building wants… what?" Cole wondered.

"I think we're dealing with a Beyonder," Rainette stated.

Staffelbach and Joss looked back and forth between her and Cole. "Sorry," Cole said. "I am not familiar with the term."

"Beyonders are what my coven call things that exist outside our range of understanding," Rainette explained. "There are things in the vastness of time and space that have existed since before time. Lovecraft actually wrote about some of them in his novels."

"What's it doing in New York?" Joss wondered.

"Someone would have to have summoned it," she said with certainty. "The reason for the ectoplasm is that it needs to form a body out of the stuff so it can affect our world. My guess, and that's all this is right now, is that whatever attacked us wants to become a part of this existential plane. It wants to interact with our world on a more effective and permanent basis."

"Would this be a bad thing?" Staffelbach jumped in.

"Yes," both Cole and Rainette answered at once.

Cole shrugged again. "I was simply not familiar with the term," he clarified. "But Faerie speaks of these things you call 'Beyonders'. They are prevented from entering other frames of space and time for a reason. It is one of the main reasons why the Hedge was formed around Faerie in the beginning. To allow something like that into this world would be disastrous."

"He's right," Rainette agreed. "The problem is, I don't know if we can fight something like that."

"We can't," Cole told her. "Let the Order handle it."

No one seemed to like the idea. "I am almost against the idea," Cole said. "But the Order took over the community of fey and other creatures here in New York ages ago. They also have knowledge of such things, I'm sure. This is more their jurisdiction than ours."

Joss was wearing a look of discontent. "They have the canister," Cole reminded him. "We can tell them what we think is after it. Willhiem is their spy, so he will pass the information on. If we try and take the thing head-on, it will erase us from existence."

"You're up to something," Rainette said flatly, giving Cole a look.

Cole smiled. "I had time to think while I was on suspension. If the Order wishes for us to be their lackeys, they must pay the price for it."

"Meaning?" Joss asked.

"Section Thirteen will not be their kamikaze pilots," said Cole, standing. "If the Hermetic Order of the Golden Dawn wishes to dominate New York City, they must pay the price of being the gods of this town. We tell them what they're up against, point out how ill-equipped we are at handling the situation, then move on to our next assignment. Either they somehow send the Beyonder, as Rainette calls it, back to where it came from, or are wiped out."

Everyone was looking at Cole now with mixed expressions.

"Cold," said Staffelbach.

"Practical," admitted Rainette.

"Wrong," stated Joss. "But as you said, none of us knows how to handle this, so I guess that makes it the Order's problem."

Joss reached for his desk phone and dialed a number. "I need to speak with Agent Willhiem," he said. "It's important."

Cole smiled at the thought of Willhiem's face when he heard what Joss had to say. While Joss spoke on the phone, something dawned on him about the day before.

"You recognized the alien that came out of the breach during the show," he said to Staffelbach in a lower voice. "I meant to ask—how?"

"That was the Offworld Outlaw," Staffelbach said, before lowering his voice as well. "He was a comic book character back in the late seventies. I used to read some of the reprints before they got discontinued."

Cole frowned. "Wait," Rainette said. "Are you telling me that a character from a comic book came out of one of those breaches yesterday?"

Cole walked over to Joss's desk just as the inspector hung up the phone. "I need to use the computer," he said. "Something Staffelbach said has given me an idea."

"About what?" Joss asked as Cole slid down into his seat.

"The *Captain Sharky* show," he said, bringing up Google Images. "One of the creatures that came out of the rift yesterday looked like a comic book character."

Cole's fingers flew across the keyboard. "See for yourself," he said while row after row of stills appeared on screen. "It's the same guy that interrupted the broadcast, right, Staffelbach?"

"That's him," Staffelbach confirmed, nodding.

"This makes no sense," Rainette insisted.

"Maybe it does," Cole countered, punching the keys again. "One of those things went by the name 'Kongazilla'. Let's see if that brings something anything."

Staffelbach's eyes widened. "It's the gorilla," he said, pointing to one of the JPEGs on the bottom row. "See that little plush toy?"

Cole clicked on the icon. "It was a toy made by a subsidiary company back during the Godzilla movies craze," Cole read. "But this says the company went under years ago."

Another search pulled up yet another lead. "Batty Batchwork," said Rainette. "I think I remember him! He was part of a kid's educational show. I think they only made one season of it."

"A comic book character," Joss rattled off, deep in thought. "A plush toy, and a puppet from a kid's show. What do they have in common?"

"Nothing," Cole answered. "By themselves, at least. They were all made years ago, and then forgotten about. And they all tie into the *Captain Sharky* television series some way."

"But none of these had anything to do with *Captain Sharky*," Staffelbach insisted. "It said at the bottom of that other page that the Kongazilla toy was discontinued before Captain Sharky first aired."

"And yet," Cole pointed out, "there were more breaches in the *Captain Sharky* recording studio than any other place in the building."

"But the building was sealed off," Rainette insisted. "Marianne assured me the spell worked. They won't be getting through that way."

"But there are other ways," Cole countered. "Time and space are not two-way streets in the grand scheme of things. Those things seemed determined. If it weren't for the potion you gave me to spread around the building, they might have succeeded. The gorilla and the bat couldn't hold the breach open long enough. Also, I think it might be wise to arrange police protection for the actor that plays Captain Sharky, just in case."

"I'm having a hard enough time dancing around my superiors' sensibilities as it is," Joss moaned. "None of them want to hear a word about monsters jumping through holes in space. Now I'm supposed to get clearance to protect the star of a kid's show from them?"

"You took an oath," Cole said teasingly.

"Get out of my chair," the man growled, giving it a swift kick for good measure.

"There's something we're missing," Cole said as he stood. "This all ties in with the *Captain Sharky* show. Is the police database system back up to speed yet? I want to have a look at those files."

"What files?" Staffelbach asked.

"Information on the *Captain Sharky* show," Cole said. "Since those 'monsters', as Joss put it, are so interested in it, I'm convinced it's at the center of this mess. Everything they've done has been to hurt the station, or that show in particular, some way."

"All of that stuff you looked up was old," Rainette reminded him. "Maybe it has something to do with that time period?"

"That would have been around the time the show first started," Staffelbach said, thinking hard. "Which would have been before I started watching it. Corhagen might know something, though."

Both Cole and Rainette frowned at the same time. "Where is he, anyway?"

All but Joss turned to stare at the door. "So I wasn't the only one expecting him to walk in just now?" Staffelbach asked.

"I don't know where he is at the moment," Joss said. "But I'm about to find out. In the meantime, though, use my computer to pull up anything the police have concerning the *Captain Sharky* show."

Cole reclaimed Joss's chair, brushing his hand against Joss's discreetly as the inspector walked around his desk. The database was already open. As Joss had said, the new upgrade was not very cooperative, but with a few well-placed Faerie swear words, Cole managed to coerce the computer into working properly.

"Don't make me reformat you with a hammer," he warned under his breath, punching each key much harder than necessary.

"Anything yet?" Staffelbach asked, leaning over Cole's shoulder.

"There's the big scandal you and Corhagen were talking about," Cole said, nodding at the screen. "About the puppeteer on the show being accused of child molestation. Some stuff in here about traffic violations and public drunkenness."

"What's that down there?" Staffelbach pointed at a highlighted article at the very bottom of the screen. "Something about a lawsuit?"

Cole brought the file up. "'Psychiatrist Wins Lawsuit Over Banned Episode!'" Cole read aloud.

"A banned episode?" Rainette asked, coming around to see for herself. "Banned because of what?"

"'The case of Davenport vs. NYTV13 was settled today thanks to the ruling of Judge Hawthorne,'" Cole said. "Apparently, there was some kind of lawsuit back during *Captain Sharky's* third season."

"That sounds familiar," Staffelbach said, leaning forward now. "Keep going."

"There's not much to say," Cole replied, scrolling down the page. "A psychiatrist named Davenport sued the TV station because of the content of one of the episodes, claiming it was harmful to children. It doesn't say what the episode was about, however."

"Look at the date, though," said Rainette. "Isn't that around the same time as that comic book, and a little after the Kong-thingie plush toy?"

"She's right," Cole said. "Let's see if the database has anything on this Davenport."

A few clicks later, Cole hit pay dirt. "Here he is," the sidhe said as the page came up. "Dr. Patrick Davenport, a psychiatrist and professor of child behavioral study at NYU. He received tenure in 1982, and retired from teaching a couple of years back."

"Let me see something!" Rainette seized the keyboard and mouse, making Cole back up in the process. As he did, Cole felt his head unintentionally brush against Staffelbach's chest.

"Got it!" she declared triumphantly. "It says that the psychiatrist brought the NYTV13 studio to court over an episode about imaginary friends."

"What?" Staffelbach almost climbed over Cole in an effort to see the article for himself. "You're kidding me?"

"Dead serious," she insisted. "It says that two weeks before the case was brought to court, *Captain Sharky* aired an episode about how it was okay for children to have imaginary friends. Apparently, this Davenport guy pitched a hissy fit in public and demanded the episode be banned from the airwaves."

"Did he say how?" Cole asked from underneath Staffelbach.

"Oh," Staffelbach said, climbing off him. "My bad."

"Quite all right," Cole said, shaking off the smell of Staffelbach's skin. "Does the article say why he thought the episode was harmful?"

"Just some pop psychobabble bullcrap about how the episode encouraged impressionable children to be introverted loners as opposed to outgoing, productive members of society. The case caught a lot of media attention locally."

"Hold on a second," Staffelbach interjected. "This guy managed to bring his case to court in less than two weeks?"

Cole checked the article date. "Almost two weeks from the date the episode aired," he replied. "That does seem a little suspicious."

"Let me check something." Rainette pulled out her smart phone. "I've got a program in here that gives me alerts for significant events in the Pagan community," she explained. "It's a long shot, but maybe these dates mean something. There could be relevance to the amount of time between the episode airing and the date it was taken to court. Either that, or...."

"What?" Cole asked, when she didn't finish.

"I don't believe it," Rainette whispered. "The equinox."

"What about it?"

"What's an equinox?" asked Staffelbach.

"A balance of sorts," Cole replied, before Rainette could answer. "The year is divided into four major events. Solstices are when day or night are at their peak, depending on the time of the year. By contrast, an equinox is when the time between day and night are shared."

"It's more complicated than that," Rainette insisted, shooting Cole a glare. "Equinoxes are holy days for Pagans."

"And Faerie," Cole reminded her. "Witches actually took the idea from us."

"Which is pure bullshit," Rainette countered. "Countless human civilizations marked the solstices and equinoxes as significant dates long before the Tuatha De Danann settled in Ireland. To bring this conversation back to the matter at hand, the episode that was banned? It aired on the day of the vernal equinox that year."

It felt as though a heavy weight hit Cole in the chest. "The banned episode," he said, turning back to the screen. "The article said that the episode told children it was okay to have imaginary friends."

Staffelbach gasped. "I remember now!" he exclaimed. "I read about that episode when I was in junior high! The site I worked on back in high school had a whole forum thread about that."

"And you just now thought about it?" Rainette marveled.

"Never mind that," Cole insisted. "What was so bad about it?"

"Eh, not much," Staffelbach replied, looking down at Cole. "At one point near the end of the episode, there was about a minute or two where Captain Sharky told all the kids watching to make up their own imaginary friend."

"And then the episode got banned?" Rainette frowned. "I don't get it."

"I do," said Cole.

"What?"

"You do?" Rainette asked, sounding unconvinced. "How?"

"It was the spring equinox," he said, looking back and forth between them. "The time of the year when spring, the season of creativity and new life, is at the peak of its power. On that day, every child tuning in did the exact same thing at the exact same instant."

Rainette's frown slowly turned into a look of pure horror. "Oh, shit."

Cole smiled grimly. "The power of spring," he concluded. "And the imagination of children all across Manhattan."

Staffelbach was completely lost. "So, those things we've been fighting," he said, looking around. "They really are some kid's imaginary friends?"

"Tulpas," Rainette correctly. "Most likely, anyway. Another word for them would be thoughtforms, creatures made out of pure human thought and brought to life by willpower."

Something occurred to Rainette then. "But to create a tulpa, don't you need some type of religious or mental symbol of concentration to give the tulpa power to manifest?"

"They were children," Cole reminded her. "They had the TV set."

Rainette fell silent for a moment. "Okay," she admitted finally. "In America, that would probably do it."

"You said that the show was a hit in this region from the moment it aired?" Cole asked Staffelbach specifically. "Picture hundreds of thousands of human children, the imaginations of so many kids across an island, coming together on the day where spring's power is at its fullest. All that energy, all that youthful creativity and wonder, connecting through the direction of an altar they sit before each day."

"The television set." Rainette nodded. "Like I said, only in America."

"I've watched young children and how they sit in front of the TV," Cole went on, trying to explain his reasoning to Staffelbach now. "It is like unto an altar of worship for them. They sit before it to draw strength for the coming day. So one day, this altar tells them to create an imaginary friend, and they do it."

"All of them did it," Rainette added, looking a little ill now. "All across Manhattan, and with that much power, it's a wonder only a few disgruntled tulpas came out of the woodwork."

"Okay," said Staffelbach, his mind racing now to keep up with them. "So how come some of the tulpas look like comic book characters or plushies?"

Rainette gave a one-shoulder shrug. "The images already had a basis in reality," Cole pointed out. "They were already a part of this world, so it was easier for those particular tulpas to take shape here."

"Look down there," Rainette said, pointing back to the computer now. "It says in that article that after Davenport won the court case, NYTV13 had to broadcast a retraction, telling kids that they should give up their imaginary friends and go play with real children their own age."

"And thus," Cole finished, "the thoughtforms were abandoned. The *Captain Sharky* show inadvertently created dozens, maybe more, of them, then told the children that they shouldn't play with their self-made friends anymore."

"Wow." Staffelbach's eyes were almost the size of saucers now. "That's pretty awful."

"And now they want revenge," Rainette added. "And my coven just stuffed them all back into their little cubbyhole. I should call them so they'll know what to look out for. Joshua, one of my coven brothers, has studied Tibetan lore, and there's supposed to be all sorts of information about tulpas in his books. He can help them batten down the hatches."

"Wait," Staffelbach said, halting her. "Corhagen and I were able to hurt them when we were inside that weird pocket space of theirs. How did that happen?"

"You were?" Rainette frowned, but continued pushing buttons on her phone. "That I can't explain."

"Offhand, I would say it's because, in different ways, you and Corhagen are both slightly more childlike," Cole explained. "I have never been a child in this world. I was raised as a sidhe, and childhood in Faerie is not like it is here."

"I have a Peter Pan complex?" Staffelbach cocked an eyebrow as he said this. "Is that what you're saying?"

"You have a child's sense of wonder," Cole said, getting to his feet. "It's nothing to be ashamed of. You see the world differently. Those tulpas were created through the power of children. Because you never let go of your sense of wonder, they became vulnerable to you in their home space."

Staffelbach considered Cole's words for a moment, then nodded. "That made no sense to me whatsoever, but I'll take it as a compliment."

"Good for you," Rainette said dryly as she hung up her phone. "Now let's get the hell out of here and go find Marcel and the others. I just got off the phone with Joshua. According to him, the ritual spell won't hold back a tulpa for very long. Thoughtforms are unlike regular spirits, so a binding spell won't seal them permanently."

"Of course," Staffelbach muttered as they all made tracks for the door. "Why would it ever be that easy?"

All three collided with Corhagen, who opened the door to Joss's office in time to get knocked backward into the hallway outside.

"Where's the fire?" he muttered, shaking his head.

"Vallimun went looking for you," Rainette said, closing the office door behind them. "Did you find him? We've figured out what those things at the TV station were."

"I know," Corhagen replied. "About Vallimun, I mean. Joss sent me to bring you guys down to the parking garage."

"Why?" Cole didn't like the look on Corhagen's face for some reason. "What's happened now?"

"Willhiem called a meeting," the detective replied, and there was a strange glint to his eye he wasn't able to cover up completely as he spoke.

"Willhiem doesn't order us around," Cole reminded him, getting angry. "Vallimun is in change of the Section."

"Not anymore," Corhagen responded curtly, turning away. "Word just came down from the brass. Until further notice, Agent Willhiem is the liaison between Section Thirteen and the rest of the NYPD, and has the right to veto any actions we take. Effectively, he's just become our new boss."

No one else moved. Rainette, ever the eloquent witch, summed it up for all of them.

"Well, fuck!"

MARCEL was taking the situation the hardest.

"I did not sign on to this to become a lackey for the Order," he whispered, cold fury rolling up from him like icy wind. "My clan was furious when I told them what I'd done. If they learn of this, I will be exiled."

No one was dumb enough to come near him. Cole had expected the ogre to put his impressive fists through the walls, but thus far, all Marcel had done was tense them every other word or so, as if imagining them around Willhiem's throat.

"Don't tell them?" Rainette, meanwhile, offered.

Marcel cast a glance at her. "We are already in exile, *Ta-chet*. If my clan casts me aside, I will have nowhere to go, no home to speak of."

Cole's eyes widened slightly at the use of the term, which was something the ogre clans used to describe an intended lifemate, but said nothing. Clearly, this wasn't the time, and he suspected the ogre had used the word unintentionally.

"They are waiting for us," he said, keeping his voice calm. "I am not happy about saying this, but everyone here needs to decide what they are going to do from now on."

It was only the three of them now. Staffelbach had gone on ahead with Corhagen to meet up with Joss while Cole left with Rainette under the pretext of helping her find Marcel. In reality, he had been thinking that Rainette would need help keeping Marcel under control. Nevertheless, it was good that they had a minute to themselves.

"What do you mean?" Rainette demanded.

"Marcel and I hail from Faerie," Cole reminded her. "You are a witch, and Joss was transfigured by the Goddess herself."

Rainette's eyes widened. Marcel looked up sharply at that. "When?" the ogre wondered.

"How did that happen?" Rainette was actually turning a little pale now. "The Goddess made his arm that way? Is that how he got his new powers?"

"Yes."

Rainette didn't look pleased by Cole's curt reply. "I just assumed you had a spare arm and eyeball lying around somewhere in a box," she muttered. "Katalina was always talking about what a pack rat you were. I can't believe you got Danu to regrow a whole arm for someone."

"It will not be without consequences," Cole said gravely.

"The sidhe were always of the opinion that Danu favored them above all others," Marcel stated dryly, before he added, "for the most part, at least. If she was willing to heed your request, you must mean something to her."

"I am no one anymore," Cole reminded him. "My home was taken from me before I was of age, and then my mother had no further use for me. Only Titania saw something of value in my existence, and even that didn't last for very long."

Cole stopped himself before he said too much. After letting out a deep breath, he said, "My point is that most of the Section consists of those that the Order would consider a threat. They might make allowances with you, Rainette, since you are a witch, but other than Corhagen and Staffelbach, we are all hazardous to whatever agenda they're conspiring."

Rainette snorted. "My coven hates the Order," she spat. "We've been a proud thorn in their collective side for years. Believe me, I'm not happy about this either."

"Fine, then." Cole gave her a nod. "Then we need to decide whether we're going to stay and present a united front, or leave and make the best of things before the situation deteriorates."

No one said anything.

"Well?"

Rainette frowned and looked hard at Cole, as though she were seeing something different about him. "You're up to something," she finally concluded.

"You have a plan?" Marcel asked.

"Not yet," he replied. "Nothing definitive, at least, but if the Section wants to survive whatever the Order is trying to do, we have to stick together. So, are either of you staying?"

Neither looked as though they wanted to answer. Marcel spoke up at last. "Before I answer yours, I have a question of my own."

"Go on."

Rainette stepped back, watching the two suspiciously now. "I want to know why you seem determined to stay," Marcel pressed. "Don't you have more to lose than either of us if you stay behind?"

"Probably," Cole replied.

"Then why are you doing it?"

"For the same reason I joined in the first place," Cole answered, before turning his back to them. "I'll be waiting in the garage, if you're coming."

Before he had taken three steps, Rainette rushed up to his side. "I can't leave you alone," she said. "Not after the fiasco you led us into on Staten. Someone has to stick around and keep you boys out of trouble."

Marcel lumbered up behind them, favoring his left side slightly so that he loomed more over Rainette than Cole. "I will stay," he said crisply.

"Glad to hear it," Rainette teased. "Oh, and sweetie, they know."

The look on Marcel's face was priceless. "Oh," was all he had to say in response.

"Besides," Rainette added mirthfully, "we can always quit later."

"So, WHERE are we going?"

Willhiem had been in the middle of giving a speech. Apparently the party had started without them. Cole had made sure to put enough force behind his words to cut the man off. When the IA agent turned around, he was wearing an uncharacteristically irate expression that rapidly melted away at the sight of the three of them approaching together as a group.

Staffelbach was smiling behind Willhiem's back now. Vallimun gave Cole a cautioning glance, but it was Corhagen who seemed the most put out. Cole ignored him for now and gave Willhiem a withering stare.

"Were we late?" he asked the mortal. "I wasn't aware of a time limit."

"We've been asked to investigate the building that was attacked by the Beyonder," Joss explained, speaking around Willhiem as if the man weren't there. "The TV station case has been put on the back burner for now."

Cole nodded. "Did Staffelbach have the chance to explain what was really going on at the station yet?"

Willhiem looked back at Staffelbach before giving Cole his full attention again. "What's been going on?"

"They're tulpas," Rainette broke in. "About thirty years ago, give or take, an episode aired on the *Captain Sharky* show that encouraged kids to dream up their own imaginary friend. This episode just so happened to air on the morning of the vernal equinox."

Inspiration struck Cole. "The Order wouldn't happen to know something about that, would they?" Cole pressed. "According to the reports, a psychiatrist took the station to court over the episode and won the case very quickly. Was he by any chance well-connected in this town?"

Willhiem drew himself up. "I can't say," he replied. "Perhaps. If the collective imaginations of children across Manhattan could create tulpas together, such a thing would have definitely been discouraged."

The fact that the man answered at all surprised Cole. "However, that was before I joined the Hermetic Order," Willhiem continued. "Will the coven's spell be able to hold the tulpas back?"

"Not for long," Rainette said. "Someone from my coven is looking into it."

"Good," Willhiem said, smiling. "Now, since you all were late, I think a quick briefing is in order."

Joss stepped forward. "According to our new liaison," he explained, "something managed to get inside the building at one thirty this morning."

"It tore an inconspicuous hole in the side of a wall, maybe three feet wide, and slithered in," Willhiem said. "The creature was able to drill past our defenses with relative ease, but we think the smaller body didn't have enough power to stay stable."

"They found a small puddle of ectoplasm in the room where the canister is supposedly being kept," Joss finished.

"It's learning," Rainette surmised, sounding fearful. "It's realized that too big of a body draws unwanted attention, and is far too massive to keep stable. So it made a smaller body for itself, thinking that would get it inside."

"But the body was too small," Staffelbach said from farther back, catching on to their train of thought. "The batteries ran out."

"Effectively," Cole agreed. "But this being is learning more about how this world functions and keeps making adaptations to compensate."

"We would like for Section Thirteen to figure out a means of destroying this Beyonder," said Willhiem.

Cole didn't have to guess who the mortal meant by "we." "Why does it want this canister so badly?" he wondered aloud. "It has to have some significance."

Willhiem smiled. "You mean to tell me you don't know?"

Instantly, Cole hated the tone in his voice. "I was told it was a medical experiment," he said. "Are you implying something?"

For Willhiem, solstice might as well have come early. "It might have started out that way," he admitted. "But we took a sample from the canister to ensure its contents weren't harmful. The fluid inside is a protein soup filled with nanomachines."

"We knew that already," Joss interjected.

"Did you know that the robots were programmed with an alchemy cipher?"

No one moved.

"Sorry," said Staffelbach. "What?"

"A code," Corhagen quickly explained. "It's for working alchemy, I think."

"The machines inside the liquid were given the alchemy code?" Cole frowned. "Well, I guess David can't be called a fool. Never tell more than you have to."

The smile on Willhiem's face faltered a bit.

"So the canister has some kind of fluid in it filled with machines that know how to do alchemy?" Joss asked.

Willhiem shot him a glare. "From what we've gleaned so far, the machines themselves don't work. The process they're using is still very primitive. This was most likely why the project was shelved, though I am curious as to why someone would attempt such a thing to begin with."

"If you know who the canister belongs to, you must know who funded the project," Cole pointed out. "So why bother asking?"

Joss looked at Cole curiously.

"David's mother has what you call Alzheimer's Disease," Cole explained softly. "She has been unconscious for some time now. Her body is weak, but it is the mind that has taken the most damage. David has been frantically searching for a cure. My guess is…."

Cole paused, giving Willhiem a look before continuing. "…this was another one of his dead ends."

"How could he have cured Alzheimer's with alchemical nanomachines?" Rainette asked. "That sounds like a real stretch to me."

Cole shrugged. "He's been chasing rainbows for a while now, as the saying goes."

"And you aren't able to cure her on his behalf?" Willhiem broke in.

"Healing was never my talent," Cole said. "My gifts lie with the dead."

"Are we done?" Joss asked Willhiem in a curt voice. "I would like for my team to get going. We still have to clean up the mess at the TV station once we're done here, assuming the 'brass' is okay with us picking the investigation back up once we're done with your problem."

In the end, those who could fit inside Cole's vehicle comfortably rode with him. Rainette sat in the back of the police van Willhiem had commandeered, beside Marcel. Before the witch left, she assured everyone that Marcel would be in no danger, loud enough that Willhiem overheard. Cole wasn't fully certain the Order lackey bought the ruse, but it was enough for the time being. The Order didn't need to know about Rainette and Marcel's new relationship to put everyone in danger. Staffelbach rode in back with Corhagen, who was looking out the window at traffic. The quiet was apparently getting to the younger officer, because after a moment more, he leaned forward between Cole's and Joss's seats.

"So," Staffelbach began. "Alchemy? Like, turning lead into gold?"

"That's just a myth," Cole replied, watching the van in front of them. "True alchemists value knowledge over precious metals."

Staffelbach looked disappointed.

"It also takes years of study to master," Cole added. "At least, that's what I'm told. I've never dabbled in the Great Art myself."

"What happens if you study alchemy, then?" Staffelbach asked as he sat back in his seat. "Could that guy you were talking about really cure his mother with it?"

"I really don't know," Cole said, turning sharply down a familiar side street. "David is my godson, so if it were possible, I'd have a difficult time talking him out of it. I know he wants to cure his mother more than anything."

"Why didn't he tell us that in the first place?" Joss asked, gripping the passenger door's handle tightly.

"David knows how I feel about human magic." Cole had to swerve to avoid getting sideswiped by a truck running a red light. "Have we got time to pull him over?"

"Leave it," Joss insisted. "I want to see more of that building while we've got Willhiem's clearance to be there. Anyway… David?"

"As I said, David knows I'm usually mistrustful of human spells," Cole went on, catching up to the van again. "He might have been worried about how I would react."

"If you say so."

They arrived at the Order building not too long after that. The remainder of the ride had gone by quietly. Corhagen climbed out of the car before Cole even had the chance to park it.

"What's with him?" Staffelbach wondered as Corhagen walked off in the distance.

"Ain't no telling," Joss replied dismissively. "Corhagen's been moody lately. I suspect his pregnant wife has been giving him a hard time."

"As if she needs to use conception as an excuse," Cole bit back. "One could almost call her present state an improvement compared to how shrill she normally is."

Staffelbach laughed as they both got out of the car. "It's moments like these that make me glad I'm into guys."

The building had seen better days. The damage left by the Beyonder, or whatever it had been, was still apparent. Cole noticed several spellcasters standing outside, muttering words under their breath as they extended an open palm out toward the building at close distance. When Cole passed through the doors, however, he felt no disturbance. Either their magics were not for keeping him out, or he was no longer a blip on the Order's radar. Neither seemed all that likely, given what Cole knew about them.

Willhiem was leading them out of the general loading area that they'd stood in last time. The feeling of shock and fear still lingered in the air for the sidhe, as well as the shame of how frightened he'd been. Cole tensed his muscles, as if testing the strength to ensure it was still there, and vowed to find this thing, if only for the satisfaction of killing it personally.

Sidhe warriors were not cowards, after all.

The first door they passed through took them down a hallway with solid white walls. Behind the paint and plaster, Cole could feel the presence of iron. The sensation only got more intense as they climbed down a flight of stairs. The building had been fortified to withstand a heavy assault by the fey. Apparently, the higher-ups in the Order were paranoid about their precious secrets getting out. More mundane methods of security had been employed as well, however. Cole spotted several security cameras the farther they went, along with what looked like laser sensors.

At the end of the stairs, they took another hallway to the right that curved into an L-bend, then split like a "T" at an intersection. Willhiem led them to the right again, with Marcel bringing up the rear next to Rainette, naturally. The corridors in this area were on the small side, meaning the ogre had to stoop down so his horns did not graze the ceiling. Cole thought that anyone they met along the way would have a devil of a time squeezing past him, assuming they didn't react in the more predictable way of running away in fear. Strangely, though, the area was deserted.

Up ahead, Willhiem stopped at a dead end in front of a complex-looking door that could not have been more conspicuous. The slab looked like a vault used at a bank. Its dull black coloring contrasted sharply with the white of the walls. Willhiem stepped forward, unfazed by the sight of it, and pressed his palm to a plate on the wall, just to the side of the vault door.

"We put the canister here," Willhiem explained, as if that weren't obvious. "This is one of our more secure areas. Normally, allowing anyone without clearance to see this would be expressly forbidden, but given the circumstances, I was told an exception needed to be made."

"Is this where they found the ectoplasm puddle?" Cole asked.

"It is," Willhiem answered without turning around. He was currently pressing his eye up against an iris reader of some kind. The machine it was connected to beeped in response, then flashed a cross emblem on its screen. Willhiem remained perfectly still as the air around him rippled slightly.

"That machine can read auras?" Rainette asked, clearly impressed in spite of herself.

"There have been some new advancements," Willhiem said dismissively. "Though this machine is still leagues slower in producing a match."

A thumbs-up sign appeared on-screen. "Usually, anyway," the agent said, popping the door open. "You may enter, but refrain from touching anything you don't need to."

"How are we supposed to examine the crime scene if we don't know what parts of the area are off limits and what parts are okay?" Joss asked pointedly.

Willhiem, at the very least, had the decency to appear chastised. "Fair enough," he acknowledged. "I suppose the consequences are inevitable."

Joss paused once everyone had filed into the vault area. "Be extra careful," he cautioned. "If you don't need to touch something, don't."

The inside of the vault looked the way Cole had predicted: each wall lined with small cubicles that had something stuffed inside of them. Nearly each object had been bagged, labeled, and in some cases, packaged so that the contents weren't discernible by glance alone.

"First off," Joss said, catching Willhiem before he slipped away, "where did they find the intrusion?"

"And the ectoplasm puddle," Rainette added.

"And the canister," Cole finished. "We need to correlate between the three."

"Why?" Willhiem asked.

Joss wasn't buying it. "You're a cop, Willhiem. You might be an IA dog and a puppet for these Order yokels, but you wouldn't be where you are now if you were stupid. This thing might not have been trying to get to the canister. Not this time, anyway."

Surprisingly, Willhiem was not the least bit put out by the insult. "You think the creature intended the break-in as a test?"

"Testing your defenses," Cole said. "To see how far it could get before being discovered, and perhaps to see how long a smaller body would last."

"Here's the canister," Staffelbach said, pointing at one of the small cubicles in the wall. "I think someone moved it, though. It's not labeled the same as the others."

"Be careful," Joss warned. "We don't...."

Whatever Joss had been planning to warn Staffelbach about was left unsaid. Staffelbach stepped on something wet on the floor that sent his feet flying out from under him. Cole winced as his head banged into the wall on his way down, causing the shelf of cubes to rattle. The canister in question tipped out with its lid wide open, splashing its contents down onto his head before rolling across the floor while Staffelbach sat in a mess of sticky red fluid, looking pissed at himself.

"I believe the contents of that canister were worth a great deal to the right buyer," Willhiem remarked dryly.

"Then why was it open?" Rainette asked as Marcel gave Staffelbach a hand.

Willhiem frowned. "That is unusual. The canister should have been airtight. Simply jolting the wall like that wouldn't have opened it."

"Unless something opened it before we got in here," Joss suggested, while Rainette picked the cylinder up off the floor, revealing that the top had indeed been tampered with. "In which case, maybe that thing got what it wanted and left."

Willhiem was looking at Vallimun seriously now. "That would not be acceptable," he said. "The whole point of keeping the canister's contents locked away was to prevent such a disaster."

"Not our fault," Joss replied. "You brought us here to investigate a potential break-in by an otherworldly source."

"I'm aware of that," said Willhiem.

"If those nanomachines were programmed with the alchemist's cipher," Rainette warned, still holding the canister in her hands, "then that thing might use them to build itself a new body—one it could live in permanently."

Willhiem looked slightly pale now. "Which would be a disaster."

"Again," Joss reminded, giving the IA agent a smug look. "Not our fault."

Willhiem shot Joss an angry glare. "I am under the impression that you and your team are less than pleased with current events," he stated. "Exactly how is that supposed to be my handiwork, though? Since when I have ever meant you or your team harm?"

"You don't get it," Joss replied as he motioned for the others to pack up. "We know you're with the Order, and that they were the ones who arranged it so you would spy on us for them. We know you aren't on our side, Willhiem. Even if none of this was your doing, it doesn't mean you won't personally stab us in the back sooner or later."

Some of Willhiem's benign facade slipped away. "The Order isn't your enemy," he snapped back sharply.

"The hell it isn't," Joss argued. "I agreed to take the helm of the Section because I thought that was most important. I thought I could do more good this way. Instead, from day one, I've had my ass ridden by city officials and bureaucrats who don't seem to realize just how necessary we are. In the end, it comes down to money and politics, something you seem to be all about."

Joss glanced out the corner of his eye toward Staffelbach. "Someone run him home so he can get cleaned up. Cole, would you mind?"

"Not at all," Cole replied. "I suddenly feel the need for some fresh air."

Staffelbach was quiet as Cole led him out of the building. Cole almost made a wrong turn more than once, but luckily, his nose was on target. Neither man spoke as Cole pressed the button on his key chain to open the car doors for them. Staffelbach was worried about damaging the upholstery until Cole reminded him that the car was not actually a vehicle at all. In the time since he'd come into possession of it, Cole had never so much as run the SEMA through a car wash. Dust and dirt were not issues for him.

"I stink," Staffelbach grumbled as they rode along down the highway toward New Jersey. "I can't believe I spilled this crud all over me, and in front of Inspector Vallimun, no less!"

"He was too busy being pissed at Willhiem to care much," Cole assured him. "In fact, you probably did him a favor. At least we know the canister was opened."

"Sometimes I worry I'm not cut out to be a cop," he muttered after a moment. "Do you ever get that feeling?"

Cole smiled. "All the time."

"Really?" It sounded as though Staffelbach didn't believe him. "Or are you just shitting me?"

"No, not 'shitting' you," Cole promised, taking the off-ramp. "I still wonder if being on this side of the law is right for me. Don't forget, I started out in this world as an enforcer for an Irish crime boss. Being a cop feels strange, even after all that time in between."

Staffelbach laughed. "Every time I hear that, it takes me a minute or two to remember that you're not joking."

Cole smiled wryly. "I guess…."

Whatever he was about to say was driven from his mind as the road in front of him blurred. Cole gasped as pain shot through his forehead. The car swerved for a moment, drifting over into the next lane and sending a taxicab into a spin, honking angrily. Then the vehicle took over for him and righted itself, while Cole struggled to force the pain back.

It was like nothing he'd ever experienced before. He could almost swear it felt like something was stabbing out through his forehead. Cursing in Faerie, Cole gripped the steering wheel again and blinked away the tears in his eyes as the shock wave slowly passed. Staffelbach watched him the whole time, as if preparing to dive out the door into the street. His hand was gripping the handle tightly.

"*Ai'skirat*!" Cole swore. "What was that?"

"You okay?"

Cole shook his head to make sure. "We must have driven over an active ley line or something. For a minute there, it felt like something was growing out of my forehead."

A thought occurred to him then. "Is there something growing out of my forehead?"

"No," said Staffelbach, still holding on to the door handle. "You're fine. You scared the shit out of me on top of everything else, but you look the same as always."

"Good," Cole said. "Then it's a good thing we're headed toward your apartment. I assumed you were going to change pants anyway."

Staffelbach glared out the window. "I was kidding, MacColewyn."

"I know," he replied. "I was being funny."

THE two men reached Staffelbach's apartment not long after. Cole had no more epileptic fits or losses of vehicular control. Staffelbach even trusted him enough to take his hand off the door handle before the car was parked. Cole climbed out along with the mortal and followed him up to the second story. He'd always been somewhat curious about mortal dwellings and the accumulations they built up around them as time wore on.

When Staffelbach unlocked his apartment door, the sight was something to behold. The entrance was a foyer adorned with personal artwork that someone had framed, as well as photographs of Staffelbach posing with, Cole assumed, friends of his. The foyer opened out into a living room/kitchen area that had no border separating the two. Cole smiled inwardly as he glanced around the living room. Posters in black plastic frames hung on the wall, each one a declaration of Staffelbach's avid devotion to comic books. Cole recognized several classics, as well as one or two more modern fictional heroes. There were also shelves, each containing small figurines. On the coffee table, coasters had been laid out in the shape of a certain "S" shield.

"You do enjoy your comics," he noted.

"Make yourself at home," Staffelbach said, heading through the living area to the back. It was a short trip for him. Two doors, kept apart by a divider, lay pressed against the wall. Staffelbach veered toward the one on the left. "I'll be out in a moment," he said, turning back. "My roommate must have stepped out for a bit, so it's just us."

Hearing the word "roommate" made Cole think of the previous year, and how much had changed in such a short period of time.

"What is he like?" he asked.

Staffelbach had left the door opened part of the way. Cole saw him slipping out of his soaked clothes and wondered if he should turn away, then decided against it. Most humans preferred not to be watched during such moments, but if Staffelbach had wanted privacy, he would have shut the door all the way.

"What?" the young officer asked, coming back to the door in just a pair of boxers.

"Your roommate," Cole repeated. "What is he like?"

"Oh," Staffelbach said, before his face lit up. "Rich is awesome! He does his own independent comic book titles. Plus, he has a review show on YouTube called *The Jersey Comic Geek*. Sometimes we do collaboration videos together."

"He sounds interesting," Cole said sincerely.

"If he doesn't come back before we leave, I'll introduce you sometime." Staffelbach suddenly seemed aware of his lack of clothing and stepped away from the door. "Rich and I always have fun together. He's been my best friend since I moved to Manhattan."

Cole hesitated. "I had a roommate not too long ago," he admitted. "She and I got along real well, also."

"You're not roommates anymore?" Staffelbach asked absentmindedly as he picked a semi-clean pair of pants up off the floor.

"She's dead," Cole replied. "I found her that way in her room. Our loft was broken into, and she died trying to fight them off. Her funeral was held a little over two months ago. I still haven't been out to see her gravestone."

"I'm sorry." The emotion in the mortal's voice was genuine. "Maybe you ought to go and visit sometime."

"Others have said the same thing," Cole replied. "But it is not the sidhe way. We do not have graves the way that humans have."

"How do your people grieve for the dead, then?" Staffelbach emerged from his room, fully clothed. "You don't have graveyards, or memorials?"

Cole shook his head. "There are catacombs," he explained. "Though I never saw them before I was exiled. When such a thing happens, it is regarded as a very big deal. Still, we do not focus on a loved one's passing the way that humans sometimes do. It is just not our way."

Staffelbach didn't seem to know what to make of this.

"My world was very different from this one," Cole went on, looking out an open window that showed an empty building across the street. "I've lived here for nearly a human century, and it still feels like yesterday that I washed up in the bay."

"Gross," Staffelbach said plainly.

Cole gave a small smile. "The water tasted bitter. I was sure Oberon had banished me to some desolate wasteland instead of the mortal realm. Of course, the stories I'd heard about here made it sound remarkably similar."

Staffelbach offered Cole a sad smile. "I remember when my mother left me with my dad," he said, following Cole's gaze. "It was around the same time that I started to realize I was gay. I don't know why, but the two seemed to go together. I think, maybe, I started to wonder if she hadn't realized it first, and left me on my old man's doorstep because she was ashamed of me."

"Was it?" Too late, Cole realized his question would be considered inappropriate. "Forgive me. We don't know each other well enough for me to ask something like that."

"It's cool," Staffelbach assured him easily. "I don't mind answering that. She wasn't abandoning me because she knew I was gay. In fact, my old man knew before she did."

"What did he say?"

"It was just before he died," Staffelbach said, picking a coaster up off the coffee table. "When he was in the hospital, he told me that he'd known for a long time that I was gay, and that he had been okay with it for a while. I remember sitting there. It scared the hell out of me. I actually wanted to ask him to take it back."

"When did you tell your mom?"

"A few years later." Staffelbach sighed as he put the coaster down. "She came back one day after I'd started college, wanting to get in touch with me. I was angry with her at the time, so I told her, thinking it would make her go away. She didn't say anything about it for a while. Truth be told, she was more upset when I let it slip that I was moving to Manhattan."

"My mother and I haven't spoken since I left her Summer Kingdom to become one of Titania's wolves," Cole said absentmindedly.

Staffelbach looked interested. "Is that why you can shape-shift?"

"Yes," he answered. "The wolves of the Queen of All Faerie have two forms. Only sidhe are permitted to join, and once they pass the tests, she grants them the power to assume a wolf form at will."

"What kind of tests?" There was excitement in Staffelbach's voice now. "Does it hurt to change?"

"Not anymore," Cole replied. "As for the tests, I was forbidden to speak of them, and this was a vow I took to the Queen and Oberon before I was banished. Even here, I cannot break it. I can tell you that the tests vary from one individual to another. No applicant's tests are the same. Also, and this was a kind of pretest, so I can speak of it, Oberon insisted I spend a year of Faerie time in his Citadel of Pain before I officially began my examination."

Staffelbach's eyes grew wide. "Citadel of Pain?"

"Oberon's personal torture facility," Cole elaborated. "Those that go there are more times than not driven mad by the experience. I was lucky to have stayed the amount that I did."

"Why did you go?" Staffelbach sat down on the couch as he said this. "What made it worth it?"

Cole joined him, taking a chair near the edge of the couch. "I had nowhere else to go," he said quietly. "If I did not endure, I would have been homeless. In Faerie, a homeless sidhe is prey for those fey who are less than fortunate. I survived because I had to."

Something occurred to the mortal then. "Your mother didn't want you either."

"No," Cole said flatly. "She most certainly didn't."

Staffelbach grew quiet. "Do you know why?" he asked after a moment. "Mine couldn't afford to keep me. It was her, my sister, and me, but she didn't have enough money, so she left me with my dad. They'd been divorced for years. I was scared that first day that he was going to put me out on the street."

"My parents were…." Cole paused. "It is hard for me to describe, because some life bonds among the sidhe have time limits. Couples will mate with one another for a designated time, then separate. Oftentimes, if a child comes from their coupling, they stay together. In Faerie, a fertile couple is considered a shameful thing to waste. For my mother and father, however, they were brought together for the purpose of forging a peace treaty."

Staffelbach frowned. "Your parents' families were at war? They were like the fairy version of Romeo and Juliet?"

"Not exactly," Cole said. "My father was the patriarch of his house, but my mother came from a slightly larger family, which had many daughters. She was traded to my father as a wife to bring an end between their feuding houses. My father was a Winter Court noble, and my mother was Summer Court. The two could not have been a more obviously mismatched pair, but the terms of the treaty were adamant. As part of the agreement, they had to perform a ritual together. I overheard some whisper that this was how the two conceived me so easily.

"My father was in the middle of fighting a war with another faction. It was why he wanted help from my mother's house so badly. Being surrounded by winter made her powers weaken, though, so after she gave birth to me, she left my father's lands to return to her own. I grew up there without really knowing who she was. My father wasn't home much, but I was happy living there, on the whole. Eventually, though, it was discovered that my connection to the Summer Court was weakening my father's power base. He was at a crucial juncture in his fight with the Narsian ice trolls, so I was sent to my mother's court temporarily. This became permanent shortly after, however, when my father was killed in action. I learned after his death that my uncle seized all of my father's land and titles for himself, leaving me disowned and without a coin to my name."

Cole wasn't sure what was making him so conversational. He couldn't remember telling a mortal this much about his past, yet it felt good to do so.

"My mother never had much use for me," he went on, looking up. Staffelbach was watching him intently now. "I was an embarrassment to her. Children in Faerie are precious, yet my mother regarded me as a nuisance most of the time, when she was in a fair mood."

Staffelbach chuckled softly. "I can relate."

"Before long," Cole continued, "there were assassination attempts. I started to fear for my life everywhere I turned. Then someone murdered my only friend, Shuggi. Shuggi had been a product of the last sidhe-goblin war. His mother was raped on the battlefield. No one liked him much either, but they never spoke ill of him publicly. He was the finest spear master my mother's court had, and carried a volatile temper at all times. We were the best of friends until his body was discovered pinned to a wall. Someone had nailed his hands, feet, and chest with cold iron spikes to kill him."

Cole swallowed. "That was the day my Hand of Power awakened. In my grief, I accidentally raised him. The court thought he had been resurrected, until an examiner took a closer look at him. Shuggi had been facing his murderer when he died, so he knew the name of the one who'd taken his life. The man was a relatively high-ranking noble, though, one who hated the goblins with a passion, so his sentence was commuted, and I was placed in the hands of the court's personal interrogator. When I emerged, I sent word to Titania, asking to be one of her wolves."

Cole straightened up again. "I don't remember ever telling anyone that much of my life since I was banished. Forgive me."

Staffelbach blinked. "For what?"

"For unloading on you." Cole shifted uncomfortably in his seat as he spoke. "You shouldn't have had to listen to so much of my troubles."

"It's cool, dude," Staffelbach assured him. "You listened to me. Ready to go now?"

Cole nodded and stood up. "The others will be wondering what happened, but I want to take a short detour before we return to the precinct."

"Where to?" Staffelbach asked, getting to the door first. "You craving donuts?"

"Not donuts," he replied. "I want to stop by the home of the actor who plays Captain Sharky. He's been on my mind for a while now. I think he might be in danger."

"Good idea." Staffelbach hesitated as he locked the door behind him. "Could we stop for donuts afterward?"

"THIS is the place?"

Staffelbach nodded as he shut off his phone. The young officer had been able to look up the address of Marley Neezer, star of *Captain Sharky and the Magical Treasure Cave*, over the phone. Using the GPS feature, he guided Cole to a rather run-down area way out on the other side of Queens. The apartment complex was set across the street from what Cole assumed to be several abandoned buildings. Several windows on the second floor were broken. More than one had been repaired through the wonder of duct tape, but the patch job did nothing to conceal how decrepit it was. Somehow, Cole suspected the interior was going to be worse. Were his car not a product of the wild hunts, he would have worried about leaving it parked outside in the open.

"I was expecting something grander," Cole mused as they climbed out of the car.

"I guess the stories about the TV station going broke were true," Staffelbach noted. "They didn't even have the money to pay the star of their biggest cash cow. That's pretty pathetic."

"I'm glad I never became an actor." Cole reached the stairs first and kept both hands free near his guns. "This wouldn't have been encouraging."

Staffelbach was coming up close behind him. Cole caught a whiff of the young officer's scent as the wind shifted. "You wanted to be an actor?" Staffelbach asked.

"Not really," he replied. "Immortals tend to stay out of the spotlight. You never know when something might come back to haunt you a century or two later."

Marley Neezer's apartment was located at the far end of the open corridor on the right. Before they reached it, Cole suspected something was wrong. The front door was cracked open slightly. It seemed foolhardy for anyone to leave their home vulnerable that way. Drawing both guns, he moved forward at a quickened pace, giving his head a jerk to signal Staffelbach to follow. Staffelbach had already followed his lead and was holding his gun at the ready.

Sniffing the air, Cole nudged the door open with his foot and looked around. The room was empty, but it looked like a fight had broken out. A coffee table in front of the couch had been smashed to pieces. Someone had turned a busted-up recliner upside-down before ripping its innards out. The kitchen floor just ahead was covered in broken plates and scattered pots.

"Keep your eyes peeled," he cautioned.

"I'm not a rookie," Staffelbach reminded him.

"I know. I said that because I smell something. Someone else is here."

Staffelbach moved around past Cole toward the hallway running alongside the kitchen to the back. "I hear something," he said. "It sounds like a TV set."

"It is," Cole affirmed. "A football game is on."

Neither of them moved. "So maybe that's where the mystery guest is hiding?"

"And armed," Cole pointed out, stepping forward. "Stay behind me. The odds of me surviving a gunshot wound are substantially higher. If I'm gunned down, take the shooter out."

Staffelbach fell in step behind him again. "Good plan," he mused. "So long as you don't mind getting shot."

"I hate getting shot."

Both doors at the end of the hall were open. On the right was an empty bathroom with the lights turned off. Cole sniffed the air again, wincing at the stench coming from there, before turning to the left where a single bedroom was laid open, ransacked like the rest of the apartment. Signaling Staffelbach that the coast was clear, he entered with Bandersnach and Jabberwock still raised high.

Staffelbach stood beside him. "The closet," Cole instructed, sniffing the air. "They're hiding in the closet."

In response, the closet door burst open. Both men ducked as a familiar-looking elderly man wielding a golf club sprung out, yelling at the top of his lungs. The man stumbled through the scattered trash all over the floor for a moment and then swore as his body pitched forward from tripping over an old sweater. In a flash, Cole was up and caught the man before he busted his forehead on a suitcase whose contents had been dumped next to it.

"Let go of me!" the man named Marley Neezer shouted. "I haven't got any money left!"

"We didn't come for money," he said, helping the old man back onto his feet. "I am Special Detective MacColewyn, and this is Officer Staffelbach. We were at the television studio during the charity incident."

Marley Neezer stopped struggling and raised his head up to get a better look at Cole's face. "Yeah, I 'member you," he grunted. "Creepy-lookin' fella with white hair. Izzat supposed to be some new style?"

"It's my natural hair color," Cole replied wryly, releasing Neezer from his hold. "Officer Staffelbach and I came here to warn you that the ones responsible for the trouble at the station might be coming after you."

"We think you should lay low for a while," Staffelbach added. "We can arrange police protection for you as well, if you'd like it."

"No thanks." Neezer grunted again. "I've had enough trouble for one day."

"So we noticed." All three looked around the room. "It looks as though you had some uninvited guests before we got here."

"Damn hoodlums came in here looking for money," Neezer growled. Off-camera, his diction was much rougher and included several annoying sounds. "I thought maybe you two were part of their gang, or whatever, and came back to finish me off."

"You didn't call the police?"

The old man glared at Staffelbach. "No phone here," he answered. "Line hasn't been connected yet. I just moved here last week."

The open suitcase was resting lopsided at their feet. "Yet you were packed and ready to go," Cole noted. "And you automatically assumed we were here to get money from you."

Neezer froze. "Why's it any business of yours?" he barked, trying to stare Cole down. "I never asked either of you to barge in here like that."

Cole was not intimidated in the slightest. "At one time," he said, with a hint of warning in his voice, "I would have been sent here to hurt you, possibly break your legs. I've been around long enough to know when a man is in trouble. We didn't come here to hurt you today, however, though something tells me you were expecting us to."

A sour scowl fell over Marley Neezer's face.

"You owe money to someone," Cole continued. "Possibly several someones."

"Prove it," the old man challenged.

Cole sniffed the air once more in answer. "This apartment building is very old," he noted. "Yet it doesn't smell like you've been here for very long. The walls are threadbare, and the furniture is sparse. You must have moved in recently. A man facing money troubles might try to hide somewhere that no one would think to look for him, and who'd ever suspect the star of a famous television series would be here?"

"You're pretty bad at hiding," Staffelbach chimed in again. "This address was in the police files."

Neezer looked away, embarrassed. "My new landlord wouldn't let me sign the lease if I didn't give the address of my former residence."

"Which is why you were already packed and ready to go when someone broke in," Staffelbach concluded.

"You seem to know an awful lot," the old man bit back. "You some sort of college boy?"

"Much to my own chagrin," Cole replied. "We are here to help you, if you want it. You could be taken to a safe house right now. Your monetary woes aside, some powerful forces might be coming for you, and if a group of petty enforcers were able to track you down, it's a miracle the more dangerous ones aren't already here."

The old man looked away. "I don't need help from no cops," he said quietly. "Just get the fuck out, both of you, before...."

Whatever Neezer had been about to say was cut off as the entire building shook. Cole was thrown forward along with Staffelbach, and both wound up sprawled out on the floor with Marley underneath. The floor shook violently as Cole tried to get up off Staffelbach, who in turn was wrestling with Marley Neezer.

"Get off me!" the old man shouted, struggling. "What the hell is going on?"

In answer, something exploded up out of the floor, sending bits of dust, carpet, and wood flying. A thin black tentacle snaked up out of the entrance it had made and moved around as though surveying the room. Cole drew Bandersnatch and Jabberwock both out in a flash and took aim as several more tentacles burst out through the walls. These were much larger, and Cole took note before firing on the one in front of him. The bullet sliced the tentacle neatly in half, sending its attached remains back down through the hole it had come from.

The other appendages in the walls were coming farther in. Staffelbach was on his feet now and took aim alongside Cole. Together, the two opened fire.

"Right," Cole announced, before riddling a fat tentacle with bullet holes.

"Left," Staffelbach answered, taking out two smaller ones farther back.

The floor rippled beneath their feet as if in reaction to the wounds they inflicted. A second later, more thin tentacles burst up out of the floor, coiling through the air as they reached around wildly searching for their prey. In response, Cole reached down and snatched the old man up off the floor, who had smartly covered his head when the gunfire started.

"This is pointless," he said, tossing Marley over his shoulder as though he were a potato sack. "We're leaving now."

Down to one hand, Cole fired Jabberwock into the coils blocking their path as Staffelbach kept the rest off them with cover fire.

"What are these things?" Staffelbach shouted as they reached the door.

"Offhand," Cole grunted, shifting the man thrown over his back, "I'd say this is what was after the canister that spilled on you."

"I thought it was invisible or—" Staffelbach was cut off in mid shout as another appendage exploded out of the wall and grabbed for him. "Shit!"

Cole fired to keep the tentacle away from the mortal. "Being corporeal has its disadvantages," he replied. "But the explanation can wait until later."

Before either of them could take another step, the whole building shook again. Cracks appeared along the walls. A terrible groaning sound filled the apartment. Cole grabbed onto the closest thing he could reach to steady himself, which turned out to be Staffelbach. The two men were thrown sideways into what remained of a wall as a whole chunk of the apartment complex was literally ripped away with them still trapped inside.

Everything in the room was tossed about. Marley slipped out of Cole's grip as he went tumbling backward down the hallway and into what remained of the restroom. A gaping hole lay where a wall had once been. Cole had to cling to the toilet to keep from falling through it. Steeling himself, he pulled his body back up across the tile floor, now hanging at a near-vertical angle. The doorframe was just above him now. Straining his arm muscles, he dragged his body through it and looked around.

"Staffelbach!" he shouted. "Where are you?"

More tentacles, massive ones the size of black pythons, burst through the walls, floors, and ceilings. The entire apartment was ripped in half, pitching Cole forward out into the empty air below. Halfway down, he felt something snag him by the leg. The unexpected jolt sent pain rocketing through his body. If he were anything less than sidhe, the experience would have broken his neck. Rather than facing the specter of death, though, Cole stared down at what lay on the ground.

A writhing nest of tentacles waved up at him from down below on the street. In the center of it, he could see what looked like a mouth, slit vertically down the middle, surrounded by razor-sharp teeth. The maw flexed open, blinding Cole with a white light. More of the creature's appendages waved around him in a midair dance. In the distance a little further down, he spotted Staffelbach fighting against several smaller tentacles that were holding him fast in a death grip.

Without thinking, Cole drew Aed Deigh from its sheath and sliced through the black coil holding him. His body dropped like a stone as a cry of pain echoed through the air.

"Right," Cole mumbled, while the wind whipped across his face. "I cannot fly. This poses a problem, then."

There was nothing within reach for him to grab hold of. Thinking fast, Cole spun Aed Deigh around him as best he could, sending out narrow jets of fire and ice at the surrounding web of twisting, fleshy ropes. The missiles of fire and ice struck home, and Cole continued his assault on the way down, mindful of the wide mouth lying open down below.

Several smaller tentacles whipped out at him, but Cole was ready. Each time one approached, he shot another missile at them, splintering the tips. One of the thicker, heavier-looking ones came his way next, which Cole immediately latched onto with both arms and legs. Sliding down it like a pole, Cole leaped off as the tentacle began to shake and then grabbed for another nearby. Working his way down, he leaped from one appendage to the next, moving toward Staffelbach. The creature was quick to catch on, however, and began moving the mortal down closer to its mouth.

"I don't believe so!" Cole hissed fiercely, swinging Aed Deigh in a wide arc and letting loose with a hail of flames. The tentacles all around him jerked away from him in pain as they were set on fire. Cole repeated the process, then fired yet again down toward the creature's mouth.

The beast roared as the flames spread across what little flesh was visible amid the knot of flesh ropes. "Wait there, Staffelbach!" Cole shouted as he fell past the struggling mortal, who by this point was fighting off at least a dozen or more tentacle heads, some of which were attempting to tear away at his clothing.

The mouth was just up ahead. There was no way for Cole to stop. The creature was bright enough to keep its limbs out of his reach. The light coming from inside the creature shone brightly now, impairing his vision. Cole swallowed his uncertainty and fell with his weapon raised at the ready. Just as the creature's teeth would have clamped down on him, Cole brought Aed Deigh down in a diagonal arc, cutting through the blinding light. Though the blade touched nothing, the beast screamed in wild agony, thrashing around as though the weapon of Faerie had cut out its very heart.

A dark mist poured out of the gap in space where Cole had cut it. Cole was plunging through the space before he had time to bring his weapon back up at the ready. Momentum failed him at once. The plummeting ceased, and he found himself stuck halfway inside the opening he'd just made. The lower end of his body was still trapped outside the beast, while Cole's upper torso was staring into what he could only describe as the White Void itself.

If white static had a shape, a physical attribute that could be fixed to it, what Cole was seeing would be it. The world around him bled white noise. Cries came from everywhere through it, through the madness all around him. Beyond that, somewhere behind him, he could still hear the creature roaring in pain.

"He… elp… p me… e!"

Cole looked around. The sounds were coming from all over the place.

"H… hel… lp m… me… e p… ple… eas…."

Something flickered out in the distance. It seemed to appear and disappear in three different places all at once. Cole stared again.

"Help me!"

The image of Marley Neezer appeared, fading in and out for a moment before becoming somewhat solid. "Get me out of here!" the old man shrieked.

"Take my hand," said Cole, reaching out.

Before their flesh touched, the image of Marley was gone again. Cole searched the area, but there was nothing in the void but the white noise. An instant later, however, others flickered in and out, the same as Marley had. It was difficult to see, but many of these people Cole did not recognize. He had a sneaking suspicion as to who they were, though.

"Ple... se, g... t me o... f here!"

"Tak... my... nd! Do... ave... e behin...."

"... elp... s!"

"Save me! I've go... wif... an... ids!"

"Dont lea... us!"

Cole felt something grab him by the leg. Before he could reach any of the others trapped there, his body was jerked back out of the void at high speed. The shock rattled his teeth and sent pain coursing down his back. Disoriented, Cole clutched Aed Deigh tightly to keep it from falling out of his hand. The double-bladed weapon snapped its blades out automatically as Cole felt his second wind build.

It felt to Cole as though his brain had been put through a laundry spin cycle. With the creature whipping him about, and having just been pulled from the spatial void within it, he was having a hard time judging which way was up or down. Dazed, he reached out for his guns, only to find them missing.

The ride came to an end when Cole felt his body crash against something solid and fleshy. Thinking he had been slammed into another, much larger tentacle, Cole grabbed hold of it with both arms and legs. As the dizziness cleared away, Cole smelled something familiar and realized the figure he was rolling with was a human.

Coming to a stop, he opened his eyes and found Staffelbach pressed up against him. The mortal's uniform was torn in several places from the creature's assault. They had fallen down to what looked like an area of the apartment that was still partially standing. Half the walls were gone, and a portion of the roof was missing. Quickly, the two helped each other up and stood with their backs pressed against each other, looking around.

The air rustled like dry leaves scraping over a city street. Small black tendrils snaked through the holes made in what was left of the walls, and down through the large gaps. Staffelbach was holding up a nightstick now, and for a brief second, Cole was reminded of the smaller mortal taking on a crazed ogre with no fear in his eyes. There could be no doubt that Staffelbach was afraid now, though Cole would have called him a fool for trying to be brave in this situation.

"What are they doing?" Staffelbach asked quietly. His voice was breathless, but still eerily calm. The tendrils were moving around them in a rhythmic fashion now, as though pulsing to some sort of heartbeat. The small ones drifted close to them, though not so much that they came within range of either man's weapon. The creature appeared hesitant now, as though searching the air for something. It almost seemed like the small tentacles were sniffing the air, breathing in their scents.

"It feels like they're making a comparison," Cole said, his muscles taut and ready to spring like a trap. "I almost want to say that this thing is trying to figure out the differences between us."

"It can sense you're not human?"

Cole's eyes watched each tendril move. "I think it's more intrigued by you at the moment," he said, nodding at how focused the creature was on the mortal. "Maybe it's interested in you."

A smile came to Staffelbach's face as one came in too close, and he swatted it away. "How can you joke right now?"

Cole shrugged as best he could. "How can you be mortal and so calm?"

The tendrils were filling the space now, cutting off their maneuverability. "I'm pretty sure we're not getting out of this," Staffelbach said in a grave voice. "I hate it, but one thing I was told about being a cop is to expect death to find you when you least expect it. I kind of wish the instructor who told me that could see this. I don't think either of us imagined anything like this."

"I would be surprised if you had," Cole replied. "However, I'm not ready to surrender just yet."

Something caught Cole's eye then. "Forgive my lack of tact, but were you aware that you are glowing?"

Staffelbach went even more rigid, which surprised Cole, and raised a hand up. "I'm glowing," he said, an edge of panic creeping into his voice.

Something about the rhythm of the tentacles near Staffelbach made Cole take a second glance. "They're doing something," he said, going over the beat in his head. "They're trying to get in synch with you, I think."

"Why?"

Cole heard Staffelbach take in a deep breath to try and calm himself. "The stuff that spilled all over you," Cole said, keeping his eyes on alert as one near him waved slightly closer. "It was the same fluid used to give this *cho-haka* its body."

"The what?"

Cole swiped the tentacle in half with Aed Deigh as Staffelbach batted another, slightly larger one away. "Forgive me," the sidhe said. "There are no words in your tongue for this. *Cho-haka* means 'many limbs' in one of the languages of the Faerie."

"Oh."

"The chemical that spilled on you must still be on your skin," Cole continued, swiping another tendril away. "It must sense that."

Cole felt something ripple through Staffelbach's body and echo inside of him. "It's been nice knowing you," the mortal said before gripping his club. "I wish we could have hung out sometime."

"We will," Cole said firmly. "So long as we're still alive, there is a chance. I refuse to let this thing have either of us."

"Too bad," the mortal said, before moving away from the sidhe.

Cole turned sharply and saw Staffelbach moving toward the creeping tendrils with his club raised. "I think it wants me," Staffelbach said quietly. "When it makes its move, get the fuck out of here."

"You're insane," Cole said disbelievingly. "You don't know what this thing will do to you."

"I have a pretty good idea," Staffelbach countered. "Get ready."

The mortal's courage struck something deep within Cole's very soul. As he watched the creature close its appendages around Staffelbach's body, he felt one leg give way. Cole crouched down automatically, keeping his weapon parallel with the floor. It had been a long time since these words had been uttered, but he remembered them as if they had been told to him yesterday. The prayer came naturally.

"E'AV-KA MATERU N' DE HORNUS, BATRUEA Y'IKUA ME DI'YATA VERAS T'HOKU BE HO'THU MORESAU. VHINE'D DKEA IT'SHU AIMETRAS I'TZ I'E DROMUS DE EM'IRETA VBOLUSTAR."

Aed Deigh was shining. The apartment had faded away to a black, empty void. The creature was nowhere in sight.

"DO YOU WANT HIM TO LIVE?"

Cole's hands gripped Aed Deigh. "I ask for nothing," he replied, even as his tone betrayed him. "Only fools come to you and plead for mercy when the answer is in front of them."

"INDEED," Danu's whisper answered. *"BUT FOR NOW, ANSWER MY QUESTION, MY SON. DO YOU WANT YOUR COMRADE TO LIVE?"*

"I did not say that prayer to call upon you," he insisted, not answering. "It is for a warrior who is facing his last rites."

"A WARRIOR FACES DEATH CONSTANTLY," Danu countered. *"YOUR COMRADE KNEW THIS. IT IS WHY HE IS UNAFRAID TO DIE. AND YOU HAVE STILL NOT ANSWERED MY QUESTION. MY REASONS FOR ANSWERING YOUR CALL ARE MY OWN. I AM HERE NOW, MY SON, SO SPEAK TO ME."*

Cole swallowed hard. "Yes."

"YES, WHAT?" Danu's voice pressed insistently.

"Spare him as well," Cole hissed, gritting his teeth tightly. "I know whatever will come will be on my shoulders, but if you would be willing, let him live."

Something almost like mirth entered her words next. *"YOU CARE SO MUCH FOR ONES WHO MIGHT OTHERWISE MEAN SO LITTLE?"*

Cole's shoulders shook. "I have been alone for many years of this world's time," Cole told her. "It has been hard, but I made my peace with that fact as best I could a long time ago. I never intended to care this much."

"CARE AS MUCH OR AS LITTLE AS YOU LIKE," she said, sounding very near to him at that moment. *"IT MATTERS NOT TO ME, BUT FOR YOU, I WILL SPARE THIS ONE. HOWEVER, YOU WERE NOT WRONG IN THAT THERE WILL BE A PRICE."*

"I will gladly pay it," Cole said at once.

"MY SON." Danu's voice breathed over him as her words faded. *"THE PRICE WILL NOT BE YOURS TO PAY."*

"Goddammit, MacColewyn!"

Cole's eyes snapped open at the sound of his name being shouted. "Quit praying and get the fuck out of here!"

Staffelbach was screaming at him as the black tentacles slowly roped their way around his body. Rising up, Cole felt power building around him. The voice of the Goddess was gone, but he could feel her presence everywhere. The *cho-haka* was reacting to it now, moving its appendages as far from him as possible.

Aed Deigh still shone, its glow resonating with the same light being emitted from Staffelbach's skin.

Cole stood and felt wind whipping at his hair. He knew, without seeing himself, that his body was bathed in light. Here and now, the Goddess was with him. Raising his weapon high overhead, Cole let out a roar of defiance against the abomination as it began drawing the mortal away.

Charging forward, he ducked under the tendrils that lashed out to stop him, then dove around Staffelbach as the creature lifted him up off the ground.

The red blade of Aed Deigh was awash in golden flames. Cole swung the blade upward, intending to cut the appendages away. Instead, a wave of light cut straight through them, and out through the ramshackle ruins of the apartment complex.

The creature hissed in agony, dropping Staffelbach to the floor. Cole leaped away to stand guard over his friend. His eyes were glowing gold now, reflected in the brown pools that stared up at him in shock.

Staffelbach's body was blurred. Colors flashed across his exposed flesh in a pattern as his features seemed to split. Cole watched as the mortal's body phased in and out of existence in rapid synch.

"I don't fe…el so-so-so… gooooood!"

Reaching down, Cole clapped a hand around Staffelbach's neck, intending to give him something to focus on before he slipped out of phase permanently. Instead, the power within him jumped from his body into the mortal's. Light exploded between them, bathing their bodies in the same warmth.

"Mac… Olewyn," Staffelbach said, his voice getting clearer now. "What's happening to… me?"

"Focus," Cole told him, breathing into his face. "You have to concentrate. That thing will sweep you up into itself if you don't resist."

The floor beneath them bucked suddenly. Huge black python-sized appendages shattered up out of the floorboards, ripping what remained of the room to pieces and sending both men flying.

"Staffelbach!" Cole called out.

Several of the smaller tentacles snatched the mortal up in midair. "Get off me!" he screamed, thrashing about now.

"Hold on!" Cole brought Aed Deigh down, the frost-covered blade extended this time, and ran it through one of the giant-sized tendrils at it swung itself at him.

The blade pierced the creature's flesh, sending ice all along it and turning the tentacle into a platform for Cole to stand on.

"I'm coming," he said, yanking his blade free.

Leaping into the air, Cole propelled himself toward where Staffelbach hung. "Give me your hand," he cried out, extending his own. "I've got you!"

"Look out!" Staffelbach screamed.

Cole had no time to react. Another tentacle swung out from behind Cole and swatted him through the air like he was a pesky gnat. The force of the blow knocked him off guard, but threw him faster to where Staffelbach was nonetheless. The two bodies collided with one another. Cole felt the smaller tentacles snatch Aed Deigh from his hands as the rest wound around him, bringing the two men together face to face.

"Dammit!" Staffelbach swore.

"I'm not finished yet," Cole declared, fighting against his captor.

The two felt themselves being pulled down through the air toward the ground. Cole felt the power between them fluctuate as the beast's maw lay gaping open between them.

"Thank you for trying," Staffelbach said, giving Cole a strange look now. "Whatever it is you did, I think it must have come at a heavy price."

"The price was not mine to pay," Cole answered at once without thinking.

A thought struck him. "Staffelbach," he said, getting the mortal's full attention. "Do you want to live?"

Staffelbach blinked. "Huh?"

Cole leaned forward, understanding now. "Kiss me."

Their mouths touched before Staffelbach could protest. Cole felt the surge run through him into the beast, freeing his arms so he could entwine them around the mortal's smaller frame. Staffelbach moaned into him as his hands gripped the tendrils left holding him in place. The power from Cole raced through him and down into the creature, who let out a high-pitched shriek as the golden glow spread through it.

Light spilled out everywhere. The creature shone with them as it screamed its pain for the whole area to hear. Desire gripped Cole as his tongue brushed against Staffelbach's in a dance of wanton need.

Everything around them exploded.

Cole felt them falling. Shards of light whipped through the whirlwind of dust and ash. Through it all, he felt his arms holding onto the mortal as though glued there. As the ground rushed up to meet them, Cole felt something close around his body.

"MY SON," a voice whispered in his ear.

COLE came to first.

He was naked. That wasn't a high priority, but concrete didn't make for the best mattress. He could feel the dirty slab of city cement underneath, scratching away at his skin with each tiny move he made.

Opening his eyes, he saw Staffelbach close by, lying as though he'd been trying to reach out to Cole at some point and just landed in that position. Most of their bodies were covered in ash. As soon as Cole realized this, he started to sneeze. Whatever remains he was lying in, it irritated his nose something horrible.

Drawing himself up, he surveyed the scene. There were police sirens in the distance, which Cole had to remember was an encouraging sign. Unfortunately, he did not have his badge on him. Getting to his feet slowly, Cole stumbled forward a couple of feet, testing to make sure nothing was too badly damaged. His body didn't appear to be injured. The feeling brought back the memories of the past few hours, leaving him wondering what he should take care of first.

The ash wasn't just covering his and Staffelbach's bodies. Everywhere Cole turned, there were great big piles of it covering the block he stood in. Off to the side, far enough that he had to turn to really see it, was the remains of the apartment complex. It looked as though the creature had grabbed huge chunks of it in its appendages and tore them clear off. A number of the pieces were lying farther away. Part of a living room and kitchen stood on its side next to a stirring pile of ash that Cole immediately tensed at seeing. The wind shifted then, however, revealing the still form of a human.

Seeing this, Cole first checked on Staffelbach to make sure he was still alive and in no immediate need of aid. Staffelbach grunted at Cole's touch, muttered something unintelligible, then rolled over as if to go back to sleep. Finding him okay for at least the moment, Cole stood and made his way toward the other human.

The ash pile, it turned out, contained several human bodies, each of them looking a little worse for wear. Cole thought he recognized one or two of the faces. It looked as though all of the creature's victims were alive, if a little harried and in need of a shower.

As he passed one of the smaller ash piles in search of other survivors, Cole's sharp eyes spotted something glistening in the darkness. Bandersnatch emerged in his grip, in need of a good cleaning but otherwise in perfect condition. Jabberwock took longer to locate, as did Aed Deigh. Cole finally found them in the largest pile of all, on the other side, away from his badge and boots. His cell phone was alive and blinking in a different pile a little further along. After sliding the boots onto his feet, Cole picked up his items and then wandered back over to Staffelbach.

A short figure was waiting for him there, holding something in her arms.

"You hurt him!" Mary Alice shouted indignantly. "The Nihilgeister will take forever to get better because of you."

Cole blinked. "Nihilgeister?"

Mary Alice frowned petulantly. "The Triskaidekahedron gave him to us for safekeeping, and so we could move back and forth out of our home without having to wait for breaches to form on their own."

The thing in her arms shifted slightly. In the dark, it was hard to tell, but Cole thought he saw a light coming from it.

"Who comes up with these names?" he wondered aloud, turning his attention back to the girl. "They all sound like consonants thrown together."

"The Triskaidekahedron are the avant-garde of the Forsaken King," she explained, taking a few bold steps toward him. "They created the Nihilgeister out of humanity's lost faith and broken dreams."

It took a moment, but Cole worked it out. "Thirteen faces," he said. "The name means 'thirteen faces', and you're saying they created this?"

Mary Alice shrugged at the question. "They do all kinds of things. I stopped caring after she left me."

In answer, a sigil appeared on her forehead: the emblem of the Willow tree. "You have the sign of the Willow constellation," Cole noted. "And the Offworld Outlaw had the sign of the Elder tree. The Triskaidekahedron must use the thirteen symbols of the Faerie zodiac as markers for all of you."

"To keep us from dying," Mary Alice affirmed. "We weren't sure if it would be enough after the station closed down. It was how we were born, after all."

"But you just said the sigils keep you alive," he countered. "Why bother?"

In answer, the sigil on her head flickered. "She left me many years ago to pursue her own ends," Mary Alice said, stroking the thing in her arms tenderly. "Since then, I can't control my forms. The shifts come at random, making me attack the others. They were afraid that if the station closed down, I might fade away. There was no way to be sure that my sigil would keep me alive."

The shock must have been evident on his face. "They did it to try and save you," he said.

Mary Alice scoffed. "Some, I'm sure, just wanted revenge. I don't blame them for that much, but it was a really stupid plan. Now that the Nihilgeister is like this, we'll have to start over from scratch."

The blob of dark flesh in her arms pulsated, and Cole saw small tendrils wave up into the air at Mary Alice's face, as if enticing her to come closer.

"It's hungry," she said, frowning down at it. "I doubt there's enough strength for the others to travel back here once I leave, so I guess this means you're off the hook for now. Once the Nihilgeister is powerful enough to help them move through space again, though, they'll be coming for you."

Cole raised Jabberwock in reply. "I'll be ready."

Something dawned on him as Mary Alice moved to leave. "Why did you stick around to talk to me?" he asked.

Mary Alice paused. "I suppose it amused me," she said, shrugging. "Things used to not make sense to me after she left. Now that she's come back, though, my head is clearer. I've started to notice things that didn't add up before. Even if you're not, it will still be fun to watch."

"Who is she?" Cole demanded as Mary Alice faded from sight. "I saw twelve shadows about a month ago. Who is the thirteenth?"

But Mary Alice was already gone. Cole's shoulders sagged as he felt the weight of the past hour crash down on him. Ash flew into the air as police cars rushed onto the scene, lights blazing. He was naked, covered in ash from head to toe, and Staffelbach was still out like a light.

It was going to take a while before anyone made sense out of what had happened. Cole hoped and prayed Joss was in a forgiving mood once he heard all of it.

PARAMEDICS were on the scene as well. Cole passed Staffelbach off to one as they approached, hoping he was doing the right thing now that the officer's humanity was in question. Some of the cops stopped short of approaching him. Cole held his badge up to ensure they didn't simply shoot him once the people tending to Staffelbach were clear.

The crowd of policemen parted as a tall figure shoved a path through. Cole smiled on reflex as Joss reached the clearing with Rainette and Marcel in tow.

Rainette shielded her eyes the moment she saw Cole was having a slight case of public nudity. Joss merely gave Cole an odd look and said nothing as the sidhe approached.

"Couldn't have warned us ahead of time, could you?" Rainette grumbled.

"As a witch," Cole reminded her, "you should be above such things as embarrassment over the nude male form."

"I was raised Catholic," she replied defensively. "Some things don't rub off as fast as others."

Rainette paused and then peeked out from under the hand concealing her gaze. "Why are you wearing boots?" she asked. "You're naked and wearing boots. Is this some fey thing I'm not aware of?"

"The boots were the only thing that survived," he explained to everyone there. "And I don't much like how the concrete scratches the undersides of my feet. Plus, I was already having to carry Staffelbach around. Speaking of which…."

Cole turned to Joss. "There are other people unconscious in those ash piles. You might want to inform the paramedics. I don't think they're injured, but they probably need to be looked over."

The other officers on-site were already moving tentatively toward the ash-strewn region of the street. Joss motioned for the man in charge and passed the information on to him while Cole stood by calmly. One of the medics kept glancing toward him, vainly trying to act as though she wasn't finding him a distraction. Once Joss was finished, he seized Cole by the bicep and pulled him off to the side.

"Let's get you some clothes on," Joss insisted.

"There are things I need to tell you first," Cole replied, moving much slower than his lover. "A lot happened in the last couple of hours."

"I can see that for myself," the inspector responded wryly. "But you're distracting people. This is a crime scene, and I want everyone here to stay focused on their job. You making people all starry-eyed with your junk hanging out like it is won't help matters."

Cole grinned. "Imagine how much more shocked they'd be if you pulled out yours."

Joss shook his head at the thought, which only made Cole's grin widen. As they reached the edge of the area where the disaster had taken place, Cole stopped.

"My car was parked somewhere over there," he said, pointing back to the parking lot in front of the apartment complex. Or, to be exact, what was left of it. Now that he was out of the crowd, Cole could see a piece of the building lying on top of several crushed vehicles in the space where it had been.

"It isn't," Joss assured him, leading them in the opposite direction. "We found it outside the Order storage facility. It pulled up just as we were getting ready to leave, but no one was driving. It seemed pretty intent on my getting inside, so I told Rainette and Marcel to follow. Corhagen went back with Willhiem. On the way here, we overheard reports of "something" attacking an apartment complex near Queens, and an explosion. I honestly wasn't sure if you would be here."

Sure enough, the car was in the street with the door open. Cole climbed into the backseat without a word and motioned for Joss to follow. Once they were inside, the door shut on its own, and the lights inside went out. Cole reached for Joss and pulled him close.

"Hold me," he insisted.

Joss frowned.

"Just hold me a moment," Cole insisted. "I need this right now. We can go back to fighting bad guys in a minute. No one is watching right now, so just please put your arms around me."

Joss's frown was visible in the low light, but he did as Cole asked. Cole laid his head on Joss's chest and listened as the steady drumbeat coming from inside of the man's body lulled some of his fears. Joss wrapped his arms around Cole in response and pulled him close.

"What happened?" he asked.

Cole took a deep breath. "After Staffelbach changed clothes, I wanted to pay a visit to the actor that plays Captain Sharky. When we got here, his apartment had just been violated by people trying to collect money from him. It seems he has debts, and moved here as a temporary measure until he could flee the island. Before we could get him out, the Nihilgeister attacked."

"What?"

"Nihilgeister," Cole repeated. "It is what the girl called it, anyway. She said the creature was made out of broken dreams and lost hope by the Triskaidekahedron."

Joss shook his head. "Okay, slow down and go back a couple of paces so I can catch up."

"My apologies," Cole said, lifting up a little to meet his lover's eyes. "As I said, it was an eventful few hours."

Joss's gaze drifted toward the rear window, where more police cars were gathering around the ash and pieces of destroyed building.

"I never doubted that much to begin with."

"As I was saying," Cole resumed, "the Nihilgeister attacked. It tore the building apart in a manner of seconds. Staffelbach and the old Neezer man were taken before it grabbed me. After that...."

Cole's voice broke. "After that," he repeated, "I lost Bandersnatch and Jabberwock. Staffelbach was trying to fight the Nihilgeister off with his club."

"Is he going to be all right?"

"I hope so," Cole answered.

Cole snuggled deeper into Joss's embrace. "The sidhe seek out comfort in another's touch when they are under stress," he explained.

"I remember," Joss said, pulling Cole tighter to him. "You still haven't explained the part about the girl, or the Tricksaforkidswhatever...."

"Triskaidekahedron."

"Whatever," Joss grumbled. "Go on, then."

Cole opened his mouth, thought through what he was about to say, then snapped it shut again. No matter how he tried to put it, there was no way this was going to end well.

"I kissed Staffelbach."

Joss stared at Cole blankly. "Um, sorry. What?"

Cole moved away slightly. "I felt the Goddess move. She offered to help me save them. At the time, I did not understand what she meant."

"Meant by what?" Joss asked, still confused.

"She said that the price would not be mine to pay," Cole said, not looking Joss's way. "She was referring to our relationship."

Joss's brow wrinkled in confusion.

"To save Staffelbach, I had to transfer the power she gave me from myself to him," Cole explained, meeting Joss's stare now. "By kissing him."

"And?" A light went on in Joss's eyes. "You thought that meant we were breaking up?"

"I was under the impression that the term 'relationship' implies monogamy," Cole replied in a slightly harsher tone. "And that outside interaction is grounds for immediate termination."

Joss began to snicker. "Not when someone's life is at stake, Cole!"

Cole was less than amused. "Forgive me, then. I'll make a mental note."

Joss reached out in response and dragged Cole over to him. Though reluctant, the sidhe quickly gave in, for the sensation of having Joss's arms around him again was too good to pass up.

"Are you all right?" Joss insisted. "That's my biggest concern."

Cole shrugged. "Fey relations are different from humans. What I did would have been considered necessary for my survival, and not a social taboo. I wasn't sure how you would react to it, though, since another human was involved."

Joss said nothing but continued to chuckle as he held onto Cole tightly. Soon, the inspector released him so Cole could sit back up on the seat.

"We still need to get you some clothes," he said. "If you're sure everything is all right, why don't you run home, get cleaned up, then meet up back at the station? Unless you want the paramedics to look you over?"

Cole shook his head. "There is little they would be able to do for me," he reminded him. "Though our bodies might look the same, we are very different beneath the surface. Anything they gave me would most likely kill me, or have little to no effect at all. I don't appear to be injured, so I'll take my leave now."

Joss gave Cole a quick kiss before reaching for the door handle. "I'll give the word to clear a path for you so you can get out."

Cole nodded, then climbed into the driver's seat and started the car. The wild chariot purred warmly in response to his hands caressing the wheel, and Cole felt the seat beneath him shift to a more comfortable position.

"Thank you," he whispered. "My dear friend."

THE shower made him feel better. Mal whipped up something for him to munch on while the water washed away any traces of the creature's remains, as well as the lingering guilt. Cole had not experienced such a thing over sexual encounters in so long, it felt alien now to be contemplating it as he stood with his legs apart under the showerheads. It felt so good to be clean.

Yet, as the water shut off of the sithen's own accord, he could not make himself feel bad about the encounter itself. Only, rather, over how well Joss had taken it, and what it meant for their future together. That was assuming, of course, they actually had one. Cole remained unconvinced, as he toweled off, that what he shared with Joss could last. The sidhe were cynical by their nature, and Cole had experienced many failed promises in his time amongst humanity.

The more he mulled it over, the less likely it felt he had anything to look forward to besides heartbreak. It occurred to Cole that perhaps the best thing for them both would be to end it now before they crushed one another.

Then he thought of Joss's face in the car and couldn't bring himself to do it. What other mortal would have accepted things so easily?

After putting on some fresh clothes and eating his dinner, Cole searched for an alternative to his lost gun holster. He had treasured the other before its destruction at the hands of the Nihilgeister. It had been a custom job, and an expensive one at that. Mal noticed him looking around his closet and approached tentatively.

"I sense something is amiss," he said. "Misplaced your spare Nintendo controller?"

"My holster was destroyed today by a tentacle monster."

Mal blinked once. "I have to say," he stated, "I never expected to hear that statement from you so soon after moving here. What brought this on?"

"It's a very long story," Cole replied, growing very frustrated. "You'd think with all the junk I've accumulated, there would be a spare one in here somewhere."

"Indeed," Mal remarked. "Out of curiosity, what made you collect all this stuff over the years? I can't imagine you needing it often enough for it to matter, and all of it can't hold sentimental value."

"It doesn't," Cole said simply. "I figured some of it might be worth money at one point later on. Humans place strange value on old junk. That's the whole reason eBay still exists."

"I'm aware of that," said Mal, nodding. "You are aware, though, that I could simply create a new holster for your guns and blade weapon, right?"

Cole went perfectly still. "I'm sorry?"

Mal pointed down at the floor near Cole's feet. A holster, the exact same in every detail as the one he'd lost, was lying there, as if waiting for Cole to pick it up. Cole frowned as he lifted it up in his hands, testing for any slight difference in weight. There was none.

"The other one was made out of animal hide," Mal reminded him in a restrained tone. "A substance very common in nature. Will there be anything else?"

"Thank you," Cole said curtly as he slipped the holster around him. "That'll do."

The garage door was rising up on its own when he got there. Cole stopped short as he spotted Joss, of all people, standing at the mouth warily, as though unsure of what he was seeing. The car flashed its lights in reply, as though waving hello.

Joss stared at Cole as well. "'The squad car I was riding in broke down about a block away from here," he said, looking around at the inside of the garage. "For some reason, my cell phone had died. I was on my way to find a payphone when I saw the garage door. I was sure it was just a coincidence, but then the door opened and your car was inside."

"Where is here this time?" Cole asked curiously.

"A couple of miles from the precinct," Joss said, stepping inside. "I guess I should be thankful for coincidences, huh?"

"There are no coincidences," Cole countered, opening the passenger door for him. "Only the illusion of such things. Someone was kind enough to arrange things for us."

"I wonder who?" asked Joss as he buckled himself in.

"I wonder why," Cole said flatly before starting the car.

Traffic was remarkably thin as they drove the remainder of the way in silence. Cole let Joss borrow his phone so he could have someone tow his vehicle. As they pulled into the parking garage, Cole glanced toward his lover and let go of the wheel with one hand to place over his.

"Thank you for what you said before," he whispered softly.

"Said what?" Joss asked, laying the phone in the cup holder between them. "Refresh?"

"In the car earlier," Cole said. "Thank you."

Joss frowned. "Ain't no big thing. It's not like I caught you with a stripper."

Cole nodded. "Understood, then," he said, swinging into an empty space. "No strippers allowed."

Joss was laughing as they both got out. "Well, not without inviting me along. Why were you so worried about how I would react?"

Cole stopped and thought the question over. "I've had experiences with human relationships in the past," he admitted. "They always ended badly for me. I wasn't sure if this time would be different."

Joss came over to where Cole was standing between two parked cars. Checking to make sure the coast was clear, he placed a hand on Cole's shoulder and squeezed.

"I'm not going anywhere," he assured him.

"I know," Cole said breathlessly. "I just wish I could make myself believe it. The problem with being immortal is you have a long time to rake up bad moments."

The smile on Joss's face was encouraging.

"I wish I could hold you right now," Cole said earnestly.

Joss removed his hand from Cole's shoulder as a car came near them.

"Later," Joss promised. "We live together now, remember?"

Cole smiled. "Very much so. I shall have to remind you later on."

"Of what?" the inspector asked as they continued along, matching each other's footsteps.

Cole smiled and leaned in toward Joss's frame as discreetly as possible. "Of everything," he whispered invitingly. "Including how much I think I'm in love with you."

The heat between them was tangible enough that the glass fogged over as Vallimun reached for the door handle. "I look forward to it," said Joss in a heated voice. "I have a few things to remind you about later too."

No one said hello to them as they made their way to Joss's office. The silence and the odd glance here and there was enough to let Cole know word was catching on. He smiled to himself at the thought of how he might respond to accusations, and almost didn't stop when someone called out their names one after the other.

Cole looked around. "What?"

Joss was pointing to someone Cole didn't recognize, sitting behind a desk. "You've got a visitor," the man said as they approached. "She's been waiting here most of the afternoon."

"She?" Cole looked over at Joss. "Were you expecting someone?"

"She asked for you by name, MacColewyn," said the officer whose nameplate read Thorton, giving his shaggy brown hair a toss. "When I said you were out, she asked for an Inspector Vallimun."

Cole's eyes followed to where Thorton's finger was pointing. A little girl, roughly eight years or so old, was sitting in a chair up against the wall by herself, glancing around nervously every few seconds. Cole noticed she was holding her school bag closely, and had a lunch box with her. He assumed she had come here straight from school, meaning she had indeed been waiting for a while. It wasn't until he approached her that Cole realized how familiar she looked.

Joss kept a couple of paces back so as not to shock her. Cole, however, settled into the seat to her right. "Special Detective MacColewyn," he said, holding his badge up. "You wanted to see me?"

The girl frowned, gave his badge a skeptical stare, then looked Cole in the face. "You're much older up close," she said, moving in a little closer. "Stephanie said you would be younger."

It was Cole's turn to frown. "Do I know a Stephanie?"

In answer, the girl reached into her bag, pulling out a small photograph of her and another young girl her age wearing thick gloves.

"Stephanie said that I should talk to you," the girl explained. "She said that if anything happened, I should ask for a man named Tuulois MacColewyn."

The other girl standing next to her in the picture was looking away from the camera nervously, as though trying to will herself from being photographed. Something about the gloves she wore made Cole think he had seen her before, as well. Handing the picture back, he waited while Joss moved in closer to have a look at it.

"Well, you managed to find me," Cole said. "And you have me at a disadvantage by knowing my name while I don't know yours."

"Melissa," she answered immediately. "I was hoping you would help me find Stephanie. She said that I might have to pay you, but if you were a cop like everyone said, you would do it for free."

Joss looked over the photograph at him. "How did you manage to find me, Melissa?" Cole asked her.

"Google," she said at once. "You have a funny name, so I figured there couldn't be many of you in the Manhattan phone book. Stephanie was the one who told me your name, though."

Cole looked over the girl's head at Joss now. "Inspector Vallimun, would it be all right if Melissa and I continued our conversation in your office?"

"That would probably be best," said the inspector. "Miss Melissa, if you would follow us both, please?"

The girl called Melissa followed them without a word. Joss kept a slightly faster pace so they stayed out of earshot. Glancing back, Cole noticed the girl seemed too intrigued by the activity going on around her to pay them too much attention.

"What do you think?" Joss asked in a low voice.

"Human," Cole assured him. "If she's wearing a husk, it's a very convincing one."

"Could she have been sent by someone?"

Cole glanced back again. "It is possible," he said. "Though, if she were around any type of fey, the smell should have rubbed off on her. If she was glamoured into coming here, there would be signs of it. It looks as though the girl is in her right state of mind."

"Good," said Joss. "Then answer me this question: How does she know you?"

"I don't believe she does," Cole corrected him as they turned a corner together. "It sounds as though this Stephanie girl is the one who sent her. So far, my guess is Stephanie was a fey I helped at some point before I became a cop. That would explain the part about her worrying whether she needed to pay me or not."

"That's a relief," Joss muttered as they reached the stairs. "At least I won't have to arrest the girl for soliciting my boyfriend."

Cole smirked. "I'm really starting to like that word."

Melissa showed no hesitation at the doorway. Cole could feel the anxiety coming off her body in waves as he shut the door behind them.

"Relax," he said. "You came to find me, remember?"

Melissa frowned but then nodded. "Stephanie said that you helped her family a couple of years ago. After her parents died, she told me that something had killed them, and that she thought she was being followed. She made me swear to look for a policeman named Tuulois MacColewyn if anything ever happened to her, because he would be the only one who could find her."

"Offhand," Joss interrupted, looking at Cole, "do you remember Stephanie's family?"

"Not really," said Cole. "I was hired by a number of fe… people before I became a cop."

"You look like how she said you'd be," Melisa went on. "Tall, long white hair, and beautiful."

Joss smiled. "Beautiful, huh?"

Melissa looked at him as she nodded seriously. "Stephanie told me you would probably be wearing black clothes, and would be the most beautiful man I could ever hope to meet. I thought she was making that part up."

Cole couldn't resist. "And now?"

Melissa turned back to him. "It's like there are lights shining all around you, even when there shouldn't be. He does that, too, kind of."

Melissa pointed to Joss, but kept her eyes focused squarely on Cole. "I found your name in the New York City Police Department registry, but it didn't list your address. Then I saw you at the TV station and knew it must be you."

Something clicked into place. "Outside," Cole said, studying her face closely. "You were watching me outside the TV studio."

Melissa nodded. "I wanted to come talk to you, but the teacher we were with wouldn't let me. I decided I'd ask someone which precinct you were from and come speak to you here. The man at the desk told me you were out, though."

"Do your parents know you're here?" Joss interrupted again.

Melissa met his stare without flinching. "A friend at school told me she would cover for me," she explained, as though talking about the weather. "Stephanie didn't have a lot of friends at school. I was one of the only ones who would talk to her. After she disappeared, Christa, the girl who sits next to me in class, told me she felt bad about how mean she was to us, so I asked her to cover for me while I went to talk to the police."

"Clever," Cole acknowledged, ignoring the glare it earned him from Joss. "Tell me about your friend Stephanie. Why did she think someone was after her?"

Melissa reached into her bag again and pulled out the same photo from before. This time, however, she held it in her hands for a moment, as if drawing strength from it.

"Stephanie was my best friend," she explained softly. "We used to walk to school together. She was born with webbed hands and feet, so the other kids at school made fun of her. I was the only one who stood up to them. At the beginning of this year, her parents were killed in a boating accident, but Stephanie insisted something bad had happened to them. They were terrific swimmers, she said, especially her mom, and would have just swum to shore."

"Webbed hands," Cole whispered.

Melissa held one hand up and pointed at the space between her fingers. "Like, right here," she said. "She had skin stretched out in the places between her fingers, kind of like how a duck's foot looks. I always thought they would make me swim better, since I can't swim all that good."

"So, your friend's parents drowned," Joss said, scratching down several notes on a pad. "What happened afterward that made Stephanie think someone was after her?"

"She wouldn't say, exactly," Melissa replied, looking anxious now. "But she was scared all the time, and never wanted to be alone. I would catch her looking over her shoulder like she had heard something when we walked home from school. She barely ate anything during lunch."

"When did she disappear?"

Cole watched the color drain out of Melissa's face. "It was on a Monday," she said quietly. "About a month ago, maybe more. I was going to wait for her by the bus stop. Stephanie was running late, and I almost left without her, but then I spotted her running down the sidewalk. I was glad to see her, but then I saw how scared she looked. It didn't look like she was running because she was late. It looked like she was scared. Really, really scared."

Melissa paused to swallow. "She was waving at me, trying to get my attention. I looked around to see if there was someone nearby who could help. The bus stop isn't far from our school. We don't meet there to take the bus. Our parents just wanted us to get together at a place that was out in the open. Sometimes, there's a crossing guard nearby."

Melissa had to stop again and collect herself. "I turned my back for maybe a second. When I looked around, she was gone. She shouldn't have disappeared that way, so I knew something had to be wrong. I ran down the street to where I'd last seen her. Off to the side, there was this alleyway that curved off like an L-shape farther down. I was scared to go down it, but then I heard Stephanie scream. When I got to the bend in the alley, I found this."

Reaching into her bag yet again, Melissa pulled out a small woolen cap. "It was Stephanie's," she explained. "Her mother made her wear it every day during the winter. She made one for me too, so we would match. Like sisters."

Cole accepted the cap from her and held it close to his face. Breathing in, he thought he caught a whiff of something faint, something distinctly not human.

"Selkie," he said very quietly.

Joss cleared his throat warningly. "Is that the last time you ever saw Stephanie?" he asked, getting her attention.

Melissa nodded. "Did you ever tell anyone about what you saw?" he pressed.

"I told my parents," she said. "When they found out, I was told not to say anything to anyone about it. After I saw him at the TV station, though, I knew I had to do something."

"We're glad you did," Cole said, giving the woolen cap back to her. "Melissa, will you keep that cap in a safe place until later on?"

"I can hide it in a drawer under my bed," Melissa promised, slipping it back into her bag. "I was going to show it to my mom and dad, but after they didn't believe me, I decided to hide it there."

"Good," Cole told her. "Keep it in a safe place until you hear from us. We have to take care of something, but when this is over, we'd like to come and see you. I want you to show us where the alley is that Stephanie disappeared in."

"Does that mean you'll help?"

Joss stood up and walked around the desk. "I can't say much about it right now," he told her. "But you may have just given us a lead to a case we've been working on for a while now."

"For that," Cole added, squeezing her hand gently, "you have our thanks. I'm going to go see if we can't arrange for a patrol car to drop you off at your house."

"Can he drop me off at my classmate's house?" she asked reluctantly, getting out of the chair. "I'm supposed to be there right now, remember?"

Joss, as it turned out, was able to get Melissa a ride home over the phone in less than a minute. Once she was gone, both of them let out a very heavy sigh.

"You thought of the same thing I did," Cole stated unquestioningly.

"I did," Joss said. "Naryssa."

Naryssa Goodwynch. That had been the name she'd given to Cole during their first encounter. In a way, she was responsible for the Section's reforming. Naryssa's kidnapping of half-fey children and murder of their parents had been what convinced Vallimun that Section Thirteen was necessary.

Following their battle, Naryssa vanished along with her "children." The Section had been keeping an ear open, hoping to catch word that she'd returned. This was the first bite since January.

"She murdered their parents while they were out at sea," Cole surmised. "The irony must have been too great to resist. Then she waits, and has someone grab the girl afterward. If Stephanie hadn't told Melissa about me, she would have gotten away with it."

"We still have to find her," Joss reminded him. "Any idea where she would have hidden after I put that hole in her chest?"

"Spinner said something about a cabin," Cole said thoughtfully. "Though that could mean a lot of things. I had thought Naryssa would give up her mission after she almost died from that bazooka you fired at her, but it looks like she was only on hiatus."

"Thirteen children," Joss wondered. "Every thirteen years. I still don't understand that. Any new theories on why she holds to that pattern?"

Cole took in a deep breath. "As a matter of fact, I do, but I want to wait until the others get here before we get too deep into them. Plus, you still haven't filled me in on the situation with the Nihilgeister's remains."

"... SO THEY'RE going to claim the attack was the result of a gas line explosion," Joss finished. "Which is technically true, since the Nilliwhateverist did explode before we got there."

"New Yorkers are still more at ease over explosions than the idea of a giant knot of tentacles going for a stroll through Queens." Cole laughed. "I can't help but find that ironic."

"Don't be an asshole," Joss advised gently. "Were you in town when the towers came crashing down?"

"I was," Cole said grimly, pushing himself away from the wall. "That was before I met Corhagen. I called Katalina as soon as I found out, then made sure David was safe. That was before he built the castle on top of the skyscraper, believe it or not."

Joss looked at Cole. "He built a castle on top of a skyscraper *after* 9/11?"

"He probably meant it as a statement," Cole said. "Or a 'take that' at anyone else trying to invade."

"So you think the tulpas are working for those shadows you saw controlling the Whittaker kid?" Joss went on, sitting back down on his desk. "The...."

"Triskaidekahedron," Cole filled in. "The Thirteen Faces, if I'm translating it correctly. They were largely to blame for the incident on Staten Island, yes. Right now, I don't know why they wanted the Whittaker boy to work on those black rings, but it ties into a much bigger picture, I'm sure."

"Explain to me again about the zodiac."

Cole went over to where Joss was sitting and planted himself on a clear surface of the desk next to him. "In Faerie," he explained, "we have major constellations like people here do. Instead of twelve, though, we have thirteen. They are named after trees."

"And the tulpas were all marked with the rune of each constellation?"

"I only saw the Offworld Outlaw's," he corrected. "And the one called Mary Alice's, but I would risk saying they all carry the marks of the thirteen trees of Faerie."

"So, what does that mean?"

Cole thought back to the day on Staten Island when Whittaker had executed his plan. "I only saw twelve shadows in his mind," Cole said. "But they're called the Thirteen Faces. There are thirteen runes to symbolize the thirteen trees of the Faerie zodiac. That would imply a total of thirteen tulpas serving the Triskaidekahedron."

"Please, stop saying that," Joss begged. "The word is giving me a headache."

"You're just mad because you still can't pronounce it yet," Cole ribbed. "Try it with me again. You'll get the hang of it."

"No," Joss replied adamantly. "Back to those shadows. You said there are thirteen runes, and twelve shadows. So, what? One went missing."

"I would think so," said Cole. "Mary Alice said that 'she' was coming back. The shadows each have one tulpa to serve them, but one isn't there."

Joss thought for a moment hard. "Naryssa?"

"Perhaps," said Cole, though he sounded certain enough. "She started her agenda to murder the parents of half-fey children before the *Captain Sharky* show made the broadcast that inadvertently created the tulpas, but that could just mean she didn't break all ties with them, or was too injured to join the others in controlling Daniel Whittaker's mind."

"'She's coming back,'" Joss repeated. "We aren't prepared to tangle with her again so soon, and if you bring another army of the dead in, there will be too many questions for me to cover on my own."

"We knew it was going to come down to us against her eventually."

"I know." Joss pinched the bridge above his nose tightly in frustration. "I just thought we'd have more time to prepare. What are we going to do?"

"We're going to prepare as best we can," Cole said, before a knock at the door silenced them both.

"Come in," Joss said.

Rainette stuck her head through the opened crack. Behind her, Cole could see Marcel standing out in the hallway. Corhagen was somewhere off to the side out of sight, but Cole could still smell his aftershave drifting through.

"I knocked in case the two of you were… busy," Rainette said, entering. "Someone told me the two of you had been inside the office for a while now."

Neither of them said a word.

"I have some good news," Rainette went on as Corhagen entered behind Marcel, staring up at the ceiling as though riveted by it.

"Good news would be good right about now," Joss said. "I hope it's of the 'very good' variety."

"I spoke with my coven after we left the site," Rainette said. "My friend who knows about tulpas was able to work out a way to keep them sealed up inside that pocket of space indefinitely."

"It may not work," Cole warned. "The tulpas were using that creature, the Nihilgeister, to manufacture breaches in space so they could pass back and forth freely."

Rainette stared at Cole. "Nilly-what?"

"Never mind," Joss interrupted. "Even if it's only a temporary measure, let's hear it. It might buy us some time."

"The spell is pretty simple," Rainette went on. "Minus one major issue. Someone has to cast it from the other side, meaning we have to actually get there, then do the ritual and leave before the region is sealed off permanently."

"The Shadewater coven insisted this was the most effective way," Marcel added. "I made sure to ask."

"I volunteered," Rainette admitted tentatively. "Cobalt was nervous about handing this kind of information over to someone outside of the coven. He's had a few bad experiences with outsiders before."

"If we could locate an entry point into that space," Cole said, giving Joss a hopeful look, "it would cut the Triskaidekahedron off from their support, at least for a little while. That should weaken Naryssa."

"Trix-are-for-who?" Rainette interjected.

"I don't like it," Joss said, ignoring her. "It sounds too risky."

"It is," Marcel agreed.

"And yet," Cole pointed out. "It may be our only option right now."

"Assuming we can find another entry into that space to begin with," Joss said. "Still, you aren't wrong, even though I'm not happy about it."

Corhagen, who had been awfully quiet up until this point, spoke up. "What's the triskydeccahydrant?"

Cole rolled his eyes.

"Everyone, get comfortable," Joss instructed. "We've got some explaining to do."

AS ALWAYS, the hospital smelled of fluids, chemicals, and cloth soaked in human waste. Cole stood near the door, watching closely in case someone recognized him. It wasn't the same hospital he'd taken Joss out of. That one, thank Consort, had been low on security. Breaking his lover out so they could ask Danu to regrow his arm would have been much harder if Joss had been kept in this place. Nevertheless, Cole felt he shouldn't take chances by letting his guard drop.

Staffelbach's room was just a few steps away. The others waited for their turn to go in while Joss checked up on their boy. Cole wondered if Staffelbach would remember their kiss, and whether it was considered inappropriate to not behave awkwardly around him. At times like this, he wished he'd paid more attention to human social norms.

Joss emerged a moment later, looking relieved. "He's fine," he said. "He just needs a little more rest. The doctors haven't found anything wrong, but they want to keep checking."

"Why are they so concerned?" Marcel asked, giving Rainette a light squeeze as she went in.

"Because Staffelbach was involved in an explosion," Joss pointed out. "Even though they don't know what really happened, someone coming out of anything like that with little to no injuries is odd. The doctors want to know why he's suffering from severe exhaustion, but showing no signs of internal injuries or burns."

Joss looked at Cole then. "You said he went through some kind of transformation when the thing attacked you both. Will they be able to detect it?"

Cole paused. "It is possible," he replied after a moment's thought. "I'm not sure what the limitations are concerning human medical knowledge, or how it relates to what happened to Staffelbach. We still don't know what the change actually means, after all."

Joss frowned. "I hate not knowing," he growled.

"As do we all," Marcel added. "In the end, however, we have much bigger problems to attend to."

"Right," said Joss, sighing. "Those tulpas, and getting inside their stronghold."

"I was actually referring to our visitor," Marcel corrected, pointing past Joss at Willhiem, who was coming up fast from the opposite end of the hall.

"Marvelous," Cole hissed out between his teeth.

"I concur," said the ogre, before Willhiem came within earshot.

"Agent Willhiem," Joss stated flatly, taking command. "What brings you here?"

"The injured officer," Willhiem answered curtly, nodding to the group as a whole. "And the matter of Section Thirteen's plan to enter a region of unidentified space to settle the matter of the Captain Sharky case."

"We have no official plan to do anything regarding the tulpas just yet," Joss corrected. "Whatever intel the Order is going by, it's incorrect."

"Not anymore," Willhiem said, drawing out a set of papers from his coat. "The Order has selected four members of Section Thirteen to accompany me and a team of specialists to enter the region of space designated as 'Square One' in an attempt to magically seal the area off from our domain forever."

Joss was busy flipping through the file. "My name is on here," he noted.

"Of course," Willhiem replied, as though that should have been obvious. "You know your men best, and will be there to help advise the operation."

"I see mine on there," Cole noted. "Marcel and Rainette's, also."

"A strong ogre and a talented witch are good tools to have when planning an infiltration mission," Willhiem insisted. "Your talents, Detective MacColewyn, speak for themselves. I need not explain why your presence is so necessary."

"Why not Corhagen?" Joss asked. "I don't see him in this file."

"The decision was made to keep Detective Corhagen out of this mission," Willhiem said. "I'm sure his skills as an investigator speak highly of him as well, but this mission will be considerably dangerous, and require those possessing more unusual talents."

Cole almost looked toward Joss when Willhiem said this.

"That makes sense," Joss said, passing the folder back to him. "I don't suppose we have a say in this?"

"You could refuse." Willhiem smiled when he said this. "If you so chose to."

"We aren't," Joss reassured him. "I just wanted to ask. When will the mission begin?"

"In three hours." Willhiem backed away as he spoke. "Make sure you have prepared yourselves. I daresay this will not be a pleasant journey."

"Undoubtedly," Marcel muttered.

Cole turned sharply to the left as a figure in the distance disappeared into an open elevator. The air in the hallway had shifted slightly thanks to a draft, bringing with it a familiar scent.

"Hagen?" he breathed out.

Cole was moving down the hall before the others had time to realize he had moved. The elevator doors were already closed when he reached them. Cole sniffed the air again, but nothing lingered but the stale remains of hospital air.

"Something the matter, Detective?" Willhiem asked, watching closely from far back.

"I thought I smelled something," Cole said, wandering back toward the others calmly. "But it turns out I was mistaken, apparently."

"Interesting," said Willhiem as Cole rejoined the others. "Your sense of smell truly is as keen as reports have said. Having you on this mission will be a great asset to the Order."

"In regards to the Order," Cole replied curtly, "you all can kindly suck on my fat, salty sidhe nuts!"

Willhiem was left behind, caught dead in his tracks. "I see," he mumbled, after picking his jaw up off the floor. "Did you mean all at once, because the Order is quite large."

"You can all form a line," Cole said, taking his place beside Joss. "I'll wait."

IN THE end, the doctors agreed to release Staffelbach after one more night in observation. None of them sounded particularly keen to let him go. They were all undoubtedly fascinated with his miraculous survival of the Queens explosion that was now making headlines. Thankfully, Staffelbach's name had been kept out of circulation. All the news had to say was that police and medics were on the scene in minutes. The chief seemed happy that the NYPD was getting some positive press coverage for a change, which meant the Section wouldn't be crucified.

Cole could have cared less what that balding, fat ass cared about.

He and Joss went home as soon as they were assured that Staffelbach would be released the following morning. Cole kept his nose sharp as they went back to his car in the hospital garage, but nothing out of the ordinary came through the wind this time.

The two of them went straight to Joss's bedroom as soon as the car was parked. Mal was given instructions to serve dinner to them there, and to knock first before entering. As the door to Joss's chamber slammed shut, Cole lifted the big man up into his arms and held him tightly, breathing in his scent as Joss did his best to strip out of his clothes in a timely manner.

The entire room had been decorated while they were gone. "I guess Mal took the liberty of unpacking for you," Cole noted as Joss bared his chest.

"Good for him," Joss said, going for his buckle next. "I didn't really want to unpack all that stuff by myself, after all."

The most noticeable thing was Joss's computer on a brand-new desk in the corner. The screen had been turned on, showing a hand-drawn desktop image of two young women caressing each other.

"I like," Cole approved, setting Joss down on the bed so he could help with the buckle.

"We can't take our time," Joss grunted, sliding the belt out of the loops with a loud snap. "Just a couple of hours before we have to be at the meeting place, but if we're going in, I want to do this first."

Cole kissed Joss deeply, savoring the feel of their mouths pressed so tightly together. Before Joss could pull him closer, however, he moved away.

"I want to say something first," Cole said. "Given what we're about to do."

Joss frowned. "Okay, but can't it wait until later?"

Cole shook his head. "No," he insisted. "This, I've been wanting to say for a while."

Taking Joss by the hand, he led him to stretch out on the bed with his head resting against one of the thick, plush pillows laid out for him. Giving his hand a squeeze, Cole freed himself from his lover's grip and drew back a little.

"In some human circles," Cole began, "I was unfaithful to you today, but you didn't hold it against me."

Joss frowned. "Cole," he said, looking frustrated. "That isn't the same thing. I don't think you understand human behavior the way you think you do. Not everyone thinks or feels the same way."

"Regardless," Cole insisted. "You didn't hold it against me. I've thought about this before, and I want to do something special for you. I've been thinking about what I could do, but nothing seemed to fit. What I want to do might sound silly, and if you're not comfortable with it, I'll understand."

Joss continued to frown but didn't object. "Stay there," Cole said, crawling over Joss's feet as he left the bed's surface. "I need to get something first."

Joss watched as Cole ducked out of the room and took off down the hall toward his own room. A few minutes later, he returned with a black brimmed hat in hand. Joss had taken the liberty of removing his pants and socks during this time, convinced he wouldn't be needing them. Seeing this, Cole smirked before heading over to Joss's computer. A few minutes later, he was bringing up a web page and typing something in. While it loaded, Cole turned back around in the swivel chair to face him again.

"Something I never told you," Cole began again, "or a lot of other people, I suppose, was that I used to dance while I was down in Florida."

Joss nodded. "I can kind of see you dancing on stage."

"Not on a stage," Cole corrected. "I wasn't part of a theater troupe. I used to dance for money in bars occasionally, during the sixties."

The look on Joss's face made him smile. "There were places under the radar, as some people call it, where men could go looking for other men. One or two of these places would have party nights where young boys could make money by dancing in their underwear. The events were held on different days so the police wouldn't catch on."

"I'd hate to have been one of those cops," Joss mused.

"Quite a number of cops during that time hated being 'one of those cops'," Cole said pointedly. "It might surprise you to learn just how many patrons of those bars were officers of the law."

Cole turned around to check the status of his load. "I was living in a commune with what you would call hippies at the time," he went on, turning the hat back and forth in his hands. "They didn't always have money, so I would help by going into town and dancing for cash. The patrons of the bar loved me the most. It got to where the owner would arrange for a special night where I danced and no one else. During that time, no one in the commune went hungry."

The first few notes of a song began playing. Cole whirled around and paused the player before it could continue. "I haven't danced in years," he said. "After I left the commune, things became hectic, and I found other means of supporting myself. I haven't danced for anyone since then, but if you would be willing, I would like to dance for you."

Standing up, Cole slipped the hat down over his head. "We don't know what's going to happen in a few hours," he stated. "Before anything else, I'd like to give you something I haven't given to anyone in private since I left Florida. What do you say?"

Joss blinked, then nodded for Cole to start.

Turning around, Cole struck the space bar on the keyboard so that the song would play again. The opening bars of Joe Cocker's version of "You Can Leave Your Hat On" blared through the speakers as Joss rose up off the bed to sit on the edge. Cole moved toward him, moving his body back and forth like a pine tree swaying in the breeze.

When he reached where Joss was sitting, Cole turned around sharply, ducked down, and slowly moved his body up against his lover, paying close attention in particular to the huge lump concealed by the pair of tight white underwear he wore. Grabbing the lower half of his shirt in a fist, Cole took his hat off in one sweep and yanked the shirt up over his head. Once he was free of it, the hat went back into place. Grinding his hips into Joss's package, which was growing at a rapid rate by this point, Cole took the shirt into both hands and twisted it like a rope.

Squatting down between Joss's spread legs, he threw the shirt around the back of his love's neck, using it like a rope to pull the man down toward him. Before their mouths touched, Cole pulled the shirt away and slipped out of his reach. Only a second later, he was back between Joss's legs, pushing his hips harder into the swollen lump of man sausage there.

"Rule one," Cole whispered as the song continued to play. "I can touch you. You can't touch me."

In response, Joss reached up to grab hold of Cole, but he was quickly out of reach again. "Rule two," Cole continued, shoving Joss back onto the bed. "Don't forget rule one!"

Joss gripped the bedsheets in his hands as Cole maneuvered himself until he was straddling Joss like an unbridled horse. Joss was almost completely erect now. The fabric of his drawers was stretched to the hilt. Seeing this, Cole smiled and reached down to seize the obstructive garment with both hands. With one quick jerk, the material ripped in two. Cole held the two fistfuls of his prize high up overhead as he bucked and ground against Joss's engorged cock like a bronco rider.

Grabbing Joss's hands, Cole moved them until they were rubbing against his chest. "Rule three," he sighed breathlessly. "Exceptions to rules one and two can be made under the right circumstances."

Joss rose up off the bed, running his tongue up and down the cleft between Cole's chest muscles as his hands held his boyfriend in a vice grip. The two rocked back and forth together as Cole tried in vain to undo the buttons on his pants. Sensing the problem, Joss batted his hands away and drew back just enough to give him room to work. The last bit of clothing separating them was gone in a moment. Naked and sweating bullets, the two rubbed their bodies against one another as their mouths ate at each other like starved wolves.

Falling back against the bed, Joss didn't protest when Cole drew away. Turning around, he positioned himself facing Joss's feet, just above where the tower of fleshy magnificence that was Joss's manhood lay. Joss seized Cole's own fat, lengthy girth in one hand while bringing him closer to his face with the other arm. Joss sighed happily as Cole ran his tongue down the length of his nightstick before gulping down the sidhe's prick.

Together, the two lapped and sucked away at the heads of each other's shafts, grunting happily at the taste of precum oozing out between the folds of their piss slits. The heavy, fat orbs hanging down between Joss's legs swelled even further at Cole's ministrations, and upon seeing this, Cole reached out with one hand and carefully took each one in his grip. Cradling the precious flesh there, Cole gagged down over half of Joss's thick pipe in one lunge forward while giving the nut sack a hard tug. Joss grunted, but kept on going.

Below those low-hangers, Cole spotted the taint separating them from the treasured canal farther back. Lifting the sac up, Cole pushed forward until his tongue could reach the space there. With one hand, he gripped Joss's manhood and jacked up and down in long, slow strokes.

The moment his tongue touched it, Joss's body gave an involuntary jerk. "The *fuck*?" he swore, spitting Cole's cock out.

Cole grinned and licked at the place again. Joss hissed, but did nothing to suggest he was finding the experience unpleasant, so Cole disregarded any remaining hesitation. Like a cat with cream, he lapped at the spot above Joss's hole like a madman seeking salvation. Joss's teeth grazed Cole's cock as he pulled it back into his mouth again.

Moving in a furious rhythm, Joss sucked Cole's aching dick with the same fervor that Cole had used on his. New beads of sweat broke out over Joss's forehead.

"You've got to stop doing that," Joss gasped as Cole's dick popped free of his mouth. "I'm going to cum soon if you don't."

To answer, Cole shoved his tongue down into the flesh as hard as he could, licking all the way to Joss's ass. There, Cole dug his tongue into the puckered entrance and rolled it around before giving the nut sack still held firmly in his hand a good squeeze. He felt them empty, and moved quicker than a flash back up to Joss's cock, engulfing it down to the base in one swoop.

The monstrous testament to Joss's virility exploded down his throat. A torrent of his lover's seed flooded down to his belly, filling him up as nothing else on this plane could. Cole felt the man's strength beneath him fill him up, giving him all the joy and rapturous pleasure he had to offer the sidhe.

Joss's balls throbbed as they continued to pump load after load down Cole's throat. When the flood finally tapered off, Cole raised himself up off Joss's cudgel slowly, keeping his lips planted tightly around the shaft. When the head at last popped free, Joss gasped one finally time before falling back to the bed, utterly drained.

Cole was still hard and hadn't cum yet. Feebly, Joss tried to move his arm and bring Cole to his own climax, but Cole gently moved him away. Lying down at his lover's side, he took his aching cock in his own hands and pulled back and forth. Joss raised his head to watch as Cole's breathing increased. Bringing Joss to him, the two kissed as Cole's orgasm hit him, spraying cum into the air. The droplets of his seed splashed down into the thick brush of hair covering Joss's chest and stomach, sticking to it like dew on a summer tree's leaves.

A knock came at the door. "Dinner," Mal's voice called out from the other side. "Or should I come back later?"

Cole kissed Joss on the mouth as his lover scooped up some of his seed. Pulling away, Joss licked part of his fingers clean before offering some to Cole, who accepted the gift of his own seed graciously.

"I guess I can wait," Mal muttered as he stood waiting outside the door while the song started over. "It isn't as though I can say your dinner is getting cold. Good thing I thought ahead and made sandwiches."

"YOU'RE late!" Willhiem shouted.

Cole ignored the man, but Joss turned to face him as they walked past. "You said we had three hours."

"Change in plans," Willhiem replied. "We have to move in soon. The breach we found won't remain accessible for much longer, and the operation has to begin at midnight."

"Why midnight?"

Cole looked at his lover. "A time between times," he explained over the noise. "These kinds of things are preferably done at a point that is between. Ergo, midnight or noon."

They were standing in an alley. Farther ahead, men were drawing an elaborate circle on the ground where another alley intersected with their own, forming a crossroads of sorts. The air stank with the smell of salt water and sewage from the wharf less than a block away, another "tween place" for the spell to draw power on. The circle was nestled in a spot between two sets of buildings no matter which way one turned inside of it. The Order had done its homework.

Men and women scuttled about all around them, either helping with the formation of the circle, consecrating it with altar incense and blood, or fiddling with machinery. There was quite a bit of machinery to fiddle with, it turned out. The inside of one van parked in front of them consisted of nothing but computer screens and surveillance equipment. Outside the circle at each corner where the building ended, a metal cylinder had been placed. From what Cole could make out, it looked as though each one had been equipped with some sort of console. At least two Order personnel were busy tweaking them.

In the center of the circle, a spot that everyone was doing their best to avoid, Cole could make out a narrow fissure of light. The crack would jerk every so often, as though perturbed by something.

"Were you listening, Detective MacColewyn?" Willhiem demanded, interrupting his thoughts.

"No," Cole said. "I was busy trying to figure out what the cylinders were for."

Willhiem turned around at the mention of them, then smiled. "Stabilizers," he explained, smirking. "They help control the circle so that nothing comes out of the portal we're about to form that isn't supposed to. They also serve as a beacon to both aid us in finding the dimensional space we're looking for, and guide us back here."

"Why machines, though?"

"Is it important?" Joss asked him.

"It could be," said Cole. "But I'm more curious than anything. Most practitioners of the Craft prefer to keep their magic separated from their technology."

"Sufficiently advanced science always appears to be magic," Willhiem countered. "Isn't that always the saying?"

"I have no idea," Cole replied tartly.

"Let us through, goddamn it!"

All three men turned toward the sound of Rainette screaming. She and Marcel were standing just outside the barricade the Order had set up. Without a word, both Cole and Joss wandered over to where several men were attempting to restrain them.

"Stop it," Joss ordered without raising his voice. "These two are part of Section Thirteen."

The guard who turned around to face Joss was young. He also struck Cole as cocky, irresponsible, and a complete moron. The fact that he was Order material didn't surprise Cole in the slightest.

"The ogre doesn't have clearance," the young man insisted in a confident voice, before glancing over at Cole disdainfully. "Neither does he, really."

Cole had Bandersnatch drawn before the man could blink. "Just look down the hole," he hissed, barely above a whisper. "I'll send it to you via air mail."

"Detective MacColewyn!" Willhiem shouted in a tried voice, coming up from behind. "Restrain yourself, or you will be removed from this mission."

Cole put his gun away and turned to face Agent Willhiem. "An empty threat," he countered. "None of your men have experience in that pocket space. I'm the only active member of Section Thirteen left who's been there before. If you cut me out, there won't be anyone to serve as a guide."

"You aren't being cut out," Joss interrupted calmly, giving Willhiem a withering look. "Right, Agent Willhiem?"

Willhiem stiffened but didn't answer. Marcel and Rainette were still waiting on the outside of the barrier. Finally, after a moment, the IA agent motioned for the hotheaded guard to allow them through. Marcel didn't duck under the tape barrier, instead letting it snap in two across his chest.

"Hey!" the guard shouted.

Before he could finish, Marcel snatched the gun in the guard's hand away and held it up. Before the young man's eyes, the ogre bent the metal weapon clean in half. Taking the boy's hand, he slapped the now ruined piece back into his opened palm, then walked away.

"It's reassuring to see that the Order still recruits from the very bottom of the idiot barrel," Cole mused as the four of them headed back into the alley. "At least when this goes south and we wind up killing half of them in self-defense, it will be with the knowledge that we are only skimming the scum away from the top."

"Tell me about it," Rainette grumbled.

"May I have permission to bring home a few of their heads?" Marcel asked Joss hesitantly. "I am told empty skulls make excellent maracas."

"Feel free to."

The machines were alive with power. Practitioners stood on the outskirts of the circle, chanting together in unison. Cole kept his hands free and close to each gun. Rainette was holding a small pocket of corrosive water on the inside of her palm so no one would see it. Marcel simply stood beside her, as if waiting for a signal to begin tearing heads off. The fissure in the center of the circle spasmed and fluctuated, stretching out as if to grab hold of one of the chanting robed figures. The moment it touched the circle's edge, however, the barrier held it back.

The cylinders hummed in response to the magic building around them. As Cole felt the air crackle, the tops of each metal stand popped open. A blue light shone, bathing the crossroads in a florescent hue. A laser beam emitted from each of them then, striking the fissure from four different angles, making it go rigid.

From out of the fissure, the same blue hue emerged. The fissure began to stretch and distort as though in pain. Cole felt himself shudder as the barrier between worlds was ripped violently open. Everyone reacted as a white light flashed. Most shielded their eyes, but Cole felt his ears pop from the force of the hole being made.

When they looked up again, a distorted geometric shape was hanging in midair in the circle's center, where the fissure had been. The borders of it appeared to be lined with blue neon lights. Joss looked at it out of his one normal eye and blinked.

"If they didn't know we were coming before," Cole said resignedly, "they will now."

"Without a doubt," Marcel agreed.

The grunts went in first. Cole watched as several armed Order members in plain camo uniforms lined up one after the other in two lines. Two of the practitioners standing at the edge of the circle moved aside and waved their arms in synch with each other, forming a space to enter through. The men and women stepped across the barrier two at a time. Section Thirteen waited until everyone else who was going was already through before approaching.

Willhiem stepped out to stand with them. "Are you all prepared?"

"Born ready," Rainette assured him.

Drawing his gun, Cole turned and took aim at the nearest cylinder. The bullet that shot out struck through the cap atop it like a hot knife through butter, bathing the area in sparks. Several of the robed practitioners closest to it scattered. Putting his gun away, Cole seized Willhiem by the waist and tossed him over his shoulder like the mortal was a potato sack.

"Now!" Joss commanded.

All four of them charged for the portal as it began to flicker. Willhiem shouted for someone to do something, but the closest guards were on the other side already, with the rest keeping the alley covered and too far away to be of much good. The practitioners, on the other hand, ran for the opening they had made to pass into the circle. Cole saw them coming, however, and passed Willhiem off to Marcel. With his hands free, he drew Bandersnatch and Jabberwock out, firing on the first magic-users as they came toward him with their arms raised for battle.

"Down they go," he mused as their bodies hit the concrete. "Like pretty maids all in a row."

Leaping backward, he felt the space around him warp and shift while his body passed from one dimensional space to the next. Coming to a stop on the other side, he allowed his body weight to continue with the momentum, falling to the soft, quilted ground before bouncing back up into a roll. The propulsion of the ground carried him into the air high above the ranks of the Order guards, who were standing in formation in front of the rest of the Section with their guns raised, poised to fire.

Joss rolled his right coat sleeve up, exposing the peach flesh underneath to the world around them. As he held it up, the flesh melted away to reveal the obsidian and silver material underneath. With a burst of willpower, his arm glowed brightly. Joss took a step forward and stood with his legs apart, facing down the armed guards who seemed stunned by his revelation.

Cole took that as his cue. "Bombs away!"

The hail of bullets he rained down took out the soldiers in back. Joss lashed out with his arm, punching the air like a prizefighter during a training session. With each blow, however, a much larger, glowing silhouette slammed into the guards poised to shoot at him. With his free hand, Joss pulled back the eye patch concealing his other eye and switched it over. The triquetra in the center was shining brightly.

Rainette, meanwhile, had Marcel cover her as she began to launch corrosive orbs of moisture out into the crowd. Her attacks were much slower, but each one met its mark with a vengeance. Cole reveled in the screams on his way back down as the acidic touch of each strike melted skin and muscle from bone, leaving behind a half-formed mess.

Cole's boots struck the spongy ground again. Pushing against it, he launched himself back into the air as the guards began to regroup.

"Return fire! Return fire!" a voice shouted that Cole remembered belonging to the young punk who had stood in Rainette and Marcel's way before.

"Belay that order!" a woman screamed. "They're using the priest as a shield!"

Glancing down, Cole saw Marcel holding Willhiem in front of him as he continued protecting Rainette from attacks. Willhiem was doing his best to escape, but the human was no match for an ogre's strength. Confident that Marcel could handle things, Cole resumed firing down on the guards. A few ducked out of the way in time and rolled onto their backs. Before they could shoot up at him, though, Joss had slammed his mystical fist down into their bellies, knocking the wind from them. In one case, the man ended up puking all over himself.

"Fall back," the woman commanded, motioning for the others to follow. "Regroup with me!"

The other guards turned without a word and ran toward the mountain of toys in the distance. Only one Order guard remained, the same punk from before. Looking around at the odds, he ducked out of the way as Cole dove for him and took off after his comrades. Cole rolled into his fall to keep from going airborne again, coming to a stop only when Marcel held his foot out.

"Thanks," Cole said. "I thought I was going to roll into that jack-in-the-box behind you for a second there."

"You're the one who's been here before," Joss said, helping him up. "Which way?"

"Are you people mad?" Willhiem screamed. "You've destroyed the only way back and murdered half of my regiment! Those men were here to protect us, and you slaughtered them!"

"Those men were ready to gun us down as soon as the portal closed," Joss snarled, grabbing Willhiem by the throat. "You had already given the order for them to kill us the moment we were cut off from Manhattan. You were going to leave our dead bodies behind in this place!"

Willhiem gagged. "You can't prove anything," he wheezed.

"Bullshit," Joss spat, letting him go. "Your men have abandoned you, and you're in unfamiliar territory. We have the information you brought with you, a trained witch, and a sidhe warrior on our side. Those bastards have their weapons and little else. Also, they aren't going to stage a full assault so long as we have you, because if you aren't gunned down in the crossfire, it will give our position away and attract the locals."

Willhiem's eyes widened as he stared down into Joss's luminescent left orb. "You are insane," he gasped before turning to Cole. "You see what your association has done to these people?"

"Oh, quit being such an idiot," Rainette scoffed. "If it comes down to me living another day, I'll gladly dump your ass on the ground here to debate ethics if it means I get out alive."

"I am an ogre, Mr. Willhiem," Marcel reminded him, giving Willhiem a cautionary squeeze with one hand. "I was never raised to have a human being's sense of moral restraint. Mainly because most humans showed no such caution when dealing with my family."

"And I just don't like your sorry ass," Joss added. "Haven't from the start."

"Well, that clears up a lot," Cole said, looking around at them graciously. "For the record, I appreciate the sentiments. To answer Joss's question, however, we should head that way, opposite of where the others ran. I recognize some of the structures in the distance."

"Let's get going, then," said Rainette. "Marcel, give the dumbfuck a good shake or two to see if he's carrying anything useful on him I can use. He's probably carrying the data I need on some type of smart pad."

Marcel started to comply, but Willhiem quickly threw down a touch pad from his breast pocket. "Everything is in there," he insisted.

"Good," Cole said as Rainette scooped it up. "Though you might be carrying weapons, so shake him for good measure anyway."

Willhiem shouted as Marcel turned him upside-down. Suspending him by the legs, the ogre gave the Order spy a good, hard shake with each step he took. Willhiem's screams became painful yells as random items fell out of his clothing. Cole spotted an expensive-looking pen along the way and quickly snatched it up.

"You never know when we might need a pen," he pointed out to Joss, who shook his head mirthfully.

"This is insane," Willhiem spat out between painful gasps.

"Quit being such a whiny little bitch," Rainette growled, turning away from the touch pad in her hand. "I'm trying to concentrate. And, anyway, did you really think we would just walk into a trap so easily after what happened on Staten Island?"

Willhiem abruptly fell silent.

"I take it that didn't occur to you?" Cole surmised.

"I guess the problem with being stupid while pretending to be intelligent is that you begin to believe your own lie," Marcel offered.

Willhiem spat as Marcel ceased shaking him down. "What would an ogre know?" he bit back weakly.

"I could say the same for you," Cole countered. "Human."

"Don't group me with that guy," Rainette insisted, glaring over her shoulder.

"Quiet," Joss barked softly. "Remember, we're in serious danger here. We need to find cover and work out how to seal the tulpas in without trapping ourselves here."

Everyone fell silent and moved along more quietly. Cole had already warned them about the texture of the ground and how easy it was to propel one's self into the air without meaning to. The four of them had gathered shortly before it was time to meet with Willhiem in the alley. Neither Cole nor Joss had been thrilled with the idea of going on a mission with the Order, and Joss had agreed that something about the whole setup stank. The inside tip they'd gotten, though, was what really saved their collective asses.

Rainette had agreed to arrive with Marcel shortly after Cole and Joss got there. The idea was to make themselves seem less united. It had, apparently, worked better than Cole anticipated. Not only were the remaining Order foot soldiers scattered, they had the upper hand with Willhiem as a hostage. Now all that needed doing was figuring out a way home and sealing the space off before they were found. Hopefully, the Order lackeys would draw enough attention to themselves to keep the tulpas distracted.

In the meantime, it sounded as though Willhiem was slowly growing a pair back. "You can't do this," he said quietly, speaking to Joss as best as a man being held by his ankles could. "You're an officer of the law, an inspector. You can't take a man hostage and abandon others to a place like this."

"Your men tried to fire on me and mine," Joss reminded him in an incredibly cold tone. "However, you are right, though. I am an officer of the law."

Willhiem looked encouraged by this. Cole frowned but waited for his lover to elaborate.

"And for the last couple of months," Joss continued. "I've watched others above me abuse their positions and accuse me of things I would have thought better of anyone; all, I suspect, at your organization's request. Then I'm told that you've effectively been placed in charge of us to keep the Section in line, despite us having no sort of agenda against the NYPD whatsoever."

Willhiem choked as he tried to swallow. Joss kept his eyes firmly on the path ahead of them, ignoring the look of worry on his prisoner's face. "Your men came here," he finished as they came upon a small pink canopy with picnic chairs and a bright pink plastic table underneath it. "They can find their own way home. You, on the other hand, Agent Willhiem, will be coming with us."

Willhiem looked relieved as Marcel dropped him down into the nearest pink chair, keeping a firm grip on the back of his neck to ensure the mortal's cooperation.

"Why?" he asked, after a moment.

Joss smiled, and it was a look Cole almost didn't like.

Almost.

"I could arrest you right now," Joss pointed out, leaning over him. "But I know you'd be out before the ink on the warrant dried. So while the others work and make sure we aren't bothered, you and I are going to be having a nice long chat about how things in the Section will run from now on."

For emphasis, Joss held his arm up so that Willhiem could get a closer look. At the same time, his left eye flashed brightly.

"My reach is a lot longer than it used to be," Joss whispered, holding his hand out above where Willhiem's heart pounded fearfully. "You can run from me, Willhiem, but you won't get very far."

Willhiem went utterly pale.

"Now," Joss said in a slightly louder voice, having a seat in the chair opposite his. "Let's talk."

COLE wandered over to where Rainette was sitting off by herself with the touch pad in hand, flipping through the different screens containing the Order's notes.

"He wasn't lying," she informed him when he sat down on the soft ground next to her. "Everything I needed was in here, along with a few things I didn't. Between this and the information my coven brother gave me, we should be okay. It sure as hell isn't going to be easy, but if what you said about that tentacle thing was true, they won't be following us around much, regardless. The hardest part will be getting out of here before the spell locks us inside along with these things."

"I have already thought of that," Cole said, glancing at one of the diagrams on-screen. "I'm just not sure how well it will work."

"Now isn't the time to be coy," Rainette snapped, before giving the handheld device a hard shake. "Dammit! I hate these old models so much. Why the hell couldn't that bastard have upgraded?"

"Push the center," Cole instructed. "You've let it lapse into sleep mode."

Rainette looked at him but did as Cole requested. "Thanks," she muttered, when the touch screen lit up again. "Anyway, what is your idea? I know coyness is a sidhe trait, but none of us can afford it if we want to get out alive."

"Good enough," Cole said. "When Staffelbach and Corhagen were here with me the first time, a ricocheted bullet caused a fissure to open on its own. Staffelbach and Corhagen were able to affect this place when I couldn't. As I said before, I think this might be because they have some measure of childlike innocence in them that hasn't gone away as time passed."

Rainette frowned. "I think I'm getting there, but you're starting to lose me."

"Both Staffelbach and Corhagen wanted to return home," Cole explained, crouching down lower to the ground. "They needed to. They felt a desperate desire to return to their plane of existence. This place, I think, has some kind of resonance with that. Can't you feel it?"

Rainette threw her shoulders back in response and opened her shields, smelling the air and letting the sense of the place they were in fill her. Frowning, she opened her eyes and looked down at Cole quizzically.

"Yeah," she said, looking off in the distance at a derailed train set the size of a subway liner. "It's like those Santa's Workshops they have at the mall. I always hated those things!"

"Pocket spaces like this do exist," Cole went on. "But something about this one feels artificial. I believe the Triskaidekahedron built this place for the tulpas out of leftover children's dreams."

Rainette snickered. "Now you're stretching things."

Cole rose. "In the old legends of your world, the fey crafted castles in the sky out of pure light, and materialized food for guests as insubstantial as the air. Is it that unreasonable to think that whoever built this place took the ideas of children as a base? Look around you, Rainette."

Hesitantly, Rainette glanced back and forth at her surroundings. "Okay, you win," she said in a defeated voice. "I just really hate being wrong."

"The tulpas were created by the imaginations of children," he added. "It stands to reason they would feel at home in the place like this, however resentful they are toward their makers."

"Right." Rainette nodded. "So the only people who can affect this place are those that are children at heart. Where does that leave us? Staffelbach and Corhagen weren't brought on the mission with us."

"They were likely not brought along for that very reason," said Cole. "Remember, we were almost gunned down earlier."

Rainette turned toward Willhiem, who was looking quite grim as Joss grilled him. "Remind me to melt that little bastard's cock off later," she hissed.

"If you kill him, bring his corpse back with us," Cole insisted. "Once it gets cold enough, I can make it dance naked in the police lounge. For now, however, we should get back to our more immediate issues."

With a nod, Rainette brought up the figures. In a relatively short period of time, they had everything they needed. Behind them, the conversation between Joss and Willhiem had grown quiet. Marcel still hadn't moved his hand away from the man's throat, a move Cole approved of wholeheartedly. The only thing left for himself and Rainette to muddle over was a tracking spell.

"It's really very simple," she explained. "The most important thing is focus. Since we're in such a small pocket of space, all I need is the center point. The problem is, this will be harder without a focusing tool."

"Didn't you bring one?"

Rainette went stiff for a moment. "It was on my dresser next to my cell phone," she muttered out from the corner of her mouth. "I must have forgotten it, okay?"

In answer, Cole reached into his pocket and pulled out the pen Willhiem had dropped. "Will this work?" he asked, offering it.

Rainette plucked the pen out of Cole's hand with a smile. "You were right," she said, giving him a rare smile. "You never know when a pen might come in handy."

"Are you both done?"

Marcel gave Willhiem a soft squeeze for his trouble. "We need to go," Willhiem insisted, straining against the ogre's grip. "They'll find us if we don't move soon."

"We know," Cole said. "I already told them. The first time I was here, it was like having a pair of eyes on me all the time. Hopefully, what little bit is left of your hit squad will keep them preoccupied while we work."

"You'd let a bunch of men and women die in your place?"

"Gladly," Cole countered.

Marcel gave Willhiem's neck another squeeze.

"We aren't here to debate ethics with you," said Joss, getting up. "Now move, unless you're looking to get handcuffed to this place so those things will find you quicker."

Marcel forced Willhiem up by his collar and brought him along with them. "Which way?" he asked Rainette, who was busy levitating the pen above the palm of her hand.

"Northeast of here," she said, gesturing. "The reading is faint, but steady."

"Let's hurry," Cole said. "My abilities won't be as effective against them, if at all."

"Then we stay in the shadows and keep moving," replied Joss, moving to the front. "Rainette, you take point. I'll cover you. Everyone else, fall in line behind me."

The group moved along together, careful to stay sharp the whole time. Cole had both guns drawn, and Marcel kept his watchful ogre eyes on the slightest detail, while Joss took point before Rainette with his Magnum. None of them spoke a word the entire time. Even Willhiem remained eerily quiet as they shuffled past what looked like a giant teddy bear with eyes stuffed in its open mouth. Cole was perhaps the most apprehensive out of all of them. The sense that they were being watched was much fainter than the first time he was here. Rather than being relieved, it made him think something worse was coming.

"She's leading us in circles," Willhiem hissed as they stood with their backs behind a set of roller skates near the side of a Trans Am.

"I'm taking us around places that don't have much cover," Rainette corrected him, giving the pen a flick. "The rules of this place don't exactly adhere to the same principles of our plane, so my magic isn't foolproof. I'm having to compensate."

"How?"

"By being very careful," she said in a warning tone. "It's still a ways north of here, but I sense we'll be there soon. The problem, though, is I don't see any other way past that open area ahead of us."

Both Cole and Joss looked past her. "We can manage," Joss said confidently. "It's not like we have much choice."

"We could go around," replied Cole. "But that would mean wasting more time, and running a higher risk of being ambushed."

"My point exactly."

Marcel, who by this point had resorted to holding Willhiem up by the seat of his pants, lowered the man down to the soft, bouncy ground. "There doesn't appear to be anyone in the vicinity," he noted, giving the air a sniff. "I don't smell anything but that peculiar odor most humans spray in their homes."

"Same here," Cole said. "It makes tracking a bitch."

"At least we aren't being watched," Joss said, sighing with relief.

"We aren't," Cole affirmed. "And that bothers me."

"Why?" Rainette asked, turning around. "That's a good thing."

Cole looked up at the sky overhead. Like before, in the distance, what looked like a massive ceiling lay spread out above their heads. "When I was here before with Staffelbach, there were paper airplanes flying back and forth overhead."

"Paper airplanes?" Rainette was back to her usual skeptical tone. "Are you sure?"

"They were sentries, I think," Cole went on. "The skies have been clear since we arrived. The fight we had would have been loud enough to give away our position. They should have tracked us easily, but we've been left alone."

Joss frowned. "That makes no sense," Marcel insisted, picking Willhiem back up again. "Why call off their forces?"

"I don't believe they did," Cole said. "Something is very wrong here."

No one said a word. "The only thing we can do is keep moving," Willhiem insisted, struggling to loosen Marcel's grip a little. "My men are still out there."

"We were a part of your company," Cole pointed out.

"Exactly," Rainette chimed in. "Were you planning on shooting them in cold blood later on? Funny how this part keeps slipping your greasy little mind."

"I agree," Joss said. "This plan went south from the get-go. Willhiem, you tried to set us up, and now something else is wrong in this place. This mission is scrapped."

"Great," Rainette said, lowering the hand holding up the pen. "Only, how do we get home?"

Everyone but Willhiem looked at Cole. "This place responds to childlike thoughts and imaginations," he said. "I believe that, to return home, we simply must want to return home."

"Like, clicking our heels together?" Rainette wasn't being sarcastic for once. "I didn't bring my red slippers."

"Colors are superficial," said Cole. "I imagine that, for most here, that would actually suffice. We should stand in a circle first before beginning, however."

Reluctantly, as if certain Cole was putting them all on, the group gathered around. Cole slipped a pair of handcuffs out of Joss's pocket, then slapped them on Willhiem before shoving him off to the side.

"What are you doing?" Willhiem demanded loudly.

"You're a practitioner," Cole answered coolly. "Find your own way home. Besides, I don't want to run the risk of you trying to sabotage us."

No one from the Section protested. "Should we be doing this?" Rainette asked, though she took Marcel's and Joss's hands when they held theirs out. "I'm the last person to act as someone's conscience, but we're essentially leaving him behind to die."

"He betrayed us," Marcel pointed out. "In my clan, we would have feasted on his bones as punishment."

"Gross."

"Let's get the portal open before we debate ethics," Cole suggested, ducking under their roped limbs. "We can worry about who we take back with us afterward. I would rather not have him partake in this."

"You really think he could keep us here?" Joss asked.

"He is a strong practitioner of his Craft," Cole assured his lover. "Though he hasn't called on his magic yet. I suspect he is saving it as a last resort in case it brings unwanted trouble."

Rainette mused on this, then nodded in agreement. "Big flashy spells are usually more trouble than they're worth," she said to Joss, backing up Cole's words. "Plus, they take up a lot of juice to cast, which leaves the Craft-wielder drained."

"Get the portal open," Joss said to Cole in answer. "Tell us what to do."

Cole breathed in the artificially sweetened air and drew on his power. "Close your eyes, each of you, and draw on your most important memory from childhood," he said in a soft voice enhanced by the power of his glamour. "Let it fill your bodies up like a cup of warm milk. Let it take on a life of its own in your mind. This memory has to be old, and very important."

Their breathing grew more rhythmic and in synch with one another. Marcel unconsciously gave Rainette's hand a squeeze.

"As contrived as it might sound," Cole went on, "next, click your heels together. Keep that memory in your head. Make certain you don't lose it."

All three of them clacked their heels together. Rainette started off too fast, and Joss's were by far the loudest. Marcel, interestingly enough, brought the backs of his feet together with a bare minimum of noise. As they all fell into synch with each other again, Cole brought out his guns.

"Now say the words," he whispered. "You know what they are."

Joss started them off. "There's no place like home," he chanted.

"There's no place like home," Rainette chimed in.

"There's no place like home," Marcel finished.

Their heartbeats pounded together as one. When Cole felt this happen, he brought Bandersnatch and Jabberwock together, cross-drawn, and pointed them at the ground. Breathing in deeply, he let his own memories of Faerie fill him.

"There's no place like home."

The ground rolled beneath them. The stink of potpourri vanished as a foul gust of something charred rushed past them. An explosion filled the room, sending them off their footing. Joss was thrown back first, breaking the chain between them, and thus the connection they shared. The power between them was gone in an instant, melted like frost before the morning sunrise.

Cole turned toward the source of the noise and saw a column of smoke rising up in the direction Rainette had been leading them.

Joss spotted it next. "Son of a bitch!" he swore.

"My men!" Willhiem called out. "Uncuff me this instant."

"Do we go?" Cole asked Joss, ignoring Willhiem completely.

"We go," he said, getting up. "But we don't uncuff him."

Marcel had snatched the cantankerous man up off the ground and was back with them in a fraction of a second.

"Put me down!" Willhiem demanded to no avail. "You stupid ogre!"

Bandersnatch was pointed at Willhiem's forehead before the man could blink. "I could shoot him," Cole offered.

"Later," said Joss, taking point this time. "We've got bigger problems."

"Bigger problems" was an understatement. Before they were even halfway there, Cole could smell the stench of freshly slaughtered human bodies filling the air. The potpourri scent was forcing its way through as if fighting to conceal the evidence of battle, but Cole's nose would not be deceived so easily now that he had a trail. The smoke grew thicker the closer they came. Rainette started coughing as a result, and rather than let her fall behind, Marcel chose to scoop her up in his free arm.

"I can run," she insisted.

"I can run faster," he replied. "And still carry you both."

Cole nearly shifted forms, but then they were there. Before bursting on the scene, he had a gut intuition that they were about to learn what had been going on the whole time the Section had been crossing the terrain uninhibited.

Fires were burning all over the place. It was chaos no matter which way they turned. The center of the pocket dimension was an inferno. The worst came from the towering decorated tree looming above, roughly forty feet high. The small houses and plastic reindeer had been tipped over and broken to pieces, or were melting under the intensity of the heat. In front of the tree, split down the middle, was a red throne someone had gone to the trouble of attacking.

It was like something out of a nightmare. Though Cole had not been raised with the imagery, even he felt his stomach turn ever so slightly at the sight.

Santa's Village was on fire.

"Duck!"

Cole dropped to the ground without looking overhead. A low-flying paper airplane dove toward the ground, missing the tops of their heads by only a few feet. Somehow, it had been set ablaze along with everything else. The backdraft from it filled Cole's lungs with scorching heat as it collided with the ground up ahead, tossing the burning cotton snow into the air like cinder confetti.

Willhiem was glaring as Cole stood up and looked at him. "Now do you believe I'm on your side?" the mortal demanded.

"You were just saving yourself," Cole retorted. "It's what you do."

"Never mind him," Joss shouted, bringing their attention back to the village. "Do you see any of the men Willhiem brought with him?"

"I can smell them," Marcel said, keeping Willhiem in a tight grip. "They are all dead."

"I smell them too," said Cole, conceding. "We're too late."

Marcel let Rainette slip out of his arm back down to the ground. All of them watched for a moment as the Yuletide setup in front of them continued to burn.

"What the hell is happening?" Joss wondered.

"We're being punished."

Cole smelled her first and drew Aed Deigh out. Mary Alice snorted at the sight of it before looking back to the inferno. "The others are trying to control some of the damage he did. The Triskaidekahedron weren't happy with us letting the Nihilgeister be destroyed, so one of them came here to destroy parts of our home."

"Why?" Rainette wondered.

Mary Alice glared back at her as though she were being childish. "Because they can," she retorted condescendingly. "And because this place is all we have. Santa's Village was one of the first things that came into being after this space was set aside for us."

"They're destroying it because it means something to you," Marcel concluded.

Mary Alice looked back at him, nodding. "The Nihilgeister is too weak right now to take us back and forth through space. We're of no use to the Triskaidekahedron until it gets stronger, so they're making us pay."

Something stirred inside of the fire. A single figure moved in and out of the flames as though dancing in time with their movements. The sight caught everyone else's attention as the image grew clearer.

"We have to get out of here," Willhiem insisted, fighting to get free. "Get me out of these cuffs, or that thing will kill us!"

"Shut up, Willhiem," Joss barked.

"It's too late," Cole informed gravely. "They've already seen us."

"He's come to kill you now," Mary Alice told them calmly. "Maybe, if you all die, he'll get bored and go home."

"Why don't you just fight back?" Willhiem wondered.

"He is one of the Triskaidekahedron," she said before turning to go. "They are the reason we bear the thirteen sigils. Mine was given to me by the one who forsook them, but she came back. Even still, I'm too weak to withstand any of his attacks."

"It doesn't matter," said Cole, holding Aed Deigh up in challenge. "He's here now, and I'm more than ready for a fight."

"Same here," Joss added, exposing his right arm. "Let's do it."

"You'll both die first, then," Mary Alice declared before running away in the opposite direction.

The male figure stopped just outside the flame's reach. Cole was taken aback at the sight of the traditional combat armor he wore. He had never seen the armor in person, but remembered it from his time as a child in Faerie. It was the traditional armor worn by the Tuatha De Danann long ago.

The metal was light, covering the body while molding to it as though it were another layer of flesh. The colors were a mixture of black and deep purple, which contrasted nicely with the stranger's tricolored eyes. They were a mix of robin's egg, sky blue, and deep azure. The stranger's skin was blue as well, a dark ocean color. A white skunk trail crisscrossed back and forth down the coal black locks of hair hanging down to his waist. The gentleman appeared to be sidhe, yet Cole smelled something distinctly wrong about him. As he shifted his footing across the unstable terrain, one of his ears protruded from the thick curtain framing his face, and Cole saw they were pointed.

The stranger was a half sidhe, like Naryssa had been.

Steeling his nerves, Cole presented himself next to Joss, with Aed Deigh at the ready. "I am Tuulois MacColewyn, son of Colewyn, the Seventh Frost King," he announced. "Special Detective of Section Thirteen, a division of the New York Police Department, and master of the Bowling Green sithen. This is my lover, Joss Vallimun, captain of Section Thirteen and wielder of the Hand of Rage."

Joss frowned slightly. "Hand of Rage?" he muttered out the corner of his mouth.

"It sounds impressive enough," Cole whispered back. "Plus, you still haven't been formally consecrated yet, so there's still time to change it."

"I can hear you both," the man replied, giving his dark hair a flip so that his pointed ears were exposed better. "I had heard your lover was mortal. Have you chosen a new one to take to your bed already?"

"I am mortal," Joss insisted, though his voice didn't sound completely sure.

The stranger smiled. "I can see you quite clearly, Joss Vallimun, wielder of the Hand of Rage and Section Thirteen captain. No mortal has ever wielded sidhe powers before. You are no more human than I am."

He then turned to Cole. "So the legends were true, then. You have the power to bring others over to full sidhe, though I think you might have had a false start with this one. He does not smell as you do."

"The Goddess ascended the man next to me," Cole countered. "Not myself. I was merely the instrument she chose to work through."

"You never did explain to me what that means," Joss added quietly. "Or how it worked."

"Later!"

The challenger gave Joss a once-over, clearly unimpressed. "And why would the Great Lady choose you?"

"I'm shy," Joss answered cockily as the energy rippled up his arm. "But I've got a really big dick."

"Who are you?" Cole questioned insistently. "Give us your name."

"Ashwyn," he said.

"That's it?" Joss kept his right arm raised. "I was expecting something a little grander."

Ashwyn smiled. "Perhaps later on you will get your wish, ascended mortal."

A loud bang went off behind them. Distracted, Cole turned his head to find Rainette being thrown back several feet. Marcel was down on his knees, nursing a wounded arm that was soaked in far too much blood for the injury to be natural. His summation was proven a second later when Willhiem raced past, free of the handcuffs he'd been bound with, and both hands glowing green against the red of the fire. Willhiem dove into the fire, heedless of how intense it was, and disappeared.

Cole jerked back in shock as Ashwyn struck at him with a knife he hadn't been holding before. Joss was already there, though, and blocked the maneuver.

"Go!" he ordered as Ashwyn struck again.

Cole extended both blades and prepared to attack, but Joss moved in front of him. Ashwyn's assault was blocked by Joss's arm a second and then a third time.

"I said go!" Joss insisted.

"He'll kill you," Cole shouted. "Or at least try to."

"You saw how Willhiem went into that fire," Joss yelled back, moving to the side now. "If he escaped to go in there, it must be bad!"

Cole wanted to argue, but his love was right. "Don't you dare die on me," he hissed, before moving around him. "Because I am not bargaining with the Goddess to restore you a second time!"

"I will bathe you in your lover's blood when you return," Ashwyn called out victoriously. This distraction cost him severely, however, for he let his guard down enough that Joss was able to land a punch from several feet away.

Joss's mystically empowered fist reared back again before pummeling Ashwyn across the face several more times. "You and what army?" he demanded.

Smiling to himself, Cole dashed into the flames, keeping the red-hot blade of Aed Deigh out. The frostbitten piece of metal would not fare as well inside this inferno. It was impossible to track Willhiem's steps in the blaze. The fire and smoke ensured there was no scent to track, but Cole remembered that Willhiem had been aiming for the center of the burning Santa village, so Cole navigated his way toward that general area, praying all the while he would get lucky.

Some of the flames were eating away at his clothes by the time Cole emerged on the other side. Risking a quick swipe with the frost end of Aed Deigh to put them out, Cole then moved around a melted plastic house. Before, he and the others had been too shocked by the sight of this place in flames to notice the bodies lying around. The men Willhiem had brought with him were scattered about. Cole recognized knife wounds in their half-burned corpses, suggesting that Ashwyn had been there earlier. It looked as though one or two of the bodies close to him had been turned over.

Clearly, Willhiem had just left this place, meaning he shouldn't be far behind. As Cole left, though, he wondered what the mortal was searching for.

The answer came a moment later, on the other side of the burning tree. Willhiem was standing beside one of his fallen men, holding a canister up as though preparing to smash it. Next to him, several broken pieces of lumber lay piled up, the remains of what appeared to be a wooden rocking horse. The container resembled the one that was stolen from the warehouse. As Willhiem hesitated, Cole drew Jabberwock out and fired. The bullet cut through Willhiem's shoulder, making him stagger.

"You!"

"Whatever you're planning, Willhiem," Cole said, keeping his gun trained on the man, "it's over."

"On the contrary, you insipid little fairy," Willhiem jeered, clutching the canister in his right hand. "I've just won."

Cole fired again as Willhiem threw the canister down to the ground. As the bullet entered the mortal's other shoulder, the canister smashed cleanly against the pile of wood. Something thin and a poisonous shade of green flew into the air and hovered above their heads, hissing angrily as Willhiem fell to his knees on the soft, burning ground.

Cole looked up as small spears of lightning colored the same sick shade of green struck all around them. One made a beeline for his head. In a panic, Cole raised Aed Deigh automatically and sent a stream of flame out. The two forces collided in midair and held fast for maybe half a second before the glowing green worm hovering above them let out a high-pitched squeal. The flames vanished into the lightning as it was drawn back into the worm.

Fire blanketed the creature, making it hiss again. Cole watched as the thing dove toward the ground, burning a path into the quilted, spongy floor inches from where Willhiem was crouched.

"What the hell was that?" Cole demanded, stepping forward.

"Burn in hell where you belong, you soulless...."

Cole grabbed Willhiem's shoulder and stuck his thumb into the open wound. Willhiem screamed, which only made Cole press down harder.

"All right!" the mortal managed to scream out. "It's an energy worm."

Cole eased up on the pressure slightly. "What?"

"An energy worm," Willhiem repeated between clenched teeth. "The Order created it some months ago, and issued the command for me to bring it here. The worm will eat away at the fabric of this pocket space, collapsing it."

Cole's thumb sank far enough into the bullet wound to touch bone. "Your Order actually kept something like that in a place like New York City?" he spat over Willhiem's tortured howls.

"Not... dangerous... there!" Willhiem grunted. "Won't harm space plane... unless a tiny one like this."

In the distance, Cole felt something. It was hard to describe, but a moment later, an arch of green lightning shot through the smoke in the far distance. One of the toy structures crumbled in response.

"It's already begun," Willhiem went on as Cole released his hold a little again. "You can't stop it."

"So this was what you were sent to do from the start," he deduced. "Kill us all, then collapse the dimension so there was no evidence, and no more tulpas to worry about."

"Not all of you," Willhiem countered, pausing as Cole refrained from pressing into his wound again. "The Order has been wondering about you for a long time, Cole. They've got very big plans for you."

"What?"

Willhiem gasped as Cole rotated his thumb in a circle. "I don't know," he grunted. "They wouldn't tell me, in case something went wrong. But they've had their eye on you for a while, and this was just the beginning. They wanted the other members of the Section out of the way, though. That was most important."

Cole pulled Willhiem until they were facing each other. "That's all I know," Willhiem said. "Come back with me willingly, Cole. You and the Section are done for. The minute the NYPD hears my testimony, they'll throw you and your conspirators behind bars. Your boyfriend's career will be over. Is that what you want?"

"No," Cole admitted calmly, letting Willhiem drop back down to his knees. "Fortunately, I have an alternative."

Willhiem frowned. "What?"

With that, Cole aimed Jabberwock again and shot Willhiem straight between the eyes. "The most obvious answer," he said. "You fool."

JOSS was still fighting Ashwyn when Cole emerged out of the flames again. For a moment, Cole considered standing back and watching his lover duel. A quick tremor in the ground, however, reminded him of the space's imminent collapse. That, and Marcel lay bleeding in the distance next to a fallen Rainette, who was still unconscious.

When Joss moved out of the way to dodge one of Ashwyn's attacks, Cole took aim with both guns and unloaded several rounds into Ashwyn's backside.

Joss stared in surprise as Cole walked up to him. "I had it," he insisted.

"I never doubted that for a moment," Cole said. "But we have another problem. The dimension is on the verge of collapsing. Willhiem's men snuck some sort of energy worm in with them. It's like a parasite and will eat away at the dimensional fabric until there's nothing left. If we don't leave now, things will get messy."

"Forsaken scum," Ashwyn wheezed, struggling to stay on his feet. "You shot me in the back."

"I didn't feel like playing fair," Cole replied dismissively. "Those bullets have iron in them, incidentally. If you don't seek a healer quickly, they'll poison you."

"Liar," Ashwyn gasped, staggering again.

Cole ignored the severe insult. "You can stay here and let the dimension crush in on itself and kill you," he pointed out. "Or leave and show us to the exit door on your way out."

"We can just join hands like you said before," Joss added.

Cole pointed to Marcel and Rainette.

"Oh," Joss said. "In that case, better tell us how we get home. This place feels like it's going to fall apart fast."

Ashwyn glared death at both of them, but ultimately conceded. Raising his left hand, he placed a hooked fingernail at a spot in midair, pushing as though something much thicker lay there. A dark spot appeared, which magnified into a great black hole as Ashwyn swiped the claw sideways.

It was a portal. On the other side was a Manhattan street. None of the pedestrians walking past appeared to notice.

"Go on, then," Ashwyn said, getting to his feet slowly. "Before I change my mind."

Cole turned toward Joss. "I'll grab Rainette," he said. "Can you carry Marcel?"

"Why do I get the ogre?" Joss asked. "I was the one doing most of the fighting here."

The ground lurched hard underneath them. "How about we argue later?" Cole suggested. "We can both help carry the ogre."

"Good idea!"

IT TOOK longer than Cole liked to get Marcel through the portal. The ogre came to as they were bringing his legs through, and in a fit of confusion, mistook them as kidnappers looking to harvest his organs and testicles. Apparently, as Marcel explained later to a slightly injured and highly annoyed Joss, ogre testicles were a powerful aphrodisiac and medicinal substance when boiled and creamed beneath a new moon.

That being said, it still didn't make up for his kicking them both backward eight feet.

The Shadewater coven was willing to patch up Marcel's mystically inflicted wound. Apparently, dating one of their own meant he was entitled to certain privileges. Not being a fan of the hospital, Marcel endured their curious stares while they took turns applying the necessary herbs that would purge the magic poison out of his body. It helped that Willhiem was no longer alive. Spells cast by humans tended to weaken once the caster died. Cole still hadn't told Joss about shooting Willhiem, but Joss seemed to have already guessed the truth.

Cole thought this would mean they were going to fight later, but Joss never mentioned it. Either he didn't want Cole to tell him, or he wasn't bothered. Cole wasn't sure, and knew it would come to light eventually. Sooner or later, they were going to get to the argumentative stage of their relationship that so many humans did, whether over the death of Agent Willhiem or something else entirely. Regardless, he wasn't looking forward to it.

Rainette was put back in the hospital, this time because of a concussion and minor neck injury. The soft trampoline ground in the pocket dimension was apparently not cushiony enough to keep her from hurting herself. The doctors seemed to take her injuries in stride, however, and insisted she take time off from work to heal properly. Joss was all too happy to sign the paperwork needed to put her on leave.

While they were visiting her in the hospital, Marianne came by with some news. The coven had voted, and Rainette was being made their new sword maiden. Cole took this as good news, though Rainette looked slightly less than enthused. Once Marianne left the hospital room, she explained to him and Joss that the sword maiden position meant that she was the defender of the coven from this point on. It meant, in turn, that she was going to have even less free time to herself after she got better. The ceremony would be held in the woods under a full moon. Ordinarily, this would have been right away, but the coven was delaying everything until next month to give Rainette time to recover. Plus, Cole was informed later, it gave the coven time to schedule things so everyone could attend. Though he didn't say it, Cole suspected the Shadewater coven was doing this so that Rainette wouldn't come back from every Section Thirteen mission critically injured.

Willhiem's death had caused a quiet shit storm with the higher-ups, but since the Section members were the only survivors, little could be done. Their report detailing Willhiem's betrayal was scrapped almost immediately in favor of a completely fabricated version painting the human in a more positive light. For once, the brass was perfectly willing to hear their descriptions about the pocket space, though. After being informed that it had subsequently collapsed in on itself, the interrogation was over, and they were led away, back to Joss's office. It went without saying that none of this was over.

No one said it, but this was why the Section had gotten stuck doing the paperwork of other departments. Extra homework was a relatively painless smack on the wrist for shooting Willhiem between the eyes, but Cole still found the labor undignified. For that reason, it was several days after their return before they managed to locate the young girl named Melissa.

Joss tried calling her house first, but received a less than favorable response from the girl's mother once she realized why they were calling. Cole was sure he heard Melissa cry out just prior to the phone going dead. It wasn't pleasant, but he was determined to find out everything she knew. On the day they planned to visit her, however, Joss was called away to check out reports of a violent poltergeist attacking customers in a bar. The bar owner had requested the inspector by name. At first, they were all terribly suspicious, but then the man explained how a relative of his worked at the TV station, and had been told about them by his cousin. Cole offered to go instead, but Joss sent him on with Staffelbach.

The young officer seemed glad for a chance to get out from behind his desk for a little while. Ever since he'd been released from the hospital, his computer had been malfunctioning. Earlier today, Cole was sure he smelled smoke coming out of the tower. No one from the tech department could figure out what was wrong, or how the interior got fused together the way it had. It put the man in a foul mood, so he was all too thrilled to go with Cole to see Melissa at her school.

Along the way, Cole couldn't sit comfortably in his seat. It made no sense, since the SEMA had always conformed perfectly to his body. As they marched along, it became clear what was bothering him. Cole didn't want to believe it, but one look at Staffelbach confirmed everything.

He was uncomfortable being in the human's presence.

A sour frown decorated his face for several blocks. He was a sidhe warrior, an element of Faerie, and nothing about sex made him uncomfortable. That was what he kept repeating to himself, but then they turned off the main road into an unanticipated floodgate of noon rush hour traffic, leaving them stuck behind a long row of cars inching along at a tortoise's pace. It was clear they weren't getting anywhere fast. Furthermore, Cole suspected this was some sort of sign.

Finally, he couldn't take the silence anymore. "I am sorry I kissed you," he said quietly. "Had there been another option, I would have taken it."

Staffelbach gave Cole a stunned look before breaking into a small grin. "Don't worry about it," he said quietly, as though fighting back laughter. "I know it meant nothing to you."

The statement caught him off-guard. "What makes you say that?"

"I did a little research," Staffelbach admitted as the car moved forward on its own slightly. "After you told me what you were. There are a lot of scary stories out there, but most of them say the same thing about the sidhe and sex. You were just doing what you had to."

Somehow, Cole didn't like the sound of this. "Yes," he admitted. "Though, saying that it meant nothing to me isn't accurate."

Cole hesitated a moment, wondering how he should phrase his thoughts. "I have lived a long time," he explained, "and one thing about human society that baffles me is how quickly it evolves. What shocks and offends people one minute is laughed at in the next. That is how it appears to me, at least."

Staffelbach listened, clearly intrigued. "I gave up trying to figure any of this out years ago," Cole went on. "For all I knew, a kiss was serious business."

Staffelbach's jaw dropped when Cole added casually, "At least, Corhagen thought so."

"Corhagen?"

Cole glanced at the young officer, who was wearing a look of total shock. "It is a very long story," he said.

"You'll have to tell me about it sometime," he replied, grinning now.

"That is why I was worried," Cole finished, unwilling to discuss Corhagen and their history with one another for the moment. "I honestly wasn't certain how you would take having me kiss you, regardless of the circumstances."

"I understand," Staffelbach replied, laughing softly now. "But don't let it bother you. I'm doing much better now. If you want to know the truth…."

Staffelbach hesitated but then threw a hand up in surrender. "It was a little hot.

"I mean," he added after a moment, "you're with Vallimun. I don't expect you to dump him for me, so if what I just said bothers you, forget about it. I'm sorry if it's caused you any problems with your boy."

"It hasn't," Cole said. "Joss was very understanding about the circumstances. To be honest, it startled me. I expected him to misinterpret things at least a little bit."

Staffelbach smiled at him. "You're a very lucky man," he told Cole. "I hope I get lucky like that one day."

"How so?"

Staffelbach gazed out the window longingly as the traffic broke. "Someone who gets me," he said. "Who loves me for who I am, and can rock my world half as good as you did that night."

Neither of them spoke again until they reached Melissa's school.

The building was nothing like the academy on Staten Island. At least from a purely aesthetic standpoint, Cole felt the institution wasn't hostile. Several different buildings connected by crisscrossing walkways covered by overhanging canopies made up the campus. Cole parked the car in a nearby space, then walked with Staffelbach on his left up to the main doors.

Beyond them was a reception area guarded by two women. Cole expected them to put up a fight. Both froze the moment they entered.

Then they raced up to the counter as though their lives depended on it, and he relaxed. This, as it turned out, would be much simpler than anticipated.

"Special Detective Tuulois MacColewyn and Officer Staffelbach," he announced in a smooth voice. Staffelbach flashed his badge along with Cole. "We were hoping to speak with one of your students, a Melissa Beckrindle."

One left their station for the PA control nearby. "Is something wrong?" the other asked, now looking ever so slightly worried.

"Melissa came to the station several days ago, asking if she could report a crime," he explained. "A friend of hers had gone missing. We think she may have witnessed something that connects to a series of kidnappings we've been investigating."

"Beckrindle," the woman repeated. "Oh, the little girl who was friends with the Stephanie Zealskin girl, right?"

"I believe so," Cole said. "Melissa told us her friend Stephanie had disappeared about a month ago."

"It must have been awful," said the woman, looking fraught now. "She was so distraught when she came to school that day, saying that her friend had been snatched up by a monster."

"Sir?" the woman by the PA system called out, interrupting them. "Detective Colewyn, was it? Melissa's teacher said she didn't show up for class this morning."

Both Cole and Staffelbach turned toward each other. "Are you sure?" Staffelbach asked.

"I'm sure," she insisted, though not impolitely. "Ms. Hansforth said she called the parents when she noticed Melissa wasn't there, and no one answered. The other students said they didn't see her before the bell rang."

"Let's go." Cole was at the door, with it open and waiting, before Staffelbach could turn all the way around. Both women blinked at how quickly he moved, like he'd given them whiplash.

"Is something wrong?" the woman who'd gone to the PA asked.

As Staffelbach ran out the open door, Cole said, "For Melissa's sake, I hope not. If you don't hear from us in the next twenty-four hours, and no one gets hold of her parents, call the number on this card and ask for me."

Joss had gotten the cards printed the day before. Cole had seen them as something frivolous and unnecessary. Now he was thankful for not having to waste time writing the information down. He would owe his lover a blowjob later tonight as a result.

Not that this bothered him.

The card spun through the air, landing neatly between the two women on the counter. When they looked up, the door was closing and Cole was quickly out of sight.

Running ahead, he unlocked the doors and started the car ahead of Staffelbach. The officer wasn't breathing hard when he jumped in.

"It has to be the Naryssa woman," he said, snapping his seat belt into place while Cole threw the car into reverse. "But I thought she only took kids who were half fey. Why would she kidnap Melissa?"

"We don't know that she did," Cole replied gravely. "They said she never showed up for school, and the teacher couldn't get hold of the parents. Neither is very likely if the family is dead."

"Right," said Staffelbach. "In that case, punch it."

It was a very good thing that Melissa had left her contact information with the officer who had driven her to her friend's home. Staffelbach got the information from their precinct over the phone before it shorted out on him.

"First my computer, and now this," he snarled. "What else is going to fuck up on me today? Oh, turn left here!"

Cole complied, nearly riding up on the sidewalk, and sped down into the residential area. Melissa had said she lived close enough to the school to walk every day, so they were outside her house in minutes.

Cole could smell blood as he exited his car. "I think they're already dead," he warned Staffelbach as they walked toward the front door together. "Be prepared for anything."

Both of them had their guns drawn as they reached the doorstep. The welcome mat had been kicked aside as if to illustrate a point. The front door was closed all the way, but when Cole knocked, it sprung open cleanly.

"The lock was broken," Staffelbach noted. "Not a good sign."

"Police!" Cole shouted, nudging the door open the rest of the way with his foot. "Anyone here?"

Silence answered.

"The kitchen," Cole said, sniffing the air. "We check there, then sweep the house. I'm fairly certain there's a body, so when we find it, you make the call. I'll search the rest of the house in case Naryssa's goon squad is still lurking somewhere."

"You think they'd stick around?"

Cole nodded grimly. "I'm hoping they did," he said. "I owe them one."

When they reached the kitchen, the source of the blood smell became apparent. A man in his early forties was lying on the floor. Or, more specifically, part of him was. The lower half had been ripped off and tossed on top of the refrigerator. The legs were hanging down limply like a passed-out drunk. Down on the tile, the upper half was facing up, staring at the ceiling, wearing an expression of stunned shock. Melissa's father had bled to death as the realization that he was half the man he'd been sank in. It would have been comical were Cole not feeling remarkably guilty at the moment.

He'd spent too much time around humans in the past century.

Staffelbach gagged behind him. "I know," Cole said quietly, putting Bandersnatch away. "Believe me, I know, but I need you to stay with me right now."

Staffelbach nodded. Cole gave his shoulder a quick squeeze as the man composed himself before backing away slightly.

"Where's the mom?" Staffelbach wondered, looking around. "In the back of the house, maybe?"

Cole hesitated as he glanced down. "Actually, you may be standing in her."

Staffelbach leaped back out of the puddle of clear water he had been standing in, and looked down at Cole in confusion as the sidhe sniffed there.

"A naiad," he declared, getting back up. "She must have been a powerful one to live so far from…."

Cole stopped as his eyes caught sight of a fountain out the window in the backyard. "Check that," he amended. "This naiad was simply prepared."

"So the girl was one of Naryssa's victims?"

"Perhaps," said Cole, looking around again. "Or maybe she killed the parents and the girl to silence them all. Killing parents could be considered a hobby of Naryssa's, so perhaps she did it this time out of habit."

Cole drew Bandersnatch out again. "Call it in," Cole ordered. "I'll be back once I check the rest of the house."

The smell of blood continued to waft from the kitchen and nowhere else. Cole searched every room, feeling his bones itch the entire time with hope that one of Naryssa's helpers had stayed behind to face him. His disappointment choked him when he came to the last room and found nothing. This room, however, was clearly Melissa's, and was marked by the signs of a struggle. Cole had often heard of the living habits that many children her age kept, but the broken window behind the bed left little doubt that a fight had broken out here. It looked as though this was where Melissa had been taken from.

After coming to this conclusion, Cole turned around to leave, but stopped when he noticed one of the drawers in the dresser next to the door. It had been left slightly open. Dragging it open, he searched through it quickly, but found nothing. Thinking, Cole swept the room with his eyes again, wondering how much of the wreckage was done on purpose, and which parts had been caused by Melissa's kidnapper. It would have been easy to hide evidence in a mess like this.

Turning around, he headed back down the hall to the living room, where Staffelbach was still on the phone.

"We're going to need a full forensic team," Cole said. "Once you're done, I want you to help me look for the cap that Melissa brought with her to the station."

Staffelbach pulled the phone away. "A cap?"

"She brought it with her to the station," Cole said. "It belonged to her friend, Stephanie. She found it in the spot where her friend was taken. Melissa said that Stephanie never went anywhere without that cap."

"Okay," Staffelbach said once he'd hung up the phone. "Why is a cap so important?"

"It may have been why Melissa was taken in the first place," Cole replied. "Assuming this wasn't just another part of Naryssa's...."

Staffelbach waited as Cole fell silent. "What?"

"I hear something," Cole said softly. "Outside, coming from...."

Running to the door, Cole stuck his head out and looked around. Above, in the sky, a bright ball of fire was coming down fast toward the house. The minute Cole saw it, he turned around and dove back into the building.

"Run!" he shouted, grabbing Staffelbach by the arm.

"What is it?"

"Fireball!"

Both were in the kitchen in seconds. Staffelbach didn't hesitate when Cole steered them toward the big glass window showing the expanse of the backyard. As their bodies crashed through it, the house was rocked by a massive explosion. The force sent them flying, stopping at a roll on top of each other next to the deceased naiad's fountain while the structure behind them went up in flames.

Then, they heard roaring.

"That can't be good," Staffelbach said, getting up.

Flames were expanding out of the smoking wreckage. As some of the black clouds parted, a pair of hands rose out of what was left of the ceiling. Two feet, made entirely out of fire, stomped down onto the dry grass, igniting it. The creature shook itself off as it manifested fully in the yard directly behind the fiery home of the dead Beckrindles.

"Flame golem," Cole identified. "She must be getting impatient."

Staffelbach stumbled back in awe of the titanic creature and bumped against the naiad fountain. Both of his hands touched the rim at the same time. Cole felt a sudden burst of power emanate from the Section member as the golem took a step toward them.

Staffelbach's skin lit up like a motherboard. Lines stretched down his skin, connecting at points on his body where bright alchemical circles were glowing. Electricity flared, racing down his arms into the fountain and ionizing the air. Cole smelled ozone as the fountain collapsed into itself.

The golem took another step, which was all Staffelbach needed. The fountain was gone now. In its place was a thick strip of black hose running out of the earth into Staffelbach's new arm. A silver metallic device was attached to it now, looking like something out of a science-fiction film. It might have been some kind of blaster weapon. Cole wasn't given long to speculate, though.

As shocked as Staffelbach was, he wasted no time in aiming the thing. The fire golem roared as he bore down on them, opening his mouth wide enough that Staffelbach didn't have to worry much about missing his target. The hose jerked, and a stream of water exploded out the tip of the arm cannon into the flame golem's face. The creature recoiled in pain as steam rolled out of its head.

"Um, just out of curiosity," Staffelbach shouted, backing up slightly, "how are you doing this?"

Cole looked at him. "I'm not," he replied stiffly. "If I were, I wouldn't have bothered with a middle man. This is all you."

The stream of water drifted away from its target as they spoke. Staffelbach noticed, and adjusted before the golem could recover.

"How am I doing this?" he wondered loudly.

"Later," Cole said, bringing out Aed Deigh. "We take care of this thing first!"

The frost-tipped blade shone brightly against the March sunlight. Cole took aim as Staffelbach brought his free hand down on top of the water cannon.

"Better turn up the pressure," he said.

The machine clicked and hummed in response. A much thicker, more impressive spray burst out of the gun's nozzle in answer.

"You ready?"

Cole took aim with his frost blade and nodded. "Always."

The flame golem had begun to shrink. Cole sent a wave of ice into its chest while Staffelbach poured on the water. Within moments, it was reduced to the size of a garden gnome.

A real one, not the plastic kind.

"Allow me," Cole said, stepping forward.

"No, please," Staffelbach said quickly, moving around him slightly. "I insist!"

One quick shot reduced the manufactured monster to a puff of steam that faded into the atmosphere. Staffelbach's smile quickly faded as he looked down at the device still attached to his right arm.

"How do I get rid of this, now?"

Cole frowned as he looked the machine over. "I have no idea."

Silence hung in the air between them for a moment. Off in the distance, however, the explosion had drawn the attention of the neighbors, and their cries drifted over the fences to Cole's ears. In front of the two men, the Beckrindle home lay in flaming ruins.

Staffelbach swallowed. "I know I'm calm right now," he said quietly, unable to take his eyes off the water cannon stuck to his arm, "but inside, there's a panic attack ready to boil over."

"Don't worry," Cole said, projecting calm into his voice with glamour. "We can figure this out."

"Figure what out?" Staffelbach wondered, looking at Cole now with horrified eyes. "MacColewyn, what's happening to me?"

Cole frowned as he spotted a crowd gathering through the flames. "I don't know," he acknowledged at last. "I really don't know."

J.L. O'FAOLAIN was born the youngest, with four older sisters, in the backwoods of the Deep South. Those that have braved getting to know him have attributed this to being the root of his growing insanity. A teased bibliophile in his youth, O'Faolain spent his years prior to getting published as a cook, laundry man, delivery boy, grease monkey, and retail stocker. He has a plethora of skills and abilities, none of which would work well on a job application. In his spare time, O'Faolain enjoys weightlifting, philosophy, deconstruction, reading, writing, porn, and the Internet in general. Aside from becoming a successfully published author, he would very much like to pilot a giant robot while Two-Mix's "Rhythm Emotion" is playing in the background. Either that, or travel the world in a dirigible. In short, the general consensus by all, including himself, is that he is a mighty strange fellow.

The Thirteenth Child

J.L. O'Faolain

http://www.dreamspinnerpress.com

The Thirteenth Pillar

J.L. O'Faolain

http://www.dreamspinnerpress.com

www.ingramcontent.com/pod-product-compliance
Lightning Source LLC
Chambersburg PA
CBHW070057030726
47506CB00002B/498